Sweet Figs, Bitter Greens

Donna L. Gestri

ISBN: 1-4802-7808-4
ISBN-13: 978-1-4802-7808-0
Library of Congress Control Number: 2012921461
CreateSpace, North Charleston, SC

For
Brandi Danielle

Music boxes have within,

melodies they carry with them,

once they open music fills the air.

The Melody Within
Rigoletto
Giuseppe Verdi

The Salvatori Family

Maestro Rinaldo Salvatori	born February 1892
Giuliana Ardito Salvatori	born October 1900
Dante (Dan)	born February 1927
Felice (Phil)	born November 1927
Lucilla (Lucy)	born September 1930
Augustino (Tino)	born August 1933

In the name of pity, my beloved pardon
the error of a loving soul;
among these shadows and these groves,
Oh God, it will always be hidden!

From "Per Pieta, ben mio"

Cosi fan tutte

Music, Wolfgang Amadeus Mozart
Libretto, Lorenzo da Ponte

Prologue
August 2016

Lucy was not aware of the secret life of wasp and larvae hidden within a fig as the ripe fruit's sweetness saturated her taste buds. Her long, thin fingers plucked another fig from the dish on her lap, and she popped it into her mouth.

"Not as good as the ones at Villa Positano. I'll never understand how Tavis didn't like them."

"Gram, your chin is sticky," said Julie, her twenty-eight-year-old granddaughter. "Here, let me clean you."

"Who's Tavis, Gram?" Nineteen-year-old Tony helped himself to a fig.

"Tavis Gregg."

"Tavis Gregg, the old-time movie star?" Julie's eyes filled with tears. "Oh, Gram," she said softly.

Walking briskly through the garden, Annie, Lucy's oldest daughter, joined the group. "I've freshened Gram's bed for her nap." She turned to her mother. "Are you enjoying the figs, Mom?"

Lucy nodded. "Yes. Yes."

Annie looked at her daughter. "What's the matter?"

Julie shook her head and turned her back to her grandmother. "I just don't understand how she could go downhill so quickly. She's saying nonsensical things again. Last week she wanted to know if we had reserved her seat for the Palio in Siena. Now…" She pointed sadly at the woman analyzing her half-bitten fig intently, "…she shared figs with Tavis Gregg."

Annie looked at her mother and smiled. "How about we take you inside, Mom? You can save some of those figs for later, you know."

"If Val sees them, he'll finish them up."

"Oh, Gram," Julie murmured again.

"Hey, at least if she thinks Grandpa is still alive, she won't miss him so much," Tony exclaimed.

"Shut up, you, before she hears you," hissed Julie.

"Never mind, you two. Let's bring Grandma inside. There's something I want to show you."

Annie maneuvered the wheelchair in the direction of the dusty-pink stucco house.

Once they had settled Lucy in her bed for an afternoon nap, Annie went to the dresser and opened the bottom drawer. Rummaging through the long unused scarves and stockings, she emerged with a small, dark-blue velvet pouch. Opening the neck of the pouch, she shook a crystal heart with a tear captured in its depths into the palm of her hand.

"What's that?" asked Julie.

"Tavis Gregg's heart."

Chapter 1
September 1936

Lucy made herself as small as possible under the teacher's desk.

"Lucilla Salvatori, climb out from under there this minute." Sister Paul Francis's tone was exasperated and none too kindly.

Lucy peeked with one eye at the long black skirt blocking the desk opening. The long rosary beads hanging from the nun's waist swayed gently as Sister Paul tapped her foot.

"If I have to call your mother to get you out from there, you are not going to be a happy little girl. You are wasting my time and the class time. I am going to count to three and…"

"Sister?"

A hand tugged at Sister Paul's skirt. She looked down to stare at the little boy standing next to her. She arched an eyebrow, and it almost disappeared under the tight white headband across her forehead.

"Sister, let me try and get her out."

"Are you her friend?"

"Uh, yeah, sure. I'm her friend."

"Then be my guest, young man." She turned to look at her first-grade class. "The rest of you open the readers on your desks. Quietly. I expect this book, and all the rest of your new books, to be covered by tomorrow. That's your homework for tonight."

"Hey, Lucy," hissed the little boy kneeling down under the desk, "I'm Jimmy."

Lucy turned to face him full front.

"Hi," he said.

"I don't know you," Lucy sobbed.

"Sshh. Don't let Sister Quietly hear you. Sure, you know me. I'm Jimmy. Everybody knows Jimmy. I pass your house all the time. The big pink one on the corner, right?"

Lucy looked at him and nodded.

"See? We're practically neighbors. I live up the next street in a circus tent."

Lucy looked at him quizzically. "There's no circus tent up the street."

"Yeah, well, people act like that's where I live. I don't care. C'mon. I need a special friend. We can walk home together. Will you be my special friend?"

"OK."

"Then come on out and sit at your desk before Sister Paul has a monkey."

Lucy giggled and crept out.

"OK, Sister, we're coming through. But I kinda think Lucy and me should sit next to each other."

"You do, do you?" She looked at the little girl's tearstained face. "Oh, all right. You…" She squinted at the first-day name tag. "Phyllis. Move to where James is sitting. James, you move next to Miss Salvatori. Quietly."

Dinner at the Salvatori table was a bustling affair. With the children in position, Dante, nine, Felice, eight, Lucy, six, and little Tino propped on two pillows at age three, mother Giuliana called to Maestro that dinner was ready. From the music room, Rinaldo Salvatori crossed the entryway and seated himself at the head of the table. Bowing his head, he led the family in saying grace. Then, shaking his cloth napkin at his side, he placed it on his lap. Giuliana served her husband two ladlesful of her homemade lentil soup with spinach and pasta. The Maestro took a sip of wine while she filled the children's bowls.

"So, how was the first day of school?" he asked no one in particular.

"Phil has Sister Mary Joseph," declared Dan. "He's dead."

"If you do what you are supposed to, Phil, you should not need to worry."

"I don't know. She sticks people in the wardrobe for punishment."

"I'm sure that's a rumor," soothed Giuliana.

"No, Ma. It's true. And there are no windows in there. She closes the door."

"We'll see about that," huffed Giuliana, mostly to herself.

"How was your first day, Lucy?" asked the father of his only daughter. Lucy's thin legs swung under the table rapidly. Her long straight hair almost covered her face as she bent forward.

"I was afraid," she whispered.

"Afraid? Afraid of what?" Maestro questioned.

"I don't know. I just was. I don't like school."

"Well, you'd better change your mind kid, 'cause you have to go," warned Dante.

"I know. But I don't want to."

"It will get better, *cara*," her mother promised soothingly. "It's just new to you. You'll see. You'll make friends, and it will be fun."

"I already made a friend."

"Wonderful! What's her name?"

"It's a boy. Jimmy. He said he lives in a circus tent up the street, but I think he's kidding."

"Hey! You mean Jimmy the midget? Yeah, he should be in first grade too!" Dan announced.

Maestro put down his spoon. "Is that who your friend is, Lucy?"

"I don't know. What's a midget?"

Giuliana put her hand on Maestro's arm. "A midget is a small person."

Lucy looked confused. "I guess he's small. Almost everyone in the class is smaller than me. I'm too tall."

"And you should be happy for it," Maestro said pointedly.

"The difference is that Jimmy will never grow up to be too tall," Giuliana explained. "He's a dwarf and dwarfs never get very tall."

"Oh. Well, he walked home with us today, and he's my friend. He said he'll walk to school with me tomorrow. Dante and Phil run ahead with their friends and leave me alone."

"What!" exploded Maestro. "You two should take care of your sister. You walk with her and don't leave her to make friends with…with…that boy."

Lucy piped up. "He's a nice boy. He made me not so afraid."

"Lucilla, I have spoken!" Maestro said darkly.

The thought of facing Sister Paul Francis's pointer and staccato instructions without Jimmy's steadying gaze compelled Lucy to challenge her father.

"Why can't we be friends, Maestro? He says please and thank you, and he makes me laugh."

"I am the father, and I know what is best," Maestro exclaimed, pushing his chair back from the table. "Do not question me."

Again, Giuliana touched Maestro's arm. "They're only children, *caro.* Let it be." She ladled a bit more soup into his bowl.

Chapter 2
September 1937

Sitting on the front step, chin in hands, Lucy mused on the last day of summer vacation as music drifted through the screen door from a Baldwin piano. She was to be in Sister Margaret Unis's class, the tallest nun in the school. In the world, probably. Lucy's stomach clenched in anticipation of the following day. She rose and went indoors to stand next to her mother at the piano. When Giuliana finished the composition, she turned to her daughter.

"Are you sure you wouldn't like to take piano lessons like Dante does?"

Lucy shook her head.

"But darling, you have a natural ear. You sit down and play already. Wouldn't it be better to be able to read the notes?"

"No."

"I don't understand you."

"I don't want to have to get up on stage like Dan did at the concert. I almost threw up just watching him."

"Ah. What if I tell the teacher you will not be in the concert?"

"No, Mama, I don't want to."

The screen door opened and Maestro entered. He placed his Panama hat on a hook of the coat rack and his walking stick in the bin below.

"Ah! My beautiful girls! How are you today?"

"We are fine, *caro,*" Giuliana said as she brushed his cheek with her lips. "You look all hot and tired. Let me get you a cool drink."

"Get something to cool my temper too," Maestro added.

"What's wrong?"

Maestro pulled a crumbled program out of his jacket pocket. "Look at this program for *Cavelleria Rusticana.* Does that look like a laurel wreath to you? It looks like a crown of thorns to me. Worse…read… *Cavellerio Rusticano*! What is this printer, *stupido*? Six thousand programs, all wrong! He took too long to print them, and now they're useless. The opera opens Friday night. He'll never fix it."

"Calm down. Of course he'll fix it. He's new, and he wants your business. You should not be doing this anyway. If Joe can't handle it, I'll come into the city tomorrow and go to the printer myself. *Basta.* Change out of your suit, and I will make your drink."

Maestro gathered up the mail from the entryway's side table and went to sit in his chair in the parlor. Scanning the return addresses, he took one envelope and put the rest aside. He ripped it open and slowly read the long letter. Giuliana entered the room with iced coffee on a tray just as the letter drifted to Maestro's lap. She was startled to note tears in his eyes.

"*Caro,*" she cried, setting the tray down on a round table in the center of the room. "What is it? Is it the letter from Italy?" She glanced at the paper on the floor, noting that the ornate handwriting was different than the script on the letters her husband usually received from his hometown of Ventotene.

"*Il Professore* has passed away," he said, referring to his mentor, Gaetano Ripolli. "Suddenly. Without warning."

"He was not a young man. Was it his heart?"

"*Si.* He was eighty-eight."

"God rest his soul."

"His sister has written me. She has other news."

"What is that?"

"He has remembered me in his will. The equivalent of twelve thousand dollars."

Giuliana sat down, her hand at her throat. "*Bedda Madra.* That is an enormous amount of money."

"*Si.* You know his last words for me."

"I am sure I do."

"Destiny has decided!"

Chapter 3

Ventotene, the remaining peak of an ancient volcano, sits in the Tyrrhenian Sea off the coast of Italy. To this island, where Roman emperors had banished relatives who fell into disfavor, Rinaldo's parents, Adela and Marcello Salvatori, banished themselves shortly after they married. They enjoyed the sleepy reclusive island, scantily inhabited and quietly anonymous. The ancient Romans had built a magnificent harbor and from there they could travel to Naples or farther when the need arose.

Unlike many of their neighbors who emerged from their pink or white houses to fish, to cultivate trees laden with figs, apricots, peaches, and plums, or to work the fields of green lentils and beans, the Salvatoris were tailors of the highest artistry. Their short, chubby fingers dissolved in a blur as they mended, altered, trimmed, and created costumes for the grand operas of Italy. Such was their skill, the frantic impresarios were willing to put up with the inconvenience of dealing with them long distance. During costuming crises, the Salvatoris would travel to a theater and be gratefully ushered in by the now-frantic director. Having solved the catastrophe, they were paid handsomely for their services, would have been offered a complimentary box seat, would have enjoyed the production, and would have retreated before the last "Bravo!" had been hollered.

Rinaldo was the joy and momentum of their lives. He was a big boy from a young age, good-looking, with his father's black hair and his mother's black eyes. He would play among the caves and tufa arches or sit by the harbor and conjure stories about the crags in the cliffs, which took on the shapes of fantastical characters. Most of all, he looked forward to trips to the Teatro di San Carlo in Naples or the Teatro Constanzi in Rome when he accompanied his parents on their business trips. All aspects of the opera seeped into his blood: the music, sets, staging, voices, story, and performers. Back home he would sit by the harbor or a Roman ruin and sing what his perfect musical ear and memory had imprinted on his heart.

It was as he was singing "Celeste Aida" on his way home from school that Gaetano Ripolli picked up his drooping head from his chest.

"Stop! You, who are singing. Come here."

Rinaldo halted abruptly and turned back. "*Si, Signore*?"

"Who are you? What is your name?"

Rinaldo scrutinized the man more closely. He did not know him, rather unusual on this small island. The man was blind.

"I am Rinaldo Salvatori, *Signore.*"

"How old are you?" he asked gruffly.

"Nine years."

"Where did you learn to sing like that?"

"I learned the song at the opera, *Signore.*"

"But who taught you to sing?" When Rinaldo didn't answer, he repeated his question. "I *said,* who is your teacher?"

"I have no teacher."

* * *

Gaetano had been a well-established and well-loved baritone on the opera stage. On his fiftieth birthday, while celebrating at a resort with his wife and son, a ferocious fire broke out. Gaetano lost his family and his sight, and was physically disfigured by the blaze.

After almost two years of recuperating and bitter swallowing of condolences, reassurances, and poorly disguised pity, he brought himself to Ventotene to live what he hoped would be the short remainder of his life, in solitude and away from the memories. His sister Norma would have none of it. She dragged her children and husband to Ventotene with her. He was a fisherman; he could fish anywhere. Giovanni was a mild man, happy with his catch of the day, a few figs, and a glass of wine. She set up housekeeping in her brother's house and had a piano sent at great trouble and expense. Gaetano, however, never approached the instrument. He did, however, cease bellowing for his sister to go home. She did not listen, anyhow.

Such was the purity of Rinaldo's voice on that day, a pain of longing gripped Gaetano's heart. He sat upright in his chair, a shadow of his former stage presence finally emerging.

"Indeed, that is obvious," he commented to the boy. "I will be your teacher."

A long and loving relationship developed. The *Professore,* as the boy now called him, coached Rinaldo in all aspects of vocal training. They worked on breath control and diaphragmatic respiration, *verismos* and *bel canto* styles, color, timbre, vocal expressions, diction, and phrasing. He introduced him to all the memorable tenor roles, from the light lyric genre to the dramatic ones. Rinaldo soared. His introduction to piano virtuosity was equally successful and by his seventeenth birthday, *Il Professore* announced, "There is nothing left I can teach you. You must go to the Conservatory in Milan."

"That will cost a lot of money," the now six-foot-three Rinaldo replied.

"I have already spoken with your parents. We will all see you through."

"I will have to pass an audition."

"You will pass."

Three years later Rinaldo returned to his small island, vocally without peer in his class and instrumentally, both piano and violin, accomplished.

"Will you be returning to the Conservatory?" *Il Professore* inquired.

"No."

"You are ready to take on the great roles at the grand houses? I can get you auditions."

Rinaldo turned his black eyes on his mentor. Their depths were as troubled as a restless volcano. "I hope you can understand this, *Professore.* I cannot appear onstage. When I have done so during my studies, I have been extremely unhappy."

"But word has reached me of your successes. You are well received and exuberantly anticipated on the great stage."

Rinaldo nodded. “I am not unaware of this. However, when I look out on the audience, my throat clenches, my hands sweat, my head throbs, and my heart jerks like a wagon on a bumpy road. No, I want to be an impresario of my own opera house.”

The professor, sixty-three now, and well aware of how life must be filled with a beloved purpose, nodded. “It will take you many years of underling labor to achieve that goal.”

“I am going to America.”

“Your parents?”

“They cannot figure into it.”

“You have severed them from your life, Rinaldo.”

“It must be that way.”

“Your talent surpasses your youth, but your youth overshadows your wisdom.”

“Do you think it is a mistake for me to cross the ocean?”

Il Professore’s sightless eyes widened with love and sorrow for his cherished pupil. “Destiny has decided.”

Chapter 4

Giuliana stuck a crisp white hankie, edged in pink and monogrammed with a pink *L*, in the breast pocket of Lucy's navy-blue uniform jumper. "Don't forget to put on your beret. It's by the front door."

"I feel sick."

"Lucilla, it's impossible that you feel sick every morning for two weeks and then are fine once you get into the classroom. I cannot walk you to school. Tino is still sleeping."

"Let me check my schoolbag again."

"You've checked it forty times. You have everything. Even if you didn't, it wouldn't be the end of the world. Now, hurry. You don't want to make Jimmy late. He's probably waiting on the corner for you already."

Lucy reluctantly grabbed her schoolbag and shuffled down the stairs. For good measure she slammed the front door, just to be sure her mother understood how unhappy she really was.

Jimmy was on the corner, his squat little figure walking in circles around his strapped books on the sidewalk. He looked up and waved at Lucy. "Hurry up, will ya? If we reach after the anthem, we'll get detention."

Lucy picked up her pace.

"Did you remember your 'Propagation of the Faith' nickel?" he asked.

"Yeah."

"My mother said I can have a birthday party this year. Are you going to have one? It's coming up."

"I don't know. I feel sick."

"You're full of baloney. You know, someday I may be sick or something, and then what are you going to do?"

"Stay home."

"Yeah. Your folks won't let you. Hey! Let's try this. Let's walk backward and maybe you'll think you're walking home instead of going to school."

Lucy turned around and moved with slow steps in reverse. After several yards she revealed, "I still know where I'm…" Down she went over a raised square of sidewalk.

"Ow!" she cried out. She had a bad graze on her back upper thigh and a mean-looking cut on her palm that was bleeding.

"Oh boy. Now you've done it." Jimmy pulled out his handkerchief and tried to wipe her up.

"Hey, squirt!" yelled out a boy on the other side of the street. "What, did you punch your girlfriend in the leg?"

"Nah, he took a bite out of her," said his snickering friend. "From where he is, it looked like a bone."

"At least I wasn't kneeling in the front of the lunchroom yesterday during lunch," Jimmy shouted back.

"Jerks," Lucy mumbled, straightening herself out. "What happened in the lunchroom?" Lucy walked home for lunch with her brothers and was unfamiliar with the lunchroom regulations.

"He was talking before grace and some Sister I don't know made him kneel in front of the room all through lunch."

"I'm glad I go home for lunch."

They reached the school yard just after the bell rang to line up by class. The monitor by the gate halted them.

"Aw, c'mon, don't write us up," begged Jimmy.

The superior but benevolent seventh grader looked at him. "All right, little guy," he said, mussing Jimmy's hair. "I'll let you two go this time."

The two raced to their class line. “That was close,” Jimmy whispered.

“He messed your hair.”

“So what? We don’t have detention, do we?”

* * *

Maestro stode down the block swinging his trademark walking stick and whistling an aria from *La Traviata.* The stick had been a parting gift from *Il Professore* those many years ago. The shaft was hand-carved cherrywood, and the handle was carved into the shape of a lute. *Il Professore* had thought it was a fitting accoutrement for his flamboyant student with the long straight hair and affinity for fine fashion. Maestro never ventured outside his front door without it. That, along with the Panama hat atop his erect stature, drew curious stares from passersby and catcalls from the neighborhood children.

“Hey, Tonto!” someone would shout out. “Where’s your horse?”

If Dan or Phil were within earshot, they would whack the offending heckler on the head. Deep down, however, they wished their father looked like other dads and played ball with them or squatted down to teach them the finer points of winning a game of ringer.

Maestro entered the front door and sniffed the air. "Ah, what is that I am smelling?" he called out.

Giuliana hurried out of the kitchen, wiping her hands on a towel. "*Osso buco.*"

"Magnifico."

"It is a celebration dinner. Tonight we tell the children the good news."

The screen door at the back of the house slammed.

"Ma! Hey, Ma!"

"In the front, Phil." Giuliana rolled her eyes at Maestro. "He's been in the yard since he got home from school. Something has been eating his tomatoes."

"Ma! Oh, hi, Maestro. I saved two of them. That's all. The rest are gone. Mr. Coltri next door said he saw a raccoon around."

"All right," Giuliana said, taking the fruit from him. "It's the end of the season anyway. Go wash up for dinner. We have an important announcement."

"What? That Dante didn't get detention?" he asked with an impish grin.

"Don't be fresh. Go upstairs and clean up."

Maestro's eyes followed Phil up the stairs. He looked at Giuliana. "Has Dante been getting detention?"

"Only once or twice. He talks out in class. He's high-spirited. Not a big deal."

"I want to know if it happens again."

Giuliana kissed his handsome cheek. "I will yell it from the rooftop. Now you go change too."

* * *

The aroma of Giuliana's osso buco was almost as tantalizing as the rich tangy flavor of the incredible veal shanks. The children looked like miniscule adults as they dove into the delicacy, unaware that many of their friends would have turned up their noses at this feast and begged for a hamburger. Crisp Italian bread was passed around and used to lap up the luscious gravy. When forks clattered against the dishes and napkins were as soiled as the children's messy faces, Giuliana announced, "Maestro has something important to tell you."

Maestro looked at each of his children individually. "This is an important day in our lives. Today I made a downpayment on a building on Eighth Avenue in New York City."

"What's a downpayment?" asked Dan.

"I paid part of what the building costs. I still have more to pay every month until I pay the owner the whole amount. Who knows why I bought this building?"

"To teach your voice lessons instead of in the music room?" asked Phil.

"No, he teaches lessons at the Academy too," Dan informed his brother.

"That is true. But that was a good guess," he added, looking at Phil. "No, the reason I bought the building is that we are going to have our own opera company! The Salvatori Opera Company."

The children looked at him expectantly.

"This is very exciting," Giuliana explained further. "Maestro is going to put on wonderful operas, and he is going to do it so everyone can afford to go to them."

"Why can't everyone go now? To the Academy or to the Met?"

"Because it is too expensive. It will also be a place I can give new people a chance to practice and show their talent. Like when I was a boy and *Il Professore* helped me."

"Will we have our own seats?" asked Lucy, who had viewed a few operas from the wings of the Kings Academy.

"You will have a throne," her father said with a smile.

"It won't be too high up, will it?" Lucy asked with a quiver in her voice.

"Don't be a moron; he's only kidding," Dante said with a snort.

"Don't be rude to your sister, or there will be no *panna cotta* for you," Giuliana warned.

"Panna cotta!" the three older children exclaimed while Tino yelled out, "Pan cot for me! Pan cot for me!"

"Yes, panna cotta. A special dessert for an Allelulia day," Giuliana announced with satisfaction.

Chapter 5

Maestro gazed upon his beautiful wife as Giuliana descended the staircase. She was one of those beautiful Italian women whom men adored and women admired. Giuliana had not succumbed to the finger waves and short curls of the '30s. Her bounteous chestnut hair was pulled back in an elegant chignon. In startling contrast to her dark hair were the blue eyes that sparkled almost violet in certain lights. Her slender figure was considered tall at five foot eight. After thirteen years of marriage, Rinaldo still gasped as he followed her regal descent down the stairs. She was dressed in a gown he had insisted on purchasing. The body-skimming gold silk was covered with small clusters of gold sequins in a small floral pattern. The two-tiered skirt had a slight train, and the neckline dipped in the back.

"My beautiful wife. I feel like Radamas," he exclaimed, referring to the prince in *Aida.* "I want to build a throne for you next to the sun."

Giuliana laughed lightly. "You already have. And it has cost a minor fortune."

"Tonight will tell the story."

"You look like a king," she stated with pride. In tuxedo and cape with top hat in hand, Rinaldo cut an imposing and very handsome figure.

"Where are the children?" Giuliana inquired in a worried tone. "They are too quiet."

"Mrs. Coltri has Tino. I have set the others in the parlor and warned them that if they moved or messed themselves, they would not be attending the premiere tonight.

"Maestro! The car is here," screeched Phil, standing by the parlor window.

"*Andiamo,*" Maestro called out, shepherding his brood to the waiting limousine.

* * *

It had been almost a year of frantic and hard work, but the opera house was now ready. The stage could hold three hundred people if necessary, the theatre three times that number. To keep costs down, the orchestra was kept to no more than thirty-six musicians. The sets and backdrops were not as grandiose as the Metropolitan, but here too, Rinaldo looked to save money. On costumes, however, he would not scrimp. He had a seamstress for the opera house, an expense his managing director fought against. The box seats, mezzanine, and balcony were elaborately carved and gilded. An amazing crystal chandelier, similar although smaller in circumference to the one he had seen in the Opera Company of Philadelphia, hung from the ceiling. The season was decided upon, not without much debate, and talent was gleaned from his own students, recommendations, professionals who owed him a favor or who wanted to help, and itinerant hopefuls who lined up to audition.

* * *

Joe Gallino, the managing director, had approached Maestro with a season list he thought was doable for economic, talent, and crowd-drawing reasons. Maestro scanned the list and crossed his pen through the first entry.

"No. No *Rigoletto.*"

"Why not? It's a favorite among opera lovers."

"I do not like it."

"How can you not like it? It's Verdi!"

"I know very well who it is," Maestro exploded with an exasperated tone. "We will not do it."

Eventually they settled on a season of twenty operas, which included *La Traviata, La Boheme,* and *Madama Butterfly*.

Joe was almost out the door when Maestro called to him, "Don't ever bring up *Rigoletto* again." Joe turned to face the impresario. "We will never put it on at the Salvatori Opera Company."

* * *

True to his word, the seats for the operas were within the workingman's entertainment budget. The prices were thirty-five cents, fifty cents, and ninety-nine cents for the best seats in the house. They sold out.

For this first performance of *La Traviata,* Maestro allowed one rehearsal with the orchestra. He wanted the musicians to become familiar with their pit and the sounds they made and heard from there. In all the previous rehearsals, only a piano accompanist had been employed. It was expensive to pay an orchestra for rehearsals. This was the sacrifice that had to be made to keep the costs down. It was his dream to bring opera to the masses; he ignored the naysayers and skeptics.

If the scenery moved a bit slowly as the crew pushed and pulled, or if the backdrops wavered in the breeze of the moving actors, the audience did not mind. The costumes were stunning, the music was magnificent, and the voices moved many to tears.

At the end of the performance, the crowds would not sit down. Shouts of "Bravo!" filled the theater. They soon changed to demands for "Il Maestro Salvatori!" The tenor who sang Germont stepped into the wings and grabbed Maestro's arm.

"Maestro, come out."

"No, no…," Maestro implored, resisting.

"You must. The people love you."

Unwilling to flaunt his discomfort, Rinaldo joined the cast in the footlights.

"*Grazie mille,*" he said. "You honor me with your attendance and your approval. I hope you will return many times over to the Salvatori Opera Company." He glanced up at the box where Giuliana was with the children. She was standing and clapping and waving at him. The children were not to be seen. They must have fallen asleep at some time during the production.

Maestro retreated to the wings, and Giuliana gathered up the children and joined him.

"It was magnificent, darling. I'm more impressed than you could ever know."

"There was not one *fischio,*" Rinaldo pointed out happily, referring to the whistles that signified the contempt of an Italian opera-loving audience.

"This was an Allelulia opening night," she whispered.

* * *

The reviews came in, and they were gratifying. Violetta, the soprano role, was recognized for her accomplished musicality and her feverish coloratura in the first act. She was recommended for being able to upstage her surroundings. The tenor, Alfredo, had a tone that was smoothly beautiful and disarmingly musical. Perhaps in time, with training, he could impart his lyrical voice style with some of the "oomph" needed in many roles. The chorus number, "*Noi siamo zengarelle*" was delightful. And if the sets made the reviewer feel like he was at times "bobbing on a raft in the middle of the Atlantic Ocean," he had never seen more superb costumes, even at the Metropolitan.

On another evening when Bruna Castagna, the famed mezzo soprano, came to see *La Boheme,* she insisted on visiting with the Maestro after the performance.

"Maetsro Salvatori," she gushed. "You have created a temple of hope for the young artist here. I am much impressed."

"*Grazie.* I am honored by your presence and kind words."

"I heard good things about your endeavor, but I found it difficult to believe. Now I see it is all true. I did not expect much; yet in my lifetime I have never been so impressed."

Maestro conveniently ignored the first part of the diva's remarks as he stepped into his role of impresario. On the marquee under the title, he instructed his stagehands to spell out: "'In my lifetime I have never been so impressed'...Bruna Castagna."

The next two months sold out. Maestro was leaving the theater at eight o'clock after organizing some last-minute details for the opening of *Le Nozze de Figaro* the following evening. He stepped through the side door and walked to the corner of Eighth Avenue on which the marquee and billboards fronted. There he saw two young boys hurling eggs and tomatoes at his theater.

"Hey, you!" he hollered. "Stop!"

The boys took off like a shot, dropping eggs behind them like deranged chickens. A beat cop happened by and blocked their progress as Maestro reached up to them and grabbed a firm hold on one of the two culprits.

"What's happening, Maestro Salvatori?" the officer inquired.

"These two thugs were throwing eggs and tomatoes at the opera house."

"Really? Did you think we put up with this kind of nonsense around here, fellows? Whatsa matter? You don't like opera?" the officer questioned, giving the shoulder of the one he was holding a shake.

"It was just for target practice," one boy said as way of explanation.

"Hmmn. Where did you get the eggs and tomatoes?" the officer asked.

Neither answered.

"I thought as much. You're coming down to the precinct with me. We're calling your parents."

"What's the matter with you boys? If you get eggs, you should at least bring them home to eat. Your family is so rich?" Maestro said sternly.

"Will you come down to the station, Maestro, and press charges?"

"Let me call my wife, and I'll be right down."

When Maestro reached the police precinct, the boys' parents were just arriving. One fourteen-year-old, Jamey, was being manhandled by his mother. The other boy, Valentino, stood shamefaced in front of his mother and his father, who was in a wheelchair. Maestro strode past them to the arresting officer.

"This is the gentleman whose theater these two boys vandalized."

"I'm very sorry, sir. I don't know what Valentino was thinking. He is usually a good boy," the father said, extending his hand. "I am Charles LoMuscio."

"I have sons too," Maestro replied. "Who knows what they are thinking sometimes?"

"Valentino will be at the opera house the first thing in the morning to clean it up. He will be missing school, but this is a more important lesson. I thought I taught him better than this."

Jamey's mother was still berating him loudly, and a cop had to disengage her fingers from his red, twisted ear. Maestro looked at Valentino's tight flushed face and tried to discern if his shame was for himself or for his wheelchair-bound father. He walked to the side of the room, indicating that the arresting officer should follow him.

"I'm not going to press charges. The father is making the boy clean up. That's good enough for me. Give them a stern warning about if it happens again."

* * *

The next morning when Maestro arrived at the opera house at eight, the two boys were busy with scrub brushes and soap and water. He said, "Good morning," to them, nodded, and went indoors. Later that afternoon, around four o'clock, he was passing through the lobby on his way to the box office. A lone figure stood inside the front doors. As he walked closer, he saw it was Valentino LoMuscio.

"Back again, young man? I checked out your work at lunchtime. You did a fine job of cleaning up."

"I just came back, Mr. Salvatori, to say how sorry I am for what I did. I never did anything like that before. Jamey sometimes has crazy ideas, and we were bored, and…I'm not trying to blame Jamey. I shouldn't have gone along with it. So I'm real sorry, and you don't have to worry about me doing something like this ever again."

"How old are you, Valentino?"

"Thirteen."

"You ever see an opera?"

"No, sir."

"Would you like to?"

"It looks like it must be pretty fancy inside, and I like music all right."

"Well, for being such a brave boy, I tell you what. You ask your parents if you can all come to see *Le Nozze de Figaro* tomorrow night. You and your mother can sit in my family's box, but your father must be in his chair at the end of the aisle. I do not have any aisle seats empty tomorrow night."

"Gee, Mr. Salvatori, that would be swell."

"I hope I see you tomorrow night."

* * *

The next evening, with hair slicked back and a jacket with too-short sleeves, Valentino joined his mother in the Salvatori box. Mr. LoMuscio sent his apologies. Only Giuliana and six-year-old Lucy were at this performance. Val barely glanced at the skinny little girl, but Lucy took a good look at her first criminal.

After the performance Maestro brought the guests backstage. Val was in awe of the bustle, sets, props, and costumes laying all about.

"This is like being in a fun house," he announced.

"You think so, eh?" Maestro said with a chuckle. "So, you told me you were bored the other night. You no have schoolwork to do?"

"Yes, sir, but I finished it."

"He's a good student. We don't know what got into him the other day," his mother explained.

"How would you like to work here after school some days and some weekends? We can always use another pair of good strong hands."

"I would love that, sir! Ma, can I?"

"That's very generous of you, Mr. Salvatori."

Maestro laughed. "Well, you would have to stay home at night and do your studying. At least you won't be throwing eggs anywhere."

"I'll never do that again. Ever."

"I'm sure that's true. OK. You're hired. But if your mother tells me your schoolwork falls off, you're fired. You understand?"

"Yes, sir. Thank you very much."

After the duo left the theater, Lucy turned to her father. "Why would you give that boy who did a crime and almost went to jail a job in our opera house? Suppose he steals something or kills somebody?"

"He's not going to kill anyone or steal anything. I can tell. He's a good boy. He deserves a second chance. His father has troubles. He can use a helping hand raising a son. I know about sons," he added, striking his forehead in mock exasperation.

Chapter 6
1938

"Very good, Shirley." Mrs. Harris praised the little third grader who successfully gave the answer to the number of states in the United States. "Who knows who the president is?"

Several hands shot up, but Lucy's hands were primly in her lap. Jimmy, seated in the desk next to her, waved his arm while trying to facially nudge Lucy to raise her own hand.

"Very good, Thomas. Who knows the vice president?"

The room was still as Lucy whispered to her ink-well, "John Nance Garner."

"Anyone?"

Jimmy couldn't stand it anymore. He reached over and grabbed Lucy's elbow and thrust her arm in the air.

"Lucy!" exclaimed Mrs. Harris, delighted to see her shy but brightest student contributing.

Lucy felt her face flush red, and her mouth go dry. She shook her head slightly.

"Come on, Lucy. I know you know it. Tell the class."

Lucy raised her eyes imploringly to Mrs. Harris. The sweet-faced woman only smiled and nodded at her. She had a nurturing demeanor, a welcome relief from the stern sisters of her first two years.

"John Nancy Garner."

"Wonderful! Almost perfect. It's John Nance Garner."

"Haaa," screeched Mario in the third row. "Nancy is the vice president!"

The class broke into laughter.

"Settle down, Mario. I don't recall you knowing the correct answer. That was just a slip of the tongue," she said with a comforting tone. "Wasn't it, Lucy?"

Lucy nodded while Jimmy tossed a quickly made spitball in Mario's direction.

* * *

Over grilled cheese sandwiches and pickles, Lucy recounted her big moment to her mother.

"Jimmy made me," she explained.

"Well, good for Jimmy! See, nothing terrible happened to you," Giuliana pointed out, sweeping her hand over her daughter's silky hair. "Maestro is going to be late tonight. He is auditioning sopranos for *Tosca.* The Tosca he had cast has an illness in the family. So why don't you ask Jimmy to come home with you after school?" she added in a conspiratorial whisper. "I will make graham crackers with chocolate pudding for a treat. Good idea?"

"Maestro will yell a high C if he finds out," Dante warned.

"No one will tell him, eh?" Giuliana replied.

"Why don't he like Jimmy anyway?" questioned Phil. "He's a real good kid."

Giuliana sighed. "Some things have no answers. It is the way it is with your father. I cannot change this thing. Now hurry and finish your lunch, or you will be late for the bell."

While the boys distracted Giuliana at the front door, Lucy snuck into the kitchen and took six huge Sicilian olives from the container in the refrigerator. She hid them in a pouch she made from Cut-Rite wax paper. Hiding the olives behind her back, she kissed her mother good-bye. As the three siblings returned to school, she distributed the booty. Giuliana watched until they were out of sight. She chuckled to herself and went to check if the bottomless container needed refilling.

* * *

Mrs. Harris clapped her hands and called for attention. "Everyone get settled. I have exciting news."

Desktops slammed down and schoolbags shuffled underfoot as everyone settled in for the afternoon. The children looked at their teacher expectantly.

"Are we having a procession for some holy day and have to bring in a dime for a flower?" asked Bobby, the wise guy in the class.

Mrs. Harris stifled a smirk. "No, Sister Genevieve told the faculty at lunch that we are going to have two programs this school year. Your parents and relatives will be invited to attend. The first will be a Christmas show, and the first, third, fifth and seventh grades will perform. The spring show will be for the even numbered grades."

A general buzz erupted in the room. Lucy reached over and hit Jimmy's arm. He turned to face panic in her wide brown eyes.

Mrs. Harris was still rambling on excitedly. "Our class is doing a skit about Santa's workshop. We will nominate candidates for the lead roles of Santa Claus, Mrs. Claus, Rudolph, and the chief elf, Wilbur. The rest of the class will be elves and reindeer. Everyone will have at least one line to say, and the entire class will be singing a song titled, "With a Ho and a Hee and a Tap, Tap, Tap."

When all was said and done, Jimmy was Wilbur and Lucy was assigned to be a very miserable elf, Verna.

"This is the worst day of my life," Lucy moaned as she and Jimmy walked home. "You made me answer a question this morning, and Mrs. Harris made me a talking elf this afternoon. I'm going to be sick."

"You're not going to be sick. You don't do that anymore."

"I feel it in my sto…watch out!" Lucy lowered her voice. "That's Strega Titzi walking in front of us."

Jimmy checked it out. "Sssh. Don't let her hear us. Quick! Duck behind this car."

The two children hid behind a parked car on the curb. As Strega Titzi hobbled down the block, Lucy and Jimmy made progress by running forward and then ducking behind another car every few paces.

"What are you two up to?"

Lucy and Jimmy both looked up in relief at Giuliana.

"That's Strega Titzi," Lucy warned, still whispering.

Giuliana glanced up the block. "It's not nice to call an old lady a witch."

"She puts spells on people, everyone says," Lucy insisted.

"She chases kids away from her house. She comes outside with her broom and yells in Italian."

"Well, maybe she's not so nice, but you don't have to hide from her. She won't hurt you."

"She threw a rotten tomato at my brother once," Jimmy informed her.

"That wasn't a nice thing to do, no matter what your brother was up to," Giuliana conceded.

"He wasn't doing nothin'. He was playing stick-ball with his friends."

"All right. Never mind. Are you coming back to the house, Jimmy?" Giuliana asked.

"Yes, ma'am. Did you make the graham crackers and chocolate pudding?"

"I sure did."

"I hope you made a ton 'cause I can eat a lot more than you think."

Giuliana smiled fondly at her daughter's friend.

* * *

Maestro paced the floor of his office and growled at Joe. "My mind is made up."

"You are crazy! You know that? This is a big production and you take the chance of an empty house. Or worse—*fischi* from the audience and acid from the critics."

"If that happens, they are the fools. Fools without ears. Dai Jiang's voice has a natural sweetness that enfolds great power. Furthermore, unlike many sopranos we know, she can act."

"She is Chinese! Who ever heard of a Chinese Tosca?" Joe exploded.

"So? Chinese, Italian, Portugese! Who cares? She is riveting on the stage. What? Because she is Oriental, she should be resigned to singing Cio-Cio San her whole life—who, by the way, is Japanese but no one takes particular care for that! I have seen Oriental girls in that role and they were laughable. *Terribile!*"

"You are asking a great deal of your audience."

"Eh, by asking the impossible we get the possible."

A dark curly head stuck itself in the doorway.

"Excuse me, Maestro."

"What is it?" Maestro asked his stage manager.

"Leticia has just stormed out of the building."

"Why now?" Maestro said, dropping in his chair and running his hand through his long hair.

"Because she claims Vincent is holding his note too long and loud on purpose."

"Let her go. Rehearse around her."

The young man nodded and left.

"I guess if Leticia doesn't return, you can always put China doll in her place," Joe remarked snidely.

Maestro glared at him. "I have spoken. The discussion is over. When are the audio men scheduled to arrive?"

"They rescheduled for tomorrow. Are you going to tell everyone that you are having speakers put in your office so you can hear everything that goes on in the theater?" Joe inquired.

"Sure, sure, why not? When the cat is missing, the mice dance. Let them know that the cat has big ears."

Joe left the office, and Maestro picked up the phone. The number rang twice and was picked up by a sweet voice.

"Hello?"

"Dai? This is Maestro Salvatori. I am happy to tell you that you will sing the lead in our production of *Tosca.*"

There was an audible gasp at the other end of the line. "Oh, Maestro! I am forever in your debt for this opportunity."

"Just don't let me down, Dai. There is much ado about you being Chinese."

"Sir?"

"*Si?*"

"Dai is my surname. Chinese names are written in reverse from American names. My given name is Jiang. It means river."

"Ah, thank you for telling me. Perhaps you will agree to reversing your name for the program and marquee? Jiang Dai sounds better."

"Whatever you would prefer, Maestro."

"*Buono.*"

Chapter 7

The Whispering Statue hung listlessly from Lucy's hand. Even Nancy Drew would not be able to devise a scheme to keep her from appearing on the school stage that evening. Her class had been aflutter all day. She smiled thinly and tried to participate in the enthusiasm, but only Jimmy knew her true feelings.

"Gee, Lucy, your family owns a whole theater. This is baby stuff for you," he cajoled.

"I sit in our box or am backstage. I never have to look at the audience."

"Don't you want to make your folks proud?"

Lucy nodded. "But I won't. I'm going to get sick in front of everyone."

Now she looked at herself in her bedroom mirror for the twentieth time. Hair in pigtails with a floppy red hat on her head. Two round red circles on her cheeks and red lipstick on her lips. She liked that last part. Her tent-style red dress had white pom-pom buttons down the front.

"Time to go, Lucilla," Maestro's voice called from the foot of the stairs.

At the school, the children parted from their parents.

"Remember, sing from here," instructed Maestro indicating his diaphragm.

"Just try to smile, honey. This is a fun thing you are doing."

Lucy scowled and headed for her assigned classroom. As the head elf, Jimmy was dressed in shorts and a top of emerald green.

"Hey, Jimmy! Are you wearing your own elf clothes for a costume?" asked Billy.

Lucy turned on him in a fury. "You'd better shut up, Billy, or I'll never help you with your math homework again," she warned.

"Oh…Lucy's saving her boyfriend. Look at Mutt and Jeff sitting in a tree, k-i-s-s-i-n-g," he chortled.

Lucy marched over to Billy and punched him in the stomach. "Watch out, or I'll trip you on the stage, and you'll go sliding across like a seal. I know how to do stage stuff!"

Billy stood slightly bent with his mouth agape. Most of the class also turned to look at Lucy in wonder. Mrs. Harris discreetly turned her back and stayed out of it. Lucy was doing fine.

* * *

"Wilbur" marched across the stage, arms and legs pumping in frustration. "What is going on, elves? Why are Santa's toys so far behind schedule?"

"The wings keep falling off the airplanes," said Murray the elf, holding up a wingless toy plane.

Rose stepped forward. "The smokestack keeps falling off the ships," she explained, holding up a sample.

Silence. More silence.

"What else is going on?" Wilbur asked loudly. He turned his back to the audience to stare at Lucy. She stared back.

"What else is going on, Verna?" he repeated, sidling up to Lucy.

Silence.

"Is there a problem with the train?" he asked, grabbing it from her hand and waving it around. "Maybe something with the wheels?"

Lucy looked at him and nodded. Wilbur crossed his eyes and stuck out his tongue at her. She was so surprised that she started to laugh.

"So what's going on?" Wilbur repeated.

"The wheels keep falling off the trains. The glue is no good." *What now? Pound my hand!* Lucy pounded her hand on the worktable. "Somebody messed up the glue! What shall we do?" she continued with a frown.

Wilbur moved downstage. "No sense frowning. No point in getting all upset. This is the happiest time of year. Here's what we'll do…" He pulled a toy chest from the wings and proceeded to hand out small wooden hammers. "Now everybody smile, and we'll get the job done. With a ho and a hee and a tap, tap, tap." The elves broke into song and some semblance of a dance. As Lucy moved forward, she could see her mother and father smiling broadly. A small glow of pleasure started in her stomach, traveled to her heart, and reached her face. She linked arms with the other elves as they kicked their legs, crashing into each other's ankles. She leaned a bit forward and looked at Jimmy in the center of the chorus line. He saw her and winked. She winked back.

* * *

The New York Herald Tribune: "As Tosca, Jiang Dai's voice purred on the soft legato phrases and blazed on the high end of her range. The climax at the end of act one was a *coup de theatre.*"

The New York Daily News: "Never before has there been such a dramatically riveting performance of the role, Tosca. Jiang Dai captured the tragic plight of her character with true inner motivation."

Maestro relaxed back in his chair and let the satisfying accolades rush over him. He was happy for his young singer, but he was more relieved that his expectations had been fulfilled. He was vindicated. Through the speakers on his wall, he heard the pianist begin playing for the rehearsal of *La Giaconda.* He needed to go speak with Josie about the costumes for this massive undertaking.

"Hey, Maestro." Phil walked into the office. "My arm's starting to hurt."

Maestro looked at his red-paint-flecked son. "All right. Stop painting. I didn't tell you to paint all morning."

"I know, but these are big flats. Where you going?" he asked as Maestro strode toward the door.

"To talk to Josie."

"Can I come with you?"

"Of course. But don't be rearranging all her threads like you did last time."

"I put them in a better order. I have a system."

"When you are in charge of the costumes, you can use your system. Until then you keep your hands to yourself."

Josie's sewing machine hummed loudly as she pushed yards of blue velvet under its needle.

"Josie," Maestro said. "Josie," he called louder.

Josie took her foot off the treadle and turned. "Maestro!" She noticed Phil behind him. "Oh, Felice! Come in, *caro.* How are you doing?"

"I've been painting, but I'm taking a break." He looked at the windowsill covered with potted plants. "Your plants need watering. I'll do it."

"Thank you. He is a real, how do you say it? Farmer Gray."

"He's the only one in the family who is. He takes care of the backyard all by himself in the summer." Maestro paused. "I come to discuss the costumes for *La Giaconda.* You know the setting is Venice, and the pageantry of the costuming must be unequalled in opera. I want to splurge on the costumes for this opera. We will use silks, brocades, jewels, and furs. I think you may need an assistant. Is your friend available to help out?"

"I don't know. I will ask her. I am sure she can use the money. But if she cannot, I will do it myself. Not for you to worry."

Phil returned with a pitcher full of water. "Maestro, can I eat my lunch in here with Josie? She was teaching me about cutting patterns last time."

"Sure, sure. Are you going to be a tailor now? I thought you were going to be a stagehand."

"I am going to be everything!" Phil exclaimed happily.

* * *

Giuliana set the big square box in front of her husband.

"*Mamma mia,*" he kidded. "I hope it is not *capuzzella*!" he groaned, comically shivering at the thought of the lamb's head delicacy he so despised.

"I would not do that to you on our fifteenth anniversary," Giuliana assured him. "Open it. My parents will be here any minute to watch the children. Our reservation is for seven o'clock."

Rinaldo pulled apart the big bow on the box. From the depths of mounds of tissue paper, he withdrew a magnificent Panama hat. "It is wonderful!" he exclaimed.

"It is one of the finest made. Do you see the diagonal weave pattern on the crown?"

"I am looking at the purple ribbon."

"It is satin with three folds."

"It will match my socks."

* * *

When Rinaldo arrived in America at the age of twenty, it did not take him long to find work as the assistant managing director at the Kings Academy of Music. After checking out his resume, contacting his references, and observing his musicianship, the Academy was thrilled to have him join their staff. As soon as he was able, Rinaldo began giving private vocal lessons, and many of his students found themselves on the Academy stage in a reasonable amount of time. In 1915 he combined being the artistic director for operas produced during the summer at Ebbets Field with his other pursuits. By 1922 he was the most successful managing director Kings Academy had ever had.

Rinaldo worked on embellishing his dapper fashion image whenever he could afford to splurge. He took regular trips into the city to see what was being featured. With his Panama hat atop his longer-than-usual hair, and swinging his ever-present walking stick, the well-built and handsome thirty-year-old made a striking presentation. As he walked through the men's department at B. Altman, his eye fell upon the salesgirl behind a counter. He stopped in his tracks as he stared at the most beautiful woman he had ever laid his eyes upon. Her dark luxurious hair was pulled back off her face, revealing a long slender neck and a perfectly shaped jawline. Her oval face was perfection, and when she smiled at her customer, his heartbeat broke into an *arpeggio.* He summoned his dignity and approached the counter.

"May I help you?"

Her voice was as full as the most magnificent aria ever written.

"I am looking for a pair of black socks."

So overwhelmed was he by her presence, Rinaldo made the purchase and left without his change.

The next day he reappeared.

"Hello again. Did you come back for your change?" Giuliana asked with a twinkle. Her voice was slightly accented. Was it possible she was also Italian?

"No, no. I came for a pair of brown socks," Rinaldo declared. "I forgot I needed brown socks."

The next day he returned and asked for navy-blue socks. "Perhaps you should check your wardrobe so you could get all your shopping done at once," Giuliana suggested with a smile.

This time Rinaldo managed to smile back and find his tongue.

"But then I would not have the opportunity of seeing you. Seeing you is the highlight of my day."

Giuliana blushed and said, "Will that be all, sir?"

"*Si, signorina*?" he inquired hopefully.

"*Si, Signore.*"

On the next two successive days, Rinaldo reappeared, asking for tan socks and gray socks.

"Oh dear," Giuliana moaned after completing the transaction.

"What is it, Giuliana?" asked Rinaldo, having successfully asked her name the day before.

"I will have to see if my manager can order purple socks. It seems you have bought all our colors. If we cannot get them, I don't suppose I shall ever see you again."

"That will never happen. I will grow a third foot before I allow that to happen."

The couple began seeing each other. Giuliana found purple socks as a gift for Rinaldo for their first Christmas together. His purple socks became a trademark that were often mentioned in newspaper articles about the Academy and its director. Soon Rinaldo was courting his Florentine prima donna. Giuliana Ardito was eight years younger than he but had come to the United States with her family two years before he did. Her father, Dante, was a physician and her mother, Anna, a housewife. They lived in Brooklyn. Giuliana was an accomplished pianist and had been continuing her studies at the famed Institute of Musical Art, the precursor to Julliard. Both were thrilled to have met someone who shared their love of music.

Rinaldo rented a car and took Giuliana on a trip to the Catskill Mountains. As they sat on a huge boulder, with the Hudson River below them and a sky slashed in pink and purples punctuating the sunset, Rinaldo stood with his back to the view. With the sun behind him, he looked like a god. He spread his arms and sang Radamas' aria from *Aida*, "Celeste Aida," skillfully substituting Giuliana's name for the heroine.

Heavenly Giuliana, divine shape,
mystic garland of light and flowers,
you are queen of my thoughts,
you are the splendour of my life
I would like to give you your sky back,
the sweet breeze of the fatherland:
to put a regal garland on your heart
to build up a throne for you next to the sun.

At the conclusion, he fell upon one knee and withdrew a ring box from his pocket.

"Giuliana, when I look into the future, I see you standing beside me. My love for you is total and will endure for all time. You will never have to wonder if I love you; you will know for sure in the deepest recesses of your heart. Giuliana, *mi amore*, will you marry me?" He opened the box to present a diamond-shaped sapphire surrounded by diamonds that he had begun to save for on the day he bought the tan socks.

"Rinaldo, of course, I will marry you. I adore you," Giuliana replied, standing and walking into his embrace. Their kiss was as warm and deep as the setting sun.

"Did you have a doubt?" Giuliana teased.

"No, *amore*, how could I? Destiny has decided."

* * *

They married in 1924 and moved into an apartment in Brooklyn to be close to Rinaldo's work. Giuliana helped with setting up his vocal lessons and his many appointments with people in the opera industry. She began referring to him as Maestro, and it soon stuck. They were deliriously happy. Rinaldo was devoted to his bride; no buxom diva or calculating student could stir his interest. Giuliana was proud of her talented and handsome husband. She trusted his judgment implicitly; she reveled in his attentions to her, and she prided herself on creating a home he was happy to return to each night.

Chapter 8

1939

The summer was drawing to a close, and the Salvatori children were both elated and sad. They had festooned the front hall with a Welcome Home sign, and the dining room was bedecked with paper chains. Maestro was returning from his summer tours with the opera company. He was finishing up the summer series tour with a production of *Madama Butterfly* in Yankee Stadium. Dan and Phil were looking forward to spending the last week of summer vacation at a camp upstate. Lucy, however, was saddened to know that with her father's return, there would be no more carefree days of playing with Jimmy at each other's houses. Nonetheless, the family didn't feel complete when Maestro was away, and they had been busy all day helping their mother make homemade spinach ravioli.

Maestro entered the front door and inhaled the tomato sauce and roasted veal aromas emanating from the kitchen. He could hear the giggles of the children's voices coming from upstairs. But what was that rhythmic clanging coming from the parlor? He hung up his hat and cane and went to investigate.

Tino was seated in the middle of the floor with an array of overturned pots and pans. He was using two wooden spoons to keep time with "It Don't Mean a Thing" as it blared from the tabletop Phillips radio. He was obviously having a high old time and keeping incredible rhythm. Maestro headed into the kitchen.

"My prima donna," he exalted, heading straight for Giuliana at the stove and taking her in his arms.

"Rinaldo. I'm so happy to see you. Welcome home." She nestled more comfortably into his arms and kissed him again.

"Do I have time before dinner?"

"Sure, sure. At least a half hour. Why don't you change and lay down for a bit? I will call you."

"Do you care to join me?" he inquired with a wicked leer as he rubbed his hand on her backside.

"And take a chance on ruining this feast I have been preparing all day?" she teased. "Shame on you." She swatted his backside with a slotted spoon.

"All right. All right. I will just dream until later." As he left the room, he stopped suddenly and turned. "Since when has Tino been playing along with the radio?"

"He began just after you left. I know," she said, nodding her head in wonderment. "He's wonderful, isn't he?"

"I will buy him a set of drums immediately, and we will look into getting him lessons."

"He'll like that. Also, it will make cooking a whole lot easier if I can have my pots and pans back in the kitchen."

* * *

Two days later Giuliana stood on the sidewalk talking to her neighbor, Rita Ruggiero across the street.

"I'm telling you, that wicked old lady put the *malocchia* on me!" Rita assured Giuliana.

"You can't really believe that!"

"What? Your family doesn't know about *malocchia*?" She threw up her hands before Giuliana could respond. "We've sidestepped it all our lives, not always successfully. I called my mother. I've had it! She's going to give me the cure."

"Cure?"

"Sure. To get rid of that witch Titzi's evil eye."

"Why did she give you the evil eye?"

"Sam has been parking his car in front of her house. A few times. What? He's supposed to ignore a good parking spot because she wants the curb clear? She's not even the owner; she's only a tenant. She and her sister don't have a car. Anyway, the other day Sam goes to get the car, and there are eggs smeared all over the windshield. He knew it was her. He rang her doorbell and yelled at her. She didn't even deny it. She said she had been trying to make the car grow wings so it would fly away from in front of her door. Then she laughs at him. Sam tells her she really is a crazy old witch and maybe she should rub some raw eggs on her behind so she could fly off on her broom."

"I can't believe he said that to her," Giuliana interjected.

"Believe it. He was furious. The next day, I pass her house on my way to my cousin Flo's, and she's sitting by the window. I can see her glaring at me and muttering something. When I reach Flo's, I trip on her front step and crack my face on the doorknob. Look at this black eye! I look like Primo Carnera! I've climbed those steps a thousand times…and now this!"

"That could happen to anyone."

"Then this morning, I bring in the eggs and milk from the milkbox, and a yellow jacket attacks me.

I dropped the eggs and broke ten of them! Eh?" she surmised, squinting knowingly at Giuliana. "I have the *malocchia.* Oh! Here's my mother now. You want to help?"

Giuliana glanced across the street and was surprised to see Maestro strolling purposefully down their street midafternoon.

"I'm sorry. I have to see why Maestro is home so early," she said breathlessly as she hurried across the street. "Rinaldo! Is everything all right?"

"No! We have a problem. Marco has the chicken pox, and I can't find another child to fill in to play Little Trouble in tomorrow's performance of *Butterfly.*"

"You called the Academy?"

"And the Metropolitan. No children are available."

"Will you use a doll?"

"No, no, no," he insisted as they reached the front door. "We were not playing it as a baby. Marco is nine years old. The same as Lucy."

Giuliana looked at him suspiciously. "What are you thinking?"

"I want Lucy to fill in."

"Rinaldo! Are you losing your mind? She won't want to do this. Besides, the part calls for a boy."

"It has been played as a girl before. In the Belasco play, it *is* a girl."

"Lucy is not yet nine, and besides, she's tall for her age."

"She is not much taller than Marco. Josie said she can alter a costume for her in no time."

"*Caro*, do not ask this of her."

"Why? She did a wonderful job in the school play last year. She had to speak and sing and dance. Here she just has to be on stage and look cute."

"Rinaldo, please, you of all people should understand how she will feel."

"I need her. Yankee Stadium is sold out. Where is she?"

Giuliana opened the tap in the kitchen where they now stood. She filled a glass with water.

"Lucy?" Maetsro called. "Where is she?"

"At Jimmy's."

"Jimmy's! Why is she there? What did I say about that?"

"Rinaldo, be reasonable. They are classmates and friends. The summer is long. Children must play."

"We shall see," he retorted as he headed back to the front door.

"Rinaldo, don't embarrass yourself! Do not show anger!" Giuliana pleaded as she ran to the front door after him.

Rinaldo turned to face her. "You wait here."

Maestro crossed Stillwell Avenue, dodging a couple of cars in his haste. He stood outside the Ferraro house and shouted, "Lucy! Lucy!"

Lucy came to the front door, looked behind her at Jimmy, and scampered down the stairs. Jimmy walked out onto the front stoop behind her, followed by his mother.

"Mr. Salvatori, is everything all right?" asked Mrs. Ferraro.

"*Scusa, Signora,* but Lucy must come home now," he replied, his accent getting thicker with his annoyance.

"Let me give Lucy some of the cookies I baked. The children were just going to sit down for milk and cookies."

"No, *grazie.* She has cookies at home." He looked at Lucy. "Where she should be right now."

Mrs. Ferraro walked down her steps. "Mr. Salvatori, is there a problem I don't know about? Because it seems to me that you are not happy when Lucy plays with Jimmy."

"I am *not* happy, *Signora,* but it seems my family does not care to respect my wishes."

"If your reasons are what I think they are, you are a simpleminded fool for all your fancy clothes and airs."

Maestro turned, grabbed Lucy's arm, and strode down the block.

"Remember, Mr. Big Shot. After the game, the king and the pawn go back in the same box. All that's left is for God to decide."

Maestro marched Lucy home without saying a word. "Into the parlor," he ordered when they stepped indoors. "Sit."

Lucy obeyed.

"Lucilla, I need you to play Little Trouble in *Madama Butterfly* at Yankee Stadium in two nights. Marco is sick with the chicken pox."

Lucy stared at him with her mouth open.

"You do not have to say a word. You do not sing. You just sit and sometimes you walk. Josie is fixing you a beautiful costume. More beautiful than a movie star you will be!"

Lucy continued to stare agape as her eyes filled with tears.

"Why you cry?" Maestro asked, exasperated. "You help your papa. It's a good thing, no? You do it because it is a good thing to do something your papa wants instead of something he does not want. No?"

Lucy nodded sadly.

"*Buono*! Tomorrow you come to the opera house with me, and you will try on your costume. We will go over what you have to do. Then I tell you what! On

Monday I won't go to work, and I cancel my voice lesson. The whole family will go to the World's Fair! Now, are you happy?"

Lucy looked up. "Yes, Maestro," she whispered.

* * *

Giuliana entered her daughter's bedroom. Lucy was reading *Little Women.*

"Did Maestro scold you about Jimmy?" Giuliana asked her as she sat on the bed.

Lucy shook her head. "He didn't say anything. I'd rather he yelled. This opera is worse punishment."

"Oh, Lucy. This isn't a punishment. Your father needs your help."

"Why can't Dante or Phil do it?"

"They're not home! They're at camp!"

"We can go get them before Friday night."

"No. Maestro wants you. We get the boys on Sunday. He doesn't want to cut short their holiday."

Lucy smoothed her hand over her book. "I wish I had sisters. Then he could pick one of them instead."

"I will be there. And Nonna and Papi."

"Can Jimmy come? I'll feel better if Jimmy is there. He makes me feel brave."

"You won't be able to see him. Yankee Stadium is very big."

"I don't care. I'll know he's there rooting for me."

Giuliana made a decision. "All right. But we can't tell Maestro. It's our secret. I will go to his house tomorrow and give his parents three free tickets to come." She smoothed Lucy's hair off her face. "Now, you feel better?"

Lucy nodded.

* * *

Giuliana rang the doorbell and waited. Mrs. Ferraro came to the door. Seeing Giuliana, she closed the door partway and spoke through the opening.

"Yes? May I help you?" she asked formally.

"Mrs. Ferraro, first I want to apologize for my husband's behavior yesterday. I do not know what he said, but I am sure whatever it was, it was not a happy thing to listen to."

"Hummph," Mrs. Ferraro grunted.

"I am sorry. He is truly a good man, but with certain things, I don't know what to say, his mind is like a tornado behind a closed door."

Mrs. Ferraro opened the door wider. "You seem like a nice lady. I know my Jimmy thinks you are. Only for that reason will I let Jimmy continue to play with Lucy. I like Lucy, but there are enough mean people in the world that Jimmy doesn't need to go looking for them."

"I want to give you these. Free tickets to tomorrow's performance of *Madama Butterfly* at Yankee Stadium. Lucy is going to be in it. She is playing Little Trouble, and she desperately wants Jimmy to be there. It would be my honor if you all come."

"I am sorry Mrs. Salvatori; I cannot accept these tickets. Tell Lucy I am sorry too. But I will not go see any show that your pea-minded, fancy-pants Indian husband puts on."

"Oh!" gasped Giuliana. She backed away from the door. "I understand. Again, I am sorry."

* * *

The stadium was filled, and the audience was exuberant. The reviews for this outdoor event were mediocre. The baritone was unimpressive as Pinkerton and sounded hoarse in his aria. The sets were spare and non-evocative, and the sound system was inconsistent. Little Trouble, however, was endearing in her brief appearances.

* * *

"Let them criticize," gloated Maestro on Monday as the family rode the special subway line to the World's Fair. "The best advertising there is. Joe said the season is selling out rapidly. It doesn't bother a dog to get pelted with bones."

Lucy tugged on her mother's arm. "Mama, I didn't see Jimmy all weekend. Did he really say he thought I was great?"

"Sshh," hushed Giuliana. "Yes, he said that. Now gather your things; it is almost our stop," she instructed as she turned her sorrowful face from her daughter.

The children were exuberant as they raced through the fairgrounds.

"Stay together, or I will tie you all to a leash," shouted Maestro as he garnished more than a few stares himself. His striped pants could not camouflage the purple socks that peeked from his black and white shoes as he walked in giant strides after the children. The family asked a passerby to take a snapshot of them in front of the Trylon and Perisphere, the tall steel-framed structures covered with stucco that were the visual icons of the 1939 New York's World's Fair. They then took the escalator in the Trylon and proceeded into the Perisphere to view the perfect world of the future.

Happily they bounced from exhibit to exhibit, wondering at the animated figures and devouring foods that rarely emerged from their mother's kitchen.

At the RCA building, Maestro went into a tirade. "I have been trying to get them to broadcast a piece of one of our operas from here. So far they have stalled us with every delay tactic you can imagine. There are not many places it can be broadcast, but it would still be a wonderful advertisement. *Allora,* I will have to try harder."

As the children nodded sleepily on the subway ride home, Phil asked, "Maestro, can we go to the World's Fair another time?"

"Yeah, that would be great," Dan agreed, studying the Washington inauguration commemorative coin he held in his hand. "But more than that, I want to be around to see that world of tomorrow they keep talking about!"

Chapter 9

Lucy was desperate to have the "Dorothy" shoes that had appeared in the shoe store on Eighty-Sixth Street just weeks after the premier of *The Wizard of Oz*. They were shiny red patent leather with a sequined red bow on the toe. A very small squat "high" heel made it even more alluring.

"I've already bought you new school shoes, play shoes, and dress shoes for the school year. We are not buying red shoes that match with nothing," Giuliana explained again in reply to the ceaseless begging.

"Then I will save my money until I can buy them myself."

"Good. I like that idea very much. Now, here is a nickel for you and one for Jimmy. Buy yourself a treat after you run my errands. Take these shoes to the shoemaker and tell him heels and tips. Here is the ticket for Maestro's shirts at the Chinese laundry. Pick up a loaf of Italian bread with seeds at the deli."

"OK, but Ma, if I get all As…" Lucy began.

"Go! Go wait for Jimmy in front and stop pestering me."

Lucy danced along the curb as a sanitation water wagon drove by, playing tag with the water, and she managed to get fairly soaked before she saw Jimmy approaching.

"Hi!" she called happily.

"Hi, back. You're all wet. You're gonna get in trouble."

Lucy shrugged. "Here's a nickel from my mother."

"Wow! Thanks. Where we going?"

"First, to the shoemaker," she said holding up her father's shoes.

"Boy, your father's got big feet."

"He's so tall, you know. Oh! Sorry, I didn't mean to talk about that."

"What? You think you can't talk about how tall someone is around me? That's dumb, Lucy."

"You're right. It's like you couldn't say the word 'fraidycat around me," she said with a grin.

Jimmy punched her arm. "You're nuts, ya know?"

"Jimmy, did you really think I was good when you saw *Madama Butterfly?* I haven't seen you since that night."

"Huh?"

"Since the opera at Yankee Stadium. My mother said you liked it, but I haven't seen you."

"Oh, sure, Lucy…" Jimmy stammered. "You were great."

"What was your favorite part of the whole thing?"

"Uh, you! And the frankfurters."

"I didn't see that they were selling frankfurters. I felt like an ant surrounded by all those people, so I really didn't see anything."

They entered the whirring, slapping, banging world of Tony's Shoe Repair. Tony looked up from his buffing machine.

"What I do for you?"

Lucy handed him the shoes. "Heels and tips, please."

"You sure you no want taps on the heels?" he asked with a smile.

"No. They're my father's."

"He's a dancer, no?" he joked.

"No, sir. He puts on operas. And he can sing. But he only sings at home." Lucy thought about it. "Or with his voice students. He only dances with my mother for sure."

"Oke. Justa heels and tips. No taps. Too bad."

As they left the Chinese laundry, two kids skated by, calling, "Hi, Jimmy," and a housewife sweeping her sidewalk stepped aside and greeted, "Hello, Jimmy. Almost time to go back to school."

Jimmy raised his stubby arm in reply but didn't respond.

Ahead of the two friends at the deli counter was Strega Titzi. Lucy went around the corner of the counter and waited for the owner to spot her. Jimmy, not taking note of the elderly woman, stood on his tiptoes to retrieve a red package of Dubble Bubble gum from its display. As the box toppled over and Jimmy scurried about trying to collect the scattered merchandise, Strega Titzi let out a screech.

"Devil boy! What you doing? Try to steal my bag?" she inquired, raising her black drawstring satchel and swinging it as if she was going to hit Jimmy in the head with it.

"No, ma'am. I'm just picking up this gum I dropped."

"You do on purpose, but you can't get me. See? I know your kind. My bag is wrapped on my wrist. You no take!"

"I don't want your bag."

"*Signora.* I'm sure Jimmy bumped into you by accident. He's a regular customer, and he's a good kid,"

Carmine the owner said soothingly. "Here, look. I'm giving you an extra two slices of capacola for your trouble."

The elderly woman flicked her hand at Jimmy. "Stay away from me, or you be sorry."

Jimmy scooted over to stand by Lucy. Jimmy stuck his thumb between his index and middle finger and shook it upside down toward the floor. "I heard this gets rid of the evil eye if she's giving it to me," he whispered.

* * *

Dan, Phil, and their friends were playing baseball in front of the house. Jimmy looked longingly as Paul hit Dan's pitch and began to run the bases.

"Want to come inside?" Lucy asked, sensing her friend's anguish.

"No, thanks, it's getting late. I gotta get home."

"Ok, watch out! Here comes my Red Ruffing pitch," warned Dan as he wound up.

The batter struck out, and Jimmy waved good-bye as he headed home.

* * *

"Lucy! Come down here and help me put the olive spread on these crackers. Dante, turn off that baseball game and bring the selzer bottles into the dining room. Phil! Where is Phil? Felice, where are you?" Giuliana hollered.

"Ma, you're acting a little crazy," Tino said as he stuck toothpicks in cheese cubes.

"She always gets crazy before the company comes," Dante concluded.

"We have two special guests today. Rocco Pandiscio and Annunciata Garrotto are joining everyone else who you're used to."

"Who are they?" Phil asked as he entered from the back door.

"Two famous opera singers from the Met. *Uffa*! Look at you all covered in dirt. Why were you in your garden at this time? Go upstairs and get washed. I want you and Dan to take the guests' jackets, capes, or whatever they have and bring them upstairs and lay them on the bed. Neatly." She twirled to the stove. "*Uffa*! I was almost burning this eggplant. Tino, get away from the cookies."

"I want to fix them nicer on the dish," Tino explained.

"They are fine," Giuliana said, moving him away. "Here. Fold these napkins. Lucy, stir the sauce."

Two hours later the house was alive with guests laughing, sharing stories, and discussing the recent invasion of Poland.

"It is time to play round robin," Maestro announced, tapping his walking stick on the floor. "Sit. Sit, everyone. Anywhere."

Forty-five people scattered about. The children sat on the floor, along with a few other guests their age.

"For the benefit of our two newest guests, let me explain the game," Maestro offered. "We start with one person singing a few lines from a song. You can choose any word from those lyrics and sing another song starting with that word. Felice, you want to keep the record of who sings the most songs?"

"OK, Maestro," Phil agreed, relieved not to be expected to sing.

"Who wants to start?" Maestro asked.

"I will start because I have to go inside and stir some pots," Giuliana stated. "Let me think. Hmmm."

Giuliana started them off with "Blue Moon," and soon the players were laughing and arguing. Giuliana ran relays to the kitchen as she tried to finish preparing the meal and join in the game. She sang "The Way You Look Tonight" with a carving knife in her hand. While everyone had something sarcastic to say about her pose, a soft, clear voice filled the room. Lucy was singing the middle verse of "Over the Rainbow." Her voice was pure and disarming, and her ardor was heartfelt. Rocco stood and called out, "*Brava*," while the other guests clapped with enthusiasm.

"I had better watch out for you standing in the wings from now on when I perform," Annunciata speculated kindly.

"I'd sure like to see the sap who's gonna find a song with *lemon drop* in it," Phil said with glee.

Maestro and Giuliana didn't respond to his outburst. They didn't even hear it. They just stared in awestruck wonder at each other.

As Guiliana retreated to the kitchen, she murmured to herself, "Allelulia."

Later that evening, before the couple went to bed, they checked on the children to thank them for their help. Lucy was reading in her room while Dan studied the baseball cards sprawled on his bed. Tino was sound asleep on his side of the room he shared with Phil. As they entered, Phil quickly flipped the sheet forward on his bed.

"Thank you for all your help today, Phil," Giuliana said. "You should be getting to sleep now."

"OK."

"Lay down, and I'll tuck you in," she said, approaching the bed.

"That's OK," Phil said, trying to slide off the bed. A rattling noise followed him.

"What is that?" Maestro asked.

"What?" Phil asked, standing ramrod straight next to his bed.

"That noise," said Maestro as he pulled the sheet up. "What's all this?" Nickels and dimes were scattered like confetti on top of the sheet. "Where did this money come from?"

"People."

"What people?" asked Giuliana, not really wanting to know the answer.

"The people who came back upstairs to get their purses and jackets and hats."

Tino woke up and rolled over.

"They tipped you?" Maestro inquired.

"Yeah. They tipped me. For doing a good job," Phil obliged.

"And because that's what it cost to store your stuff in the bedroom. Like a coat check in the theater, Phil said," Tino explained groggily.

"Did you ask for this money, Felice?" Maestro asked sternly.

"Kind of."

"*Bedda Madre*!" Giuliana cried. "I can die of shame. I want to die this very minute."

"Don't die, Ma," Tino begged.

"I'm not dying, Tino. But I may kill your brother. How could you think we would approve of this?" she asked, bewildered.

"I didn't. That's why I didn't tell you. I was doing a job. I needed some money so I charged. It was cheap. Like Maestro. Give a good performance, but don't overcharge the customers. I was doing business like Maestro."

"Well, now we will have to tell everyone that we do not charge people to set aside their coats. And you, young man, are bringing that money to the poor box at the church."

"It was quite enterprising of him, *cara,*" Maestro said, looking at Phil's crestfallen face.

"You stay out of it," Giuliana snapped.

"All right. I'll bring it to church. Can I keep some of it to buy all of us ices when the truck comes around?"

Maestro started to speak, and then looked at Giuliana.

"All right. You can treat your brothers and sister."

"You too. And Maestro. I was thinking. Turns out Lucy has a great voice. You can save money by hiring her to sing in the chorus. Maybe then you could raise our allowances."

"Thank you for the advice, Phil. I will take it under consideration," Maestro said, trying to maintain a serious expression. "Good night now."

As they climbed into bed, Giuliana still could not get over Phil's antics. "Lord, help us," she said with a sigh. "That kid is a lollapalooza. Who knows what his next scheme will be."

"He'll keep us on our toes. That's a good thing," Maestro declared.

"I think he's going to turn me gray."

"Then you can borrow a wig from the theater. I'm sure Phil will give you a discount on the rental."

Chapter 10

Filing through the turnstile at the Highlawn Avenue subway station, the Salvatoris headed for the San Gennaro feast in Little Italy, a celebration in honor of St. Gennaro, the patron saint of Naples. Maestro was from an island near Naples. He didn't talk about it ever, but he always enjoyed listening to people who came from that area tell their stories. Maestro had preceded them into the city earlier in the day. Several of his singers were going to perform arias from various operas. He had gone ahead to check on the sound system, the placement of the huge Salvatori Opera Company banner, and the preparedness of the eight musicians, getting paid dearly for their services.

Guiliana led the family through the throng of people, her parents, Dante and Anna Ardito, chaperoning the group from either side. The appetizing smells that assailed them aroused immediate appetites in everyone.

"Don't you be stopping," Anna scolded her husband, Dante. "It'sa no time to eat now. We're finding Rinaldo."

"I come to eat and listen to the music. Not to be a shepherd dog," groaned the aging physician. His quiescent tone, however, was one used in rote counterattack to a spouse of forty-four years.

Up ahead, Giuliana could see Maestro talking with a man in a loud striped suit. She eased up to his side just as the man was exclaiming, "I am sure your company is very talented; however, I contacted the Metropolitan for singers, and they send me second best."

"Perhaps Signore Johnson asking me, with much persuasion by the way, to come here today does not so much say what he thinks of Salvatori as where he holds you in his esteem," Maestro said. "But no problem. We can go."

"No, no. People are expecting opera. They will get opera. I'm just saying I should have been told ahead of time."

"Not my job. You talka to Edward. I'ma doing him a favor." Maestro's accent became more pronounced as evidence of his annoyance. He turned to Giuliana and slipped his arm through hers.

"Trouble?"

"No. He expects Caruso to rise from the grave to sing at his feast. Now listen. Four of the singers brought costumes, two did not. You think that is all right, or should they all sing in street clothes?"

"They are all individual arias, no? Let them wear the costumes."

"*Buono.*" He turned to go backstage and then made a quick twirl, pivoting on his walking stick. "I almost forgot! I ran into Mayor LaGuardia, and he promised to use his connections to get us television time at the World's Fair in the spring. I'll be sure *not* to mention the San Gennaro feast in our credits."

Giuliana patted his arm. "Don't be getting all sour. That man is not important."

An hour later, after the family had feasted on sausage with peppers and pork braciole, they headed back to the stage area for the performance. Only Papi Ardito was still eating the *polpi,* baked baby octopus seasoned with sesame seeds, paprika, and olive oil.

"Yuck, that looks disgusting, Papi," Lucy informed him.

"You say? Hey, Dante, this is a cousin to the fried calamari you were so busy eating at our house last week."

Lucy looked at the plate again. "Well, the calamari wear a better costume."

The announcer, the man in the striped pants, approached the microphone. While he greeted the assembled crowd and described the order of the singers and their arias, Thomas Griganti, dressed in his costume as Pagliacci, approached Maestro.

"Maestro," he said hoarsely.

"*Si?*"

"I cannot sing."

"What happened to your voice?" Maestro asked in a panic.

"I've felt poorly all day, but now, it is almost done. I cannot sing."

"But the people are expecting *Pagliacci.* They love it."

"I am sorry. I cannot," he said, trying to clear his throat.

"I can see that. I hate to give that *stunade* up front the satisfaction."

Josie, accompanied by her boyfriend, spoke out.

"Maestro, I have a suggestion."

"Happy to hear it."

"Why not let Tomaso stand in front in his costume and lip sync? You can sing Canio's song from back here."

"Preposterous!"

"Why is that? You have a magnificent voice. Tomaso is your pupil. You know exactly how he will sing it."

"It's a good idea," Tomaso choked out. "We can tell the audience what is happening. Better yet, why don't you just go out front and sing? You can't fit in my costume, though. It would be too small."

"Absolutely not! It is not done."

"Didn't Mayor LaGuardia say he was going to be out front?"

"*Managia!* OK, I do. But you will stand out front and lip sync. No one is to know who is doing the singing. *Capisce?*"

The announcement was made, and Maestro took his place with a microphone out of the audience's view. On cue from the musicians, he sang "*Un tal gioco, credete mi,*" an aria in which Canio warns the villagers that while everything on stage is an illusion, life is reality. He admonishes that in this real world, transgressions will be met with real punishment. Tomaso did a beautiful job of lip-synching to his mentor's words; however, he could not know that out of sight, tears were streaming down Rinaldo's face.

Out front, Guiliana gasped. She recognized her husband's luminous voice from the fifth note sung. She signaled her mother to watch the children, and maneuvered her way through the throng. She waited until the thunderous applause had abated and then ran to Rinaldo's side. Seeing his tears, she ushered him away from bystanders. As she reached up and held his face in her hands, she wiped away his tears with her thumbs.

"My love, why tears? It was beautiful."

Maestro shook his head. "I cannot escape my destiny. I will pay for my sins. I can feel it in my soul."

She covered his mouth with the tips of her fingers and then kissed him gently.

"You talk foolishly. Superstition."

"I fear fate will take revenge on the sins of my heart."

* * *

Dante darted from one technician to another as they set up the equipment to transmit a live radio broadcast of that evening's performance of *Don Giovanni* from the opera house.

"Here, young man, you want to hold this for me for a minute?" one of the workers asked.

"Sure," agreed Dante. "When will it be ready?"

"Soon."

Maestro stood in front of the orchestra pit giving last-minute instructions to his Donna Anna. "You're anxious, and it's getting a little sharp up top. Try it again."

The soprano tried again.

"Better," he sighed. "Try releasing the tension in your forehead and jaw. Like this." He exaggerated, relaxing the wrinkles in his own forehead in demonstration, and hoped he would actually release some of the accumulated tension in the process.

"Maestro," interrupted Dante, grabbing his father's arm.

"I'm working. What?"

"Can I stay for the broadcast? Can I have the radio turned on just behind the seats and watch the show live and hear it on radio at the same time?"

"*Uffa*! No. Either radio or take a seat. Not both. Now go. I have to straighten her out," he said in a low voice and pointing his head toward the stage.

Dante walked dejectedly down the aisle.

"What's the matter, kid?" the technician he had helped asked.

Dante explained.

"Here you go," he said, handing Dante a set of headphones. "If your father says it's OK, you can watch and listen at the same time. You'll sit by me."

"Jeepers, mister, that's swell," he cried and ran off to the costume room to tell Phil of his good fortune.

* * *

Dante couldn't stop talking about his radio experience for two days as he prepared for the big ball game against the Bay Ridge Barracudas. The teams were informally organized by fathers in different neighborhoods, and they set up playoffs to coincide with the excitement of the World Series.

Dante stepped into Lucy's bedroom. "Tino, don't you want to come to the game?" he asked.

"No," answered Tino, sitting on Lucy's bed. "We're playing jewelry store." Giuliana's jewelry box was opened on the bed, and her varied pieces were lined up on the bedspread.

"C'mon, that's sissy stuff. Come watch me and Phil play."

"Do I have to?"

"No, you don't have to," answered Lucy. "Leave us alone. We're not interested in your stupid game."

"You're just jealous because the coach is taking us all out to the ice-cream parlor when it's over."

"Well, we're getting ices from the ice man when he comes down the street," Lucy retorted.

"*If* he comes down the street," Dante reminded her as he went down the stairs.

Papi Ardito accompanied Guiliana and the boys to the game while Nonna watched the other two at home. Maestro was working at the opera house.

* * *

It was the fifth inning, and Dante was pitching a successful game. He was glorying in the cheers from the Bensonhurst section and managed to retire Benny Rosa, a star hitter, on a one-pitch flyout to center. Swelled with bravado, Dante's next pitch almost knocked Bobby Coffey off the plate. When he pitched again, Bobby swung hard with a line drive that shot across the field and hit Dante in the chest. Dante collapsed on the ground and did not move. The crowd hushed and then roared as Giuliana and her father, a physician, ran to his side.

"Quick! Run to a store and call an ambulance," shouted the doctor as he put his ear to his grandson's chest. Dante remained unconscious while his grandfather's eyes darkened in a vain effort to find a pulse. Cradling him in his arms, he kept repeating

Dante's name while Giuliana sobbed onto her clenched fist as she knelt at their sides. After what felt like forever, but was in reality only two minutes, Dante's lids fluttered. His half-opened eyes had a thousand-mile stare.

"His heart is beating again. It's very fast. And erratic," Dr. Ardito declared.

Dante was whisked away from his family as they followed in close pursuit. Phone calls were made, and Dr. Ardito disappeared through a long bleak corridor to get firsthand information about his grandson. An hour later he returned with the physician on duty to explain that Dante had traumatic pericarditis from the impact to his chest.

"We are concerned about hemorrhagic pericardial tamponade," Dr. Boyar explained.

"What's that?" Giuliana asked frantically.

"It means that there's bleeding into the membrane that surrounds the heart," her father explained gently.

"Can you fix that?"

"We will have to drain it, and monitor him very closely for signs of reaccumulation."

"Is he going to be all right?"

"The situation is critical, Mrs. Salvatori. He's in shock; the beating of his heart is abnormally rapid. There are conduction problems." Dr. Boyar took a breath. "That means that there is a problem in the transmission of the electrical impulses that control the heartbeat. The good news is your son is young and healthy and regained consciousness after a short time. I am going back to check on him again," he said as he excused himself.

"I'm going with him," Dr. Ardito added, already halfway through the doorway.

Maestro strode into the waiting room, hat askew, minus his jacket, face flushed and sweaty.

"Where is he?" he bellowed.

"With the doctors. They are doing everything for him. Papa is with him."

"I want to see him," he stated, heading out in a direction he didn't know.

Giuliana ran after him and grabbed his arm. "Come. Sit here with us and pray. It is all we can do for Dante right now."

Anna Ardito pulled up in a cab with Lucy and Tino. Both children burst into tears upon seeing their parents.

"I yelled at him before he left the house," Lucy mourned. "He was probably mad at me and threw the ball bad because of me."

"Is Dan going to die?" asked Tino fearfully.

"No! Absolutely not! I will not allow it," Maestro said ominously.

“Rinaldo, hush,” Giuiliana begged. “Please, I am holding on by a thread.”

“But that thread is attached to God,” Anna comforted.

“God? What God?” Maestro seethed. “What God punishes a twelve-year-old boy for sins he did not commit?”

“Maestro!” Lucy sobbed.

“Dante has always been a good boy. He has always honored his mother and father. This is God turning his back.”

“Hush. Hush. You are upsetting the children,” Giuliana warned. “Come, we will go to the chapel.” She clustered Lucy, Tino, and Phil around her. “You wait here with Mama for Papa or the doctor.”

Inside the chapel Giuliana said to the children. “We will pray to the Virgin. She is a mother. She understands. She knows a mother’s pain, and she will ask the Almighty Father to spare us this suffering. *Allora,* we say the rosary.”

Later that evening Lucy shivered under the blanket she had drawn tightly to her chin. She listened to her parents talking in their bedroom.

“I will not listen anymore, Rinaldo. This is not your fault. It has nothing to do with you,” Giuliana insisted.

"You have never appreciated the forces of destiny," he argued, fear clutching at his heart. "God pays an eye for an eye."

"He does no such thing. He is watching over Dante right now. Our time line is drawn. We cannot know what it is. Dante's destiny is not mixed with ours."

Maestro sat on the bed, head in hands.

"If you are so worried, it is not too late. You can reach out," Giuliana urged.

"The time is passed. The pain has severed all ties."

"I am tired of this. When Dante comes home, I will write!"

Maestro started to speak, but Giuliana held up her hand. "*Basta*! I will not discuss this any further. This time, *I* have spoken. I have more important things to do than listen to your foolishness." She took the rosary beads from the top of her dresser and lit the votive candle in front of a small statue of the Blessed Mother.

* * *

"Lucy, where're you goin'?" asked Jimmy as she turned the corner instead of crossing the street to walk home.

"I'm going into the church," she explained. "I'll see you in the morning."

Lucy tugged at the intricately curved wrought-iron door grasp of the church. The heavy wood door grated open slowly. Immediately the sweetly burnt scent of recently used incense shrouded her in an aura of holiness and hope. She tried to muffle the loud clatter of the taps on the heels of her shoes as she walked up the aisle. Pausing midway, she genuflected and slid into a pew. Bending over, she pulled down a kneeler, which thumped loudly in the stillness of the church. She gazed at the tastefully ornate altar and spied a small red lantern aglow, indicating the Body of Christ was present in the chiseled gold tabernacle. Fading bouquets of roses and white carnations from a weekend wedding stood a drowsy guard along the altar rail.

Lucy looked up at the crucifix and started to cry. She didn't understand what was going on. Dante might die, her father had done something terrible she didn't know about, and her mother cried all through the night. She began to pray earnestly. A stooped, elderly woman with a kerchief tied tightly about her head retrieved a wooden taper from the bin of white sand surrounding the candles in front of the statue of Mary. Dropping a coin noisily into the narrow slot, she ignited her taper from a burning candle and quickly lit a votive light.

Lucy sat back in the pew and dug through her schoolbag. She withdrew a small purse and dropped the contents in her lap—$3.27. The money she was saving for her "Dorothy" shoes. They really weren't important anymore. Besides, Dorothy's shoes weren't red patent leather like these were. The red shoes in the store were just a bad imitation. She scooped the money back into the purse and rose. Her eyes caught the statue of St. Joseph with the flickering blue votive candles in front of him. St. Joseph, a father, the patron saint of the Holy Family. She made up her mind. She walked over to the statue and dumped her savings, coin by coin, into the slot. She lit a candle and prayed. She prayed for Dante, she prayed for her mother, and she prayed for her father whom she was afraid was going to hell, and she didn't know why. Sobs suddenly racked her small frame.

A hand touched her shoulder, and she jumped.

"What is wrong, child? Can I help?" Father Fazio's chubby face was etched with concern.

Lucy jumped up. "Good afternoon, Father," she said. "I was going to leave now."

"Sit first." He led her to the front pew. "Can you talk to me? Is there something I can help you with?" Recognition dawned in his eyes. "You are the Salvatori girl. Is your brother…doing better?"

"I don't know. I haven't gone home yet. My mother is at the hospital."

"You have been praying for Dante. I am praying for him also."

Lucy nodded. "I'm also afraid for my father."

"Why is that?"

Lucy couldn't tell the priest that her father had committed a terrible crime. Besides, she had no clue what it might be. But she was afraid for other reasons.

"He is mad at God right now. He blames God, or he says there is no God. I am afraid he will go to hell."

"Ah, Lucy. Your father is frightened. He is saying things he doesn't mean. He will not go to hell."

"But how can God forgive him when he says these things?"

"Remember in the Bible when Peter betrayed Jesus three times before the crucifixion?"

Lucy nodded.

"And do you remember at the Resurrection what Jesus said to Mary Magdalene?"

Lucy shook her head.

"He told her to tell the disciples and to be sure and tell Peter. Do you know why he specifically mentioned Peter?"

"Because he had betrayed him?"

"No. Because he knew Peter felt bad about betraying him, and wanted him to know that he was forgiven, and that He still loved him."

"Oh."

"God never stops loving anyone. When your father is not so scared for Dante, he will be sorry for what he said. He will come back to God, and God will be waiting for him."

Lucy left the church feeling immensely better. She never even thought about her $3.27.

* * *

For almost a week they were concerned about possible cardiac arrest. As they monitored the enlarged cardiac silhouette on chest x-rays, the situation remained touch and go. Repeated surgical punctures of the pericardial cavity were made to aspirate fluid. Then suddenly Dante was making progress. Maestro headed for the hospital every morning. He slipped in a back door with many of the staff; no one thought to question the imposing figure who walked with such intense purpose. On Dante's floor the nurses approached him.

"You know, Mr. Salvatori, you should not be here at this time."

"Ah, beautiful lady, but what can I do?" he'd cajole. "I have to go make beautiful music in a little while that reminds me of you."

At Dante's bedside another nurse came in to check on him, "Mr. Salvatori, visiting hours are not for another three hours on the children's floor."

"And I am not a child!" he would say with a wink. "But look what I brought for you today. Two tickets to my opera house. You come as my guest. *Sì?*"

The nurse sighed and took the tickets with a smile. "OK, but if anyone asks me, I never saw you come in."

When Giuliana arrived, he left for work, only to return later in the evening. Slowly Dante began to gain strength. He walked around the corridor and chafed at the restrictions on his activities. There were just so many books to read and creatures to mold out of modeling clay.

"Why can't Phil and Lucy and Tino come to visit?" he begged.

"Children aren't allowed in the hospital," Giuliana explained once again.

"I want to go home."

"We want you to come home. Soon. The doctor promises soon."

"I'm gonna be dumb in school. I've missed three weeks."

"The teacher understands. If you would read the assignments Phil picked up for you, you wouldn't be so far behind."

"I can't think when I start to study. I get tired."

"Then don't complain about falling behind."

That evening, Maestro arrived at Dante's hospital room door with a flourish. He was bouncing a baseball in his hand.

"Is that for me?" Dante asked excitedly. "I thought maybe you wouldn't let me play baseball anymore."

Giuliana grimaced.

"We will see in time." He pulled another ball out of his pocket.

"Why do you have two balls?"

"One is for you, and one is for Bobby Coffey. When you are well, we will visit his house and give him one."

"I think he probably has a baseball."

"Ah, but he doesn't have *this* baseball."

"What's so special about that one?" Dante asked.

Maestro stepped to the doorway and nodded his head. In stepped Red Ruffing with a big grin on his face.

"Oh my God," shouted Dante, levitating off the bed. "I don't believe it!"

"How're you doing, Dante? I'm glad to hear you're doing so well."

He sat down beside the awestruck boy and chatted for half an hour. He signed both baseballs and gave Dante an IOU for four tickets to a game the following season.

"Now, listen to me, Dante," Red said as he stood up to leave and shook the boy's hand. "Don't let this incident get you down or stop you. I don't know if you know it, but I lost four toes on my left foot in a tractor accident when I was younger. I never for one minute allowed it to make me think I couldn't do something. You remember that, OK?"

"Yes, sir."

After Red left the room, Dante turned to his father.

"Maestro, I *am* playing baseball again."

"I think maybe you are."

Dan stared at the door again and shook his head in amazement.

"You know, Pop, you're the greatest," Dan crowed.

"Pop?" said Maestro, grinning as he arched an eyebrow.

"Oops! It slipped. But it was like you're a regular father. You brought me a pitcher from Yankee Stadium instead of a baritone."

* * *

Dante's return home turned into a block celebration. As the car carrying the recuperating patient turned the corner, the crowd burst into cheers. Children held balloons, and many well wishers held homemade signs welcoming him home. The ice-cream man and flavored-ice man had staked themselves out on the curb. Since the party couldn't come into the house, Maestro handed each vendor a five dollar bill and told them to accommodate the neighbors' wishes. Dante was waving at everyone when he noticed Bobby Coffey in the crowd.

"Maestro, there's the boy from the Barracudas that swung the bat."

Maestro whispered to Phil and waved his hand at the boy and his father to come forward. Bobby, freckled and nervous, looked lost in his green wool sweater. His father nudged him gently.

"I'm really sorry, Dan. I didn't mean for you to get hurt."

"That's OK, Bobby. I didn't mean to mess up the whole game," Dan replied. "Look what my father got for you," he said, handing him the autographed baseball. "I got one too."

Bobby looked at the ball. "Wow! I can't believe it. Red Ruffing signed this, Dad," he said to his father.

The two fathers shook hands. "When Dante is all better, you bring your boy here to play with him, eh?" suggested Maestro.

"Will do," said Mr. Coffey, relieved the meeting had gone so well.

Maestro tipped his hat at the crowd and led Dante into the house, which was steeped in the scent of Pine Sol. Giuliana had been scrubbing every nook for a week before Dante's arrival. Now she was bustling in the kitchen. She sat Dante at the dining room table, all laid out as if for a holiday, and served him homemade cheese tortellini swimming in her golden chicken broth. The rest of the family, including his grandparents, sat around the table watching him eat. Just seeing him sitting at home was enough to fill them up for the moment. Later, when they had digested the full knowledge of this miracle, they would partake of the rest of Giuliana's celebratory cooking. For now, though, she refilled his bowl, announcing, "It's an Allelulia day!"

Chapter 11

Because of the rain, recess was being held in the cafeteria. Lucy and her brothers had eaten in school because of the weather. Dante was still confined to home study. Lucy ambled over to a group of girls and boys playing with jacks. Lucy was good at jacks, but most of these kids were older than she.

"Wanna play, skinny girl?" asked a sixth grader.

"Her name is Lucy," said Jimmy, who stood by her side.

"Sorry, Lucy. I didn't know your name," said the blonde girl. "Do you want to play too?" she asked Jimmy.

Before he could answer, one of the boys in the group said, "No way. Get away from us, troll. Go play with the other trolls under the bridge."

Jimmy's prominent forehead crinkled, and his shortened upper arms flailed out from his body.

"You take that back!" Lucy's shout startled Jimmy and those around her.

"Yeah? What are you going to do if I don't?"

"I'll knock you out," she replied in a fury.

"Oowee. Snow White is gonna beat me up," the boy said with a fake shudder.

In an instant Lucy lunged forward and jumped on the offender. Jimmy shouted for her to stop, but she was beyond caring. She wasn't going to stand around while someone she loved got hurt again. The boy pulled at her long hair and tried to roll away, but Lucy punched him square in the nose. As his friends hooted, the boy slugged Lucy in the eye. Phil and Sister Paul Francis and Sister Helen Marie all reached the tumbling twosome at the same time. The nuns separated the culprits and marched them out of the cafeteria. Lucy found herself standing in the principal's office for the first time in her school career.

"Miss Salvatori, would you care to explain yourself?" asked the principal, Sister Mary Agatha, looking over the rim of her eyeglasses.

"He was mean."

"And you thought that punching him in the nose would improve his behavior. Do you know he is bleeding in the nurse's office?"

Lucy didn't answer.

"Could you not have thought of another way to solve your disagreement?"

"He wouldn't take it back."

"Take what back?"

Lucy wouldn't answer.

"All right. The two of you will meet in my office at three o'clock and apologize to each other. Then you will stay for detention."

"I won't apologize."

"And why not?"

"I'm not sorry."

"Has no one taught you that ladies don't throw punches?"

Lucy shrugged.

"Don't shrug at me, young lady...which you apparently are not. Well, then, if you won't apologize you will have detention after school every day for a week. You may leave."

Lucy turned to go.

"Lucilla."

Lucy turned. "Yes, Sister?"

"Go to the nurse and have her give you an ice pack. That's one bad shiner you're going to have."

* * *

Maestro was working with Greta Gorbinsky in his studio. He had reassigned a room on the third floor to be his voice studio, thereby eliminating the commute time to and from lessons.

"When you sing, the octave jumps; it's too heavy at the bottom." Maestro played the line of music again and demonstrated. "You see? You have to even it out some more."

Greta nodded and tried again.

"Better, *molto bene*," Maestro exhorted. "Yes?" he inquired as Joe stepped through the open doorway.

"Maestro, the new conductor has been waiting for ten minutes."

"Our time is through here today anyway." He turned to Greta. "I look forward to the improvement next week. Now, get some rest before rehearsal tomorrow morning."

Maestro walked with Joe back to his office.

"I think we should consider doing Wagner's *The Ring of the Nibelung*. Sounds to me like we'd have a noble Brunnhilde in that girl. Would she be ready for the next season?"

"We won't be doing any part of *The Ring* cycle."

Joe sighed. "Why not?"

"I don't like it."

"Why don't you just give me a list of every opera you have something against? Then I won't waste my time thinking about them."

"That is all," Maestro informed him.

"Yeah, right. Until the next one."

* * *

"You wanna come to my house after school today?" Jimmy asked Lucy.

"Can't. My father's coming home early. He's bringing the Christmas tree and we're going to decorate it. My mother's making homemade pizza. We always have that when we decorate the tree. I wish I could invite you."

"Yeah, well, I could only decorate the bottom branches anyway."

"Oh, Jimmy," Lucy said fondly. "Did you get your grab bag gift yet?"

"I dunno. My mother's getting it."

"I have the best gift in the whole world. I don't want to give it away."

"So why are you?"

"Because Tino and I were fighting over it. My father brought home a box of *The Wizard of Oz* playing cards. Every card is a scene from the movie. Someone brought it to him from England."

"So?"

"So Tino and I got into a big fight over who got it first, and we didn't stop when my mother told us to. She took them away and said no one would have them. Now she says she is wrapping it up for the grab bag. I hope my father gets another box from that man."

* * *

Maestro dragged in the biggest tree they ever had. It was almost ten feet tall.

"Rinaldo! What were you thinking? Do we even have enough ornaments?" Giuliana asked.

"The children can make more if we need them. But first, I am decorating this tree special."

"Why special?"

"Because this is a special Christmas. Dante is all well and back in school. Felice got three As on his report card. Lucy is not afraid of nothing no more," he said with a chuckle, recalling her black eye. "And Tino, ah, Tino. He is going to play in a big band some day with those drums. Eh?" He turned to Giuliana. "Does he look small to you?"

"What small? He's six years old. He *is* small."

"In the Christmas play, he looked smaller than the other children."

"*Uffa*! Everyone can't be a giant like you. What? All your children have to be like you? Dante looks just like you; Lucy is tall like you..."

"And you," he reminded her. "Tino has your beautiful eyes. I hope not too beautiful for a boy."

"Enough. So what is so special for the tree?"

"*Andiamo*," he said, leading her into the kitchen. After searching for a large bowl and placing it on the kitchen table, he began searching other cabinets.

"What is it you want...before you shake down the ceiling with all this banging?"

"The Lux soap flakes and the liquid starch."

"Are you going to give the tree a bath?" Giuliana teased. When she brought them to him, she went to the sideboard to check under a pile of towels. "My dough is just about ready. I bought the mozzarella fresh at the deli today."

"Wonderful," Rinaldo replied as he added water into his mixture. "Where is the swoosh-around thing?

"What swoosh-around thing?"

"The swoosh-around thing. You know," he said, demonstrating turning the handle on a rotary beater.

"Oh. It's an eggbeater. Here," she said, after getting it out of a drawer.

"You have blue coloring?" Rinaldo inquired.

Giuliana sighed as she retrieved yet another ingredient. "What if I didn't have all this stuff for this magic you're concocting?"

"I'm home early, no? I would go get it. But I knew I could count on you."

The preparations complete, Maestro headed back to the tree. With a paintbrush he applied the soap mixture to the branches. Two hours later the magic was complete. The tree had been completely covered by a shimmery white snowfall.

"Rinaldo!" Giuliana exclaimed. "It's beautiful. I almost hate to put any decorations on it."

"It is good, no? Who says my sets are shabby?"

* * *

It was the last day of school before vacation, and Lucy was sick.

"I have to go in, Ma," she cried. "It's the party. We're having cupcakes. And the grab bag!" she exclaimed suddenly. "I'll miss the grab bag!"

"Lucy, you've been throwing up all night long. You can't go in. I tell you what. Your brothers will give your grab bag gift to Jimmy to bring to class. Jimmy can pick out a gift for you."

"Suppose Sister won't let him."

"Of course she'll let him."

"Maybe we can just let me keep my own grab bag gift."

Giuliana looked at her daughter with a piercing eye. "I'm not that stupid, young lady. You lost that right when you disobeyed. I'm sure Jimmy will pick out something perfectly fine."

Jimmy did his best. He reached in and pulled out an odd-shaped package for himself. He ripped off the paper. Inside was a Buck Rogers popgun. "Oh boy," he said.

"Lucky you. Look what I got," said Billy. "A box of playing cards."

"Jimmy," called Sister Genevieve. "Are you picking out a gift for Lucy?"

"Yes, Sister." Jimmy slid off his seat again. Sister lowered the sack to him. Jimmy reached down to the two remaining boxes. He pulled up one. When he had climbed back onto his seat, he opened a corner to see what he had chosen.

"Oh boy," he said sadly.

"What you got?" asked Billy.

"A crummy box of animal crackers. She's gonna hate this."

"Tough luck."

Jimmy sized Billy up. "You want to trade?"

"What? For the animal crackers? Are you jokin'?"

"No, for the Buck Rogers gun."

"For real?"

"Sure. Yeah, all right."

* * *

Giuliana entered Lucy's bedroom. She was surrounded by books she was reading aloud to her "class" of dolls.

"I don't know how you pulled this one off," she said as she handed Lucy the mangled package.

Lucy ripped off the remaining paper and beamed. "*Wizard of Oz* cards! Good ole Jimmy."

Chapter 12

Leonie Dufrey had been born in France, but came to America when she was two years old. By the time she turned six, it was apparent she was a natural performer with an extraordinary voice. Her mother took in laundry and ironing to supplement her father's salary as a printer in order to provide Leonie with voice lessons. When she was twenty-five, she left Chicago and headed for New York. She was an extremely pretty girl with curling black hair and sparkling dark eyes.

Her figure was generous except for a tiny waist. Without care, she would be considered zaftig by her thirtieth birthday. For the next ten years, however, she could get away with voluptuous and alluring. Her slight French accent was an affectation; her shouts in the streets of Chicago during games of hide-and-seek were not outdone by any of her friends. She was destined for stardom; she was determined to take the shortest and quickest route.

These plans were derailed at the Metropolitan Opera House of New York. True, they were impressed by her talent, but she was raw, much too raw for the grand stage of the Met. They sent her to Salvatori.

"Maestro Salvatori will fine-tune your talent. We will call him personally to accept you as a student. He will give you the opportunity to perform and hone your skills. This is a wonderful opportunity."

Leonie was not happy. To expend her talent on people paying a mere fifty cents for a ticket was degrading. She determined to work her way through the Salvatori opera house with expediency. She was unprepared for her first meeting with Maestro. Tall and incredibly good looking. Eccentric to be sure, but with the talent he displayed in working with his company, the long hair and wardrobe could be overlooked. She worked hard in her classes with him because she was intelligent enough to know that he truly had something to offer her. She also worked hard because she wanted to be his prized pupil, his star. She knew she was at a disadvantage. She was a mezzo-soprano. Leading roles or even juicy roles for mezzos were few when compared with sopranos. But even the great Salvatori could not develop her upper register. It wasn't long before the improvement in her style and her technical assurance were clearly audible. She cajoled him to put on *Aida* so she could sing the mezzo soprano role of Amneris, but to no avail.

"To do a grand *Aida,* one needs horses and camels and elephants. We need magnificent sets and hundreds of extras. I cannot afford to do it well just yet. Some day but not now. I am, however, considering *La Vestale,* which many find reminiscent of *Aida.* I am speaking about Mercadante's *La Vestale,* of course. Its structure is large and imposing, and it has the requisite finale. And we can have a triumphal march, less imposing, but a march."

Leonie could feel her heart and diaphragm wince. *So typical of Rinaldo,* as she had taken to calling him to herself. *Everything is about the company; nothing about me. Another second-rate mezzo role.* At least, in this opera, the soprano did not have any arias to deflect from her own inevitable role as Giunia.

As it happened, *La Vestale* was very well received by the audience and the critics. Not often performed, they found the melodies refined and elegant, in particular the love duet between Decio and Emilia. Miss Dufrey's Giunia held a real presence on the stage with her natural voice and seemingly effortless technique. If impresario Salvatori's future productions had the same kind of imagination and talent, the opera-loving populace of New York had years of thrilling musicianship to look forward to. Oh yes. The Maestro's sacred vestal flame looked exactly like a barbecue pit run amok.

* * *

Maestro stood next to his conductor as they ran through Lucia's aria in *Cavalleria Rusticana.* He needed a productive rehearsal, as the expense of these rehearsals with the full orchestra had not been anticipated. They were, however, necessary. This production was to take place at the World's Fair, as promised by the mayor, and broadcast via television. True, televisions were scarce, but one never knew who might be at the viewing end of all those cables and wires. Someday operas might be broadcast live from the opera house by television as easily as they now transmitted by radio.

"Maestro."

Rinaldo turned to face Josie.

"*Si?*"

"I have an incorrect shipment of fabric, and I need you to look at it. I think I can use it, but it's not what we originally designed."

"All right. I have ten minutes before I have to meet someone from RCA in my office. I will be up in a minute." As he turned to look at his Santuzza, he did not notice Leonie scooting out the theater. Maestro signaled Santuzza and called out, "Sing into the mask. Sing into the mask." He turned to the conductor. "It's too dark. It must be brighter." He strode down the aisle, giving tense directions to several staff members who would be accompanying the company to the fairgrounds.

As he neared Josie's workroom, he could hear Leonie's voice raised in anger.

"It does not fit, I tell you. When I sing, my chest cannot expand. It is crushing me." She grabbed the top of her bodice and ripped it down. Her breasts, full, high, and truly amazing, bounced with their sudden freedom and then blinked saucily at an astonished Josie. Maestro entered the room and began to question, "What is the…"

Leonie turned to face him, displaying her assets to their best advantage. "I cannot breathe in this costume. It must be refitted!"

Maestro turned quickly toward the door. "*Scusa,*" he choked, fumbling his way out the door.

"You need not turn away, Maestro. Maybe you can convince this seamstress that she measured me incorrectly. Perhaps she thinks I am your puny Loretta. Ha! Am I puny, Maestro? Tell me, am I puny?"

Maestro backed into the corridor and ordered, "Cover yourself, Leonie."

Josie jumped up with a piece of blue velvet fabric. "Have you no decency?" she whispered.

Leonie stepped out of the rest of her costume. "This needs to be altered," she declared haughtily. In only her lower undergarments and crushing the velvet to her chest, she brushed past Maestro. He could feel the full softness of her breast against his arm as she passed. He felt scorched.

"There was nothing wrong with the dress," Josie said when Maestro eventually entered the room.

"I am sure. I am sorry, Josie. She is always looking for attention."

"She knows how to go about getting it."

"She will pay to repair her costume herself, or Loretta will fill in as Laura in *La Giaconda.* There is a costume she can wear?"

"Sure. Some of the chorus costumes will do fine."

"I will give her the ultimatum."

* * *

Leonie waited by the rest room down the hall from Maestro's office. As the two RCA executives exited, she made a hasty retreat inside to recheck her appearance. She had changed to a white off-the-shoulder blouse, which showcased her prominent virtues most alluringly. The straight black skirt was tight enough to suggestively announce most of what else she had to offer. Tossing her hair, she headed for "Rinaldo's" office. The door was ajar.

"May I come in?"

Maestro looked up from the paperwork on his desk.

"Ah, Leonie. I am glad you are here. I need to talk to you." He turned the papers over and sat back in his chair.

"Maestro, I am sorry about before. I should not have acted as I did. But it is not the first time I have had costume problems."

"Really? I haven't heard of any problems before this one."

"*Oui.* I try not to complain. What else can the poor girl do? I would not want her to lose her job."

"Have no fear about that," Maestro reassured her in an irritated tone. "In fact, I am requiring you to have the garment repaired yourself. If you have a problem with that..."

"*Oui, oui.* I will do so. As I said, I am sorry for my temper. Do you forgive me, Maestro Salvatori?"

"Do not let it happen again."

Leonie walked over to the desk and leaned forward. Her breasts were almost fully displayed. Rinaldo turned his chair halfway and looked out the window behind him. Suddenly he felt both Leonie's hands on his shoulders. "You do forgive your little Leonie, don't you, Maestro?"

"Sure. I forgive this time. There better not be a next time. Now leave."

"Oh, Maestro," she whispered into his ear and leaned against his back. "I have something I need very much to discuss with you."

"What is that?" he asked impatiently, rising from his chair. He turned to face her. She was adjusting the shoulders of her blouse farther down her arms. She was definitely alluring.

"I think perhaps I should be the one singing Lola in *Cavallaria* instead of Loretta. She does not have my fire. Don't you want fire when your opera plays on the television?"

"Loretta is a wonderful performer. It is her role."

"*Oui,* but I am better. No?" Leonie walked around the desk and stood face to face with the Maestro. "You know you want to do this for me, Maestro. You want to be my mentor in every way, no?"

"You'd better leave now, Leonie,"

"Rinaldo, I know you do not mean that. I see it in your eyes when you teach me my lessons. I see you want to teach me other things. There are a few things I can teach you also. Do you not want to learn from me?" Leonie picked up Rinaldo's right hand while pulling down her top with the left. She placed his hand on her left breast. He felt like it was on fire, but he couldn't remove his hand. She held it there insistently.

"Kiss me, Rinaldo."

He broke away and turned fully toward the window. She did not need to see what was going on with him.

Leonie walked over and closed the door. She pulled her top over her head.

"I promise you will not be disappointed. We will be good for each other. I will be on television, and you will know pleasures you have never known before. We can be discreet. I know how refined you are. I like that about you." She began to unzipper her skirt. The slight clicking of the zipper teeth was enough to bring Rinaldo's full attention back into focus. He did not turn from the window.

"Stop whatever it is you are doing. Compose yourself and walk out of this room. We will not discuss this ever again."

When he heard the door open, he swung around. "One false move, and you will be out on Eighth Avenue singing for a cup of coffee. Choose your suckers more wisely next time, Miss Dufrey."

With fury in her eyes, Leonie stepped through the doorway.

"And Miss Dufrey…"

"*Oui?*" she responded without turning.

"I will always be Maestro to you."

* * *

When he composed himself, Maestro returned to the theater to oversee the rehearsal. He sat in the fifth row center, but found his attention diverted back to what had transpired in his office. Should he have fired Leonie? What she had proposed was not unheard of in opera companies. It would be a shame to lose her, but could he trust himself? He was used to beautiful women; he was used to women's inviting glances. He had never considered it. Yet no one before had ever been as bold as Leonie. For a moment, just for a brief moment, he had felt a weakening. Was it lust or was it the power? He enjoyed his total control of the opera house, a world he shaped and devised as he saw fit. He could forget about the cruelties, poverties, deceptions of the outside world.

Here he conjured up a safe environment of encouragement, hope, and escape both for his company and for his audience. He *was* the impresario. He could have strayed many times in the fifteen years of his marriage, but he never had. He loved and respected Giuliana. He wouldn't endanger their relationship for control of the Metropolitan itself. Yet, just for an instant, he had thought it could be wildly passionate with Leonie. He shifted in his seat. No, he had actually thought, *I can teach her what passion is about. I can bring this infantile diva to her knees.* Rinaldo felt himself relax. *Ah, so it was the power.*

Joe came hurrying down the aisle. "Maestro, a telegram for you."

Maestro raised his brows in question.

"I don't know," Joe said, handing it it him.

Maestro ripped it open and scanned the message. He lowered the telegram to his lap.

"Everything OK?" Joe asked.

"*Si.* I am being honored."

"Honored! Wonderful. For what?"

"No thanks to you," Maestro chuckled. "First Lady Eleanor Roosevelt is giving me a commendation for giving Jiang Dai the role in *Tosca.* It is for giving opportunities to minorities."

"Well, congratulations," Joe said sincerely, extending his hand.

Maestro shook it and sat back in his seat. He crossed his legs.

I am relieved it is not for giving opportunities to the French.

* * *

The children were already in bed by the time Rinaldo reached home that evening.

"Can I get you something to eat?" Giuliana asked.

"No. Just some coffee. I ate at the theater. Not good, but I ate."

Maestro retreated to the parlor and took off his shoes and tie. Giuliana brought in coffee for the both of them.

"Will you be ready for the fair next week?"

"I think so. The cast sounds good. I suppose we should plan on doing *Pagliacci* and pairing it with *Cavallaria* next season. Half the work is done."

"Good idea."

Rinaldo sipped his coffee. "Oh!" he exclaimed, settling his cup into the saucer. "I almost forgot." He rose and padded into the entryway to get his briefcase. He returned to his seat and pulled out the telegram. "Look what arrived today."

Giuliana read the missive. "Rinaldo! How could you almost forget? This is wonderful. I'm so proud of you. When will you receive it?"

"I do not know yet. Sandra will call the number they gave."

Giuliana studied her husband. "Is something wrong?"

"No. Why do you ask?"

"You look drained."

"It's been a long day."

"More than that. You are distracted. Upset."

Maestro smiled at her. "My love, you know me too well. *Si*, I had an upsetting incident today." He told Giuliana about Leonie, starting with the scene in the seamstress's room and ending with her exit from his office. He left out certain details, for sure, and emphasized his horror and disgust.

Giuliana watched Rinaldo as he spoke. There was a faint glimmer of sweat on his upper lip. He ran his hand through his hair repeatedly. His tongue moistened his lips as he did when he was telling a story. A secret was hidden in his eyes as in the depths of a volcano. She listened carefully to the quality of his voice. Hmmn, but not *that* secret, of this she was certain.

Chapter 13
1940

Lucy stood in the alleyway, stunned and soaking wet.

"Oh my God!" cried her friend Joanne. "Ma! Ma!" she yelled up at the window.

"I'm going home," cried Lucy, racing down the alley. She flicked her wet hair from her face and scooted down the block. She could feel water dribbling down her back. She raced around the corner, nearly knocking a five-year-old neighbor off his tricycle. She slammed through the front door instead of going around back.

"Ma!" she screamed.

Giuliana got up from the piano where she had been playing. "Lucy, you've been told not…what happened to you?"

"Strega Titzi. Strega Titzi threw a pot of water on me," she sobbed, the full impact of her fright and humiliation catching up with her.

"She did what? Why? What happened?"

"Nothing. Joanne and I were playing hit the penny in the alleyway between her house and Strega Titzi's. She looked out the window once and told us to go play somewhere else. Joanne told her mother and she told us to ignore the old witch. That's what she said, Ma, honest. So we kept playing, and then Strega Titzi came to the window again and threw a whole big pot of water at us. Except it got mostly me."

Giuliana flushed with anger. "She did, did she? Come with me."

"Please, Ma, I don't want to go back."

"You're coming back. Go. Go put on dry clothes first. I will wait for you."

Phil stepped out of the kitchen and came down the hall. "Can I come?"

Giuliana stood by the door, one hand on the glass knob, a picture of maternal indignation. She didn't even hear Phil. As soon as Lucy returned, she whisked her out the door. Phil trailed behind them. At Strega's house she rang the doorbell. When the old woman opened the door, Giuliana lashed into her.

"How dare you? Who do you think you are? How dare you throw water at the children?"

"They make too much noise. I tell them to stop, but they no listen."

"That's your excuse? You really *are* an old witch. What are you so busy doing that the sound of children playing disturbs you? Whipping up a potion to bring a dead rat back to life? Why don't you make yourself a magic potion to mind your own business, eh? I warn you, you ever bother my daughter again when she is playing with her friend, I will call the police. I have friends in the police department. They will arrest you and throw you in a jail cell to rot. You hear me?"

"Ma," Phil said, tugging at his mother's skirt. "Ma. Calm down. She's an old lady. You're scaring her."

"She should be scared." She turned back. "You hear me? Never again. *Capisce?*"

Giuliana took Lucy by the hand and went down the steps. She saw the old lady looking at them from the window.

"Don't you stare at me. You hear me? Your old evil eye doesn't work on me!" Giuliana shouted before she stomped down the block.

Phil lingered behind. He went into the small garden in front of the house and started gathering up debris around the rose bushes. He saw the old lady watching him suspiciously from the window. He stood up and called to her.

"*Signora*, your roses are sick. See the black spots? You got bugs too. You've got to keep it clean under these bushes. And prune them. Do you know how to prune roses?

"Go away, boy of bad mother."

"Yeah, well, I've got to go now, but I'll come tomorrow and show you what to do, OK? If you want, you can squish these bugs in your fingers. There aren't too many yet. See ya."

* * *

That evening the tale was told and retold over dinner.

"Enough," Giuliana finally said. "Pretty soon Lucy will have herself drowning under Niagara Falls. Help me get the strawberries, Lucy. Strawberries and cream will cheer us all up."

Phil looked at his father conspiratorially. "She was wild, Maestro. Like a lion or something."

Maestro smirked. "Ferocious, huh?"

"I never want to get her that mad, let me tell you."

"Good advice, Felice. I'll remember that."

* * *

The next afternoon Phil returned to the *Signora's* house. He rang the bell.

"Here I am like I said."

"Go away."

"I would except I can't stand to see your roses dying for no reason. See? I brought my pruning shears."

Phil went back down the steps and began clipping away. "If you get me a garbage bag, I'll pick up these stems and all this dead stuff. See how your leaves are yellow?"

The old lady disappeared and returned with a garbage bag. After he had finished cleaning up, Phil asked, "Do you have a pail?"

"Of course I have pail. What am I, a queen?"

"Can I come inside?"

"I don't know. Your mother might say I bake you in oven."

"Nah. She won't bother you anymore. You know, you did almost drown my sister."

"Hummph."

"Let's fill the pail with water. Get me a bar of soap." Phil began soaping up the water until it was cloudy and a bit sudsy. "Meanwhile you chop some garlic."

The old lady got a cutting board and the garlic. "We gonna feed the roses?" she asked.

"You have mineral oil?"

"Sure."

"OK, mix the garlic with the oil."

When that was done, Phil told her. "This has to sit together for a day. I'll come back tomorrow and finish."

The next afternoon, Phil arrived, carrying a spray bottle.

"OK, now we're going to mix the garlic oil with the soapy water and put it in this spray bottle. When we spray this on the roses, it should get rid of the bugs."

"It's a lot of work for a few flowers."

"You got them, you gotta take care of them. You can't just let them die. Or else you're going to wind up just having to chop them all down. Is that what you want?"

"No, they nice. I would miss."

"So you'll do what I say, OK? When you water them, water from the bottom. Don't get the flowers all wet. Got it? I'll come by in a few days to see how they're doing."

"Wait a *minuto*," *Signora* said, disappearing into the house. "I have this for you." She handed him a lollipop.

"Thanks."

"When you come, I show you my herbs. You like?"

"Yeah, that would be super."

"You come alone. No bring anybody else."

"OK. No problem."

Chapter 14

"Rummy!" Dante laid down three twos and the six, seven, eight, and nine of hearts.

"I don't wanna play anymore," moaned Tino. He turned from his seat on the front steps to face the street. "You win all the time."

"How do you expect to learn if you quit playing?"

"I'm tired of rummy. When is Mama coming home?"

"Soon. What do you think you'll get for your birthday tomorrow?" Dante asked soothingly in his role as temporary babysitter.

Tino perked up. "I want a five-piece drum set."

"You make enough noise with what you already have."

"It's not noise. I'm really good. Mr. Sansone says so."

"Yeah, OK, I guess you are. Someday I'll put you on the radio."

"How're you gonna do that?" Tino asked, facing his brother again.

"I'm going to work on the radio. I've decided."

The front gate rattled and both boys turned to look.

"Hi, can I come in?"

"Hi, Danita. Sure, the gate's open."

A pretty thirteen-year-old girl walked over to them. "Hi, Dante," she said shyly. "I have your mother's Avon order from my mother."

"She's not home right now, but I'll take it." Dante extended his hand for the bag.

"Let me see," Tino said, grabbing the bag from Dante.

"Put it down," Dante said. He shook his head. "I'm watching him until my mother comes home."

"Want help?" the girl offered, inching closer to Dante. He was so good looking. Wait until she told her friends she had been so close to him.

"I don't need two people watching me. I'm practically seven."

"Nah. Thanks, though," Dante answered, crushing Danita's hopes of a more fairy-tale ending.

Danita backed away. "Whose class are you in?" she asked, referring to the St. Mary class assignments for the upcoming school year.

"Sister Helen Marie."

"Me too!"

"Then I'll be seeing you around."

"OK. Bye, Dante. Bye…uh…"

"Tino. It's really Augustino, but everyone calls me Tino. It's funny, huh? Cause I was born in August."

"Keep quiet," Dante hushed him. "Here comes Ma."

"Hello," Giuliana said to Danita. "Everything OK, Dan?"

"Yeah, Ma. Bye, Danita."

"Come on in, Tino. It's time for your bath."

"Bye," Danita sighed. Bad timing. If Mrs. Salvatori had come a few minutes earlier, maybe she could have been left alone with Dante on the stoop.

Darn! She hoped her mother planned on selling more Avon on this block real soon.

* * *

"Can I have bubble bath, Ma?" Tino asked.

"Sure. I'll fill the tub; you get undressed."

A short while later, she told Tino his bath was ready.

"I can get in myself, Ma," he announced. "I'm seven."

Giuliana started to object and then let it go. Her baby was growing up.

"All right. But I'm standing outside the door until you're sitting down safely."

"I'm in."

Every so often Giuliana checked by the door. "Are you all right?"

"I'm fine."

"Are you washing yourself, or are you just playing?"

"I'm washing."

"I'll be checking that in a few minutes. I want to wash your hair."

"I can do it."

Five minutes later Giuliana entered the bathroom. "Let's see how my big man is doing." She looked at the parade of rubber toys floating in the water. "What is that doll doing in there?" she asked, aghast.

"I made her a mermaid. See? I tied a washcloth over her legs. She's teaching the fish to dance in the water. And I beat the drums, see?" He banged his right hand along the rim of the tub while his mermaid splashed to the beat.

"Tino! That's Lucy's Liguria Girl doll. Give her to me." She grabbed the doll from his anxious hand. "She's got a cloth body. I hope you haven't ruined it."

"I took her clothes off. They're all dry on Lucy's bed."

"But her body is soaked through. What were you thinking?"

"That I wanted a mermaid in the tub."

"I hope we can hide this from your sister until it dries out. *If* it dries out. If not, you're going to be in big trouble, little man."

"I thought I was a big man."

"Not when you do stupid things. Was that your doll to play with?"

"No. But I don't have a doll."

Giuliana rinsed his soapy head with water and helped him out of the tub.

"You should have asked Lucy's permission before you took it."

"Aw, Ma. She would have said no."

Giuliana swatted his bare bottom lightly. "That's for knowing the answer was no and doing it anyway. Not a smart thing for a seven-year-old to do."

* * *

Lucy enjoyed the crisp washed smell of the freshly laundered clothes as she hung them on the backyard clothesline. In the winter she wasn't allowed to dangle over the second-story window in Phil and Tino's room and hang the clothes. On the coldest winter days, her mother would retrieve the frozen clothes and call them *baccala,* meaning they were as stiff as the salted codfish. If they could get away with it, the siblings would grab the stiff clothes and pretend they were life-sized dolls until they began to droop and bend like the Scarecrow in *The Wizard of Oz.* Today Lucy had only hung two pairs of socks when her friend Joanne appeared. Her father was on vacation; they would like it if Lucy could join them on a trip to the beach.

"Let me ask my mother," she said as she ran indoors.

Giuliana wasn't entirely in favor of this jaunt.

"First of all, I am nervous to send you off to Coney Island without me."

"Ma, I'm almost ten," Lucy cried.

"Second, you have two baskets of wash to hang. You know your father warned you about completing your chores before other activities."

"Why doesn't he have chores? He's in Washington; he took Dan and Phil with him. Why don't they have chores? They get to see the Capitol."

"Mostly they are with your father working. You will go to the Capitol one day."

"Yeah, right. What? To clean the White House?"

Giuliana sighed. She didn't want to admit she agreed with Lucy, but the child had a point. The male jobs around the house, landscaping, painting, and repairing, were mostly handled by hired hands. Rarely did Rinaldo lift a hammer or screwdriver. The boys took out the garbage and helped lift and carry things but otherwise were pretty devoid of duty.

"All right, go. I'll tell Joanne you're putting on your swimsuit. We won't tell your father, OK?"

"Thanks, Ma," said Lucy, bounding up the stairs.

* * *

The Brancatos took the subway to Coney Island. Under the weight of blanket and towels, lunches and beach toys, they lumbered through the hot sand to a spot where the ocean was clearly visible.

"Water, water!" screamed Joanne's three-year-old brother, Joey.

"I'll take him in," said Mr. Brancato.

"You girls wait right here on the blanket. I'll be right back, and then we'll go in the water," promised Mrs. Brancato.

"Where is she going?" asked Lucy as Mrs. Brancato headed back in the direction from which they had just come.

"She's going under the boardwalk to take off her corset," replied Joanne.

"What?"

"She wears a corset on top of her bathing suit until we reach here. She has a bad back."

"I don't think my mother has a corset."

"I thought you had to wear a corset when you got big."

"I don't think so. But you have to wear a brassiere because your ninnies keep growing till they're really big."

"I saw my grandma once in the bathroom by mistake. I wonder how old you have to be to get ninnies that big."

"I don't know. Mine are the same as they always were."

"Me too. Here comes my mother," Joanne said as she struggled to get her hair under the tight-fitting bathing cap.

"Ready, girls? Let's get into the water. The rope is that way," she said, pointing in the direction of the heavy, coiled, yellow rope attached to buoys in the water.

Slowly they inched their way into the water, squealing at the small waves that attacked them as they sidestepped down the rope to waist-deep water.

"OK. Hold on tight. If a bigger wave starts to break on us, put your head into it like you are going through a window."

For several minutes they screeched and laughed as they dodged breaking waves or kicked their legs, all the while maintaining a firm grasp on the safety rope.

"Hey, lady, can you move down a bit with your girls so we can all stand here together?" a woman with a small army of children inquired.

"Lady, you can cut off my hands, but we're not moving from the rope," Mrs. Brancato informed her.

"Daddy's waving at us," Joanne announced several minutes later. "Do we have to go in? Let's pretend we don't see him."

"He wants lunch. Let's go in."

"Can we come in again later?"

"We'll see."

After eating Italian bread sandwiches of peppers, potatoes, and eggs followed by plums and cherries, the girls had to content themselves playing in the wet sand by the shoreline for an hour. To go back into the water any sooner was to run the risk of getting a cramp.

"Hey, girls! Want to play a little catch?" Mr. Brancato asked, tossing around a beach ball he had just inflated.

"Yay!" yelled Joanne as Lucy watched in wonder as Mr. Brancato threw the ball at them, danced around, and caught their tosses at him by backing into the water and falling on his backside with his legs flailing in the air. Joanne howled with laughter, and Lucy wondered how many other fathers acted so silly with their children. Later she watched Mr. Brancato dig a hole deep enough to bury Joey up to his chin. When he dribbled ocean water onto Mrs. Brancato's face as she tried to nap and she screeched, Lucy said she must have hit a high C.

"A high seal?" asked Mr. Brancato and then proceeded to make seal-like noises while he flapped his arms and toddled around the sand.

* * *

When Giuliana put her freshly bathed daughter to bed that evening, she asked how her day at the beach had been.

"Fun," she replied. "Did you know that all mothers cook and worry about their kids, but some fathers are like kids and like to have fun?"

"Your father is fun."

"So far I've missed it," Lucy murmured as she nestled into her pillow.

* * *

The rhythm was kept in fits and staggers as Tino played on his five-piece drum set, trying to keep time to a practice recording on the record player. When he stopped and started once again, Maestro, seated in the parlor, asked, "What is wrong with him tonight? I don't want to tell him to stop practicing, but I'm getting a headache."

"He's had a bad cough for a few days. I've been waiting for Dr. Marino to get back from vacation, but maybe I should take him to see someone else."

"See if you can take his drums too. I can't study with all that racket," Dante suggested.

"Never mind. Go up to your room to study. Why did we buy you that desk anyway?" his mother scolded.

"Hey, Dan, we're getting up a game of ring-o-levio. Want to play?" asked Phil, bounding into the room.

"Felice, why are you so dirty again?" his mother asked.

"I was working in my garden. If you don't let me climb to get those figs, we're gonna lose them."

"I'll get someone; don't you climb," Maestro said without looking up from his newspaper.

"Are you sure you did all your homework?"

"Yeah. Sister Cornelius only gave us math because it's her saint's name day. Happy St. Cornelius! Whoever the heck he is."

"Ma, my throat hurts," Tino cried as he entered the room, drumsticks in hand.

"Peace," murmured Dan.

"Hey! Don't move. I think I can help you. I'll be right back," said Phil, dashing out the door.

"Come back here—all filthy dirty. What will the neighbors think?" yelled Giuliana, but Phil was already headed down the block. Ten minutes later he raced in again and headed up to the attic. "I'll be right back," he assured everyone.

"You know, he's just screwy," Dan commented.

"What are you saying?" Giuliana asked, exasperated.

"He just is, Ma. Always in the garden like it's the Garden of Eden or something. Or else he's working at the theater, free of charge, no less. I mean, it's good for you, Maestro," he added, addressing his father, "but he works as hard as some of your real guys. Or else he's helping the girls in the sewing room. He makes them laugh, and they love him. Why wouldn't they laugh with that screwy stickin' up hair he has anyway? But on top of all that, he's the best ballplayer in the neighborhood. He's just screwy."

"I'm glad you've had time to figure your brother all out. How about you spend less time judging your brother and taking apart the radio —"

"Who took apart the radio?" Maestro interjected.

"...and more time keeping your room clean." Giuliana paused. "What's he doing in the kitchen now? Phil?"

"I'm fine. Be back in a minute," he yelled.

A few minutes later Phil came into the room with a steaming cup of tea.

"What's this?" Giuliana asked.

"For Tino. It's a special tea for his cough. Thyme and a little sage. Sit down, Tino, and drink it while it's hot. You have to drink it hot."

"Where did you learn this?" Giuliana asked.

"I know about gardens, Ma," Phil replied, setting the cup down for Tino.

Tino took a sip. "It's hot."

"Drink it if you want to feel better," Phil advised.

A few minutes later, Tino tried again. "It's disgusting."

"Doesn't matter. Just drink it."

Within the half hour, they noticed the drumbeat from the music room continued without pause.

"I'm so glad he's feeling better," Dan said with a sigh. "Isn't it his bedtime yet?"

Chapter 15

Giuliana sat on the edge of their bed with the letter in her hand. She had found it a bit difficult translating from the dialect it had been written in, but she was pretty certain she understood the essence of it. The writer explained her mother was not well, and she was writing in her stead. The Salvatoris had died in the past year. Marcello had not been well for a while. Adela tried to care for him, but she was not well herself. Four months after Marcello's passing, Adela threw herself off a cliff overlooking the sea. It was a spot where the couple used to like to sit and remember their son singing out over the water. She had left a note for no one to be sad. It was better this way. She couldn't go on without Marcello. She had, however, left another note for Rinaldo. It was only to be given to him or a member of his family if and when one of them should turn up in Ventotene.

"I have determined to take it upon myself to discuss another matter with you. I am breaking no promises, as far as I know. When my uncle bequeathed Rinaldo money several years ago, he was following instructions given him at one time by the Salvatoris. However, nowhere is it written that I cannot tell you that the money was not my uncle's. It was left to my Uncle Gaetano by the Salvatoris for Rinaldo.

I am sorry to be the one to express this sad news to you. The Salvatoris were private people, but those who came to know them thought that they were brave and good. I liked them very much and shall miss them.

Francesca Mantovino.

Giuliana lay back on the bed and covered her eyes with her arm. What to tell Rinaldo? Could this news destroy him? He had a perpetual scab in his heart covering the self-inflicted wound. He tried never to pick at it, afraid the bleeding and pain would start anew. Yet it was always there, rough and itching, at the slightest reminder. He would not look for a way to heal the wound. About this he was adamant.

I will tell him his parents have died. I cannot tell him how his mother chose to leave this world. And I will tell him about the inheritance. He should know they never stopped loving him.

* * *

Lucy changed out of her school uniform into a flowered jumper and pink blouse for her family birthday dinner. Nonna and Papi were coming, as was "Uncle" Joe from the opera house and Joanne and her parents. This was a big one. Ten. She had been hinting for a wristwatch for a month. She headed for the kitchen where her mother was preparing her favorite manicotti. Entering the kitchen, she caught Tino with his fingers in the bowl of pink frosting.

"Ma! He's touching the frosting," she groaned.

"Augustino, what did I tell you?" Giuliana cautioned.

"I get to put the candles in, right?"

"Only if you behave."

"The pink looks pretty, Ma. What kind of frosting is it?"

"It's just butter cream with food coloring."

"I told her to make it pink," Tino informed her.

"Why do you have polish on your nails?" she asked Tino.

"*Uffa*!" Guiliana exclaimed. "I forgot. When I was putting it on, he wanted some."

"Not every nail, see?" Tino said, pointing out that every other nail was a bright pink. "My nails are in costume for your birthday."

"No, they are not. Lucy, take it off him before the company arrives."

"Ma!" Tino wailed.

Lucy grabbed him by the arm and headed him for the stairs. Maestro entered just as they neared the front door.

"Ah! My birthday girl! Come, let me give you a kiss," he said with a smile, dropping his cane in the stand and opening his arms.

Lucy ran into her father's arms. Maestro hugged her and then noticed Tino examining his fingernails.

"What's on your hands?" he asked.

"I was just taking him to wipe it off," Lucy explained. "He was playing." She turned to Tino. "Come on. Let's skedaddle."

Maestro walked into the kitchen and buzzed Giuliana's cheek.

"My daughter looks more grown up every day, and my son is wearing polish on his nails."

"Oh, you saw," Giuliana said with a sigh.

"Eh. I've seen worse at the theater," Maestro mentioned philosophically.

* * *

During dinner Joanne's mother commented, "I am named after St. Lucy too. She is my mother's favorite saint. We tend to have poor eyesight on her side of the family, and she prays to St. Lucy to intercede for us."

"Lucy is not named after the saint," Maestro replied.

"No? Is it a family name?"

"Family? Ah, our extended family, perhaps," Maestro said with a laugh.

"Don't be telling that story," Giuliana warned.

"Why not? It's a good story?"

"It's embarrassing," Giuliana said looking around the table.

"What embarrassing? This from the daughter of a doctor? No. Listen. Giuliana was not supposed to have the baby for another two weeks. We decided she would enjoy a night out, so she came to the King's

Academy. It was opening night for *La Scala di Seta.* You know it?" he asked.

"I'm afraid not," said Lucy Brancato.

"It's an *opera buffa,* a comic opera by Rossini," explained Joe.

"The title means the silken ladder," Maestro continued. "It has a lively, melodious overture. Some will say it is shallow, but audiences tend to enjoy it immensely. So. The soprano in the opera is named Giulia. The mezzo is Lucilla. I happen to be conducting the orchestra this evening, which is another reason Giuliana had come. So Lucilla begins to sing her aria, '*Sento talor nell' anima*'..." Maestro hummed a few lines. "Just as she begins..."

"Maestro, the children..." Giuliana warned, looking at the youngsters.

"So after a minute I hear this small commotion behind me. Do I turn to look? It is not proper etiquette. Yet I am remembering that my wife is sitting in the fifth row, and the noise is not far behind me. Eh?" He shrugged dramatically.

"I turn a little. I see some people standing. I hear voices saying, 'Sit down in front.' I turn some more, and I see Giuliana stepping over people to get to the aisle. Now what do I do? My arm stops moving, the orchestra keeps playing, but then Lucilla stops singing and walks off the stage in a fit of rage. So? No singer…I take off down the aisle after Giuliana. She tells me the baby is coming, and she has left a flood on her seat and on the floor. We call…"

"Why was there a flood?" asked Phil.

"I spilled a drink," Giuliana answered.

"There's no drinking in the theater," Phil reminded her.

"It was a special exception because your mother felt hot because she was having a baby," Maestro interrupted.

The adults around the table all nodded their heads in agreement.

"So we get to the hospital and *allora,* finally, a baby girl. We name her Lucilla because the doctor tells me she came out singing, and we already know that singing is what got her moving in the first place!"

"Have you seen this opera, Lucilla?" asked Mrs. Brancato.

"No. Maestro has never put it on since."

"I am waiting for you to be old enough to sing the part."

"Oh, Maestro," Lucy said, bowing her head and blushing.

After the candles had been blown out and cake distributed, a mountain of presents was placed before Lucy. Among them she received a pearl necklace and bracelet set from Uncle Joe, a white fur hat and muff from her grandparents, and a Nancy Drew mystery, *The Clue of the Broken Locket,* from Joanne and her parents with a promise of an outing to see the latest Nancy Drew movie at the Marboro Theater. Through all the unwrapping, her eye had been on the long, narrow box her mother was now handing her. Lucy's heart skipped an expectant beat. Ripping off the gold paper, she opened the lid.

A fountain pen! A fountain pen?

"Hey, Luce, what is it?" asked Dante.

Her voice caught in her throat. She mustn't cry. She mustn't hurt her mother and father's feelings. Her father was beaming at her.

"A pen," she replied.

"Not just any pen," Maestro informed them. "It is a Conway Steward fountain pen. From England."

"It's beautiful," said Joanne, admiring the green marble design.

"Just in time," announced Mrs. Brancato. "You fifth graders begin using fountain pens in a couple of days."

"It's called a Dinkie," Maestro explained further.

"What?" asked Lucy.

"A Dinkie. I have a new bottle of blue-black ink for you to bring to school with you."

"Thank you, Maestro. Thank you, Mama. I love it."

"What do you think of this teacher they have instead of a sister? Miss Tuccio?" asked Mr. Brancato.

"I don't know. I'm spending this money to send her to Catholic school, and she doesn't even get a sister. Plus, she's very young."

"Let's see. Maybe she is good. For the girls, at least," Maestro theorized.

"She's very pretty," said Joanne. "She's getting married in December. A snowball wedding, she said." She turned to Lucy. "Lorraine Tuccio is going to be in the wedding party. She's her niece."

"She's in Jimmy's class. We're not in the same class this…never mind," Lucy paused.

"This has been a lovely evening. Thank you both for inviting us," Mrs. Brancato said.

After the guests left, Lucy retreated to her room. She cried quietly into her pillow over the fountain pen, and her parents, who couldn't take a hint.

Three days later, the class opened their pencil cases and pulled out their new fountain pens. They were to begin writing in script with ink for the first time. As most students pulled out the standard black or blue pen, Lucy tried to inconspicuously begin writing with hers.

"Look at Lucy's fancy pen, Miss Tuccio," cried Maria.

"That's lovely, Lucy," remarked the teacher.

"It's from England. It has a big name, but it's called a Dinkie."

"A Dinkie?" said Billy with a laugh. "What's that? A Dinkie for a stinky?"

The class began laughing. Soon others had joined Billy's chant, "A Dinkie for a stinky!"

"Enough. Quiet down, everyone, and get to work."

Lucy's face burned. Her stupid father! Why couldn't she have a Schaeffer or Parker like everyone else in the school?

Within the half hour, there were ink splotches in everybody's black and white notebooks and blue fingers that suggested a grape-squeezing contest.

"Hey, stinky! How does your Dinkie write?" asked Billy, tired of copying practice sentences out of the penmanship book.

"Shut up," Lucy warned.

"Lucy, that is not acceptable language. One demerit." Miss Tuccio turned to Billy. "And one for you also, Mr. Russo."

I hate my father! Why can't he be like other fathers and buy something ordinary?

Chapter 16

Lucy turned to look at the trail her bright red galoshes were leaving in the snow.

"The snow's pretty deep. I thought we'd get a snow day."

"Me too," said Jimmy who was plodding with difficulty across the mostly unshoveled sidewalks.

Today he carried no books. Since the homework load had gotten heavier, his father drove to the convent on his way to work and dropped off some of Jimmy's books. His teacher would bring them to her classroom and slip them into Jimmy's desk. On his way home, Mr. Ferraro would pick up whatever books were needed for that evening's homework. Jimmy couldn't manage to carry all of them anymore. He refused to pull them in a wagon. This morning Mr. Ferraro had delivered all the books to the convent.

"Hi, Lucy," said a girl's voice reaching up to the pair. "Hi, Jimmy."

"Hi."

"I'm Danita. I'm in your brother's class."

"Which one?"

"Dante. Is he going to school today?"

"Yeah. He's meeting up with some friends first. They're probably throwing snowballs around right now."

"Do you know if he's taking the exam to get into Catholic high school this weekend?"

"No. He decided he wants to go to Lafayette."

"Oh," Danita said sadly.

"It's brand new, you know."

"I know. Well, see you around," she said as she met up with another eighth grader turning the corner.

"She likes Dan," Jimmy remarked.

"Yeah. They should all form a club."

"Who?"

"All the girls who like him. I had one girl offer to help me with my math homework so she could come over the house. I could help her with hers, I bet," Lucy snickered. "Dan doesn't care. He's not interested in any of them."

"I don't see why she cares. She'll go to an all-girls high school, and he'd go to an all-boy," Jimmy wondered aloud.

"Probably dances. The high schools get together for dances."

"Oh, dances," Jimmy said with a wince. Another hurdle yet to be faced.

"You should have come to the church for Miss Tuccio's wedding on Saturday. She looked beautiful."

"I don't even know her."

"The bridesmaids were all in red and carrying red and white flowers. Lorraine was all showing off because she had lipstick on and these red lacy gloves."

"Big deal."

"Lorraine's such a show-off. Did you see her for Halloween? She was an actress. An actress," Lucy said scornfully. "For what? Horror movies?"

"Why do you hate her so much?" Jimmy asked after picking himself up from a spill.

"She just thinks she's so smart, always asking me what I got on a test. I usually beat her anyway. I was so glad we weren't in the same class this year, but she still runs up in the school yard and asks what I got on my report card."

"You don't have to answer her. Just ignore her."

"That's what you do, isn't it, Jimmy?"

"My mother says I can't pay attention to what the idiots say. I'm as big as I want to be about things."

Lucy opened the door to the school building and held it open for Jimmy.

"We're lining up in the cafeteria, I guess," Lucy said.

"I go straight to my room. See ya later," Jimmy replied as he struggled up the flight of stairs. On ordinary days, he was line monitor, which meant he was last in line. He was proud to be assigned the job of looking out for malingerers and making sure no one propped open the doors as they went through them. He had this job for two years in a row. He never really made the connection that his class was always the last one to enter the building. With him at the end of the line, he couldn't tie up the swift procession to the classrooms. Stairs, like windows and most furniture, were just another Mount Everest for the determined little man.

* * *

The 1940–41 school year drifted into memory along with the triumphs and failures of the Salvatori children. Phil handled two weeks detention after setting worms from his garden in each penholder crevice on the desks in his classroom.

By the time the students returned from lunch, the squirmy creatures were writhing not only on the desks but also on the chairs, floor, and in one boy's open inkwell. Lucy managed to beat out Lorraine Tuccio's average by 0.6. The middle finger on her right hand displayed a permanent blue-black ink-stained callus on its inner side, betraying the hours she spent doing her homework. Tino turned out to be masterful at marbles. as evidenced by a bagful of winnings, including his prized 1933 World's Fair "Berry Pink" marble. Dante had begun to learn how to operate a ham radio and was in a perpetual state of supplication for his own system and permission to apply for a license. But now, on the Friday before graduation from St. Mary's, he had bigger problems. There was a school dance for the graduating eighth graders, and attendance was pretty much mandatory. He stood awkwardly in his navy-blue suit and striped tie and continued to bemoan the fact that he had to go and that his mother was one of the chaperones. Giuliana turned on the record player one more time.

"Let us practice the dance again before we go."

"Ma, I'm not gonna be dancing with anybody."

"You say so. We'll see. Better you should be prepared a little."

So they one–two–three–foured around the parlor while Phil hooted, and Lucy tried to imitate them from the entryway.

At the dance, pretty much as predicted, the girls in their party dresses stood to one side as the boys congregated in circles on the other side of the auditorium. Music played, but only the chaperones swayed in time to the music. Eventually several of the girls ventured forth and danced with each other. The boys gulped punch and a few got into a game of leapfrog on the stage until the janitor broke it up. Dante followed a few of his friends outdoors, but refused to get involved in smoking some pilfered Lucky Strikes. He wasn't going to mess up his entire summer if his father found out. He drifted back into the building but stood outside the auditorium door. Danita was returning from the girls' room with several friends when she saw him there.

"Hi, Dante. Like the dance?"

"Not particularly."

"I'll meet you inside," Danita said to her friends. The girls giggled and departed. Dante shifted uncomfortably.

"I'm kind of sad that we can't all stay together for high school," Danita observed.

"Yeah. We've known everyone our whole lives."

"It's like a family breaking apart."

"I guess."

"You don't like to dance?"

"Nah."

"I thought you would. Your family being so involved with music and all."

"Yeah, well, that's singing and stuff. We don't do ballet or anything."

"This isn't ballet."

Another song drifted into the hallway from inside the auditorium.

"Dante, will you give me a small good-bye present?" Danita asked.

"Present? I didn't buy any presents for anyone."

"No, I mean right now."

"What?"

"Will you dance this one dance with me?"

"I don't think…"

Danita stepped up close to him and picked up his left hand with her right one. She started to move slowly to the music, "I'll Never Smile Again," thinking dramatically, as fourteen-year-old girls will, that the lyrics were absolutely true. Dante's right hand found her waist as his mother's lessons automatically kicked in. They shuffled to the music, sweaty hands clenched, hearts pounding. Danita smiled up at him sweetly, and Dante noticed for the first time that her eyes were hazel and that her nose turned up at the end in the cutest way. At the end of the song, they broke apart awkwardly.

"Thank you, Dante," Danita whispered. Standing on tiptoe, she kissed him right on the lips. Then she turned and hurried into the auditorium. Dante stood motionless lest his heart be jarred outside his shirt. He peered into the room after her, but she didn't join the gaggle of girls standing in the corner. Instead she went to get a cup of punch, spoke a few words to his mother, and then stood dreamily leaning against the stage. Dante sat on the bottom step of a flight of stairs. Why wasn't Danita going to Lafayette anyway?

* * *

Sunday Mass had just finished and the congregants were recessing out of the church when Sister Genevieve ran up to Father Fazio and whispered in his ear. He hurried to the microphone at the pulpit and spoke out, "Brothers and sisters, your attention, please. Kindly remain where you are standing or take a seat next to you." While several people scattered for a quick exit, Father Fazio waited for the bustle and rumble to settle down.

"I have just been given extremely upsetting and frightening news. The Japanese have attacked Pearl Harbor in Hawaii."

One loud resounding gasp filled the church, followed by a tumultuous uproar.

"Those of you who would like to leave now, please do so in an orderly fashion. We will say the rosary. When we have completed beseeching Our Lady's intercession during this horrific time, you may leave the church. May God be with us all."

When Giuliana and the children reached home, Maestro was seated beside the radio. Their eyes locked as he shook his head at her. The family sat in frightened silence as they listened to the reports as they became available.

"See?" Dante finally interjected into the tense stillness. "If I had my ham radio license, I could have helped our country now."

"Let us hope the war doesn't last so long that you and your brothers will have to face the enemy."

"No!" gasped Giuliana. "It cannot last that many years!"

There was a knock at the door, and Lucy returned with her grandparents. Everyone hugged and spoke at once.

"*Basta!*" announced Anna. "Giuliana and Lucy, *andiamo.* I have brought vegetables for minestrone soup and pork to make braciole."

"Mama, I was planning to prepare…" Giuliana began to argue.

Anna put up her hand. "We need a hearty meal. We cook for strength against the enemy; we cook to keep our family close at home; we cook to calm our fears. *Andiamo.*" She led the warriors into the kitchen.

Chapter 17
1942

Rinaldo stretched along the sofa's length and rested his head on the arm. His purple-socked feet dangled over the end. The house was quiet; Tino was at a Saturday drum lesson and the others busy with their friends. He draped his arm across his forehead and sighed.

"Do you have a headache?" asked Giuliana as she passed the doorway.

"A slight one."

"Is something wrong?"

"No. Yes. Maybe."

"Which is it?

"*Don Giovanni* is an excellent production, but the house is only half full. It did not even get reviewed.

No one can think of opera at a time like this. Also, we are in rehearsals for *Carmen,* and I am ready to hurl Leonie at a bull if I had one."

"What is she doing?" Giuliana inquired with more interest than the typical diva antics usually aroused in her.

"She is clashing with the conductor over every note. She stops mid-aria because she can hear the crew working in the background. How can we be ready to open if the crew can't work? She refused to sing in the lighting designed for 'Habanera.' Felice came up with an idea, and she loved it! Can you believe it? Then she berated the lighting technicians for being outdone by a fourteen-year-old boy."

"Why don't you replace her?"

"She has ripened into the richest mezzo soprano I have ever heard. The Met will steal her after *Carmen.*"

"Humpph! Good riddance if you ask me."

"She was giving Josie a hard time with her costumes too. But then I had a brilliant idea. I suggested we resurrect the idea of a matador outfit in the final scene. It was quite the sensation when Rosa Ponselle wore one. For now, Leonie is happy." Rinaldo stared off into space. After a while, he said softly, "I am almost fifty years old."

Giuliana sat in an armchair.

"Yes! Shall we throw a big party? A Sunday gathering with friends and singing, games and dancing!"

"No," Rinaldo said, swinging his long legs to the floor. "No big happy party. I am in no mood to celebrate this."

"But why not, *caro*? You have much to celebrate."

"*Si,* I have you. That was the unexpected blessing in my life. I never thought to marry. Music was to be my sole mistress; the opera house, my shelter."

Giuliana crossed her legs. "Not to dig up old bones, but I have heard stories of mistresses other than music."

"All before I met you. I was not supposed to meet someone and fall in love until I was good for nothing else. And then I was not supposed to have children."

"But God had other plans. I told you that when we decided to marry. God would shape our family, and we would love it whatever shape it took."

"*Si.* And again, we have been blessed. But now I see time slipping away. Dante is in high school; Felice has better ideas than me at the opera house. Lucy will be smarter than both of us. She is *un bella ragazza,* the beautiful young girl you were that I never knew. And Tino. My little Tino has pictures of that Superman ripped from those magazines he reads taped all over his walls. This Superman is his hero. When we decided to have children, all I ever wanted was to be their hero. Now, this man in the cape is Tino's hero. The boys have baseball heros..." His voice faded.

"Rinaldo, the children adore you. Why are you making yourself sad for no reason?"

"Sometimes, I know, they are ashamed of me. The one thing I feared most, I have accomplished. I am too old to change. I am an old man."

Giuliana rose and sat on his lap. She draped her arms around his neck.

"I do not want you to change. You are much too handsome for anyone to think of you as an old man." She played with his hair. "We could color these few strands of gray, but frankly, I think they make you look even more handsome and important. Your appearance has matured into the role of impresario."

Rinaldo kissed her. "Then I am content."

"Good. Listen to me. When you walk home and see some of the women neighbors standing outside and talking, I want you to hurry inside."

"Why is that?"

"Because they all find you immensely appealing, and I fear they are plotting to kidnap you away from me."

Rinaldo raised his eyebrows in surprise and then squeezed Giuliana tightly.

"Ahh, you," he said with a chuckle as he rubbed his nose in her neck.

* * *

Don Giovanni was playing to half a house, and no one was happy. The cast, orchestra, crew, and staff had all gathered in the theater seats prior to the performance to hear Maestro inform them that there would have to be a cut in pay for this production's run.

"I hope after the initial shock of being at war, people will turn to us for renewal of their spirits. Until then, things will be difficult. More important, we have lost Jerry and Stu to the war effort. May God be with them in what lies before them."

Phil listened to the somber announcement from the wings. As the orchestra tuned up, he charged for the sewing room. As the first act neared its end, he stood in the wings once again. As soon as Juan and Leporello's lines were completed, Phil strode out onto the stage in front of the closed curtain.

"Ladies and gentleman. May I have your attention, please."

People rising from their seats for intermission paused or stopped midstride.

"I am Felice Salvatori, the Maestro's son. I can tell you are the people who love the opera as much as

I do because you and I are here and half the other people who claim to be afficionados are not," he pronounced, waving at the half-empty theater.

A ripple of laughter ran through the crowd. Those standing took a seat.

"Those of us who are here should not be deprived of our music because of fickle phony audiences. But we will be affected because an opera house costs a lot of money to run. I can tell you this because that is the excuse my father gives me for my allowance being so cheap."

The laughter from the audience was even heartier. Phil continued.

"You know my father has tried to make the opera ticket a price you can easily pay. People said he could not do it, but he has kept his promise to you about this. Now, it is your turn. I have here a hat from one of the operas. It's pretty deep; I don't know whose head fits all the way in here, but they say opera singers have big heads, so I guess it's true."

Laughter.

"Anyway, I am going to pass this purple hat around. By the way, have you ever seen a bird with a feather this color?" he asked, pointing out the bright mauve feather sticking out from the brim. "I haven't. But it would be a shame if he lost this feather for no reason. So if you would pass this hat from person to person and put in what you could, it will allow us to continue putting on the operas for people who love them." He bent down and handed the hat to the conductor to pass along. "Now I have to get off this stage before my father reaches me. I may lose my puny allowance altogether for doing this." With that he walked off the stage to tumultuous applause.

Maestro was already in the wings. "What was the idea of that?" he asked.

"I heard you say you were in trouble. I took care of it. No big deal," he said, shrugging.

Maestro headed to the sewing room. "Josie, did you hear what happened? Did you see Phil take the hat?"

"I saw him take the hat, but he didn't say why."

Maestro told her what happened. Joe entered the room with the filled hat, plus a filled fire bucket as the orchestra struck up the second act.

"Maestro, I think there is close to five hundred dollars in here. Look at all the dollar bills. We had to empty the hat once; it was overflowing."

Maestro shook his head in amazement. He looked at Josie. "Felice is one amazing boy."

"Yes, he is," she agreed.

"Never mind that. He has to do this for every performance this season. The kid's got real stage appeal. We won't get five bucks if you or I try that trick. Can you bring him to every performance?" Joe interrupted.

"I will try, but his mother is not going to be happy."

"Yes, she will," Josie whispered.

* * *

The reviewers turned out for opening night of *Carmen* as they were already curious about stories they had heard of the young impresario's intermission antics. Phil had enhanced and polished his spiel to the point where his father warned him several times to cut back on the *opera buffa*. Unfortunately, Josie standing in the wings applauding with delight did little to encourage obedience.

The cries of "Bravo!" were wild with delight at the end of the performance. Leonie Dufrey was described as a riveting dynamic singer who could act. She exuded a natural sensuality that complemented both the voluptuousness of her thrilling voice as well as the voluptuousness of her exhilarating figure. The bolero pants accrued their own praises in the press.

"She will be impossible to live with," the conductor warned Maestro the following evening. "She has already handed the orchestra a list with more notes on it than the score of the opera."

* * *

The house was unnaturally quiet when Rinaldo entered and slipped out of his winter coat and hat. Music played softly from the record player, and he could see candles glowing on the dining room table, which was elaborately set for two. He had prepared himself for a surprise birthday party, which he imagined Giuliana had planned. Entering the kitchen, he announced, "Home early, as I promised," indicating that the clock said 5:45 p.m.

"Happy birthday, my love," Giuliana greeted him as she swept across the kitchen to kiss him.

Rinaldo held her at arm's length and looked her over. "What is this costume?" he asked with a leer.

"You like?" she said with a grin as she twirled for his benefit. She had on a flouncy multicolored skirt and a red off-the-shoulder peasant blouse. Her hair fell wild and free, and her makeup had been applied as though she were going to a premiere.

"You look ravishing," he said. "I think you are auditioning for *Carmen*?" he teased.

"I hear that role is managed quite successfully," she replied, handing him a Manhattan. "Go inside and relax. Dinner will be ready in a few minutes."

"Where are the children?"

"At my mother's for the night. The whole night."

Rinaldo lowered himself into an armchair and considered. The blouse was almost exactly the one Leonie wore on the day she tried to seduce him. Was it possible Giuliana knew something? No, it could not be.

"Dinner is served, Rinaldo," Giuliana announced, leading him into the dining room.

Wine was poured in crystal glasses. Wild asparagus wrapped in prosciutto drizzled with a balsamic reduction sat invitingly on the appetizer plates.

"Where did you get these asparagus at this time of year?"

"I have been planning this for some time. Nat, the produce man, made a deal with the devil to get them. I know how you always love them."

"Mmm," he agreed as he stuck another stalk into his mouth. "This can be an aphrodisiac."

"I hope so," Giuliana said wickedly as she picked up one in her fingers, threw back her head, and lowered it into her open mouth.

The next course was a seafood risotto, which included clams, prawns, scallops, and halibut. It was accompanied by peas and mushrooms with sage and a tossed green salad.

"This tastes like the Tyrrhenian Sea is outside our back door. I can almost smell the air of Italy."

"That is the orange skins I am roasting in the oven."

"Ah. Is that in some way involved with the dessert?"

"Oh no, my love. Dessert is something very, very special. Are you ready or do you want to digest a bit?"

"Will I drown if I jump right into it?" he said with a smile.

"You may," Giuliana considered. "I tell you what. Why don't you go upstairs and dress down."

"What does that mean?"

"Oh, just get as comfortable as you want. I have a few things left to prepare. Then I will call for you. Stay in our room until I call."

"This is very mysterious.'

Giuliana kissed her fingertip and touched his lips with it. "Go."

A short time later, Rinaldo heard her calling. He opened the bedroom door. Music was coming from Dante's room. He entered there and saw that the door leading to the attic was open and flickering fingers of light were beckoning from beyond. Slowly he climbed the stairs. When he reached the top step, Giuliana commanded, "Wait there until your banquet is complete."

Rinaldo surveyed the unfinished room. Candles arranged on the windowsills and various pieces of abandoned furniture gave the space an ethereal glow. A travel trunk draped in one of Giuliana's favorite tablecloths stood in the middle of the floor. The cloth puddled in pools at the base of the trunk. The air was fragrant with Phil's drying herbs. Thyme, oregano, basil, rosemary mixed with the orange skins and Giuliana's own floral perfume. The sky was a perfect midnight blue outside the window as frost began to accumulate on the panes.

Giuliana stood watching him as she lifted her blouse over her head. The childish breasts of her twenties had ripened into full luscious globes after nursing four children. She lowered her skirt over her narrow hips and long, lean legs. Rinaldo's suspicion that she had not been wearing any undergarments was confirmed. He took a step forward, but she raised her hand to halt. Turning, she reached for her handpainted Italian pedestal fruit bowl. Piled high were strawberries that had been cut in half, dipped in egg white and coated with sugar. Carrying the bowl with her, she lay across the trunk. Slowly, she gathered several berries and laid them on her thighs. She stretched out and reached for more fruit, continuing to arrange them between her legs, on her belly, in her navel, around her torso.

Carefully, she stretched her hand for more and laid them on her collarbones, shoulders, breasts, and eyes. With a Mozart concerto glorifying the air around them, she whispered, "Your sumptuous feast is ready, Maestro. Enjoy." She placed the final strawberry on her lips.

The attic should have been cold, but neither of them could have vouched for that assumption. Rinaldo made the final climb into the room, almost forgetting to duck under a few precarious beams. He stood to Giuliana's side and removed his shirt. He sat on the floor to remove his shoes and socks and couldn't resist. He gathered the strawberry from her lips into his own and said, "I love you."

Her body arched in desire, destroying a bit of the tableau. "Rinaldo," she whispered, "no speaking until you have finished your dessert." Carefully, she rearranged the berries while he removed his pants.

Bending over her, he took the berries from her eyes into his mouth. "I want to look into your eyes," he said. "*Uffa*! I forgot. No speaking." Swallowing, he moved to her thighs where he gathered the berries with his tongue and lips. Moving to her navel, he removed that berry with his teeth and brought it to Giuliana's lips. She opened her mouth and took it on her tongue before capturing Rinaldo's lips with her own. He found his way back down the table to her torso and then traced a line of sugar with his tongue. Giuliana started to laugh.

"You will destroy the mood, Rinaldo," she warned as he continued to lick where strawberries had recently lain.

"I think not," he concluded. "I do not leave crumbs on the table." He brought his lips to her breasts and took much more than the strawberry with each mouthful. Giuliana groaned and held his head to her chest, but Rinaldo would not be stopped. He went in search of the berries he had seen her place between her thighs. He nuzzled there, probing, darting, insisting he had seen her put many more fruits in that region than he had found.

Finally, when Giuliana cried out, "Please, Rinaldo, there are no more strawberries left in all America," he rose and straddled her thighs. A foreboding creak alerted him to the realities of this unrestrained banquet, and he stood, indicating Giuliana should do so also. Removing the tablecloth, he laid it on the floor, pushing the trunk out of the way. Together they settled themselves, older and passionate, young and wanton, familiar yet unexplored, oblivious to the hard floor or the cold air around them.

Afterward, Rinaldo lay on his back with Giuliana's head on his chest.

"I adore you, my wife. Every breath I take is in ecstasy of loving you."

"Happy birthday, Rinaldo. I bless the day your soul was conceived."

Early stars appeared in the sky, peeking through the frosted windows at the lovescape before them. The winter wind in the trees whistled gently through the rafters like a chime announcing a promising tomorrow.

* * *

Three weeks later, while listening to a live broadcast of *Carmen* on the radio, Giuliana was astounded to hear an announcement during intermission. It seemed MGM had offered Leonie Dufrey a contract. What would the diva do? Giuliana grappled with the possibilities and made a bet with herself as to the outcome. When Rinaldo came home, she was sitting prettily in bed, reading.

"How did it go this evening?"

"Brilliant. This production is sold out. Even standing room."

"Anything interesting?"

He sat on the seat from Giuliana's vanity table to untie his shoelaces. He looked up at her mischievous face and wondered to himself, *How does she know these things? They were only at the opera house this afternoon.*

"Yes. Leonie was offered a contract to go to Hollywood. They got wind out there of all the hoopla surrounding this production and sent a scout. She is breathless with excitement and acting so sweetly haughty, she's lucky no one pulled some kind of stunt on her during the show."

"What is she going to do? Give up singing for film?"

"If she had her way, she would have been out the door permanently tonight."

"She'd leave just like that?"

"That's Leonie. Anything for her art," Maestro said sarcastically.

"So I've gathered."

Rinaldo stood and finished undressing. "I told her if she broke her contract, I would contact friends in high places in Hollywood."

"Which friends would that be?"

"I know people. Several have been to our operas." He paused. "*Carmen* is sold out. I considered letting Loretta take over the role just to be rid of Leonie. But we're sold out because people want to see her." He climbed into bed and reached over to kiss Giuliana.

Giuliana turned out her bedside lamp. "So she goes to Hollywood," she said with satisfaction. "Only one thing, Rinaldo."

"What?"

"I hope you're not disappointed you didn't sample a French croissant before settling for the Italian pastry at home."

"*Buona notte, Giuliana mia.*"

Chapter 18

A whole nickel! How to spend it? Phil and his friend Paul joined Henry to pick up a few items for his mother in the new supermarket. It was convenient having much of what you needed under one roof, but loyalties to local shopowners were strong, and the new establishment was still trying to validate itself to the community.

"Hey," said Henry. "There's Strega Titzi. Let's shake up a bottle of soda and open it in front of her."

"Leave her alone," Phil replied fiercely. "She's just an old lady."

"Aw, she's a grumpy old witch. I'm gonna knock down a bunch of cans in front of her and watch her dance," said Henry with glee.

"You do, and I'll punch your lights out," warned Phil. "Why are you such a hood?"

"Oh, come on. It's not like I'm gonna bump her off. Just want to put a little scare in her like she does to all the little kids."

"Just get what you came for, Henry, and spend your nickel. Let's get going," said Phil in exasperation.

As the boys were checking out, there was a sudden commotion near another register.

"All right, lady. You're coming inside while I call the cops," the manager said, gripping Strega Titzi strongly by the arm.

"I no take nothing. I no take," the old lady cried hoarsely.

"Yeah, well, we've noticed missing inventory a lot lately after you've been visiting. Now there are two cans of beans and a sauerkraut in your satchel here. Tell it to the cops."

"Get a load of this," said Henry with a laugh. "The old witch is a shoplifter."

Phil looked at the trembling old woman as the manager led her to the rear of the store.

"You go on ahead, guys. I'll catch up. I have to do something," Phil said as he took off after the store manager. "Hey, mister," he said, just as the duo were entering the dark recesses at the back of the store.

"What?"

"She didn't take the stuff."

"What do you mean? How do you know?"

Strega Titzi turned to look at Phil. Her face paled, and she hung her kerchiefed head.

"Those guys and me were talking about playing a trick on her. So I put the cans in her bag. I thought it would be funny when she got home and found them. She didn't take them herself."

"Are you telling the truth, young man?"

"Yes, sir."

The manager let go of Strega's arm. "OK, you can go this time. But I have my eye on you." Turning to Phil, he added, "I should call the cops on you. It's still stealing."

"Yes, sir."

"I'll give you one more chance. If you mess around again, I call the cops, and you're barred from this store. But I'm calling your parents. Do they have a phone?"

"Yes, sir."

Phil followed the manager to the back office and watched nervously as he dialed the number. Minutes later Giuliana arrived, angry and mortified. She spewed a lengthy tirade all the way home and then sent Phil to his room until his father came home.

"This behavior is completely unacceptable," Maestro roared in a thunderous voice. "I cannot believe that a son of mine would do something like this."

Giuliana, who had had some time to calm down, spoke up. "It is my fault too. This is what comes of calling someone, *strega,* a witch. Soon others think she does not matter and treat her that way." She backed to the doorway of the dining room where they were standing and looked at the three siblings who she knew were sitting on the stairs. "Do you all hear this? No more Strega Titzi."

"There will be sharp consequences for this, Felice."

"Yes, sir."

"There will be no baseball or stickball or any other kind of ball for the entire summer."

"OK," Phil mumbled sadly.

Maestro seemed to be thinking. "That includes no going to Yankee Stadium or anywhere else to see a ball game. You have no right to cheer celebrities if you cannot treat the person you pass on the street with respect."

"Yes, Maestro."

"And you will go and apologize to this old woman. Dante…," he called.

Dante came running into the dining room. "Yes, sir."

"Walk with your brother to her house and make sure he apologizes."

Twenty minutes later they returned.

"Did he apologize?" Maestro asked Dan.

"Well, he went into the house. I wasn't going into that spooky house, but I saw her answer the door, and he went in."

"Good. Now we eat and then listen to what's happening in this crazy world on the radio."

* * *

The next evening Phil sat on the front steps watching Dan and his friends play stickball. The block was quieter somehow; several of the older young men on the block had already been drafted and left for overseas. *Everything seems weird now anyway,* thought Phil. *I don't care if I can't play ball. It's not the same when you know guys are out there shooting guns and getting shot at.* Visible over the top of the hedge, a kerchiefed head came bobbing down the block with the military stride of an aged general. The determined *Signora* appeared at the gate, fiddled with the latch, and marched up the walk.

"Is your father home?" she asked Phil.

"Yes. What are you doing here?"

"Never you mind. You open the door."

They walked into the entryway.

"Ma, Maestro," Phil started to call, but they had already seen the visitor from their spots in the parlor.

"*Signora...*," Maestro began.

The old lady put up her hand. "I no talk long. I just come tell you. Felice did not do what he say. I take cans. I put in my bag. He tell man with iron hand he take, but no, I take. I sorry your boy get in trouble. He a good boy and no should be punished."

Giuliana's hand flew to her chest, and Maestro shifted uncomfortably.

"I don't understand, Phil," began Giuliana. "Why would you lie about this?"

"I go now. You take the punish off the boy."

Maestro looked at her well-made housedress with bric-a-brac trim and perfect buttonholes. It looked handmade by an artisan.

"*Signora,*" interrupted Maestro. "Why did you need to steal the cans of food? Are you hungry?"

"*Si, Signor*e. My sister and me have trouble since the war. We no have much money, so I think...she no know I take. Summer now, the vegetable grow; it be better. I no take from crazy man store anymore. His potatoes are rot, anyway." With that she turned, opened the door, and left.

Giuliana stared at Phil. "Why on earth would you take the blame for something you didn't do?"

"Gee, Ma. That guy scared the whiskers off of her. She was all shaky and trembling. He was really in a lather. I felt bad for her. I thought she was gonna have a heart attack on the spot."

"So you give up your ball games all summer for her." Maestro made the statement softly.

"Phil, this was a noble deed. Truly. But you cannot go around taking the blame for things when you feel bad for people you don't even know." Giuliana took a step and wrapped her arms around the boy.

"Well, you see, Ma, I kinda know her. Remember when she threw the water at Lucy? Well, I've been helping her with her flowers and stuff since then. She's taught me about herbs. Remember when I fixed Tino's cough? That was Signora Titziano's remedy. Sometimes she tells me stories—"

"Signora Titziano?" interrupted Maestro. "Her name is Titziano?"

"Yes, why?" asked Giuliana.

"I only hear Titzi," Maestro stated.

"The kids call her that. Strega Titzi. I said it before. What's wrong?" she asked, observing Maestro's suddenly pale face.

"I must check this out. Phil, you go. You go play ball with the boys."

Phil opened the door before his father changed his mind.

"Phil. I'm proud of you."

When the boy left, he turned to Giuliana. "Josie's last name is Titziano."

* * *

The newlyweds found an apartment on the Lower East Side. It was small, a tiny kitchen, small parlor, and a bedroom with a window that opened up over a narrow courtyard where tenants dumped slop from pails and other household waste. In the heat of the summer, the stench became so unbearable, the window had to be kept shut. They often slept on the parlor floor during these months. The subway, however, made access to Giuliana's job at Altman's and Rinaldo's job at King's Academy an easy commute.

Street life in this part of the city was colorful. The pushcart vendors cried their wares: singsong, operatic, shouts, and hollers. The produce man clopped down the street with his horse and wagon, calling, "If you come out, come out to buy; if you don't come out, I'll go home and cry." Another childless young couple shared the cost of a gallon of "Biancolino," homemade bleach, with the Salvatoris as both couples' laundry needs were less than those families with several children running around. Giuliana would skip in a hopscotch court or duck under a jump rope that some neighborhood girls were turning as she hurried home to prepare dinner for Rinaldo. Once in a while, on a Saturday night, they would go to a Chinese restaurant and have egg drop soup, chicken chow mein with rice and noodles, an egg roll, fortune cookie, and ice cream for a quarter a piece. Rinaldo wasn't particularly fond of the food, but he knew Giuliana enjoyed it. When Giuliana became pregnant, she worked until Christmas of 1926 in defiance of her parents' and Rinaldo's objections.

Late afternoon on a crisp, cold February day, Giuliana went into labor. A chain of events was set in motion. She hobbled to her neighbor's door to tell her the news. The neighbor called one of her sons from outdoors. He was sent two blocks down to get the midwife. The neighbor then went down to the corner candy store to call the hospital in Brooklyn where Giuliana's father worked. Dante Ardito raced home by bus. While his wife changed clothes, he called Rinaldo at the Academy using their phone, the only one on the block. The anxious almost-grandparents headed for the subway to go into Manhattan.

The midwife was already with Giuliana in her tiny bedroom. After checking on his daughter, Dante retreated to the parlor with his wife. Anxious and harried, Rinaldo burst into the apartment. "How is she? Where is she?" he asked.

"*Uffa*—where is she. On the roof. In your bedroom; where you think?" Anna cried brusquely.

Rinaldo opened the bedroom door that was partially closed. Giuliana was raised by several pillows, flushed and sweating, her hair plastered in wet curls around her face.

"How are you doing?" Rinaldo asked as he entered the room gingerly.

"This is hard work," Giuliana huffed.

"She'sa doin good. She strong girl. You leave. No bring bad luck," the midwife ordered.

"I'm OK. She says the baby is coming fast. Go stay with Mama and Papa."

An hour later Giuliana was still in labor, and Anna was in the kitchen preparing a frittata and coffee. A scream cut the air, and Rinaldo raced to the bedroom.

"Is she all right?" he yelled, afraid to enter the room and get chastised by the midwife.

"The baby is coming, Rinaldo. Sing to me. Sing *Celeste Aida.* Let the baby hear music as he enters the world. Let him hear his father's voice."

So Rinaldo sang as baby Dante greeted the world; he kept singing when he heard the first cries and continued the song as he slid down and sat with his back against the wall, knees and head both bent in relief.

The midwife exited the room after handing the baby to Giuliana. She looked down at Rinaldo on the floor next to the door and said, "You have a son."

Rinaldo stood. "Is he fine? Is he good all over?"

"He isa perfect. He looka like you."

Rinaldo entered the room while the Arditos stood in the narrow doorway.

"Look, Rinaldo. He's beautiful. He has your hair, your forehead." The baby let out a wail. "Your mouth."

Rinaldo looked at his son and kissed his wife. She was not surprised to feel his tears wetting her face.

* * *

Two weeks later Rinaldo made a direct turnabout as he reached the subway station as he returned home from work. He had forgotten a score he needed to work on in his office. He reentered the building, retrieved the music, and noticed a light flickering under the costume room down the hallway. He headed for the room, grasped the doorknob, and flung the door wide open. Huddled in a far corner on a makeshift bed, covered with an assortment of costume capes and robes, lay Josie, one of the young seamstresses who helped out at the Academy on occasion. She gasped in fright at the intruder.

"Josie? It is I, Maestro Salvatori." He moved closer to her.

Josie sat up. She was wearing a coat under her other coverings.

"What is going on?"

"I'm sorry, Maestro. I will leave." She started to rise.

"*Aspetta.* Wait. Why are you here at this time of night?"

Josie's voice caught in her throat. Eventually she squeaked out, "I have no place to go."

"What of your home? Your family?"

"My mother threw me out."

Rinaldo considered this. "Gather your things. We will get something to eat, and you will tell me the story." As she started to protest, he raised his hand. "Just do as I say, or I will have to tell the board that you are living in the costume room."

They found a diner, and he insisted Josie order a complete meal. From the way she attacked it, he could tell she was ravenous. He sipped his coffee and studied the small, pretty girl with curly hair, dark eyes, and bow lips almost too small for her face. She had just turned nineteen, worked in the garment district in the city, but on occasion, when the Academy needed extra help with costumes, she sewed on a piecework basis. Now she took a sip of her chocolate malted and looked sadly at Rinaldo.

"I am with child," she said simply.

"The father?"

"He is gone. My mother is disgraced. She says I disgust her. I came home from work one night, and she had my clothes in bags in the hallway. She told me never to show my face around her again."

"You have no other family?" Maestro inquired.

Josie shook her head. "About a year ago my father and sister died in an accident. My mother couldn't do this if my father was alive. I stayed with a friend's family a few days, but I couldn't keep imposing. I have one aunt, my mother's sister. I went there, and the other tenants said she had just moved. I went back to our old apartment, and my mother was gone too. I cannot find them." She lapped up the pot roast gravy with a big piece of bread and stuffed it in her mouth. "So I began sneaking into the Academy at night before it closed. Everyone knows me, so no one questioned me. Then I hid until everyone had gone and went to sleep in the costume room."

"This cannot continue, you understand," Maestro said gently.

Josie didn't answer. Finally she said, "I don't know what to do."

"Tonight you will come home with me. You will sleep on the couch. Tomorrow I will try to find other arrangements for you."

"Oh, Maestro. Thank you, but this is not your problem."

"If one of my best sewers is not getting a good sleep, then it is my problem," he said gruffly.

Giuliana was surprised yet gracious to the unexpected guest. Josie stayed with them for five nights, and then Maestro made arrangements for her to rent room and board at the home of one of the conductors at the Academy. He paid the rent until Josie accumulated enough savings to take care of it herself. In the meantime he hired her full time at the Academy costume department, paying her equal to what she received in her previous job and time and a half for overtime. She was, in all fairness, the best seamstress in the company, even though she was one of the youngest.

When Josie began to show, Rinaldo would stand for no idle gossip or cruel comments. If you had a problem with an unmarried pregnant girl working at the Academy, you were welcome to leave. One day Josie came to Maestro at the end of the day.

"Maestro, can I speak with you?" she asked.

"Of course."

"I need your help. I am looking into where to put my baby for adoption, and I need your advice on which place looks safest and most honest."

"You have the names?"

She nodded and handed him a piece of paper. As he scanned the list, she broke into loud, convulsing sobs.

"Josie, Josie. What's wrong? Come, sit," he said, leading her to a bench against the hall wall. "Now, tell me. Why are you crying?"

"I can't bother you anymore, Maestro Salvatori. You've been so good to me."

"I'll decide that. Tell me."

"I don't want to give up my baby. I love him already. But I can't take care of him. I have to work, and there's no one to care for him. I know I have to do it, but my heart is breaking all the time." She took the handkerchief Maestro handed her and wiped her eyes and nose. "It will, perhaps, kill me to never see him again, but I have to do it."

Rinaldo sat for a long time without saying anything. Finally, he turned to Josie and took her hands in his. "I have a thought. I cannot promise you because I have to talk with my wife. But it has been done before. People cannot afford to raise one more child, and a relative takes the child to raise as their own. I am thinking maybe my Dante would like a baby brother or sister."

"Oh, Maestro!"

"I cannot say for sure. This will not be easy to tell Giuliana. But if we have your baby, you will be able to see it every little while."

"That's all I'd want! That's all I'd need! To know she's all right."

"We shall see."

* * *

It took Rinaldo three days to broach the topic with Giuliana. She sat by the parlor window with the baby at her breast and looked out at the trees budding with the promise of renewal. She smiled at her husband. "This may be the best time of our lives, *caro.* We have our perfect son and so much promise for our tomorrows."

"Truly. We have been blessed. Some others are not so fortunate."

"I know."

"Remember Josie?"

"Of course. You told me the child shows. Is she managing all right?"

So Rinaldo told her.

"Are you asking this for real, Rinaldo?" she questioned incredulously.

"*Si.* It is not unheard of."

"But I already have an infant."

"He will be about nine months when her baby is born. You will be able to nurse him like your own."

"She will want to be his mother too."

"No, no. She knows she cannot. She wants only to see him once in a while."

Giuliana gazed out the window. "Rinaldo. Is this your child?"

"Giuliana! Oh, my love," he cried, running to her side. "No. It is not. Never. No. I swear on the head of my son, Dante," he cried, caressing the baby's head.

Giuliana leaned her head back on the chair and closed her eyes. Dante loosened his grip on her and looked up at his mother. He turned his little head and looked at his father. Giuliana looked down and played with his dark, straight hair.

"Let me think, Rinaldo. I cannot answer today. Let me think. And pray."

* * *

Rinaldo waited three days. He never brought the topic up. Giuliana laid Dante down in his cradle at the foot of their bed. She climbed into the bed and sat on top of the covers.

"No one can know," she stated.

Rinaldo shifted and turned to look at her.

"We can take him, but no one must know. It is our child. She must agree to this without argument. Only my parents will know."

"We can try."

"No. Not try. It must be. You will tell the people at work that I am with child. I will not come to the theater anymore. We will tell the neighbors and then when the child is born, we will move. These neighbors will not know when I have the baby, and the new neighbors will think it is ours to begin with."

"I will look for a house starting tomorrow. I promised you we would look for a house, and we will begin now."

"We will give her pictures, and you may take him to the Academy sometimes when he is older. I will bring him to the Academy myself when he is an infant. She must agree to this."

"I will tell her."

"One other thing. You will pay a midwife to say I am the mother. It is the information she will bring to the office of records. The birth certificate will say we are the parents. If Josie ever says differently, I will have her locked up as a crazy person and a threat to our child. I will have the papers to prove it."

Maestro studied the fierce fire in Giuliana's eyes. She had already usurped the motherhood of this coming baby. If Josie balked at one detail, there would be no agreement. Giuliana leaned down and kissed Dante's head. She whispered softly to him, but Rinaldo could not hear what she said.

* * *

Josie agreed to all Giuliana's stipulations and was happy to do so. During her eighth month, Maestro told her he had found the perfect house and was going to bring Giuliana to see it the coming weekend. If she loved it as much as he was sure she would, he would buy it.

"Before we move in," he promised Josie, "I will take you to see it so you know where the baby will live." He had taken to calling the child "the baby" instead of "your baby" when speaking with Josie. "It is only a few blocks from my in-laws' home. Also, my father-in-law is a doctor."

"That is good." She hesitated. "It is good that the baby will have grandparents."

"Have you found your mother?"

"No. I looked and looked. She has disappeared. I am finished. She is no longer in my life."

Maestro shook his head. "You will never be able to erase her from your mind."

"I will do it," Josie insisted stubbornly. Then, rubbing her belly, she said shyly, "I do have one request if Giuliana will agree. If it is a girl I would like her to be named Felicia. Happiness. Or a boy, Felice. Because, no matter what, I am happy for this baby. And even though it will never know who I am, I want it to feel the happiness in its soul."

* * *

The house was a grand dusty-pink stucco on the corner of a treelined Brooklyn street. Waist-high shrubs surrounding the property were circled by a wrought-iron fence and gate. The front yard was divided by a walkway that led to three steps, a small porch, and the front door. The entryway was wide, with a flight of stairs to the second floor slightly right of center. To the left of the entryway, the huge dining room would hold a grand table. A place where food was more than nourishment. A setting of reassurance in family, approval, and self-worth. Beyond that, the kitchen was bright and large with an adjoining pantry. The parlor and what would become the music room were on the right side of the entryway. A small bathroom with space enough just to do your business was next to a door leading to the basement Another outside door opened to a large yard where a fig tree and a peach tree lorded it over an otherwise unkempt display of flowers and shrubs. Upstairs were four bedrooms and one bath, and above them an unfinished attic. Giuliana was in love.

"Yes, yes, yes!" she shouted as she ran down the stairs. Rinaldo stood in the dining room looking outside the big window. He smiled in satisfaction. It would be a little difficult in the beginning, but they would manage. Giuliana deserved a palace for her growing family.

Two months before she gave birth, Josie moved into a small one-room apartment. When she went into labor, only the midwife and Rinaldo were present. An envelope passed hands, Rinaldo kissed the girl's sweaty forehead, and promised her she would never be sorry. The little furniture he and Giuliana owned had already been moved to the new house. He went downstairs to the waiting cab that would take him to his in-laws', where Giuliana, he, and Dante had been living the past four days. Thankfully, Josie had delivered almost right on schedule. Tomorrow the family of four would move into their new home. He climbed into the back of the cab holding the newborn, whose light blond hair already stood in spikes above his head. Rinaldo kissed his head. "Destiny has decided, Felice," he whispered.

At the door of her parent's home, Giuliana stepped forward with outstretched arms. She took the baby from her husband and carried him into the kitchen. The sweetness of his innocence erased all fears. Next, she studied his light hair, grayish-almond shaped eyes, and button nose. He didn't look anything like Rinaldo. From what she could tell, he didn't look anything like Josie either. The baby opened his mouth in a wide yawn and settled more comfortably into her arms. She felt her doubts slide like a river over rocks. Giuliana smiled. "Welcome to the family, son."

Chapter 19

Rinaldo put one grocery bag down and pushed the doorbell. The blinds in the window moved, and he saw Signora Titziano peering through them. A minute later the old woman opened the door.

"Good evening, *Signora.* May I come in?"

She didn't answer but opened the door wider and shuffled back into her apartment. Rinaldo picked up the bag, stepped inside, and closed the door with his foot. He rested his walking stick, tucked under his arm, by the door.

"I've brought you some groceries. Can we put them in the kitchen?"

Still wordlessly, she led him through a small parlor, a smaller dining area, and into the kitchen.

It smelled like his attic with drying herbs hanging all over the room. He placed the bags on the table.

"Here is milk, eggs, and butter. Do you have a refrigerator?" he asked, looking around.

"An icebox," she said, indicating a small one that stood in a corner.

"There is fruit, some vegetables, crackers, jam, soup…don't tell my wife I bought canned soup," he added conspiratorially, "cookies, tuna fish, and pasta."

"Why you do this when I make your boy trouble?"

Maestro sat down. "What happened is over. We will not talk about it anymore. Can I have a cup of coffee or tea? I haven't been home yet."

She shuffled to the stove, her slippers scuffing along the old floor tiles, and put up some water for tea. Neither spoke while the water came to a boil. Maestro again studied her housedress, which was well made, although plainer than the one she had worn on her "mission" to his house.

After she poured the water over tea bags and sat down to join him, Maestro asked, "How is it that you and Felice are friends?"

She took a sip of her tea and pulled away from the cup as it burned her tongue. "He do it. He come and work with garden. I rent here. Upstairs rents too. The owner not around; he no care for garden. But I lika flowers. I usa herbs, and we eat vegetables.

Felice make it better. I give him a drink, a cookie. We talk. We play cards, *briscola*, hearts. We play *sette mezzo*. He tell me about the school, the ball games, you, you family. I feel like I hava family."

"What happened to your family?"

"You no want to hear."

"I do."

"You will no let Felice come here anymore."

"I promise that will not happen."

She pushed the cup of tea away from herself and folded her hands as if in prayer.

"I hava husband and *due*, two daughters. Elisabetta, we call Bessie, and Giuseppina is Josie. Bessie is my girl; Josie is her father's. He crazy for her. I tell, after a while, I get the jealous. I'ma sorry it hap, but it hap. Once, I fall offa the trolley when it start to move as I get off. I hit my face on street. Breaka my nose; scratcha my face. Bernardo act like no big deal. 'You ok,' he say. 'Nothin' the time won'ta fix.' Then Josie fall two steps in front of house. Her knee cut deep, there'sa the blood, and she cryin' like her leg fall off. Bernardo goesa crazy. Pick her up and run to hospital. He buy her toy; he feed her pastina." She pressed her hands flat on the table. "That'sa how it was. The girls get big; it'sa the same. One day in summer, Bernardo rents automobile. We goin' on picnic in up New York. He no drive much; he no know so much about the automobile. So we drive where he goin', a place with the lake, but he get'sa lit' lost. He pulls to side of road; it's edge with no fence, no wall, no nothin'. He say, 'We have to turn around.' He get back in automobile and turn around. But before we start to go front again, he go back and whoof! Car go over edge. We fall, fall, fall, and stop." She paused, picked up her cup, and sipped. "Bernardo is dead. Bessie is dead. Justa me and Josie we live."

"Where is Josie now?"

"I no know."

"How come?"

Signora Titziano let out a big sigh. "This issa the bad I do. Josie come a home one day and say she in family way. I am *furioso.* I *knew* my Bessie the better girl. I tell her to go. Leave the house. No come back. She cry; she beg. But I get even with Bernardo. I show him he no teacha Josie the way to be. My Bessie no get the family way. I put all her things in the bags. She find when she come a home that night. She leave. I never see again."

"She never came home again?"

"I no know. My sister, Rosa, and me, we move here to Brooklyn. It's a cheap than New York, and I no have Bernardo work anymore."

"And her baby?" Maestro prodded, although he now knew the ending to the tale.

"I no know. Is a boy, girl? God only know."

"Would you like to find Josie?"

She looked at Maestro, and his breath caught as he saw her eyes fill with tears.

"*Si. Si,* I like to see. I tell her I was *stupido.* I have the anger at her father, so I throw it on her. It was bad. I miss; I miss but she live life now with no mother. Maybe she marry; maybe many children. I no know. I never know."

"Maybe I can find Josie," Maestro said, laying his hand over hers.

"Who you? Angel *di Dio*?" Angel of God.

Maestro gave a dry laugh. "No. Believe me, I'm no angel. There are no clouds in heaven waiting for my return. Don't give up hope, *Signora.*" He rose to leave.

"You letta Felice come here?"

"Yes, of course. Whenever he wants."

As he left the room, he heard her mumbling, "I bad mother. *Dio, Dio,* I bad mother."

* * *

The children settled in bed, Giuliana joined Rinaldo in the parlor. As she sat on the couch and reached for a magazine, he set aside his newspaper.

"I visited Signora Titziano this evening before coming home."

Giuliana paused mid-reach and sat back in the cushions.

"You did?"

Rinaldo nodded. "I brought her a few groceries."

"That was kind."

"I didn't use any of our ration coupons. I used gift ones."

"I didn't ask."

"She talked about Josie."

"So she is her mother."

"Yes. She is sorry now. With age comes wisdom. I am going to see if Josie will consider seeing her."

"Why are you getting involved, Rinaldo?"

"I must."

Giuliana's fist pounded the chair. "No," she exclaimed, standing and walking to the center of the room. "You do not ease your own conscience on the back of my child."

"What are you saying?"

Giuliana lowered her voice to a whisper. "She will find out Felice is her grandson. Before you know it, the whole neighborhood will know."

"Josie has always played by the rules you set fourteen years ago. Why do you think she will talk now?"

"Because it is her mother. No, Rinaldo, you promised. Time does not change that."

"Of all people, I thought you would be happy to see a reconciliation between a mother and child."

"There are others involved here. The old woman spread thorns around. Now she can't expect to go around walking barefoot."

"I trust Josie will not say anything if I ask her. I do not even know if she will agree. She is bitter, as she has a right to be."

"Tell me what you know."

Rinaldo repeated the story he had heard earlier from the *Signora.*

"I am sorry, but I do not feel differently. I do not want her to know about Felice," Giuliana said firmly at the end of the recital.

Rinaldo knew it was useless to try to persuade Giuliana against something she set her mind to. At least right away.

"All right. Signora Titziano will not be told. But I must tell Josie I have found her mother. If she chooses to meet with her, I will tell her—no, I will order her not to break her word to us."

Giuliana bit her inner cheeks. She did not trust Josie not to talk. "I'd rather you stay out of it completely."

"I already told the old lady I would search for her daughter."

Giuliana felt her eyes fill. "All right, Rinaldo. Tell Josie. But the next time there is something I must do that you disagree with, I am reminding you of this. *Capisce?* Understand?"

Rinaldo rose and went to take her in his arms. "When do I ever disagree with you?" he asked lightly.

She shrugged off his embrace and ran upstairs.

* * *

"I'm not interested." Josie cut off Maestro midsentence.

"Josie, she is so sorry."

"I don't care. If she had been a true mother, I would have been a mother to my own son. She took that from me. I don't forgive."

"We've done right by Felice. We love him the same as the others. Do you resent us for this, Josie?" Maestro said imploringly.

Josie's features softened. "No, of course not. You saved him and me. I know you and Giuliana are the best parents he could have ever had. But Maestro, there is a hole, a hole as big as that Grand Canyon inside of me." She stiffened. "She shot the cannon that put it there. No."

"Someday you are going to regret this decision, but it will be too late."

"Never. I had forgotten her until you brought her up."

Maestro laughed bitterly. "Not so, Josie. I know this to be true. It is God's little joke on mankind. The memory of one's parents and children is the one part of the human body that God has forged with immortality."

Josie sat in her chair as if to work. She slumped slightly.

"Think about it, Josie. Don't decide in anger. Think perhaps that she has changed and can now be the mother you always wanted. Think that when Tony and you marry and have children, you can give her grandchildren. You can be more generous with love than she was with you. She will see; she will understand, and you will both mend. Think about it, Josie."

Chapter 20

1943

Lucy sat straight up at her desk and tried to look as proper as possible. Of all the luck for her final year at St. Mary's, she had Sister Bulldog as her teacher. Oh, she had a real name, Sister Grace Alphonse, but everyone called her Sister Bulldog. Her lower jaw jutted out from her habit, and her teeth seemed to be in a permanently clenched setting. When the steel gray eyes behind her rimless glasses weren't staring you down like an attack dog ready to pounce, they darted about, not missing the slightest movement of air within a radius of three miles. The only saving grace was that Jimmy was back in her class for this, their final year together.

Sister Grace, who must have been about a hundred years old, sat on the edge of her desk, enumerating the classroom rules. She flicked a pointer around for emphasis, and every so often, Joey Califano, whose reputation preceded him and was assigned a seat directly in front of her desk, was tapped on the head with the pointed stick.

"If you've bothered to observe, you will see that the blackboards, front and back, have been divided lengthwise into eleven sections each. Each of you will be assigned a spot at the blackboard. That is your designated spot; you do not change it. Understood?"

A general murmur of affirmation spread through the room.

"There are two divisions. First division and second division. Every person in the odd-numbered seats in each row is first division; the even numbered seats are division two. Is everyone following?"

Lucy's brain began to swirl. What was this division stuff? If getting to the blackboard was so complicated, how were they supposed to function while doing actual schoolwork?

"When I call your division, you go up to the board. You pick up your piece of chalk, and you do whatever the assignment is. It may be a math problem out of your book; it may be diagramming a sentence; it might be spelling; it might be summarizing a chapter in the history book. I will be watching your board work very closely."

Uh-oh, Lucy thought. *This must be what I heard about heads getting cracked into the blackboard if you get something wrong. She's nuts.*

"Let's practice," Sister Grace droned on. "Division One."

There was a general scrambling as twenty-two children raced to the boards. One terrified young girl raised her hand and called out, "Sister?"

"Why are you wandering around like a hobo?"

"Sister, there's no place for me at the board."

Sister Grace looked around at the standing students. "You," she said, indicating a small blond boy with her pointer. "Do you see your desk?"

The victim looked. "Yes, Sister."

"Is there someone still sitting in the desk in front of you?"

"No, Sister."

"Did you pass math in the first grade?"

"Yes, Sister."

"Count the seats in your row."

"One, two, three, four, five..."

"Stop there. What number are you?"

"Six."

"Is that an odd or even number?"

"Even."

"And what did I say Divison One was?"

No answer.

"Did you hear me? What number seats belong in Division One?"

"Odd?"

"Odd. So, you do have ears. Maybe nothing between them, but you do have ears. Come here."

Summoning his last bit of courage, he trekked to the front. Sister Grace tapped him on the head with the pointer. "Sit down in your number six seat."

Lucy was in the second row, second seat, very close to Sister's desk. Her throat had constricted, and her teeth tingled with anxiety. She looked at Jimmy, standing at his spot by the blackboard, barely reaching the chalk tray. After so many years, she had a natural antenna where Jimmy was concerned, and she knew he was panicked and mortified.

"Division Two."

The first bunch seated themselves as the second group raced forward.

"All right. I see Division Two is smarter than Division One," Sister Grace concluded. "Now, each time you use the board, before you return to your seats, you will erase your section. Three people share one eraser. You hand the eraser to one another. That does not mean you slide it across the chalk tray or hurl it at one another's heads. I see a flying eraser or chalk eraser marks on uniforms and the perpetrator will get detention. Understood?"

"Yes, Sister," the class said in unison.

* * *

There were rules for classwork, homework, asking a question, asking to be excused, answering the door if someone knocked, and for lining up. Lucy was in crisis mode. She had been assigned as homebound line leader, and the lunch bell had just rung. But she had to talk to Sister Grace. God knows, she didn't want to, but she had no choice. After she led the line down the flight of stairs to the outside door, she ran back up the stairs instead of heading home. Peeking through the narrow rectangular window, she saw Sister Grace still sitting at her desk. She tapped a short, pleaful knock and opened the door. "Sister?"

"Why are you back here? Aren't you a homebound for lunch?"

"Yes, Sister. I'm sorry, but I had to talk to you."

"Something so very urgent. All right, Miss…"

"Salvatori."

"Yes. Lucilla Salvatori."

"Everyone calls me Lucy, Sister."

"How nice for everyone, Lucilla. What do you have to tell me?"

“Sister, Jimmy Ferraro won’t be able to reach the blackboard. He’ll be embarrassed, plus he won’t be able to do the work. That doesn’t mean he won’t know the stuff you’re asking, but he can’t reach.”

“Do I look blind, Lucilla?

“No, Sister.”

“I am aware of James’s, uh, disadvantage. I don’t need a welcome committee to bring it to my attention.”

“I’m sorry, Sister. I’ll go to lunch now.”

“You’d better not be late returning, Miss Salvatori,” Sister Grace called after her.

Lucy would have been surprised to see the impressed smile that covered the elderly, but not as ancient as commonly believed, nun’s face.

* * *

The students buzzed all through lunch break about what new terrors would be in store for them that afternoon. Lucy was the first homebound to reach the school yard, dragging Tino behind her, who was upset because she would not waste time pulling off the green olive caper before leaving the house. When they reached the classroom, there was a new enigma on the blackboard. A long rectangle, thirty-six inches wide by six inches high, divided into five segments, adorned the black slate.

"Every afternoon, when we return from lunch, we will pray the rosary. You should all be carrying rosaries with you every day. Today is the only day you will get away with it, if you are found deficient. A word to the wise." Sister Grace walked to the board. "Each of these boxes represents one of the mysteries of the rosary. Today is Wednesday, so we pray the Glorious Mysteries. Tomorrow will be the Joyful, Friday the Sorrowful. Here I have a box of colored chalk." She held it up for the class to see. "The person reciting the mystery of the rosary for us to respond to—we will go in order down the rows, day by day—will choose someone to draw the picture in the box."

This doesn't sound too bad, Lucy thought.

"Here are copies of what the pictures should generally look like." Sister Grace handed out mimeographed pages on which were little figures with round heads and halos and swooping lines suggesting the robes of biblical times. There was the stable for the Nativity and kneeling mourners by a cross for the Crucifixion and so on. "I expect you to follow this directive for the most part. I will allow some latitude in creativity. However, if I start to see bats flying out of the cave with the resurrected Christ, all personal flourishes will be forbidden. Understood?"

"Yes, Sister."

"Then let us begin. Paul, choose an artist and begin the Glorious Mysteries."

"Uh, Robert Ravino."

* * *

After the rosary was completed, Sister Grace produced a step stool from the back of the room. It was a foot wide and had two steps leading to the platform. There was a small handrail on the left side. She put it at the end of the front blackboard.

"Division One."

Twenty-two children once again scrambled, while the boy in desk number six held onto his seat for dear life. Jimmy glanced at Lucy with a grin. No words were exchanged as Jimmy headed for the left corner stool. Along with everyone else in the room, he began spelling vocabulary words. He barely even noticed that one of the words was *miniature.*

As the year progressed, never had this group of children encountered such wheeling and dealing as in the attempt to be chosen as one of the Rosary artists.

* * *

"Put this note in the milk box, Tino," Giuliana instructed. "I need more of everything for the get-together on Sunday."

Tino took the note and read it.

"This is so rude, Ma."

"What are you talking about?"

Tino read from the paper. "One extra gallon milk. Extra half pound of butter. Two pints heavy cream."

"So?"

"Can't you say, 'Dear Milkman. I would like'—whatever you need—then 'thank you very much'?"

"Oh, for goodness sakes. It's a business. He sells; I buy. We're not pen pals."

"I think it's rough sounding."

"Next time I'll write love and kisses," Giuliana said with a laugh as she turned the flounder she was frying for dinner.

"I don't think Maestro would like that. But you could write 'Cordially yours' or something."

"I tell you what. You write the note however you like. Just put it in the box so I get what I need."

Tino set about redoing the note. Unfortunately for Giuliana, for a ten-year-old boy he had a meticulous handwriting. When the milkman delivered the milk the next morning, he glanced at the note to see what else was requested.

Dear Mr. Milkman,

I hope you will have a good day. It can't be fun getting up so early every morning. We are having a party on Sunday. I will need an extra gallon of your milk, which is very good, an extra half pound of butter, and two pints of heavy cream. If any of the dessert is left over, I will put it in the box for you. I hope you have a very nice weekend. Cordially yours, Giuliana Salvatori

The milkman scratched his head and looked around. He glanced up at the house to see if perhaps Mrs. Salvatori was hanging out the window gauging his reaction. Come to think of it, he'd better just leave. He had seen Mr. Salvatori. The guy was a giant.

* * *

The guests were scattered throughout the entire bottom floor. The music-minded congregated in the music room performing, discussing theory, or expounding on various performances they had seen. The parlor was filled with the strategists for the war effort, while the dining room simultaneously hosted a card game and a bingo game. Those draped on the stairs tended to be younger and in a flirty mode. The doorbell rang, and only Tino, who had relinquished his spot at the drums to a stagehand from the theater, heard it.

"Hello, Tino."

"Josie! Maestro didn't say you were coming today."

"He doesn't know. Is he home?"

"Sure, hold on." He ran from the entryway without inviting Josie and her fiancé, Tony, inside.

Shortly Maestro appeared. "Josie, Tony! How good to see you. Come in, please. Join us," he added graciously.

Josie shook her head. Others at the theater had been guests at these Sunday get-togethers over the years, but she had never been asked to attend.

"Thanks, Maestro Salvatori, but I happen to have my family car this weekend, and we were just taking a drive. Josie was showing me the Kings Academy where she used to work sometimes, and we kind of wound up near here," explained Tony.

"Good, good."

"So I thought, since we were so close…and I'm never really in Brooklyn anymore…so Tony thinks… and I…"

"We were wondering if you could show us where Josie's mother lives," Tony interjected.

Maestro's eyes widened in surprise. It was over a year since his original efforts to get Josie to relent.

He had tried several more times, but he had never seen evidence of any softening on her part.

"Let me get my jacket," he said. "Please step inside while I do."

"I don't want you to leave your party," Josie pleaded.

"They will still be here when I return. Believe me. We haven't eaten yet."

Giuliana moved from the music room to the kitchen and caught sight of Maestro scurrying out the door. She ran to the front window and caught the barest glimpse of Josie as they headed down the block.

"Lucy," she called, catching sight of her daughter trying to maneuver her way up the stairs. "Did you see who was at the door?"

"Nope."

"I did," said Tino, exiting the dining room. "I just learned a magic trick."

"Was it Josie?"

"Yeah. And some guy with her."

"What did she want?"

"To talk to Maestro. Hey Ma, can I call Maestro, Pop?"

Giuliana's eyes clouded. She calculated the obstacle course on the stairs and hurried through the hallway to the basement stairs instead. As she clambered down the steps, resignation etched her grief-stricken face.

Chapter 21

The Quest of the Missing Map. Lucy's hand snatched the book off Sister Grace's classroom library shelf.

"Got it," she congratulated herself.

Sister Grace stood behind her observing her selection.

"Lucilla, you are such a good student. Those Nancy Drew books are for the pupils who make reading into a chore."

"I love Nancy Drew, Sister. I missed this one."

"Well, then, enjoy it. But here," she said, reaching out for two books. "Choose one of these too. *My Antonia* or *The Good Earth.* I know you will enjoy either one."

"All right," Lucy said choosing *The Good Earth.* She recognized it had been made into a movie, although she had not seen it.

"Good," Sister said. "You must not get lazy. You must stretch your mind, not feed it only pablum. Can you hand me my satchel?" she said, pointing to the bag hanging on the doorknob of the wardrobe. Sister had assigned Lucy to be her personal assistant, and she often helped her set up the classroom, take attendance, and run interference if someone knocked at the door.

"How is your satchel coming, Lucy?" Sister asked. Once a week she taught sewing as a useful diversion to the class. The boys hated it. Lucy was pleased enough to learn how to hem and such, but she wasn't very good at it.

"Well, I finally have the knack of the running stitch, but I don't know if my mother will want to use the bag, even if it is just for clothespins."

"She'll use it," Sister said confidently. "Can you run outside and see if James Ferraro is in the schoolyard after lunch? Ask him to come up; I want to talk to him."

"Am I through, Sister? I'll stay outside until the bell rings."

"That's fine. Put on your jacket."

Ten minutes later, Jimmy entered the room. Sister observed his sweaty face.

"James, I want to talk to you about something. I have noticed that you are an excellent writer."

"That's good. I thought I was in trouble or something."

"Not this time," Sister Grace retorted, smothering a smile. "I would like to put out a small newspaper for the school. And I would like you to be the editor. Would you be interested?"

"Really? Me, the editor? I guess. What kind of stuff in the paper? About the war?"

"No, although you may mention it on occasion. Just about things that happen to people in the school. Maybe someone has a new baby brother or sister, or someone wins an essay contest. You'll have to be a reporter. You'll mention upcoming events like the Christmas pageant. You could write a review of it after it is over. You may write one editorial per paper."

"What's that?"

"You can write your opinion about something. So let's say you didn't like a certain rule in the school, you could write why that is. It would have to be serious and well thought out and not a crybaby kind of story. I, of course, will approve everything you write before it gets printed. I may insist you change a few things. Are you interested?"

"Yeah, Sister, it sounds…"

"Yes, Sister."

"Yes, Sister, it sounds nifty. Can I complain about how we can't talk before grace in the cafeteria before lunch begins?"

"You may. If you give a sound and logical argument."

"How about you Sisters have to give a sound and logical argument why we can't?"

Sister Grace had to grin. The corners of her mouth almost touched her ears. "The reason, young man, is so that the Sisters on lunch duty can hear themselves think for a few minutes before pandemonium breaks out."

"Oh. Then I guess if nothing can come of it, I'll find another cause."

"Take your seat, Jimmy," Sister said, calling him by his preferred name for the first time. "No sense in your going back downstairs. The bell will be ringing in two minutes."

* * *

Christmas was once again a quieter holiday than in the past as the war waged on. A young man on the block had been killed, and out of respect, no one on the block displayed decorations on the outside of their homes. Gifts were fewer, the holiday meal not quite as festive. The family stood around the piano and sang carols to Giuliana's accompaniment, feeling blessed to have their family circle intact. Whenever Maestro was given extra ration coupons as a gift from a city official, a show business personage, an entertainer, or supplier, he used them to help stock Signora Titziano's pantry. Jimmy arrived at school one day to find that thick, heavy ropes were tautly suspended by metal bars on each end of the stair railings leading up to his classroom. Being able to hold onto them made his ascent and descent so much easier. A firm warning came from administration that anyone found playing games with the new railing would be suspended.

* * *

Several girls were in the classroom helping Sister Grace organize packets of information about graduation requirements for the eighth-grade parents. The school year's end was still several months away, but no one could accuse Sister Grace of not taking every step she could think of to ensure the whole procedure would run smoothly. While they sorted and collated, Sister sidled over to Lucy.

"Lucilla, I was wondering why you never joined the school choir. You have such a beautiful singing voice. I've heard it when we sing 'The Star Spangled Banner' or when we sing hymns in church."

"I don't know. I guess when people first started joining, I was too shy."

"It's a waste of your talent."

"The choir sounds good without me."

"I've tried to get her to join," interrupted Joanne, who had been eavesdropping.

"I hope you join when you go to high school. When you raise your voice to God, especially a soprano," she added, giving a Lucy a friendly nudge that almost made her fall over in surprise, "your notes reach the closest to heaven."

When the task was complete and the girls were leaving, Sister called upon Lucy once again.

"Lucilla, I have a favor to ask of you. In two weeks we have a golden jubilee celebration for one of our Sisters. It is at the Knights of Columbus hall. I was wondering if you were available to play the piano as a bit of entertainment. You don't have to stay at the party, although of course you are more than welcome to join us, as are your parents."

"Sister, I don't play piano."

Sister Grace's eyes darkened and her lips pressed firmly together. Lucy shifted uncomfortably.

"You've probably heard me play, Sister. What I mean is I don't read music. I've never taken a lesson. I play by ear."

"Really! That's astounding. God certainly has been bounteous in the gifts he's showered upon you. Well, we might have expected a bit of Beethoven or Mozart, but I'm sure we will be very happy with Berlin and Gershwin if you would indulge us."

"Sure, Sister. If I can just play requests, I'll be fine."

"You really should consider taking lessons. Don't waste these gifts."

"OK, Sister."

As Lucy turned to leave, Sister Grace called out, "Thanks, Lucy."

Chapter 22
1944

Dante entered the house with his redheaded friend, Wayne Higgins. Juniors at Lafayette High School, the boys were cocky and full of swagger while being self-conscious and insecure.

"Hey, Ma, have you seen Phil?" asked Dan, bursting into the music room and interrupting Lucy's piano lesson with her mother.

"Can't you see we're busy here?"

"Yeah, but this is important."

"I think he's drawing up plans for the summer vegetable garden in his room."

Dan and Wayne charged up the steps.

Phil was stretched out on the floor in the room he shared with Tino. He looked up when his brother unceremoniously burst into the room.

"Wayne's dad has tickets to the Golden Gloves tomorrow night. Want to come?"

"Nope. I'm going to the movies with a bunch of kids."

"Aw, c'mon."

"No thanks."

The boys headed back downstairs just as Lucy was leaving the music room.

"Did you make Beethoven grateful he was deaf?" Dan asked lamely.

"She's a better pianist then you'll ever be, especially since you've stopped practicing," Giuliana advised him.

"Maybe Lucy wants to go to the Golden Gloves," Wayne kidded.

"Yuck," she replied.

"I'll make some calls tonight. It would be a shame to waste the ticket," Wayne said.

"Why don't you ask Jimmy?" Lucy suggested.

"Jimmy? Since when do I do stuff with Jimmy?" asked Dan.

"It wouldn't kill you. He's been a bit down lately. His bicycle was stolen, and his folks can't buy a new one."

"Well, I'm OK with it if you are," Dan said to Wayne.

"That's the midget guy, right?" asked Wayne.

"Yeah."

"Well, as long as he's not afraid someone will throw him in the ring, it's OK with me."

"All right. Let's go down to his house and ask him."

* * *

Sister Grace sat with Jimmy as they pored over his newsletter galley.

"Jimmy, I think there are a few too many mentions of Lucy in this paper."

"I can't help it if she does a lot of stuff. She won the spelling bee; she made honor roll; she led the eighth grade in rolling the most bandages for the war…"

"I don't think the rest of the school needs to know that Lucy painted her room peaches and cream."

"Oh. OK." Jimmy picked up the pen and crossed that item out of the "In the News" column. "Is that it, Sister?"

"Yes, Jimmy. Be careful walking home."

Sister Grace looked fondly at the little man as he toddled out the door. She looked over his editorial one more time.

...The lights were so bright, I don't know how the fighters could see each other through their squinting eyes. When the bell rang, the coaches yelled like the results would have an effect on the World War. Romeo put his guard up, but it didn't deflect a direct blow to the head. His own gloves smashed against his face from the jab. Romeo let loose with an upper cut that sent Clooney reeling. His body crumbled like a clay pot hit by a slingshot...

In the end all I could think was that if God has given you a healthy body with long arms and legs, wouldn't it be better to use those arms to reach out and pick an apple, push a baby carriage, swing a baseball bat, or save a drowning swimmer? It seems to me in that way, you would be practically touching the sky.

Sister Grace's eyes filled with tears. She could never adopt one of her students, but Jimmy was the son of her heart.

* * *

Grace Marie Nast emigrated to America when she was ten years old. Twelve years later the family welcomed the happy and unexpected blessing of a baby boy, Niklas, to the family. Twelve years older, Grace doted on her baby brother and was responsible for most of his care. As he grew older, he loved playing pranks on his older sister. They sang together in the church choir, and he toted her guitar to gatherings where they entertained family and friends. On more than one occasion, Grace would have to pull out socks or balls of yarn that her brother had stuffed inside the instrument unbeknownst to her until she began to play. Niklas was not thrilled when at the age of thirty his redheaded sister decided to become a nun. She had been teaching in a poor neighborhood, but felt an even greater calling. Grace was so happy and sincere in her desire to serve the Lord that he never let on about his true feelings.

One morning in 1926, Nick, as he was called, awoke with a fever and upper respiratory infection. By the next day he couldn't walk and was diagnosed with polio. He resisted the iron lung, a metal coffin-like device that aided respiration. He did agree to try the "convalescent serum," which was made from the blood of monkeys and humans who had recovered from the disease. Never losing his sense of humor, he greeted his sister, Sister Grace, with loud baboon cries when she visited him in the rehabilitation clinic.

Once he returned home, Sister Grace enlisted Nick's wife in some of her own ideas about her brother's weakened limbs. He had muscle spasms and much pain. Grace had researched medical texts on muscles and suggested they wrap the affected limbs with hot moist compresses. She recommended daily massages along with exercising his limbs. The latter met with resistance by her mother as this was against the prevailing medical theories, but Nick agreed with the sense of it. In the meantime Sister Grace enlisted every nun and priest she knew to add her brother to their prayer list. In time, with braces, Nick managed to get around. He used a wheelchair when needed, as he fatigued easily and was often in pain.

Always crafty, he made his home user friendly for the disability. With the help of his father, they constructed footrests and lower tables so his arms rested comfortably instead of being elevated when he sat in his wheelchair. Because baths were so much more soothing than showers, they invented a seat that could be swung over the tub and lowered into the water to ease the strain of climbing in and out.

He spent a few summers in the early '30s in Warm Springs. He underwent two surgeries and spent weeks recovering and receiving therapy in the center's pools. He was there one time when President Roosevelt arrived at the train station. He recognized that the president was wearing braces as he maneuvered his way down the train ramp. He watched as Roosevelt drove a Ford convertible using hand controls, and made a mental note to research that option for himself. When he had the opportunity of chatting with the president one evening, he told him of his love for woodworking. After returning home, he received a set of the finest quality woodworking tools from the president. The man's vitality, enthusiasm, and nondefeatist attitude became the driving force in Nick's life.

Nick was a newspaper columnist. He learned about Sister Elizabeth Kenney of Australia and traveled to Minnesota in 1943 to interview her. Sister Kenney was not a religious; her title referred to her military rank as chief nurse. He was astounded to realize that his own beloved sister's prayers and intercessions were not the only reason his life with polio was so much richer than his original prognosis. Instead, he learned that her methods of treatment coincided with what Sister Kenney was finally being recognized for in the treatment of polio.

When Sister Grace approached him about her pupil Jimmy, he was moved by the plight and pluck of the young boy. He happily spent his evenings working on a stool for blackboard assignments and designing a workable yet affordable banister to ease his climb. There weren't enough ways under the stars for him to repay his sister for giving him the life that everyone thought ended for him when he was thirty-six years old.

* * *

The wheelbarrow bumped along on the sparkly concrete sidewalk as Phil pushed it filled with spring gardening tools to Signora Titziano's house. Down the alleyway, into the small backyard, he maneuvered his cargo. As was his custom, he set to work without herald and planned to visit with the *Signora* afterward. He was out of sight, cleaning debris beneath the high concrete porch. Voices drifted down to him, and he was about to stand and announce his presence when he recognized Josie speaking. He paused with a handful of dead leaves in his hands, trying to decipher why Josie from the opera house would be here.

"Mama, when I told you I had something to tell you, you gave me your word."

"I'ma keep it. But it is get more hard. Ev' time I see I want hold him like grandson. I want know what he's a doing. You gonna marry Tony, and your son no there. Notta right."

"I gave my word seventeen years ago. I'm not going to break it now. You should just be grateful that he came into your life unexpectedly. I'll bet Papa had something to do with that."

"All right. I keepa quiet. But can I tella Rosa?"

"No. I'd think you'd honor this to the last detail. Maestro Salvatori has been so good to you during these difficult times. Leave the boy in peace. He has a wonderful family who adores him. "

"Whatsa not to adore? He's an angel."

"Let's not be crazy. I adore him too. But he's an angel with a crooked halo. Just mischief…but no angel."

"He's a my angel."

"I'm glad. And maybe he *will* be at the wedding. Tony is going to ask him to be a groomsman. We're only having a small reception in a restaurant, but we hope he can be there. All these years of being together at the opera house…" She paused. "We're pretty close. I don't think he would find it odd."

She turned to her mother once again. "Mama, are we clear on this? Do you think it hasn't been difficult for me? Every time I see that shaggy head of hair, I want to brush it off his forehead. It used to stick up, now it hangs down. Why? I want to know what he does to it. Does he put on his shirt first or his pants? Each time he makes a suggestion at the theater that is a success, I want to shout out, 'That's my son.' When the plants on my windowsill thrive,

I want to explain that he got that through my side of the family. But I don't. And I won't. And neither will you."

"That'sa right. I listen. I'ma hap to have my girl back. I takea the boy like glass of wine. Small sips. *Basta.*"

Phil fell back on his heels. What did this mean? Josie was his mother? Signora Titziano was his grandmother? He waited until the two women were safely indoors, hid his wheelbarrow as best he could, and moved stealthily down the alleyway. Cutting across a neighbor's small front yard to avoid detection, he ran home to his bedroom to dwell on what he had overheard.

* * *

"Ma, did you pick up my suit from the cleaners? I can't find it," yelled Dante.

"It's in the hall closet. It would get crushed in your closet," answered Giuliana, wiping her hands on a dish towel as she exited the kitchen. "Wait," she called as Dante headed for the front door. "Where are you going? Did you order the corsage for Kathy? Is it Kathy or has it changed again?"

"Yes. I'm going with Kathy. No. I haven't ordered the flowers because she can't decide whether to wear a pink dress she bought or a yellow one still sitting in some store."

"If she doesn't decide until the day before, just order one with both pink and yellow flowers. Also, I want to know where you're going after the junior prom."

"Aw, Ma. No one knows yet. We're just gonna go to Coney Island, or maybe one of the guys' uncles will set aside a section for some of us in his club."

"Make plans, Mr. Romeo, and let me know. Dinner in an hour," she advised as he opened the front door, revealing Maestro. "Ah. You're home. Schedule a talk with your son about how to treat women."

"Now what?" groaned Dante as he slipped outside and shut the door behind him.

"What's going on?"

"First he was going to the prom with Angela. Then Phil tells me it changed to Mary somebody because Angela got mad at him for spending an entire afternoon with Mary working on something or other. Now, at last roll call it's Kathy. It would serve him right if at the last minute he had to take his thirteen-year-old sister."

Maestro had an amused grin on his face. "He takes after his father. The women can't resist him."

"Is that so? Then talk to him about how it feels to get your wings clipped," she retorted, heading back to the kitchen.

Rinaldo caught up to her and spun her around. He gave her a long, hard kiss. "It feels pretty good."

"Now you're on the right trolley, buster," she commented. "Come inside. I have some excellent prosciutto you can try."

Giuliana set some thinly sliced Italian bread and nearly transparent prosciutto on the table between them. She poured red wine provided by their neighbor, Mr Coltri, who made it in his basement.

"How is *Otello* going?"

"I'm having problems with Richard. He comes by correct breathing naturally. His scales, even his modulations, natural. I thought he only needed finishing touches. But now, when he sings Otello, something is missing. When I hear music sung, the air is sculpted into a triumph of sound. When Richard sings, all the sculptor's tools are there, but they don't create anything memorable. I've been working with him, but I can't find the missing key. This could be the biggest miscasting in eight years."

Phil stood in the doorway. "Ma? Maestro. Can I talk to you?"

"Sit down. Have some proscuitto," Giuliana said, rising to get another plate.

"No, thanks."

Giuliana seated herself and looked at her normally voracious son in surprise. He looked edgy and uncomfortable.

"What's so serious, Felice?" Maestro asked.

"The other day I went to Signora Titziano's to work on her garden. She didn't see me in the backyard."

Giuliana moved forward in her seat. A tingle akin to sharp electric shocks skipped along her spine.

"She was talking to someone on her porch and suddenly I realized it was Josie. From the opera house," he added, looking at his father.

Maestro now sat forward also and cleared his throat raspily.

"Anyways, I heard something. I'm pretty sure I got it right." Phil looked first at his mother and then at his father. "Am I adopted? Is Josie my mother?"

"*Caro,*" Giuliana moaned on a breath of despair.

"Yes, Felice. Josie is your natural mother. She was alone, abandoned by her family and was going to give you up for adoption. But she couldn't bear never seeing you again. I thought she might hurt herself. Your mother and I decided we wanted you to be our second child. You are not adopted. If you look at your birth certificate, you will see that we are named as your parents. That is so no one could ever take you away from us. Once you came to us, that was it. You belonged with us. Your mother nursed you and loved you with every shred of her being. No one could question that you are ours."

Tears streamed down Giuliana's face. Her voice came out of a tight, convulsing throat. "Perhaps we should have told you. I should have trusted that you understood that we love you equally to your brothers and sister. But I never wanted you to doubt. And, God forgive me, I never wanted to share you."

Phil spread his hands on the table. "So, Dan isn't my real brother? He always says I'm the one ziti in a bowl of spaghetti. I really hate that he was right." Phil leaned back in his chair and put his hands behind his head. "It also explains why he gets all the girls." He brought the chair back down with a thud.

Maestro and Giuliana looked at each other. This was not the anticipated reaction.

"So how come no one knew that the *Signora* was Josie's mother?"

Maestro explained the story as he knew it.

"Yeah. I could tell she was lonely and mad about something. Yet I liked her for some reason. Now I know. Blood. Funny, huh? How something in me felt something?" He looked at his mother's gray face. "It doesn't really matter, though. Blood or not, I mean. You love who you love."

At a loss for words, Giuliana and Maestro just sat and stared at their son. Finally Maestro added, "She named you Felice, you know. For happiness. She wanted you to know that you were born with happiness."

"That worked out. I am happy. Thanks, Maestro, Ma. Except, is that why I'm the one to share a bedroom with Tino while everyone else has their own room?" he asked with a twinkle in his eye. "You know, I can't start calling Josie Mother or anything. That would be really strange. I mean, she's not. My mother. Really."

"No, she's not, Felice. Your mother sat up with you when you were sick, read to you, cleaned your scrapes, did your homework with you, and paddled your behind."

"So this really doesn't change anything, does it?" asked Phil.

"Not a thing," replied Giuliana firmly.

"Hmmn. It really should, though."

"What do you mean?"

"Well. You would never ask someone not a member of the family to take out the garbage. I don't think that should be my chore anymore." Phil smiled his disarming grin at his parents.

"You know, you're a real smart aleck. I'd like to know where *that* came from," Maestro retorted with relief coating his every word.

"I guess we'll never know. Just like we won't know where I got all that charm people keep mentioning."

Giuliana got up and walked around the table. She took Phil in her arms. He stood about an inch taller than she. "My children are all gifts that God gave me. But you, you were the surprise package under the tree. The one I didn't ask for, but the one that fills my heart with laughter. I love you."

"I know, Ma. I love you too. You too, Maestro," he added, turning to his father. "But if you don't mind, don't go telling the others. I really don't want to have to put up with the crap they're going to give me if they find out."

* * *

"Jimmy, I want to talk to you about this editorial you wrote for the final newsletter." Sister Grace sat at her desk, the red pencil held between her fingers tapping the copy.

"What about it?"

"I have to wonder why you feel this way." She picked up the draft and read: "'Of all the archaic social customs foisted upon teenagers, the school dance is the worst. Stumbling around in awkward proximity, stepping on each other's toes, deadly minutes of deafening silence or gales of laughter descending on a comment not meant to be humorous…' Why do you think this is what the experience will be like? In the past, it seems to me the graduates were happy for this final celebration together."

"I've heard stuff like this. I think it would be better if we took a trip to the Statue of Liberty. Or went to Radio City. Anything but the dance. You have to wear a suit…"

"I know the girls love to dress up. They are already talking about their dresses."

"So maybe it's just what I think."

"Why is that?"

"Because, Sister, I'm just gonna be standing there by myself while everyone dances."

"It's also been my experience that at your age very few people actually dance together. It's more the *idea* of a graduation dance."

"Yeah, well, maybe you haven't noticed, but a few people in the eighth grade are kinda paired up already for the dance. Just my luck, everyone will be Fred Astaire and what's her name, and I'll be by myself."

"Lucy would never leave you out. She'll dance with you."

"No, she won't. And I won't dance with her. I wouldn't embarrass her that way. And she wouldn't embarrass me. We'd look stupid together. Besides,

I'm like her brother. That's what I am, her brother. The brother that got sold to another family." Jimmy's face contorted in annoyance.

"I think it will ruin the dance for Lucy if you don't attend. Nonetheless, I want you to think of a more uplifting editorial for your final piece. There is no need to put a damper on everyone else's good time because of your own misgivings."

"Sister, it's just one more problem in my life. Dances. And I have a whole lifetime of school to still deal with it."

"If there's a problem, there's a solution. If there's no solution, there's no problem."

"Well, I don't see it."

"I've never known you to be faint of heart, James Ferraro."

"You've never seen me try to dance either."

"Rewrite your editorial and have a little faith. Deal?"

"What's the deal, Sister? What am I getting out of it besides feeling left out?"

"One hundred in English for the term. And two tickets to Radio City if the dance turns out to be the worst night of your life."

Jimmy slid out of his desk and scurried up to Sister. He stuck out the pudgy hand on his shortened arm. "OK, Sister Grace. You've got a deal."

* * *

"Boys, I want you to help your sister clean up after dinner tonight. I have a meeting at the school to go to," Giuliana announced as she rose from the dinner table.

"Is it that note from Sister Grace?" asked Lucy. "What's it about?"

"Yes, it's from Sister Grace. The meeting is in your classroom. I don't know what it's about. Maybe it's about graduation. Dan, scrape those dishes. Don't be throwing that stuff down the sink. I have to change."

Rinaldo entered their bedroom moments after her.

"I have to ask you something."

"Talk while I change."

"Josie asked me if we'd allow Phil to be a groomsman in the wedding party."

Giuliana halted pulling up her stocking. "Doesn't Tony have brothers? Friends?"

"Yes. They're overseas. Remember, he's 4-F. For his eardrum, I think."

"Oh."

"His uncle is the best man, and a friend who was injured but is recuperating is the other groomsman."

Giuliana fastened her stocking. "I knew it would come to this. Trying to edge themselves into his life more and more."

"Giuliana."

She stared back at him.

"Phil is almost a man. He will do what he will do," Maestro said softly.

Giuliana put on her other stocking. "It is Phil's decision. Ask him if he wants to do it. If he says yes, tell Josie to ask him. But if he says no, you tell Josie that I said no, she can't ask him. I don't want him to have to be forced to tell her that he isn't interested. It's too much pressure. Let him decide."

Rinaldo kissed her cheek. "You are very wise." He left the room and returned downstairs.

Giuliana hurried into the bathroom and closed the door. She tried to be quiet as she retched desperately into the toilet bowl.

Chapter 23

A "Congratulations Class of '44" banner hung over a haystack. Various cutouts of farm animals were scattered beneath the stage as were wheelbarrows filled with flowers or fruits and vegetables. "Decorations courtesy of 7th grade, Class of '45" was written on an easel sitting near the auditorium door.

Lucy entered the room with Joanne. Her hair had been shortened into a fashionable page boy, and she couldn't refrain from touching the bouncy cut of it. Her white cotton slightly flared dress had short puffy sleeves and an emerald-green sash. She self-consciously maneuvered to a group of friends in her open-toed shoes with the tiniest of high heels. Just as the girls began questioning the theme the seventh graders had chosen for them, Sister Grace called for attention from the stage.

"Ladies and gentleman. Welcome and congratulations on successfully completing eight years of study at St. Mary's. We have a special treat for you tonight, courtesy of many of your parents. I'd like to introduce you to Hank Monroe." A man in his thirties crossed the stage in overalls and a straw hat. "Hank is a square dance caller, and he is going to teach you all how to square dance. He also has music for other group novelty dances. He'll play records of the popular music that you're all fond of too. This dance is for all of you, and your parents didn't want you standing around staring at each other after buying all these new clothes for the occasion."

Nervous laughter filled the auditorium.

"So, let's get started. Have fun. Congratulations, once again. Believe it or not, I will miss those of you who were my pupils. Sister Helen will have a few words to say later on to her class."

Once the party got going, the graduates had an uproarious time. They circled to the right and circled to the left. Pairing of couples lasted only for moments as Hank quickly instructed the dancers to promenade. Halfway through the evening, Sister

Grace spotted someone at the entrance. She hurried over and plastered a big kiss on his cheek.

"Nick! I'm so glad you could stop by. The children are having a wonderful time. They only stop to drink some punch or catch their breath. Look, look, there's Jimmy."

"He looks like he's having fun."

"He is. I can tell. Thanks so much for finding a square dance caller."

"Not as difficult as you might have thought, given we live in New York."

"The parents couldn't have been more generous donating money to pay for him. Honestly, I don't think one of them spilled the beans to their children."

As the dance ended, she raised her arm and waved Jimmy over.

"Jimmy, I'd like you to meet my brother, Nick."

"Nice to meet you, Jimmy," Nick said, bending a bit stiffly at the waist.

"Jimmy, Nick made your stool for the classroom. He also designed the rope banisters."

"I wondered where that stuff came from," Jimmy responded.

"When my sister saw you on her roster for last September, she called me up right away. You know her…she wasn't letting anyone get away with her infamous blackboard divisions."

"Yeah, I wouldn't have minded missing that so much. Although, Sister, I never got an eraser thrown at the back of my head like just about everyone else."

"I suppose you always had the correct answer, or I couldn't read your chicken scrawl writing." She turned to her brother. "Jimmy will be attending Boody Junior High School in September."

"Good luck, Jimmy. Grace, er, Sister Grace has told me what a firecracker you are. Don't let the bullies get you down." He raised a pants leg slightly, revealing metal braces. "I got polio almost twenty years ago. I was lucky enough to learn from the best that you don't let anything stop you from doing what you have your heart set on. I wanted to tell you that."

"Thanks."

"Sister Grace also told me that you're a newspaper writer."

"Well, I wrote the school newsletter. I may do that when I grow up."

"If you decide that's the direction you want to head in, you contact me at the *Daily News.* I'll get you summer work. It won't be anything glamorous, but you'll get to see what it's all about."

"Wow! That would be nifty."

The three turned when a roar went up from the dance floor. Joey Califano was spinning on his backside in the middle of the circle, his arms and legs raised in the air.

"Always the class clown," Sister Grace huffed as she hurried over to intervene.

"He's always been off his nuts," explained Jimmy to Nick.

"Before I leave, would you like to see my car?"

"It's something fancy?"

"Oh, I think you'll be interested." He put his hand on Jimmy's shoulder and paused. "Here comes my sister. Just let me say good-bye." He turned to Sister Grace. "I'm bringing young Jimmy outdoors to see my car, then I'll be going."

"Thanks so much for coming. Give my love to Irene."

The siblings hugged as Lucy made google eyes at Jimmy as she returned from the restroom.

"Luce, you want to see Nick's car?"

"Sure. I can use some air. Is it OK, Sister?" she asked.

"Certainly. Just don't go driving off with him," Sister replied with a smile.

Jimmy was amazed to see the hand-controlled vehicle. He hoisted himself into the driver seat for the full effect. "I'd have to sit higher to see better over the steering wheel, but other than that, I could drive this car."

"Of course you can. So the sooner you start saving money to buy your own automobile, the sooner you'll be on the road when you turn eighteen."

"Maybe I'll start working at the *Daily News* right away."

"I'm afraid it's too late for this summer. Next year contact me around March, and I'll set you up. Here's my number," he added, handing Jimmy a card. "Should I walk you two back to the school?"

"Nah. It's just half a block. We're fine."

"Good meeting you, Jimmy. At last."

"You too. Although I didn't know about you till tonight. Sister never mentioned she actually came from a family."

Nick hid his smile as he slipped into his car and waved good-bye.

"Let's sit on the church steps for a few minutes," Lucy suggested as they passed in front of the building. "The school steps are getting crowded. The dance is really fun, huh?" Lucy stretched her legs in front of her as she tried to wiggle her big toes sticking out of the shoe tips.

Jimmy sat with his elbows on his thighs. "Sure is. I guess there's no tickets to Radio City for me."

"I was so scared of Sister Grace last September. Now she's my favorite teacher ever. I hope the nuns at St. Aloysius are not horrible."

"At least you're starting with a whole bunch of new people. Most of the kids in the ninth grade at Boody have been there since seventh grade. Except for the Catholic school transfers. I'm going to miss you being in my class."

"I'll miss you in school too. I'm going to miss having boys in the class, period. I can't imagine. All girls. Supposed they're all like Lorraine Tuccio?"

"There's people from here going to St. Aloysius."

"I know," Lucy said, but her tone betrayed her dismay.

"Hey, if you need me, I'll ride the bus with you. We'll stand backward the whole way so you can pretend we're going home."

Lucy laughed. "Didn't work then; won't work now. Anyway, it's a different kind of nervous. It's not knowing what to expect or what's expected of me. Taking a bus, making new friends, the whole 'they're not going to put up with that in high school' thing." They sat in companionable silence for a while. "Look," Lucy whispered. "There's Peggy and Steven by that tree. Sister will kill them if she catches them." She moved slightly and faced Jimmy. "Have you ever kissed anyone?"

"Besides my mother and cousins?"

Lucy pushed him playfully. "You know what I mean."

"Lucy, who am I going to kiss?"

"I'm thinking I'm never going to find out about kissing until I'm an old lady, since I'm going to an all-girls school and all."

"There's dances and stuff."

"Maybe. But I don't think the fun part of high school will be the same as public school. Aren't you curious? About kissing, I mean."

"I guess."

"Do you want to kind of try it? Just to see what it feels like?"

"You and me?" Jimmy asked incredulously.

"Uh-huh. Just so we know what to expect for the future if it ever happens."

"I guess we can." What had Sister Grace said about his never being faint of heart? If that fluttering inside his chest meant anything, his heart was having a major attack of some kind.

Lucy moved right next to him. "Let's close our eyes like in the movies and turn our heads to the side."

"This sounds like a science experiment," Jimmy noted, trying to sound nonchalant.

"Well, it is, kind of. We want to do it right. OK, here goes."

Lips upon lips, soft, slightly pursed, an exhalation of held breath.

Jimmy was not only faint of heart; his whole body turned to Jell-O and was sliding off the steps.

"That's kind of nice, Jimmy."

"Uh-huh," he agreed. How could he have traveled as far as the stars when he hadn't budged an inch on the step beneath him?

"At least now we'll both know what to expect," Lucy said with a checkmark to her mental to-do file. She leaned back and stared at the stars, totally unaware that her Jimmy antenna was completely turned off.

* * *

Joy and sorrow jockeyed for position all through the rest of the summer of '44. Dante worked at WABC Radio for forty-three cents an hour. He rode into the city every day on the subway with his father, a cap on his head, having decided he did not yet have the flair to carry off a Panama hat. His fondest wish was to talk on air. Lucy began taking vocal lessons with her father. He was flabbergasted at her voice, which rang out with a power and richness that highlighted brilliant upper registers.

Dante Ardito, MD, seventy-six, passed away quite unexpectedly from a heart attack. Anna found him sitting with a cup of espresso, his head bent over a medical journal, a lit cigar still in his hand. The older boys coped well and were dutiful and helpful at the funeral parlor. Lucy and Tino were shaken at the loss. Their grandfather was the masculine source of cuddles and tickles in their lives. He took them bowling and held the seat of their bicycles when they learned to ride. He modeled clay with them.

In fact, they had sculpted an entire Nativity set out of special clay that they baked and painted. Each of the children had made their own sheep under their grandfather's tutelage. When they thought the set was complete, their grandfather had sculpted one more piece. It was a replica of the dog he owned as a boy in Florence, a black and white collie mix with a fluffy tail and droopy ears. The dog, Galileo, sat at the foot of the manger every year.

This coming Christmas everyone would wonder what became of Galileo. Only Lucy knew that she had searched her grandmother's basement until she found the stored Nativity set. She placed the clay replica of Galileo under the pillow on which her grandfather's head rested. She had cried when she felt his cold, stiff face. As difficult as the loss was for the youngsters, they would have been surprised to learn that Maestro, awash in a grief so acute, required comforting each evening behind closed doors.

Josie asked Maestro to give her away. One day at the theater, Phil gave a hilarious performance on how his father should walk Josie down the aisle. Two days later he escorted Giuliana to her seat in the church with dignity and took the photographer aside to request a photo taken of the two of them. He planned to give it to her at Christmas.

Tino went to the summer camp his brothers had attended a few years earlier, but called up asking to return home after three days. He refused to elaborate, but insisted that he hated it.

Jimmy and Lucy managed to capture the last blush of childhood playing board games, a beach jaunt with the Ferraro family, and a movie outing to a double feature of *Going My Way* with Bing Crosby and *Girl Crazy* with Mickey Rooney and Judy Garland. Jimmy shared the angst of the height-challenged hero's plight and related to the poignancy of Judy's song, "But Not For Me." Uncomfortable, he made a big deal about it being a sissy movie, much to Lucy's annoyance.

Lucy's forest green uniform arrived, pleated skirt, blazer, and appalling inverted soup bowl-shaped hat. She and her mother shopped downtown for the mandatory white gloves to complete the uniform and new underwear, which included a full-length slip and her first brassiere. She astounded most everyone who knew her when she sang the small role of an unnamed young girl in her father's production of *L'Amore Dei Tre Re* when the role's soprano had to return home to Ohio due to a death in her family. There was not a hint of a tremor or misgiving in her demeanor either before or after the show.

Chapter 24

White gloved hands folded primly in her lap, Lucy surveyed the bus route she would be taking for the next four years. St. Aloysius Academy, a well-respected all-girls Catholic High School, sent an unusually high percentage of young ladies on to college. They also offered a commercial program of education, but that wouldn't be available until junior year. Giuliana had given Lucy a pep talk at breakfast, encouraging her to take advantage of any challenges the curriculum offered.

"Dan is planning to go on to college next year, and there is no reason why you can't also. You might be a doctor like my father. Wouldn't that be wonderful?"

"I'm not going to be a doctor, Ma. I don't like science."

"Don't decide before you take high school science classes."

Tino entered the kitchen, meticulous in his St. Mary uniform of navy slacks and tie. "The belt you gave me to strap around books is worn out."

"It will hold fine."

"It's cracked and ugly. I don't like it."

"I can't look for something else now, Tino. We'll search tonight, OK?" Giuliana said with exasperation.

Tino pulled out a chair and plopped into it.

Lucy patted his hand. "It's not important, Tino. Forget about it."

Lucy watched as two seniors boarded the bus. They were recognizable by their off-white blazers. Neither had on their hat and gloves. They looked so knowledgeable and important, as if the world's wisdom had been imparted to them in the last three years. The sole purpose of this final year at the Academy was to lord it over the peasants. Lucy walked solemnly behind the seniors when they disembarked and noted that the soon-to-be despised gloves and hats were only put on within yards of the school grounds.

The freshmen "women" were given a lecture on Academy rules in their homeroom class. No talking in the halls between classes. No talking in the cafeteria until after grace. Choose three girls to sit with at lunch; the tables in the cafeteria sat four. You sit in rows according to grade level and are served accordingly if you are buying lunch. Here are your coupons. Ten in all. Any infraction results in the loss of a coupon to be followed by detention and credit lost on your conduct grade. No going to the locker room during the day. You either carry your books or hustle back to your homeroom to exchange books for what was in your desk.

Lucy was given her daily schedule: English, Algebra, World History, Biology, Latin, Religion, Music.

"In a week you will be voting for a homeroom president. Get to know each other," the Sister of St. Joseph nun standing in front of the room advised. The familiar habit was not comforting. The woman had not cracked a smile. The girl in the desk next to Lucy raised her hand. She was all wild dark hair and bushy eyebrows.

"What are we going to do with Latin, Sister? Are they going to have women priests?"

"Are you trying to be clever, young lady? Because if you are, you haven't succeeded. Your name?"

"Louisa Livalli."

"Well, Miss Livalli, Latin is the root of most languages. It will be invaluable to you in the future. I suggest you keep your opinions to yourself. Sister

Rita Thomas is inordinately fond of her dead language, and if she hears you belittling it, your life will be irrevocably altered for the worse. *Praemonitus, praemunitus.* Forewarned, forearmed."

The bell rang and the girls scurried to their first-period class. Sister Bartholomew stood in the midst of the frantic freshman, her four foot nine lost in the sea of green. A fussy whirlwind, she appeared to be almost one hundred years old. Her face was a raisin in a dish of rice pudding, and she ended each directive with the threat, "…or I'll take your right shoe." Before long the freshmen would join the affectionate chorus describing the aging nun as "Sister Bartholopew, she took my right shoe."

Within a week Lucy and Louisa had bonded. When homeroom elections were held, Louisa nominated Lucy for president. When she won, Lucy was both flattered and apprehensive. Sister Agnes, the homeroom teacher, took the wind right out of her sails.

"I'm always curious as to the criteria used in electing someone for office who is virtually a stranger. I've seen the office go to the funniest, the girl with the best hair, the girl with some cutesy name her parents bestowed on her. This year I see you've chosen the girl who most looks like a movie star. That certainly gives me insight into where this class is headed."

Lucy felt her face turn red. As several girls turned to stare at her, she looked down at her desk.

"Don't listen to her," scolded Louisa. "She's jealous because she looks like an ancient mummy."

Lucy raised her head and stared straight back at the offensive nun. *Oh no, you don't,* she thought. *That evil eye stuff doesn't work on me. You can't intimidate me. I'm Lucilla Salvatori, and from here on in I'm going to shine.*

* * *

In anticipation of attending a "tea" where they would be considered for possible membership in the Academy Angels, Lucy and Louisa listened to the *Hit Parade* on the radio as they experimented with hairstyles featured in the new *Seventeen* magazine. The Academy Angels was not a school-sponsored club. Their proposed mission was to help the war effort, raise money for the missions along with other charities, and foster school spirit. In fact, it was mostly a social club of forty-eight girls, only twelve new recruits accepted each year. They arranged parties with the boys from St. Michael's and other all-boy high schools, organized jaunts into the city, and attended sporting events at public high schools in the security of a circle of several other Angels.

"None of these hairstyles will make any difference unless I get rid of these eyebrows," moaned Louisa.

"Have you ever tweezed your brows?" asked Lucy.

"No, but I'm going to. Do you have a tweezer?"

"What? Now?"

"Why not?"

"Maybe my mother has one. Let me go look."

A few minutes later, Lucy returned brandishing the grooming implement.

"You first," suggested Louisa. "You have practically nothing to do."

"I'm not sure about this," Lucy said, leaning toward her dresser mirror. "Ow! Ouch! This is stupid."

"Let me see." Louisa peered at Lucy's face. "It looks good. Look at yourself. It's already more like a magazine model."

Lucy plucked a few more stray hairs. "That's it for me. You go."

Louisa took the tweezers and grabbed the magazine. "Are there any pictures of Ingrid Bergman in here? I have a feeling she may have had eyebrows like mine before Hollywood got ahold of her."

"No, she's not in here."

"That's the look I'm going to go for," Louisa announced as she got to work. A few minutes later, she turned to Lucy. "How am I doing?"

Lucy analyzed her friend's face. She looked a bit like a clown with a migraine. "You'd better stop. They're not even, Lou. The right side is thinner than the left, and this part over your nose is wider than this one," she said, pointing to the uneven brows.

Louisa stepped back from the mirror. "Oh God, that's awful. I'm ruined. They'll never accept me into the Angels. What should I do?" She sat on the bed. "Can your mother help me?"

"She's not going to be happy I took her tweezers without asking."

"What's worse? You getting yelled at or me not getting into the Angels with you?"

"What makes you so sure they'll take me?"

"They'll take you. You have two adorable older brothers and a big house for parties. You're a shoo-in."

Giuliana surveyed the damage. "I'm afraid you're going to look a bit more like Hedy LaMarr than Ingrid Bergman until the brows grow out again," said Giuliana as she evened up the over pluck.

"That's not a bad thing," said Louisa. "But my mother is going to kill me."

"Tino, get out of here. What are you doing spying?" asked Lucy as her brother leaned in the doorway.

"You could try wearing bangs to help cover your eyebrows until they grow back," Tino said before he turned and went back to his room.

Lucy and Louisa looked at each other.

"Mrs. Salvatori, how are you at cutting bangs?" asked Louisa.

* * *

A bright bouquet of rust-colored mums, dried blue hydrangeas, and dried yellow lady's mantle sat cheerily on the kitchen table when Giuliana arrived to put up the morning coffee. She had been thinking about the coconut she needed to buy to bake Phil's requested birthday cake. In front of the flowers rested an index card.

For Mom,

Thank you for being my mother. I'm the luckiest guy in the world.

I love you. Your son, Phil

P.S. Happy Birthday to me!

With unzipped emotion Giuliana slipped into a chair with weakened limbs. This child of her soul, easygoing jokester Phil, possessed a heart with a perception that pierced through all camouflage. She reached out and touched the autumnal bouquet. Her eyes filled with the beauty of the tender gesture that was her reprieve from anxiety and an illumination for the future.

Chapter 25
1945

Giuliana placed her free gift dish on the floor and took Rinaldo's arm as they sat in the darkening theater. The newsreel came on outlining the latest developments in the war. The mood was brightened with a clip about the 1945 Oscar ceremony. Giuliana popped a peppermint into her mouth and offered one to Rinaldo, who shook his head. They were ostensibly there to see *A Tree Grows in Brooklyn.* They both knew they were waiting to set eyes on Leonie Dufrey in *Dance of Desire.*

A dance hall owner in the West played by the suave Glenn Deshane is a shameless philanderer. His longsuffering, devoted wife portrayed by the ever-adorable July Winters puts up with his dalliances as she lives a comfortable yet lonely life on the outskirts of town. Leonie Dufrey was just one of several women who catch his eye. Her character, Rose Raynor, is introduced as a mousy store clerk who soon reveals ambitions to be a star in dance hall shows. A woman with a cold, calculating heart, she cajoles her way into the hall owner's bed, life, and stage. The wife's endurance finally implodes, and she shoots the amoral seductress through the heart. *Leave it to Leonie to be the one to drive America's darling, July Winters, over the edge,* thought Giuliana. *July probably requested that final scene written in just to have a go at her.* She glanced over at Rinaldo several times during the movie. He sat stiff and still, no giveaway expressions crossing his features in the light bouncing off the screen. *Rather like the Indian the children call you on the street. Why is that?* She picked up his hand and rested their entwined palms on his thigh. Rinaldo turned to her and smiled. Then he gave her the most comical, pop-eyed expression she had ever seen in the twenty-three years she had known him.

As they exited the theater, Giuliana asked, "So what do you think?"

"The little girl was superb. She steals the movie. Great role for Dunn. He's perfect—"

"You know very well which movie I mean," interjected Giuliana.

"Oh. You mean that bit of baloney? Leonie was at her best in the song and dance numbers. Otherwise, she is too big for the screen. Too exaggerated. Did you notice her eyes when she was acting? She looked like a demented Rita Hayworth in *Blood and Sand.* She should have stuck with opera. She's going nowhere in the movies. What did you think?"

"She put on weight."

* * *

The Salvatori house was hosting an end-of-school-year dance for the Academy Angels and boys from St. Peter's Prep. The kids spilled into the backyard, and Phil was on frantic security detail guarding his flowers and vegetable seedlings. Dan joined him for a few minutes to escape the blaring music in the house.

"I'm telling Maestro we can't put up with this for three more years. Or else she just has winter parties here."

"Don't be such a party pooper," Dan kidded.

Lorraine Tuccio and Meg Reilly huddled in the doorway, having followed Dan.

"Go talk to him. Maybe he remembers you from grammar school."

"I can't. He graduated high school, and he's dreamy."

"Ask what he's doing now that he's out of school."

"I know what he wants to do. I've asked around."

"He doesn't know you know. Just…"

Dan approached the door.

"Hi, girls. Excuse me," he said, trying to pass.

"Hi, Dan. Remember me…from St. Mary's?"

"Uh…"

"Lorraine Tuccio."

The infamous Lorraine Tuccio. Lucy's nemesis.

"Oh, sure. You go to Aloysius too, huh?"

"I heard you graduated Lafayette. What are you going to do?"

"I'm going to Fordham to study communications and business. I'm going into radio. That is if Uncle Sam doesn't send me to the Pacific now that the Germans have surrendered. I'll go when I get back, if that happens."

"You'd be perfect talking on the air. You have such a…a…radio voice."

"I hope so. Excuse me," Dan concluded, pushing past them.

"My brother is in the Pacific," Meg said.

"I hope he'll be OK," Dan responded.

"My aunt's husband was killed. You know, Miss Tuccio from St. Mary's."

"That's awful. I'm so sorry. I kind of remember her getting married when Lucy was in her class."

Lorraine nodded.

"Well, I'll see you around. Why don't you try and pick one of Phil's flowers?" Dan said with a grin as he stepped through the door.

"I'm going to die," Lorraine said.

"You're going to have to figure out ways to bump into him if you want this to go anywhere."

"I don't know how. He's so much older. My mother won't allow it. I'm not allowed to date as it is."

"Grease the slide for the future, like my father says," Meg counseled.

A roar went up inside the house and the two girls hurried in. Lucy was dancing the jitterbug with Dan, much to the rest of the party's delight. Having older brothers kept Lucy on the cutting edge of the dance crazes.

"That was incredible, Lucy," Louisa cried in delight. "Dan, you have to teach me some steps."

Having visited at Lucy's house all year long, Louisa was presumably comfortable enough to address Dan like an ordinary boy. No one would have guessed that her heart had derailed and was thumping over rocks and gulleys to avoid stopping all together. Meg nudged Lorraine.

"I'm next," she called out weakly as Dan and Louisa sidestepped and shuffled their way around the parlor and into the entryway.

* * *

The radio played almost nonstop in the week following the bombings in Japan. Early Tuesday evening, August 14, President Truman's voice could be heard on both the kitchen and parlor radios. The family gathered as the president announced that Japan had surrendered. They each sat stunned for a moment and then ran to embrace one another. Tumultuous cries of joy soon filled the street as neighbors rushed outdoors to celebrate their relief and joy. Firecrackers went off almost immediately, and soon the block was covered in crepe and toilet paper. Children blew on whistles and noisemakers of every kind. Tino hauled his drum set outside with Phil's help and began an impromptu session. Soon housewives emerged with cups of coffee, cookies, and fruit as the neighborhood shared in the momentous news. Maestro reentered the house looking for Giuliana. The sound of sobs led him to their bedroom. Giuliana lay across the bed, heartrending sobs racking her frame.

"Love, why are you crying? It's a time for cheers."

"Rinaldo," she choked, "Rinaldo. Our boys are safe. Our boys will not have to go to war this time. Pray with me. Pray that there is never another war like this one."

* * *

The sound of voices in the yard below woke Lucy. She looked out her bedroom window and saw Phil and a young man gathering figs from the bursting tree. With a quick brush to her pageboy, she raced down the steps and through the kitchen.

"Where do you think you're going like that?" Giuliana inquired, looking up from her cup of coffee.

"Outside. To get some figs. I want figs for breakfast. I didn't get any the other day except for what I picked off the ground."

"You're not going outside like that. Put on your robe."

"My robe is too heavy. It's for winter."

"You may borrow mine on the bathroom door." She looked at her daughter's budding figure, more ripe and enticing than the fig tree in full bloom. Young breasts pressed against the thin cotton of the floral nightgown. "I'll buy you a light robe for summer."

Lucy came down the stairs just ahead of her father.

"Giuliana," he said softly, "I spoke with…"

Lucy turned around. "It's me, Maestro. Ma said I could borrow her robe."

Maestro grasped the handrail more tightly. Yes, of course. She was still shorter, narrower in the hips and shoulders. But still, for a moment, he had been fooled. "You are getting so tall," he said lamely, pride and sorrow aiming darts at his heart.

Lucy skipped outside full of tomorrows and a desire for figs. She bent over an almost-full pail. "I'm taking some of these for breakfast, Phil. Hi," she said to the young man standing on a ladder.

"How many are you gonna eat, fatso?" Phil kidded, noting at least a dozen cradled in her hands and arms.

"This may not be enough," she retorted, staring at the handsome young man as he climbed down with his pail.

"This is Valentino," Phil said. "You know him from the opera house. He worked there before the war."

"Oh, sure. I saw you backstage."

"We met a long time ago," Val reminded her. "You were just a little thing then."

"Now she's a big thing with a little brain," Phil joked.

"Keep quiet, Phil," Lucy said. "I'm surprised the big bad giant is letting you near his golden figs," she said to Valentino.

"Actually, your father invited me to pick some. I just got out of the hospital a couple of weeks ago."

"Val was injured by mortar fire in Germany while repairing telephone lines."

"I'm so sorry. Are you all right now?"

"Yeah. My left side was gashed open pretty bad. They did what they could overseas and then sent me back home. Turns out to be a lucky break. The war ended, and I don't have to go back. I'm still on active duty, but I'm stationed at Fort Dix. I'll have my old job back at the opera house, and your father agreed to let me go to Fordham at night to major in business. On the GI bill."

"What's Maestro got to do with it?"

"I'll miss a lot of evenings at the theater while taking classes. But today I'm picking figs. He said there are more than you can all eat and more than Mrs. Salvatori wants to make preserves with. We love figs, so I took him up on it."

"If I had known fig face here was going to grab so many, I would have given you smaller pails," Phil remarked.

Lucy stuck her tongue out and retreated to the house, her hips swaying under the thin blue robe. "Hey, Valentino!" she called before going inside. "Welcome home, soldier." She tossed him one of her figs.

"How old is your sister?" Val asked Phil.

"Uh, she'll be fifteen in September."

"No kidding. She's gonna be a heartbreaker."

Phil looked at Val in surprise. He turned back to watch the door slam shut behind Lucy. "Maybe you're right. Forget what I said about the small brain. She's almost like a genius or something."

Valentino kept staring after her. *I'll be twenty-two in September, seven years difference. It's a long wait, but I have a feeling she's worth waiting for.*

* * *

The new school year was uneventful. Lucy didn't lose any coupons; Louisa lost two, one of which was for penciled eyebrows. She was still struggling for a look that suited her, and having a best friend who was perfect didn't make facing the mirror any easier. Both girls went on a movie outing with Dante and his friends. This was big news among the Academy Angels as college men were the epitome of social success.

Lucy asked Phil to keep an eye on Jimmy now that they were both in the same school again. As a popular senior, Phil could throw around his weight, but he didn't need to. If anything, Jimmy became a school mascot with his winning personality and upbeat attitude. As he and Lucy walked along Eighty-Sixth Street and strangers called out, "Hi ya, Jimmy," Lucy groaned in frustration.

"Don't you ever want to say, 'Who the hell are you?' to these people?" she asked.

"What does it matter? They're being friendly."

"They're treating you like the town sideshow. Everyone knows Jimmy. But they don't know a thing about you."

"If you want to get riled up about it, go ahead. I'd rather be recognized than scorned. I'm not going to let being a dwarf cripple me. If that means saying hi back to strangers so they think they know me and don't razz me, then that's the way it is."

"Don't get so defensive…"

"Jimmy," called a man standing in a Buster Brown Shoe Store doorway. "The shoes are in."

"Uh, OK. I'll tell my mom. Thanks, Sam," he said as he scurried past the store.

"What shoes?" asked Lucy.

"For my cousin. My mother ordered them." He couldn't see the irony in the anguish he'd feel if Lucy found out that he had to wear child-sized shoes.

* * *

Another school year drew to a close. Her finger poised over the telephone dial, Giuliana finally stuck her index finger in the circle bearing the letter *M.* She listened to the ring and swallowed hard.

"Hello?"

"Josie? It's Giuliana Salvatori."

"Oh!" The surprise was apparent. "How are you?"

"Fine. I —"

"Excuse me, Anthony, get down from there. He's a year old now and into everything," she explained.

"Yes. I've heard he's a beautiful boy." Giuliana cleared her throat. "I am calling because, well, as it happens, we have two extra tickets to Phil's graduation ceremony. Dante is working that day, and my mother doesn't feel up to attending. I thought perhaps you and Tony, or you and your mother, would like to come."

The phone was silent for several heartbeats. "I would be honored to be there. Thank you, Giuliana."

After exchanging details, the women hung up the phone. Giuliana exhaled a breath that felt stale and rancid. Stepping out the back door, she took a deep breath of sweet-smelling air. She did not feel brave; it took little enough courage to act when there was nothing left to fear. Nonetheless, the midmorning sun felt warm on her face and seemed intent upon delivering an Allelulia kind of day.

Chapter 26
1946

The clothespin bag from Sister Grace's old sewing class was filled with small gold sequined bows. Gold was Lucy's campaign color for vice president of St. Aloysius Academy, the office open to junior girls. The material for the bows was courtesy of the costume department at the opera house and would certainly outshine the opposing candidate's prissy lavender ribbon. The campaign committee of six girls headed by Lucy's manager, Louisa, had worked long hours twisting the difficult ribbon into bows. The next morning they were set to audition their campaign song for Sister Agnes. On Friday an assembly would be held, where the eight candidates for four offices would present their platform, the committee would sing the song, and the two-week campaign before voting would be off and running.

After classes Lucy and her committee sat outside Sister Agnes's office and listened to the committee of a sophomore candidate for treasurer belt out a rousing revised version of "We're in the Money." When they trooped out of the office, Lucy's girls rose in unison and entered the room to face the formidable Sister Agnes.

"Row H gets hungry awaiting lunch call…"

The girls punched out the lyrics they had composed enumerating the changes Lucy hoped to implement as vice president. Lucy grinned at their polish and harmony.

Sister Agnes folded her hands tightly on the desk in front of her.

"What song are those lyrics set to, may I ask?"

"'The Lady Is a Tramp,'" Lucy replied.

"Isn't that the most notorious banner a proper young *lady* could run her campaign under?" Sister remarked icily.

"The music lent itself to what we wanted to say."

"And the song suggests you'll stop at nothing. Despicable! If you intend to run for office in this school, Miss Salvatori, you will change your campaign song by Friday. If I don't approve of it before the assembly, Miss Simoni will win by default."

"Sister, there's just not enough time to come up with something new!" Louisa cried desperately.

"Do you choose to withdraw right now?" Sister asked, addressing Lucy.

"No, Sister. We'll be ready." Lucy turned from the nun and scrunched her face at the girls, sticking out her tongue in anger. "C'mon, girls. We have work to do."

* * *

"Can you believe it? She approves something that Snow White sings, 'I'm wishing, I'm hoping, that you will vote for me,'" Lucy snorted, singing the line, "and nixes a song that actually says something."

"I'm surprised she recognized the melody."

"The old witch probably sneaks out to movies that the Church condemns hoping to catch some student she can blindside," Lucy said indignantly.

"Well, moaning about it isn't getting us anywhere. Let's get to work," Louisa said with a sigh

On Friday morning the girls assembled before Sister Agnes to present the lyrics they had composed to "If I Only Had a Brain."

"The spirit at old Aly's
Is always up and at ease
Because we are the best..."

"We did it!" Elise, one of the committee members, crowed after Sister gave her stamp of approval.

"Of course we did," Lucy retorted in exasperation. "It's a mindless piece of nonsense that says nothing. And she's too stupid to recognize I'm laughing in her face."

The final day of campaigning had arrived, and Lucy and Louisa huddled at their sixth-period lunch table in row C.

"Hey, Lucy," called Elise, standing up in row D. "Did I forget my purse at your table?"

Lucy bent over and looked under the table. "Here it is. Catch!" she yelled, tossing the purse across one aisle and down six tables.

As luck would have it, Sister Agnes was standing in the doorway to the cafeteria commiserating with Sister Bartholomew about how, despite their best efforts, the cafeteria was always a mess by the end of the third lunch period. Out of the corner of her eye, she saw the flying missile and zeroed in on its source. Stomping down the outer aisle, she positioned herself across from Lucy's table.

"Miss Salvatori! With me," she said, pointing down in front of herself. "Now."

Lucy rose from her seat and followed the nun into the corridor.

"Was that a purse I saw sailing across the cafeteria? A purse that you pitched disregarding the possible calamitous effects it might have engendered?"

Calamity engendered? What is this? A vocabulary contest?

"I'm sorry, Sister. It was injudicious of me to be so inattentive to the possible consequences."

Sister folded her arms. "You're not as clever as you think you are, Lucilla. Furthermore, you are not made of the fabric we'd like to see in our student body officers. I am hereby terminating your candidacy for vice president. In addition, don't bother trying to run next year when you're a senior. You are not president material. I'll take one coupon, thank you. Go back to your seat."

Lucy stood for several moments with her mouth wide open. She felt the long-absent flush of shame sweep through her body and the sharp taste of humiliation in her mouth. She turned, and walking as erectly as possible, returned to her seat.

"That witch!" Louisa whispered hoarsely. "She's always had it in for you. Since freshman year."

"Can she do that? Can she fire you?" asked Ginny, another member of the team.

“She just did,” Lucy said, fighting to keep the tears from spilling from her filled eyes.

“So Katie becomes VP just like that. No glory in that victory,” Louisa comforted.

“No shame either,” said Lucy, gathering her belongings and rushing to the girls’ room.

* * *

“Come in, Mrs. Salvatori,” said Sister Agnes when Giuliana knocked hesitantly on her office door. “I’m afraid I don’t have much time. I have a world history class to teach in fifteen minutes.”

“I don’t require much of your time, Sister,” explained Giuliana. “I’m here to ask you to reconsider your position on Lucy’s candidacy before tomorrow’s election.”

“There is nothing to reconsider. I’m sorry to have to be the one to tell you this, but your daughter is not the sort of girl we want representing our school. Our officers attend various functions in other parochial high schools in the diocese, and Lucy’s behavior, and I might add, her demeanor, leave much to be desired. She is unruly and unpredictable.”

Giuliana felt a slow burn as she responded. “Sister, I believe you are mistaking youthful enthusiasm for untoward behavior. Lucy is honest, loyal, compassionate, and generous. She—"

"She flaunts her intelligence, always trying to outdo every other girl in the school. She flaunts her talents, insinuating she knows more than the music teacher."

"Sister Agnes. We are a musical family. Lucy cannot sit by and let misinformation be taught—"

"She is a showoff. Did she have simple bows in her campaign color like every other candidate? No, she distributed some burlesquey concoction for the girls who supported her to pin on themselves. And then of course, her original choice for campaign song suggests her overall attitude on how to get what she wants. Lucilla will not be reinstated in the election, and, as I'm sure she's told you, she will be ineligible to run in future elections."

"There are no second chances in your rule book?" Giuliana fumed.

"Your daughter had her second chance with the song. If I only had a brain, I would not have even given her *that* one," Sister Agnes remarked with a smirk. "Now, if you'll excuse me, I must get to my classroom. It's on the third floor."

Giuliana was dismissed.

* * *

It was April when Giuliana picked up the early-morning phone call and heard Sister Luke, the Academy's principal, on the other end of the line.

"Mrs. Salvatori, I'm sorry to bother you this early in the morning, but a terrible dilemma has developed, and I need to act on it at once."

"Is Lucy all right?"

"Oh yes, dear. This doesn't involve Lucy at all."

Giuliana relaxed. "What can I do for you, Sister?"

"It just came to our attention that through some oversight, our sister in charge of reserving the theater where we hold the graduation inadvertently forgot to make the arrangements this year. We have been unable to find another locale as they have been reserved by other schools for their own ceremonies. I thought perhaps your family, being involved in theater, might be of assistance to us in some manner," she said hopefully.

"I don't know, Sister. If all the theaters are reserved…"

"If we are forced to have it in our auditorium, the girls will only be able to have two guests present."

"That would be disappointing."

"Very."

"Sister Agnes has had too much on her plate this year. She has never been remiss about anything before."

"Sister Agnes?"

"Why, ycs. You must know her."

"I know her. Have Sister Agnes call me, Sister Luke. She and I will talk."

* * *

St. Aloysius Academy's class of '47 graduation was held in the magnificent venue of the King's Academy of Music. The following autumn, Lucy ran for president of the student body and was elected. Her sequined bows were blood red.

Chapter 27
1948

It was Lucy whom Louisa called first when she was accepted into St. Vincent Hospital School of Nursing. So, in turn, Lucy phoned Louisa and screeched into the phone. "They've accepted me! I've been accepted to Julliard."

"No surprise to me, but congratulations," Louisa offered.

"Then this will surprise you. I actually asked Wayne to be my date for the senior prom. He said yes."

"You didn't! Fantastic. Is Dan OK with it? I mean, his friend going out with his sister."

"He only said he always knew Wayne was soft in the head. But you know, he's been giving me signals.

He put his arm around me a couple of times when we were all together…"

"I know; I saw it."

"When Dan made comments about my singing in the shower, Wayne said he'd be happy to be my audience."

"Big surprise there."

"I really like him. I always have. Have you decided who you're going to ask?"

"Other than my cousin, Mario? No. I could ask your brother Phil's friend, Sal, but what's the point? My father won't agree because he doesn't know him."

"Why don't you ask Phil? He'll go."

"I like Phil all right, but he's like my brother too. If I had to ask one of your brothers…" Louisa's voice drifted off.

"Dan?" Lucy asked in astonishment. "You've never said you like him."

"I didn't want you to think I was just like every other girl in Brooklyn. Don't say a word to him, please. At least I get to see him this way. I'll die if he finds out I like him, and he couldn't care less."

"All right. I'll be quiet about it. I'm in no hurry to have him chaperoning my prom night anyway."

* * *

Sister Grace was working at her desk when Lucy knocked on the classroom door and peeked into the classroom.

"Hi! It's me."

"Lucy! Come in. It's so good to see you."

Lucy bent down and kissed the nun's cheek. "Getting ready to graduate this bunch of brats, Sister?"

"They've been a good group. I'm going to miss them. I'm going to miss all of it."

"All of what?"

"I'm being transferred to St. Joseph's in Brentwood, Long Island."

Lucy read the sadness in the elderly nun's face.

"It might be nice to get out into the country," she suggested.

"They're taking me out of the classroom. I'm going to be in charge of the library."

"Oh. I'm sorry. That's a loss for the students."

"They think I'm too old."

"You don't seem any older to me. How many heads did you crack into the blackboard this year, Sister?"

Sister Grace smiled and visibly seemed to stiffen her spine. "How's Jimmy? I haven't seen him for a while."

"Pretty busy. Did you know he has a full-time job at the *Daily News* when he graduates?"

"Yes. I'd heard. I'm so pleased for him."

"That was all your doing. Just like getting me into music. I'm going to be a music teacher, you know. Only I'll be smashing heads into the keyboard when my students mess up their scales." Lucy picked up the wrinkled hand of her favorite teacher and squeezed it affectionately. "I'll come to visit you. I promise."

"I'd like that."

"Sister…there's a job to do in that library. No one ever really taught us how to use the card files effectively. You should teach research skills so kids don't have such a difficult time in high school. You can also set up book lists for each grade level. I'd probably still be reading Nancy Drew if it wasn't for you. How about a classic books club on the high school level? I would have loved that at Aly's. You could—"

"Slow down. So I've come to this. My students giving *me* the pep talk."

"No, Sister. I only meant…"

"Sssh. I'm glad. You've made me feel better about the transfer. Maybe the old bulldog isn't totally ready for the pasture yet."

Lucy winced.

"What's the matter, Miss Salvatori? You didn't think I knew I was Sister Bulldog?"

* * *

The seniors were abuzz with prom chatter. Lucy had narrowed her gown search down to two selections. Louisa was still dateless, cousin Mario in reserve.

"I overheard something you might want to know about," Ginny said to Lucy.

"What's that?" asked Lucy, biting into her tuna fish sandwich.

"Lorraine Tuccio is going to ask your brother Dan to the prom. She figures she's said enough to him over the years that he might accept."

"She wouldn't dare!"

"She's daring. She's always been crazy about him, and this is her last shot for glory at St. Aly's...to turn up that evening with a college junior who happens to be the most gorgeous man at the prom."

"It's not going to happen."

"Why? Does he loathe her or something?" asked Darlene, the fourth girl at the table.

"Because I won't let it. I can't abide her. Remember what she pulled at the tea this year?" she asked Louisa.

"What did she do?" asked Ginny. Neither she nor Darlene were members of the Academy Angels.

"One of the freshman applicants was an extremely heavy girl with bad skin. She was really nice, though. She had a sweet disposition. I voted her in."

"Lorraine voted her out," Louisa chimed in.

"Adamantly. She persuaded a majority not to give her a chance. And only because the girl, Suzanne," Lucy added whispering, "didn't suit her standard of what an Angel should look like. She actually said she didn't want any guys to think she approved of the way that girl looked."

"There was a huge argument," Louisa informed them.

"Which is why I've been mostly inactive with the club this year. Lorraine actually said that if it makes her a terrible person, so be it. If her hell is a bunch of girls who look like Suzanne poking red hot pitchforks into her svelte figure, she'd endure it for all eternity."

"Nitwit."

"So, *I'll* burn in hell before I let my brother take her to the prom. Louisa, this is war."

"Huh?"

"Get ready because Dan will be escorting you to the prom."

"What!" Louisa squealed, jumping up and causing her chair to crash into the girl seated behind her.

"He's not going to be available to take her. But more than that, she's going to watch you dance with him all night. That should make for her own private little hell."

"I don't want him to hate taking me," Louisa said worriedly.

"Dan thinks you're great. He said you'd be a lot of fun to be stranded on an island with."

"When did he say that?"

"We were playing that game. Who would you want to be with, what book would you bring, what one necessity…By the way, I was Wayne's 'necessity.' Dan slugged him."

"Oh my God. I'm so excited. Call me the minute you mention it to him."

"Consider it a done deal, friend. A done deal. The devil is in the details."

* * *

Lucy dropped the phone into its cradle and clambered up the stairs. Not until she slammed her door shut and plopped on the bed did she burst into huge heartrending sobs.

Fifteen minutes later Tino crept down the stairs and burst into the kitchen.

"Ma?" He looked out back, walked around the house until he came to the front stoop. "Ma?"

Giuliana was sitting on the steps with the Avon lady. She looked up as Tino approached.

"I think you should come upstairs. Lucy's been crying a long time."

Giuliana's eyebrows lifted in surprise. "I thought we'd decided the yellow gown was the most flattering. She's probably having second thoughts," she said to the saleswoman.

"I know what that's about. Thank goodness Danita is happily married. Dealing with her brothers is so much easier."

"I don't know about that, but I'd better go see what set her off."

"I should have your order in a couple of weeks."

Giuliana opened the front door and climbed the stairs. "Lucy? Lucy, can I come in?"

More sobs.

Giuliana opened the door. "What happened?"

Lucy rolled over to her side. Her face was red and wet; her lashes stuck together in little clumps. "Wayne called. He can't go to the prom with me. He has a chance to go with a group of people to see the Grand Canyon, and he wants to do that before he leaves to join the Navy. A big hole in the ground is more important than going to the prom with me."

"Honey, I'm so sorry," Giuliana said, sitting on the bed.

"I thought he liked me. A lot."

"Men are strange. I'm sure there's someone else you can ask, isn't there?"

Lucy pushed herself up on her elbows. "There's this guy on the bus, Rick. I've seen him for three years, but we've only been talking this year. He works in a bank." Lucy perked up. "He's gorgeous. I noticed him the first time he got on the bus. Blond hair, blue eyes, dimples. He might say yes, although since he works he may think school dances are childish."

"How old is this Rick?"

"Same as Dan."

"Let's see what your father says at dinner."

* * *

"Absolutely not," Maestro declared, slicing a piece of white meat off his chicken breast and popping it in his mouth. He could dissect a chicken wing with a fork and knife until there wasn't a suggestion of food left on the bone.

"Why not?" Lucy cried, raising her voice more than a little.

"Because," he replied, setting both his knife and fork down, "we do not know who this man is. He rides a bus to work in a bank. Who is his family? Who are his acquaintances? What does he do in his spare time? No. No daughter of mine goes out with a stranger. It is unacceptable."

"Then that's it. I'm not going to the prom. Just take back the dress, Ma," she said with a quiver in her voice.

"I'm sure there is someone else who can escort you," Maestro said.

"Like who? I go to an all-girls school. Like who?"

"I'll go with you, Lucy, if you want," Phil offered.

"I'd rather die than show up at the prom with my own brother!"

Maestro took a sip of wine. "I have an idea. Joe has a nephew about your age. One of a zillion nieces and nephews he's always talking about. I think his name is Matthew."

"What? He's not a stranger? I've never set eyes on him."

"We'll invite him to dinner so you two can meet. He's Joe's nephew. He comes from a good family. If he's a no-good kid, Joe will tell me."

"Great."

"Give it a chance, Lucy. You never know," her mother advised.

"All right. But if I don't like him, I'm not asking him."

"Fair enough," Maestro said while carving away at a thigh.

* * *

"Fresh-made tomato and basil soup and rosemary lemon lamb chops. Bitter dandelion greens on the side. Does that sound like a getting-to-know-you meal?" Giuliana asked with a tender smile at her daughter.

"Puleez," said Lucy, slicing the Italian bread. "I hope I don't live to regret this. Talk about bitter."

"They're here," yelled Tino before he opened the front door. "Hi, Uncle Joe."

"Augustino, my boy, you're getting bigger every time I see you. How are the drums doing?"

"Great. I'm in the school orchestra even though I'm only a freshman."

"Good evening, Joe. This must be Matthew," said Maestro, joining them. "Come sit in the parlor. Giuliana and Lucy will be joining us in a moment. A drink?" he asked, indicating his own.

In a short while the ladies entered the room, and all the men jumped up, including Tino. Matthew felt his collar tighten around his neck when he was introduced to the beautiful Lucy. He had been expecting homely, if not outright ugly. She was a bit taller than he.

Lucy felt her knees buckle, and she punched her mother in the backside as they entered the room.

He was sickly thin, hands and feet sticking out of cuffs that looked like life preservers surrounding the appendages. His face was acned and picked at, his hair wetly parted in the middle and slicked down. His fleshy lips appeared to cover two-thirds of his scrawny face. When Giuliana announced dinner, Dan and Phil came downstairs sharing a joke between them. One look at Matthew, and Dan's eyes crinkled in amusement at Lucy while Phil's eyes lowered in compassion. They got through the meal, Maestro at his most jovial, and said their good-byes.

"So, what do you think?" Maestro asked.

"You've got to be kidding me," Lucy wailed.

"What did I say?"

"He's awful."

"He was gracious all through dinner."

"Gracious! He barely let anyone get a word in."

"He was nervous."

"Did you happen to notice that all he talked about was the war? The *Civil* War, for crying out loud!! That's it. It's over. I'm not going to the prom." A small sob escaped.

"You know, Valentino at the theater heard about the…er, problem, and offered to take you," Phil said.

"Valentino? He's nice, the little I've seen him."

"Too old. I told him he's too old," Maestro explained.

"What's too old? You're eight years older than Ma," Lucy said exasperated.

"That's now. When it's your age, the difference is too much."

"Lucy, for real. I'd love to take you," Phil said.

"I'd take you too," said Tino.

"Thanks, both of you. But no. If I can't go with someone that makes it the least bit romantic, I don't even want to go."

"Romantic? What's with romantic? You can't just go dance and have laughs with your friends?"

"I think you've made enough suggestions regarding the prom, Maestro," Giuliana said in a warning tone as Lucy ran up to her bedroom.

* * *

Prom night found Lucy in the kitchen cooking her first family dinner as a means of distracting herself. Dan entered to retrieve Louisa's corsage from the Frigidaire refrigerator where he had set it earlier in the day.

"I'm sorry you're not going, Lucy," he said.

"It's OK."

"Wayne is a bastard."

"I hope he falls down the Canyon. Or at least rolls partway."

"Save some of this meal for me. It smells really good."

Lucy didn't bother to respond. She had already scorched the bottom of the tomato sauce pot with a too-high flame. The sauce tasted smoky to her, but there was nothing to do about it now.

"Make sure Lou has the best time of her life, Dan, OK?"

"That won't be too hard to do."

"Don't be a smart-ass, Mr. Cary Grant. Don't lead her on; just treat her special."

"I wasn't being a smart-ass, honest to God. I like Louisa a lot. She's really special. I think it's terrific she's going to be a nurse."

"Have a great time then."

* * *

The rest of the family gathered at the dinner table as Giuliana brought in the salad bowl and a dish of meatballs and beef ribs. With Lucy following behind with a huge serving bowl of spaghetti, she gave a warning look to the men at the table that dared them to make one derogatory comment about the meal they were about to be fed. Everyone commented on how delicious everything looked, but it was obvious from the way the spaghetti hung limply and clung together for comfort that it was overcooked. The acrid burn at the bottom of the saucepan had definitely infiltrated the whole pot. Phil jabbed at a meatball twice before he managed to spear it. Hesitantly he offered the bowl to his father.

"This is really good. I'll take more salad," Maestro said, having finished his first serving before his pasta and meat.

Lucy burst into tears. "It's terrible. Don't pretend. I'm just a loser. A loser."

"Lucilla, this is not the end of the world. One little dance...," Maestro began.

"What do you know about it? Why don't you just kill me now and get it over with? Instead of doing it in bits and pieces my whole life. Why don't you put on the *Rigoletto* you're always refusing to produce? Why, huh? Saving the role of the daughter, Gilda, for me? Just put me in a sack tonight and stab me to death. Get it over with. This is all your fault," she cried, running out of the dining room and up the stairs.

"What did I say?" asked Maestro incredulously.

"Her heart is broken," said Tino wisely.

Phil sat there forcing his bouncing fork into the meatball, determined to finish it to the last bite.

* * *

The dishes were cleared, washed, and put away, the boys having risen to help their mother without being asked. Maestro retreated to the parlor, stung by the *Rigoletto* comment and more confused than ever about women. He remembered being the hero in his little girl's life. The nights he would get in late from the theater, the house dark and his stomach rumbling. He would head into the kitchen, where a covered meal awaited him. Sometimes he needed to heat it in the oven, other times it was a hearty sandwich. Oftentimes a sleepy little girl, rubbing her eyes and nightgown dragging, appeared in the kitchen and sat on a chair at the kitchen table.

As he fed her bits of his frittata or pot roast, he would describe the evening's opera, plot, music, performances, what went right and what went wrong and why. The little girl would come awake and ask astute questions for a child her age. As she got older, they discussed books she was reading or movies she had seen. Those were some of his favorite times and memories. After putting his dirty dishes in the sink, he'd pick her up and carry her into her room. Oftentimes he would sing a few lines from the opera they had been discussing before kissing her forehead goodnight.

When had those evening chats ended? When her homework became so time-consuming, she fell into bed exhausted? When her interests turned more to friends and social activities than the arts? He knew it was before he had given up those post-midnight meals in obeisance to his waistline. When had he become the man who unknowingly arranged to murder his daughter?

He was startled from his reverie by the bell. He and Giuliana reached the door simultaneously. There stood Jimmy, looking uncomfortable but straightening his shoulders at the sight of Maestro.

"Good evening, Mr. and Mrs. Salvatori. I've come to see if Lucy wants to take a walk."

Maestro took a surprised step backward, and Giuliana's hand pushed him even farther.

"That might be a good idea. One moment, Jimmy. Come in, please." She opened the door wider and stared at Maestro, just daring him, once again on this black evening, to open his mouth. He retreated to the parlor and picked up the newspaper with a big show of rustling and page turning. Lucy came downstairs and without a word stepped outside with Jimmy.

"So you want to go for a walk with your best buddy in the whole world?" he asked.

"Oh, Jimmy. It's just awful. It's not even just missing the best night of the whole four years. I feel humiliated. I couldn't even get a date."

"Well, I could have gone with you, but that would have been even more humiliating."

"Never. If my father wouldn't have made such a stink, I would have asked you. At least it would have been a lot of fun. Who cares if we couldn't dance?"

"You're the president. You should have arranged a hoedown for the prom."

The gentle reminder made Lucy smile for the first time that night.

"Let's go to the park," Jimmy suggested.

There were two boys still dangling from the monkey bars, one father pushing his son on the toddler swing, and one elderly man with a folded newspaper on his lap staring into the distance. As the sky darkened, the two young people were left alone except for the occasional pedestrian who used the park as a shortcut. They went down the slide several times and took turns spinning each other on the merry-go-round. They tried to knock someone's sneaker out of a tree using stones they gathered. Eventually they settled on the swings. They swung in companionable silence for a long while.

"Guess what?" Jimmy finally said. "I wrote the obituaries for tomorrow's paper."

"No kidding."

"Yeah, Murray, the guy who does it, had to go to the hospital. I'd been working with him for two days, and the chief told me to go for it. I wrote the obit for Charles Vagnor, the world reknowned photographer."

"I'll have to remember to look at it in tomorrow's paper. Did you do one for me?"

"What are you talking about?"

"Lucilla Salvatori, school president and valedictorian of her class, died unescorted to her senior prom. After the usual tributes, flowers, and snickers, the senior class got back to swinging with the Johnny Belmont band."

Jimmy swung around so his legs straddled the metal seat.

"Lucy, I didn't go to my senior prom either."

"I'm sorry, Jimmy. I'm only thinking of myself. You'd think I'd know better—having you to show me the way on how to overcome disappointment." Lucy swung around on her seat too. Her feet dragged in the sand while Jimmy's hung suspended in the air. She grabbed the metal chains on both their swings and gave a slight push with her hands and feet. The two friends began to move back and forth in unison.

"Someday, Luce, you'll be dancing with the man of your dreams. I know it."

"So will you, Jimmy. I mean, with the girl."

"I hope so."

From a distance, anyone watching the swaying bodies might have thought the two friends were dancing in the moonlight.

Chapter 28

1950

It was a warm day in May as Dan walked through the Lower West Side of Manhattan. He had met with an advertiser for the radio station, listened in on a recording session, and now had free time before he went on the air at four o'clock. Ahead of him, a woman in a long-sleeved, medium-blue shift hurried down the block. He kept an eye on the enticing figure until her ankle twisted on a raised section of sidewalk, and she teetered on one foot trying to recapture her balance. Dan rushed forward and grabbed her elbow.

"Are you all right?" he asked, leveling her.

"Yes, yes," she replied, straightening. "Thank yo—Dan!"

"Louisa?"

"How have you been? I haven't seen you in ages."

"I work crazy hours. How's nursing school?"

"Hard work. But good. I'm trying to get errands accomplished before my four o'clock shift. I'm on clinical today."

"Is that your uniform?"

"Yes. Except I'm missing the hat. I have to get straight to work when I go back."

"Do you have time for a bite? It's lunchtime. There's a coffee shop right on the corner."

Louisa hesitated. She really needed to get her errands done. She looked at Dan, who was smiling at her. Heart skip. "Sure. They make fantastic split pea soup."

Settled in a small booth, the two friends caught up as they awaited their orders.

"I've heard you on the radio. Your voice sounds wonderful on the air."

"Thanks. Just when I get settled, I'm sure that television will make me obsolete."

"You can go on that then. Face or voice, you'll be successful."

The food came, and Dan excused himself. "I have to wash my hands before I pick up that sandwich."

When he returned, he caught sight of Louisa's lovely round blue backside sticking out from under the booth. He also noted three male customers and the guy at the grill all in rapt observance. She backed out and rose. Seeing Dan, she raised her hand in triumph.

"Success!"

"What are you doing?"

"The tuxedo button from the dress fell off. Do you know how much time I waste searching for these stupid things before class or my shift? I can't afford to lose one." She settled it back on the front of her dress. "Have you met anyone famous yet?"

"Not really. Although I did see Bing Crosby in the hallway. Oh, and Mel Torme dropped by the station Christmas party for a few minutes."

"That must be fun. Everyone I see is either sick or in dire distress."

"Can't say you didn't expect that, going into nursing and all."

"Of course. But some days it gets you down. Well, it's almost two years down and one more to go. Lucy and I are going up to the Catskills in July for a weekend. Did she tell you?"

"No, I hadn't heard."

"How's Tino?"

"He'll be a senior in September. He actually gets some professional drumming gigs. Phil's graduating Fordham and will be working full time at the opera house. Care for a cup of coffee?" he asked, noting that Louisa had finished her soup and salad.

"I really should get going."

Dan studied her. "Do you know you have eyes like spring soil?"

"Huh? Are you saying they're muddy?"

"No. Beautiful. Rich and full of promise."

"Come off it. Have you forgotten how long I know you?"

"What?"

"All right. You have eyes like the open range."

"Which means?"

"Full of bullshit."

"Honest to God, I'm not bs-ing you, Lou. You're right. I've known you since you were all exploding hair and eyebrows."

"How gallant of you to bring that up," she kidded.

"You certainly have it all together now, Nurse Louisa."

"Thanks, Dan. I love you too," she said flippantly as she slid out of the booth. "I have to run. This was great. Say hi at home."

"Can I call you?"

"You can try. One phone, thirty-six girls. A nun on duty and no men allowed. Even our fathers. Give it your best shot. Lucy has the number."

Dan stayed in the booth and watched as she passed the window where he sat. She stopped, stuck both thumbs in her ears, and waggled her hands at him through the window before continuing on her way.

Lou, Lou, Lou, Dan mused before getting up to pay the cashier.

* * *

Julliard was buffing Lucy's musical shine beyond her expectations. The school was happy to be the one chosen to do the polishing. Some of her teachers were at first taken aback by the talented pianist/vocalist. That is, until they learned her father was the fabulous impresario Rinaldo Salvatori, and her mother, a Julliard graduate herself. Classes in innovative music theory curriculum, literature and materials of music, along with courses in conducting, composition, and performance, complemented her piano and voice studies. When she appeared on the stage, it was as if an additional spotlight had been turned on.

No one at Julliard would have ever suspected that Lucy had once quaked in an elf costume on a school stage. Among her teachers were Henry Brant, the famed composer, and during one summer, Teddy Wilson, the renowned swing pianist. Lucy and Tino threw open the windows in the house and played some mean swing duets as Rita Ruggiero and her husband, Sam, danced in the middle of the street, to the delight of Rinaldo and Giuliana. Lucy had many pursuers, but she maintained a friendly distance and for the most part socialized in groups. It was in such a setting that she joined Phil and his similarly named date, Phyllis; Jimmy; Dan and Louisa, who had finally agreed to switch a shift with someone to go with him; the infamous Wayne; John; and Ginny to a nightclub in New Jersey named the Coconut Bar. There they were entertained by a big band, a singer, Dick Valenti, and a new female singer, Rosemary Clooney.

"She's incredible," Lucy said after Rosemary's first song.

"She can sure wrap her voice around a song," Phil agreed with awe.

"I'm going to see if I can interview her for the paper," Jimmy said aloud.

When the performances were through, audience members climbed onto the stage and began to dance. Jimmy hightailed it backstage to see if he could snare a meeting with Miss Clooney. Lucy danced with all the guys except Dan, who was glued to Louisa's side. She even condescended to dance with Wayne, who regretted his decision to ever visit the Grand Canyon when she turned down a second dance and returned to their table.

Jimmy maneuvered his way through the tables, oblivious to any stares directed his way.

"I got it," he announced, waving the back cover of a folder. "She was sweet as anything. Sometimes my, er, height impairment is a distinct advantage. No one else was allowed backstage, but I charmed the owner's wife by the dressing rooms."

"C'mon, Jimmy. They're playing a cha-cha. We can manage this," shouted Lucy over the music.

When the group got up to leave, "The Way You Look Tonight" began to play.

"One more dance, guys," Dan called as he led Louisa back to the dance floor.

As she snuggled in his arms on the crowded floor, Dan began to sing with the music.

"Dan! You have a good singing voice too."

"Well, compared to my father and Lucy, I'm mostly intimidated to use it. But I can carry a tune."

"Oh, you're much better than that. A girl can get used to being serenaded."

"In that case, I'll brush up on my lyrics. Tell me, what are your favorite songs?"

"Surprise me."

"'Making Whoopee,'" he teased.

"Once a cad, always a cad."

"I have never been a cad."

"Just overindulged."

Dan considered. "Maybe. But that's all behind me now."

"What's ahead of you?"

"You, I hope, Louisa. You."

* * *

June 30, 1950. President Truman committed US troops to enforce the United Nations directive that North Korea stop its attack and return to its borders. It was called a police action under the UN as described by the newspaper and radio; it sounded like war to most Americans. Either way Giuliana clutched her chest and waited for her world to turn upside down. For a year she gathered the mail with her heart in her throat. Tino graduated high school in June of 1951 and enrolled in Brooklyn College. Mixed in between a handful of literature from the college was Dan's draft notice. The night before he left for boot camp, he sat with Louisa in his backyard after dinner with the family.

"I have something for you," he said, handing her a box.

Louisa took the oddly shaped gift and ripped off the paper. "What?" she said as six separate boxes tumbled into her lap.

"It should be at least a two-year supply of white tuxedo buttons for your uniform. I don't want you bending your pretty tush over looking for them with all those doctors prowling around the hospital."

Louisa laughed until tears streamed down her face. When the sobs began hiccupping out of her, Dan took her in his arms.

"It'll be all right, Lou."

"I'll miss you so much, Dan. Please, please, be careful. I'll pray for you every day."

"Between you and my mother, I should have a free pass out of there. If I even go to Korea." He kissed her lightly. "Don't cry. I don't want your eyes to get all muddy."

Louisa laughed. She got up from the concrete bench they were sitting on and climbed onto his lap. Putting her arms around his neck, she kissed him.

"Can I ask you to wait, Lou? It will be over two years. If you don't, I'll understand."

"Are you implying I'm no spring chicken, Dante?" she scolded. "I'll wait for you. When you return home, I'll announce it so loud, people won't need radios to hear the news."

* * *

During the sixteen weeks Dan was at boot camp, followed by another eight weeks of leadership school, Phil approached Maestro.

"I want to put on *Aida* this season."

"Don't make a step longer than your leg," Maestro chided.

"We can pull it off. I have some ideas. Please, Maestro. I want to do it before I have to go away."

"Go away?"

"Chances are I'll be drafted next. Let me get this one under my belt."

Maestro rose and faced the window. He appeared to be deep in contemplation. It was a transparent ruse to cover the emotion in his face.

"All right," he said gruffly from a hoarse throat, "put on *Aida*. Joe will be thrilled."

Phil called in some of the favors his father had garnered over the years. The mayor contacted the police. An opera singer who was now with the Met contacted his cousin, Count Yurii, who was ringmaster with the circus. He spoke with the owners and animal trainers. Lou Jacobs, the famous clown who remembered seeing the young boy Phil passing a hat on the opera stage, thought the idea was a hoot. Phil approached Josie.

"Can you get together about a dozen costumes that we will use in *Aida*? They don't have to be perfect.

You can do the finishing touches later. And gather together costumes that we could get away with. The public won't know the difference."

"What's the secret?"

"Can't tell just yet."

"All right, I'll do it. I may have to bring Anthony in. My mother is getting too old to watch him full time."

"Bring him in. I'd like to see the little guy. And make sure you bring him into the city the Wednesday after next."

Billboards arrived announcing *Aida.* Props were hastily constructed. The performers went into high gear. Luckily, most of them were well schooled in the opera, and Maestro worked at manic capacity to whip them into shape for the first performance.

On a brilliant Wednesday afternoon at lunchtime, police lines went up on Broadway, snarling traffic and redirecting motorists. Music in the distance was soon followed by shouts and cheers. The circus was coming to town and announcing their arrival with a parade of performers and animals. Oddly enough, although clowns held a huge banner for the circus, the elephants wore billboards on their sides proclaiming that *Aida* was opening the following Friday evening at the Salvatori Opera Company. Two beautiful white circus horses pulled a chariot carrying the actors singing Radamas and Aida; Amneris and other cast members floated by on rolling platforms. In between, trapeze artists performed a few stunts, and Lou Jacobs drove the fully automated mini car that he had invented. Clowns handed out flyers for both the circus and opera. Little Anthony sat on Phil's shoulders and watched the parade with glee.

"Stop bopping around, Anthony," Phil ordered. "You're going to fall off."

Josie focused her camera and took a picture of the brothers, who were for her the greatest show on earth.

* * *

Jimmy got his first byline at the paper with his article about the not-so-impromptu parade. Lucy gathered much of the student body at Julliard and asked for volunteers. They raided the costume department. Two days before opening night, Phil got his draft notice.

Aida was sold out. People clamored, and they added extra performances to the schedule. The opera was a huge success, with elephants, horses, and camels rented from the stables of Eddie Fils, who supplied theatrical animals. The triumphal procession was long and magnificent. The Julliard students marched across the stage and down the aisles while off-duty police officers and firemen whose families had free seats for future performances paraded across the stage draped in white togas. It was all Maestro had ever hoped for, and his son Felice had pulled it off. The spectacle was so unforgettable that it almost overshadowed the rich and vibrant performances. After the final bows, Phil stepped out of the wings and came through the heavy curtains.

"Thank you all for sharing this magnificent indulgence of mine. It has been a joy and an honor to bring you this production. I will be leaving it now in the able hands of my father, the Maestro, who has brought you so many unforgettable music events. I will be leaving in a few days. Uncle Sam has called me." A ripple of gasps and chatter filled the audience. "Keep these seats warm until I return. I don't want to have to start from scratch when I get back!" he said with a grin.

The audience broke into applause and took to its feet once again. In the wings where Giuliana had raced before the bows, she turned to look at Josie, who was standing beside her. The women's eyes met, and they fell into each other's arms.

"He'll be OK. He'll be OK," Josie sobbed.

"Of course he will. They both will," Giuliana agreed.

"It's a police action. Right? A police action."

"It's a war, Josie. Don't let anyone tell you differently. "It's a stinking war."

* * *

"*Mangia, mangia,*" instructed Sophia Titziano, cutting a huge slice of Swiss chard pizza for Phil. "I make justa for you."

Phil smiled and took a bite. It was delicious, but he had just finished lunch before paying this farewell visit to his grandmother.

"You want I should make a salad on side?" she asked, pouring soda into a glass for him.

"No, this is terrific. Thanks."

She sat down at the table. "I have somethin' for you." She reached into the pocket of her housedress and pulled out a folded handkerchief. Laying it on the table, she methodically opened it until it lay flat and white on the red oilcloth covering the table. A dime-sized amulet rested in the center of the handkerchief. "I make for you. It's a good luck." She opened the gold brooch. Behind a plastic window was a grayish blob of mush.

"What is it?" Phil asked.

"For your safety. A potion made with special herbs. I canna tell you what or it no work. I mix them with the special oil, and I steam them in the holy water."

"Holy water? Are you sure that's not sacrilegious?" Phil joked.

"What you say! God knows. It'sa for you good. You keep with you all time."

Phil took the amulet and put it in his pocket. "Thank you. I will keep it on me."

"Good. So, Mr. Truman, he send you Korea?"

"I don't know yet. I have to go to basic training first."

"You be careful, understand? You see good herbs, you bring them backa to me."

Phil smiled. "Will do." He rose to leave. "Thanks for the pizza. I'll want it again when I get home."

The old lady stood up and walked around the table. She reached up and took his face in her hands. Pulling Phil's head down to her, she kissed his face all over. He could feel the wetness on her cheeks.

"You no get in trouble, you hear? You tell them Sophia Titziano has the magic. They be sorry they hurt my Felice."

As Phil approached the house, he noticed a big P.C. Richard & Son truck parked in front. Giuliana stood on the curb ready to confront the driver when he emerged from the cabin. Phil hastened his steps to reach her.

"Look at this? What's he doing in there? Go ask him why he's here," Giuliana ordered impatiently.

"It's OK, Ma. It's a gift I ordered. For you."

"For me? What did you order from P.C. Richard's?"

The driver jumped down and went to the rear of the truck. "Ma'am," he said, nodding his head before he unlatched the back door.

"You'll see," Phil said. "Go inside and wait. Be surprised."

"I've had enough surprises lately, thank you. I don't think I can take any more."

"Don't be a killjoy. Scoot."

Giuliana trudged indoors and listened while Phil directed the driver into the parlor. There was movement of furniture, the opening of a carton and a bit later, a stranger's voice. The driver left and Phil called out, "OK, Ma. Come on in."

In a place of honor sat an RCA Victor television set.

"For you, Ma. To keep you company while I'm away. And Dan. The funny shows will make you think of me. There's *I Love Lucy* and *The Jack Benny Show*..."

"This is so generous, Phil, but does your father know? He was in no hurry to get one of these things."

"Yes, he knows, and he thinks it's a great idea. He would have bought one himself, he said, but when I suggested it...you know Maestro. Save a penny, save a penny."

"After dinner you show me how to work this thing."

"It's not a thing, Ma; it's a television. There's nothing to work. You turn it on; you turn it off."

"Look at that," Giuliana said, jutting her chin at the TV. "That woman is asking for money."

"It's a game show."

"How can they play games when our boys are fighting a war?"

Phil sighed. "Don't watch the game shows, Ma. Watch the comedies, OK?"

* * *

Later that evening the family gathered around the television the way they once settled around the radio before everyone was off in a different direction.

"Look. Here's that show that used to be on radio, *Life With Luigi*. Remember?" Phil asked.

As the story enfolded, Maestro asked, "Why is J. Carrol Naish playing an Italian? He's Irish, isn't he? I've met him."

"Why do you cast people who aren't Japanese in *Madama Butterfly*? Or not Italian in…"

"All right. You make your point. His accent is pretty good, anyway."

"Are we gonna watch this, or are we gonna dissect the entire show?" Tino asked from his position on the floor.

When the show finished, Lucy said, "That plot was reminiscent of O Henry's story, *The Gift of the Magi.* I wonder if all TV shows imitate literature."

"If movies are any example, I'd say no, some of the writers have never even cracked open a book," Phil suggested.

"How can you say that? Just this year…" Lucy argued.

"OK, guys. The next show is starting. Can you two college snobs settle down or leave the room?" Tino asked in exasperation.

* * *

After Phil left for boot camp, Lucy tried to help out at the opera house more frequently. She was in Phil's office, rummaging through files, when Valentino stuck his head in the door.

"Hey, Lucy, your father is looking for you. Something to do with the second scene in *Cavalleria.*"

"I'll be right with him. Val, do you know who Phil buys the lighting gels from? The lighting guys have some special requests. I can't find the info."

"I'll check it from the invoices in my office. I'm pretty sure it's Citywide Theatrical Services, though, and not a lighting company." Val was the treasurer of the Opera Company and in charge of all things financial. "Care to grab a bite to eat?" he asked hopefully.

"Thanks, Val, but I have classes this afternoon. And a rehearsal. You'd think everything would be wrapped up as we approach the bitter end, but it's as demanding as ever."

"No problem. I'll catch you some other time."

* * *

Lucy hurried backstage before the final curtain fell on the popular duo of *Cavalleria Rusticana* and *Il Pagliacci.* She was wearing an emerald satin dress. Her black shoes had an emerald-colored bow atop the new style stiletto heel that she had miraculously found at Miles Shoe Store on Eighty-Sixth Street. Her mother joined her, beginning to look a bit thin from lack of appetite since both her boys were gone. Amidst the hubbub of post production, a young, handsome man stepped up to Lucy.

"Hi. I'm Thomas DiGregorio. Tom Turner, the director of the Sayville Musical Workshop on Long Island, told me I should look up Maestro Rinaldo

Salvatori to say hello. They called him, and he put aside tonight's ticket for me."

"How do you do?" replied Giuliana, extending her hand. "Maestro is my husband. He should be along shortly."

"Mrs. Salvatori, a pleasure." He turned to Lucy. "You must be the daughter then. The resemblance is striking."

Lucy smiled and nodded but was taken aback. Her mother was a stunning woman who drew second looks wherever she went. Still, at fifty-two, she was breathtakingly beautiful. Lucy had always felt like a pale imitation of her mother. She knew men took note of her, but to be actually recognized as Giuliana's daughter gave her a warm glow of pleasure.

"Are you a singer?" asked Giuliana.

"No, ma'am. I don't do musicals. I act in straight plays. And the workshop produces a lot of great plays. I've studied and worked with them for a few years. I'm on my way to Hollywood but staying in the city a few days."

"Ah, there's my husband. Rinaldo," Giuliana called out.

She introduced Thomas when Maestro joined them.

"How's my old friend Tom doing?" Maestro asked with a grin. "One of the finest choregraphers around. He actually helped me out here a few times. So you're the young man heading West? Much luck. It's a tough business, this show business."

"Yes, sir."

Lucy found herself mesmerized by Thomas's mouth. Perfectly formed and when upturned in a smile, totally captivating. Light-brown hair contrasted by deep-blue eyes all settled engagingly atop a six-foot, well-toned physique.

"...or a drink, Miss Salvatori?"

Lucy snapped back to the moment. "I'm sorry, I was distracted for a second. You were saying?"

So much for my fatal charm. "Would you like to go out for a drink?"

"I'm sorry. A bunch of us are going over to Sardi's tonight. It's a good-bye party for Leo, the conductor. He's retiring and moving to Arizona."

"We could grab a quick drink at the Algonquin; it's just up the street from there. I'll walk you back to the restaurant afterward. Would that be agreeable to you, Maestro Salvatori?"

Maestro leaned forward on his walking stick. "Well, since you come here by way of Tom Turner... if Lucy would like to go, I think it will be fine."

"All right then. Let me get my wrap. I don't want to make too late an entrance at Leo's bash."

As the couple headed toward the backstage exit, Val passed them in the hall. He had come in especially for the retirement party and had hoped to spend some time with Lucy.

"Aren't you going to the party?" he asked, inspecting Lucy's escort.

"Sure, Val. I'll be there in a bit. See you at Sardi's."

As they walked toward Broadway, Lucy asked, "So if you're not a singer, how did you wind up at the opera house tonight?"

"Like I said, I'm in the city a few days. I love musicials. Last night I saw *Guys and Dolls.* Great show."

"Yes, isn't it? I saw it last year."

"My grandmother always played *Cavallaria Rusticana* on her Victrola. I've known the music by heart practically my whole life, it seems. Tom told me to look up your father while I was in town. So when I saw the opera on the marquee, I called Tom about getting tickets, since no one was at the box office."

"Did you enjoy it?"

"I really did. I know the story because my grandmother told it to me. I had to kind of piece together *Il Pagliacci.* I think I'll read up on it, though."

They walked over to Forty-Fourth Street as Lucy explained how she was trying to fill in for her brother Phil.

"The studio got me a deferment, for the time being anyway."

"You've already got a film then."

"Yes. Don't ask me the name, though. Every week it's something different. Here we are," he said, indicating the doorway.

They made their way to the Blue Room and ordered.

"Johnnie Walker Black on the rocks and a good merlot for the lady," Thomas ordered. "So what are your plans when you graduate?"

"I already have a list of prospective private students. In fact, I've been teaching two girls in our neighborhood for a year already. I'll also be teaching a course in piano for non-majors at Julliard in September." She sipped from the wineglass, which had arrived. "And keeping Phil's seat warm until he returns."

"Where is he now?"

"Just finishing up boot camp, then we'll know for sure. Dan is in Korea. He doesn't write much. Or the letters aren't reaching us."

They chatted for another twenty minutes until Lucy insisted she had to join the opera house party. Thomas walked her back in the direction of Sardi's. He was hoping for an invitation to join the group inside, but Lucy merely extended her hand and thanked him for the unexpected interlude.

"May I write to you, Lucy?"

"I doubt the movie star is going to have time to write."

"I don't know anyone out there. It may get lonely."

"I think you'll meet plenty of starlets to keep you occupied."

Thomas ignored her. "May I write?"

"If you really want to correspond with the mousey music teacher from Brooklyn when you have Lauren Bacalls all around you, sure." She wrote her address on a slip of paper from inside her purse. "It's been great meeting you."

"I'm bewitched," he said with a dazzling smile.

Actors, Lucy thought as she entered the restaurant. *Almost as bad as opera singers.*

Chapter 29

Maybe God just threw up his hands when confronted with Sophia Titziano's amulet. As Phil stood with the rest of his company waiting to hear his assignment, he pressed his palm against his pants leg to feel its comforting presence through the cloth. Surnames beginning with *A* through *P* were headed for the Far East. Soldiers lettered *Q* through *R* set their sights on Africa. The men whose uniform name tagged them *S* through *Z* boarded aircraft to Germany. Giuliana was numb with relief.

They received word in a letter from Dan that he was not an officer. At the last moment before graduation, the officer candidates were told they would have to agree to change their terms of enlistment from two years to five. He considered it for a second, pictured Louisa's face and his mother's tears, and excused himself, along with several others. As he lurched down the gangplank in the drizzle and darkness of a Korean night, it was disturbing to see the assembly of casualties waiting to be loaded onboard. The company moved north alternately by train, truck, or foot, sleeping in abandoned sheds, schoolhouses or in the freezing outdoors. And always, always, throngs of refugees surrounded them.

He had a close encounter with an enemy tank and watched an officer killed in a collision between a jeep and one of their own trucks. His company was nearby when an ammunition train exploded, and they watched the gray sky turn red and black. Amidst enemy machine gun fire, he slogged through waterlogged rice paddies that stank of the human manure used as fertilizer. Abandoning his poncho cape, he tried to let a heavy rainfall wash the stench of death and despair from him. Unsuccessful, he stripped off his clothes, desperate to feel clean once again. He succeeded in being savaged by mosquitoes. He stumbled on with his fellow soldiers, never convinced that this enemy could ever be vanquished, as General MacArthur had originally insisted it must. The objective now was to negotiate on the basis of agreeing to the pre-war division of Korea. If they weren't obliterating communism, why were they there?

* * *

"Are you crazy?" Giuliana moaned.

"I'm sorry, Ma. It's not for me. I've got a fill-in gig with the Glenn Miller orchestra. That's big time. It gives me a chance to travel. I don't need college for this. I'm a pro at what I intend to do with the rest of my life."

"College may keep you safe from being drafted. Now is not the time to drop out."

"It's a chance I have to take. Maybe you'll see me on television. They play on TV shows sometimes, and this is a six-month job."

"I'd rather see you alive in this house."

"Ma, I'm nineteen. You can't stop me."

"You think I don't know that?" She plopped into a chair. "Maybe the government will take pity on a mother with two sons in the service already. Maybe. Maybe."

"Maybe," Tino echoed.

* * *

The forced march of anxiety once again tugged Giuliana's feet to the mailbox. Each day she dreaded seeing the familiar Selective Service envelope, and each day she went upstairs to say a rosary of thanksgiving when it didn't arrive. Her torture was sidelined one hot July day by a mysterious envelope addressed to—she wasn't quite sure whom. When Lucy arrived home, she showed it to her. Her face broke into a grin as she read the addressee.

> To: The Mousey Musician of Brooklyn
> c/o the Salvatoris

"What is it?" asked Giuliana.

"It's a letter from Tom DiGregorio. Remember, he was backstage at the opera house a few months ago? I went out for a drink with him."

"Ah, yes. The spectacularly gorgeous young man who asked your father for permission to take you out? Maestro was impressed."

"That's him. He finished his movie. Apparently, his leading lady was nowhere near as stunning as me," Lucy said with a smirk.

"Why are you the mousey musician?"

"Oh, it's just something I said. Funny that he'd remember it."

"I'm glad it wasn't your father or Tino. Or me, for that matter. I thought someone was trying to insult us."

"Just the opposite, I'd say. He's trying to endear himself to me."

"Is it working?"

"He's making progress."

* * *

There was little the army could do to endear itself to the soldiers facing the enemy's fanaticism. It was frightening to encounter North Koreans willing to cast their lives away in suicidal charges at point-blank range. The unceasing unpredictability of where and when the enemy would turn up took a constant toll on the emotional health of the troops. It was with fervent gratefulness that Dan boarded a Globemaster cargo plane for a four-hour trip to Tokyo for R&R. He wore a parachute for the uncomfortable ride and thought how disappointing it would be if it failed to deploy, and he died vacation bound.

The getaway did prove restorative. Most people spoke English where the troops hung out. There were clean sheets and baths, food that was better than rations, and the female form to soothe the eyes. Dan amazed himself with his disinterest in pursuing the feminine diversions available to the soldiers. He thought of Louisa, wrote letters on real stationery, and took the train to outlying areas to explore. As he watched the locals indulging in the luxury of a normal daily routine, he had to ask himself… had anyone ever asked the Korean people what *they* wanted?

* * *

The quality of the government's mercy was definitely strained. Six months after Tino's birthday, he received the notice to go for his physical. Giuliana studied her slender son. Compared to her other boys, Tino looked fragile at five foot seven, an inch shorter than herself. Except for his arms, which were powerful from the drumming. They'd surely notice that if they gave him a shot. What about that slight wheeze he would get in the spring? *Somewhere between allergies and asthma,* she thought. *Maybe it's asthma. What's the matter with me,* she groaned inwardly. *I'm hoping my baby has asthma to keep him out of harm's way.*

"I'm off," Tino said as he left for the physical.

Lucy ran in from the kitchen and grabbed him at the doorway.

"Be honest," she said, staring him down.

"What are you talking about? What am I lying about?"

Lucy had heard about the physical from several acquaintances.

"Just be honest."

* * *

Tino didn't return until just before six that evening. Giuliana made a valorous effort at composing herself for the inevitable announcement of induction. When Tino entered the kitchen, she continued frying cutlets at the stove. "Dinner won't be ready for an hour, but the broccoli rabe is ready if you want a small dish. This batch is particularly bitter and delicious."

"I'm not hungry."

Giuliana turned to face him. "When?" she asked simply.

"I wasn't accepted."

Her heart leaped in her chest, but she maintained a concerned visage. She lowered the flame under the pan and sat at the table. "Sit. What is it? Flat feet? Asthma?"

"Ma. I'm a homosexual."

It didn't take Giuliana long to digest the news she had already suspected for ten years.

"You told them just like that?"

"No, for Chrissakes. They asked me, 'Do you like girls?' And I said, 'I love my sister and mother.' The doctor growled at me and said, 'Don't be a smart-ass. Do you like girls?' and I said no. Then he scribbled something on the paperwork. I heard him mumble 'damned sissypants' as I was pushed through. They kind of just sent me on my way after that. So, not to worry, Ma. I won't be a soldier." He stood up. "I'm sorry, Ma."

"You're sorry? For what are you sorry? Did they change you somehow over there? You're still Tino, right? That's all I care about. You're my Tino, and you're staying in America. Anything else is your private business."

Tino looked at her in astonishment. "Have you guys all been discussing me behind my back?"

"No one has discussed anything with anyone, ever."

"This morning Lucy told me to be honest when I went there."

"She did? She's never asked me about it. Maybe your brothers said something, or she noticed herself. Not for anything, Tino, but you used to steal my Avon when you were a little kid."

"That didn't mean I was a homosexual. I just liked it."

"Well, whatever it meant, it doesn't matter. You're a sweet, gentle soul, and it's nice to have a man around who understands things that matter to me. Like when that volcano experiment Phil was working on exploded and ruined my dining-room curtains. Your father didn't see what the big deal was, but you said you'd go shopping with me to get new ones. I like that."

"Maestro. What will Maestro say? I never intended him to know." Tino walked through the doorway. "I can't face him just yet, Ma. I'm going out. I'll be back later."

"All right, son. I love you."

* * *

Giuliana postponed telling Rinaldo why Tino wasn't inducted until they were alone in their bedroom later that evening.

"I don't know if it would have made a difference to me if he was our only son, but I feel no pain over this. As long as he can live a happy life. That's all I'm concerned about. As long as he can be happy." Giuliana's eyes dared Rinaldo to think differently.

"Do you think I'm upset? Did you think I didn't know?" he asked incredulously. "What am

I...*stunado*? His whole life he's been uncomfortable with the usual boy stuff. I guess he was too young to remember when I picked him up from that camp because he couldn't fit in. The other boys were making fun of him. I knew it then. Did I ever try to change him? Did I ever give him a hard time? Why do you look at me like I'd turn on my own child?"

"He was afraid to tell you. He thinks you'll be disappointed in him."

"I've been in theater my whole life. Do we not know hundreds of actors and singers like him? Do I treat them any differently?"

"I guess we thought it might be different with him."

"Well, just so you know...and you can tell him too, I'm insulted. Insulted that you think I'm such a monster that I'd disown my own son when I've never shown prejudice to these people in my life."

Rinaldo climbed into bed and turned on his side, turning off the lamp on the night table. Giuliana slid in next to him and lay on her back. Both lay unmoving, aware of the other's wakefulness. Rinaldo threw back the covers and padded out of the room. Giuliana listened intently as she heard him descend the staircase. A while later, he returned to their bed.

"What did you do?

"I thought of something I needed to do."

"I'm sorry if I offended you, Rinaldo."

"Don't think on it."

"It's just, well, the ladies have always been attracted to you, and I know that pleases you. And with Dan, you take pride in how the girls have always vied for his attention. Rather like a young Rinaldo." He turned suddenly in the bed. "Don't deny it. I'd get annoyed with the parade of girls, and you'd strut around like the rooster who taught him he has a cock."

"Giuliana. Where is this nonsense coming from?"

"I'm just saying. So it's only natural that I would think you'd be upset if one of your sons didn't follow in the Salvatori tradition."

"Well, it doesn't bother me. In fact, it's almost a relief. Now I only have to worry about Dan and Lucy if they—"

"Don't even say it. I thought we got past that twenty-five years ago."

"My mouth is closed. It's only an afterthought. Not my first reaction. Tino is who he is, and he's better than most."

"I am so in love with you at this moment," Giuliana whispered.

She raised herself on an elbow and bent over him in the darkness. Her lips found his in a deep emotional kiss. Rinaldo responded by running his hands along the sides of her lithe body. He tugged at her nightgown, trying to pull it over her head. She assisted frantically and lay back on her side of the bed. Lovingly, he caressed her breasts. His hands sought the familiar territory that he hadn't visited for longer than usual.

"What is this? Where is your flesh? You're skin and bones!" he exclaimed, poking at her ribs.

"I am fine. I've lost my appetite with Dan and Phil away. But I'm healthy as an ox."

Rinaldo's hands slipped under her, examining her back for protruding bones.

"You're like a skeleton. How didn't I see this?"

"I've only lost ten pounds. I had started to put on a little weight, so this isn't such a bad thing. I'm well aware of my body; I'm all right. Am I unattractive to you now?"

"Curse the day I don't want to make love to you." He bent over and flicked at her breasts with his tongue. "I was very wise to marry a younger woman. She is still beautiful and enticing while I dodder toward being an old man."

Giuliana reached down to touch Rinaldo. "From where I'm lying, it doesn't feel like you're ready for the nursing home yet."

"Not yet, my love, not yet."

* * *

Tino entered the dark house and turned on the entryway light. His father's Panama hat and walking stick were in their usual position on the coat rack. *Well, she didn't tell him as soon as he walked in the door, or they might be shredded and broken.*

He walked into the dining room and kitchen looking for evidence of upheaval. Everything seemed normal. He gulped a glass of water from the tap and went up to his room. Closing the door behind him with a sigh, he turned on the light. On his pillow lay a book. He walked over to the bed, sat on the edge, and reached for the book without looking at it. He brought it to his lap and focused on the slip of paper sticking out of the book with his name *Augustino* written in his father's hand. Cautiously he opened to where the paper bookmarked, almost afraid a coiled paper snake would shoot out at him like a child's prank. His eyes were drawn to the underlined words on the page.

> If a man does not keep pace with his companions, perhaps it is because he hears a different drummer. Let him step to the music which he hears, however measured or far away.

Tino looked at the cover. *Walden.* Henry David Thoreau. Would he have known this if he had stayed in college? His throat clutched at his father's quiet acceptance. His message of love. He discarded his clothing and hopped into bed. A light shown under his doorway through the night as he read the first of many books to widen his understanding of the world.

Chapter 30

The Warner Brothers logo filled the screen, and Lucy whispered to Louisa, “Here goes.” The title of the film, *Prairie Paradise,* rose bold and yellow from the plains of Nebraska. The cast’s names flashed bright on the screen, Lucy’s eyes darting frantically to catch the one she was searching for.

“Where is it?” she whispered. “Did I miss it? Did you see Thomas DiGregorio?”

“No. I didn’t see it either.”

Lucy felt a pang of disappointment, followed by a splash of anger. Had he lied to her about being in a movie? On the screen, legs stretched in front of a bench at the train station pulled back to let the stationmaster pass, the head lifted, and from under the cowboy hat two deep-blue eyes crinkled in the sunlight.

"Oh my God! That's him. There's Tom."

The two friends sat captivated through the movie as did the other patrons of the movie house. When the character, Match Logan, jumped off the moving train, ran back to the station, and took the stockstill actress who adored him into his arms, an audible groan of desire rippled through the theater. Lucy squeezed Louisa's hand, and Louisa choked, "You actually went out with him? Oh. My. God."

They sat in silence until the final credits ended and rose to leave, all at once too impatient to sit through a second feature.

"They changed his name to Tavis Gregg."

"Is he that handsome in person?"

Lucy nodded. "I'm dumbfounded. He's really very talented. And the movie. It was good, wasn't it?"

"It was. The story is a tearjerker, and it has a great cast."

"Of which Tom is the lead. I can't believe it," Lucy repeated wonderingly.

* * *

The buzz on the film and the young actor of promise was so positive that Giuliana dragged

Maestro to the movies to see what he described as a sobby Western. He walked away impressed with the performance and commented, "Too bad he doesn't sing."

Giuliana said wistfully, "I spoke to him when he called Lucy the other night."

Rinaldo looked over and stopped her stride with his walking stick.

"You look smitten. I can't recall you ever mooning over a movie star before."

"I'm not mooning. I could be his mother. He just kind of makes you feel all romantic inside."

"Then let's forget about ice cream sundaes and get home while your insides are all smitten."

"Are you sure you're not just trying to save the fifty cents for an ice-cream sundae?"

"We have maraschino cherries at home, don't we?"

* * *

"Have you seen *The Crucible* yet? It won the Tony for best play." Tom's voice sounded as deep blue as his eyes.

"No," Lucy replied, her knuckles white on the phone receiver.

"I'll get tickets for tomorrow night then."

"Just like that?"

"Just like that," he said with a chuckle. "It's nice being Warner's favorite son of the moment. I'll pick you up at six thirty."

"No, Tom. No sense coming into Brooklyn. I have to be at Julliard tomorrow. I'll bring a change of clothes. Pick me up there."

"Does that mean less time with you? I'm driving in from Sayville, so Brooklyn is not too far out of the way."

"Come to Julliard at six thirty instead. I'll show you around."

"You want to show me off to your girlfriends?" he asked, sounding pleased as punch.

"You are incorrigible. No, I meant I'll show you around the school."

"Better yet."

"I'll see you tomorrow night then."

"See you, Mousey," he said affectionately.

Lucy called Louisa, who had just woken up and was readying herself for her midnight shift at St. Vincent's Hospital.

"I'm going out with Tom tomorrow night!"

"Tom of Tavis Gregg Tom?"

"Yep."

"Be still, my heart." She was quiet for a moment. "When, oh when, is Dan coming home?"

"Soon, honey. Soon."

* * *

The Julliard tour went well. They sat in on an orchestral rehearsal, and Lucy introduced Tavis Gregg to one of her students, who almost fell off the piano bench when she realized who it was. Then in sunglasses camouflage, Tavis held Lucy's hand as they took a leisurely stroll to the theater district.

"Why didn't you tell me you changed your name?"

"I didn't. They did. It seems so foolish; I was embarrassed to tell you."

"Well, Tavis is nicer than Rock, I'd say."

"They did kind of work off my real name."

"I don't know what to call you, though. Tom, Tavis, Match…"

"Well, everyone is calling me Tavis, and I'm trying to get used to it. Except my family, of course. I'll always be Tom to them and butthead to my brother."

"Just so you know, Tavis, those sunglasses aren't fooling anyone. People have stopped and stared a few times already."

"I'm sure they're staring at you, Mousey."

* * *

The couple waited in a back room of the Martin Beck Theater until just before curtain. An escort showed them to their seats, and as the curtain rose, the woman next to Lucy shoved the program at her.

"Have him sign this for me, will you, sweetie?"

Lucy gave her an icy glare. "At intermission, if you don't mind."

The woman withdrew her arm.

"You tell her, Lucy. Who needs a bodyguard?" Tavis whispered.

* * *

After escaping the theater, they went for a late supper. They discussed the play, and Arthur Miller's obvious jabs at McCarthyism.

"It's upsetting," Lucy commented. "The central spokesman for rational thinking, Proctor, winds up dead in the end. It makes you wonder if the crusaders against the hysteria we're seeing have a chance of succeeding."

"Saner minds have to prevail in the end."

"Well, in case they don't, I think I'll have the baked Alaska, after all."

* * *

Tavis drove Lucy home in his rented white Buick Skylark convertible. He escorted her up the three steps to the front door.

"Wow. This is some house. Have you lived here your whole life?"

"Yes. This is the house and neighborhood I grew up in. Would you like to come in?"

"I'd love to see the inside someday. But it's really late, and believe it or not, my mother will still be up when I get home."

Lucy pulled her key out of her purse, and Tavis took it from her hand.

"I don't know when I've enjoyed an evening this much. Thanks for agreeing to go out with me. I'm just beginning to see that dating can be a hairy proposition nowadays."

"I had a great time too, Tom, er, Tavis. It was worth the looks and fingerpointing."

Tavis bent down to kiss her tenderly on the lips. "Will you come out to Long Island and visit my hometown? You'll have a nice day, I promise."

"Sure. I'd love to."

This time when he kissed her, he held her tightly. This soaring thrill from a kiss was new to Lucy. Not wanting to appear breathless, she put her head on his shoulder as their lips parted. Tavis slid his hand down her head until he was left with a cascade of soft waves slipping through his fingers.

Lucy leaned back on the door she had closed quietly behind her.

Just how many dates did you go on before you realized it's a hairy proposition, she wondered.

* * *

Lucy grabbed the phone on the second ring.

"Hello?"

"Hey, Luce, Jimmy here."

"Oh, hi."

"Sorry to disappoint you."

"What do you mean?"

"I know where you were last night," he said in a singsong voice.

"What?"

Jimmy got serious. "Listen, Luce. I'm calling to give you a heads up."

"About what?"

"The gossip page in tomorrow's paper."

An uneasy feeling akin to a thousand paper cuts started in her head and moved downward.

"Go on."

"I'm reading this. 'Tavis Gregg, Hollywood's newest heartthrob, was seen in the company of an unnamed starlet. The willowy brunette clung desperately to the actor's arm as a squadron of female fans tried to wrestle him away from her. After maneuvering their escape in a cab, the lovestruck couple made a getaway to Delmonico's. The lovely lass in the black dress dotted with tiny pink poodles and hearts had no problem scarfing down a baked Alaska while Tavis watched his trim waistline, nursing an afterdinner drink. The twosome walked to a parking garage, where they were last seen kissing and driving off into the moonlight.' I'd know the willowy brunette in that dress anywhere, sweetheart," Jimmy added, doing a Bogart impression.

"Oh my God! It's not true. Most of it anyway. We were not kissing in the car. What are we, teenagers? And we were not besieged by frantic fans. He scribbled a few autographs before our cab pulled up. This is mortifying."

"If it's any consolation, don't forget, they called you a starlet. They have no idea who you are."

"Who's they? Can't you stop the article?"

"No, it's just one story of several. The page only comes out once a week. Your luck to be the hottest new story closest to deadline."

"All right. Thanks for calling. I'm confiscating the paper before my father gets home."

"Hey, Lucy?"

"Yeah?"

"When are we gonna grow up?"

"I don't know, Jimmy. I don't know."

* * *

It was daybreak, pale sunlight trying to break through the mist. Dan and seven other members of his squad, knowing they were a good distance from the enemy lines, walked back from where they had been posted to join the rest of the company. Had they taken the wrong trail? Before them unexpectedly was a clearing. Seven North Koreans were shedding their uniforms in the open and changing into the clothes of a peasant family they had ambushed. Dan spied the naked, dead bodies on the ground, along with those of two children whose stripped clothes were tossed aside.

In unison, as the North Koreans reached for their weapons, Dan and his comrades fired at point-blank range. Blood splattered, turning the mist red. A quick nervous movement from under an overturned cart. A body crawled out. They all fired. They stopped breathing. The blood in the air seemed to fill Dan's eyes and ears and rest on his tongue. A small boy, still clothed, somehow originally overlooked, lay dead from their gunfire. No one knew which bullet did the deed, but the deed was done. Dan and a fellow from New Hampshire fell to their knees and were sick. The sun rose higher in the sky, its rays outlining the day in mourning.

And then it was over. A truce agreement was signed; all fighting ended. Dan waited six months to be sent home.

* * *

Jubilant that the war had ended, renewed by a long-distance telephone call from Phil, and happy for Jimmy that he had won a prize for an article he wrote entitled "Did Someone Say We Were at War?", Lucy waited on the front steps for Tavis to pull up in his rented car. This time a black Studebaker rounded the corner, and Tavis emerged, tan, fit, and beyond good looking. Lucy stood and met him on the walkway.

"Good morning," she called.

He reached her, put his hands on her upper arms, and kissed her.

"Good morning. I need another kiss. This is my breakfast."

Lucy laughed and obliged. "Would you like something to eat before we set off?"

"No. My mother is packing a picnic breakfast for us to take to our local beach before she goes to work at the library. You'll meet my folks later on. Hop in," he said, opening the door for her.

Mrs. Russo stepped outside to take in her milk. She took one look at the car and its occupant and dropped one of the bottles. It splattered her robe and slippers and seeped into the geraniums and thirsty impatiens. Tavis, becoming a pro at the whole Hollywood thing, waved at her.

"Good morning, lovely lady. I hear milk baths are a fanstastic beauty treatment…not that you need it."

"That's obnoxious," Lucy said with a grin.

"What? I complimented her."

"You should pay for the milk. You're the reason she dropped it."

"Should we go back?" he asked as they reached the corner.

"No. I'm only kidding. But really…," she said with a sigh, wondering what other misadventures lay ahead for them in Sayville, Long Island.

* * *

Tavis opened the unlocked door on Handsome Avenue.

"I can't believe you live on Handsome Avenue!" Lucy said with glee. "Did they rename it for you?"

"Now who's being obnoxious?" Tavis asked.

He showed her around the first floor, finishing up in the kitchen, where a picnic basket sat on the table. Nearby was a thermos filled with hot water and a note instructing them to reheat the coffee on the stove. Having made the final preparations, they set off.

"We can walk to the beach," Tavis informed her as they strolled along the treelined block. Every style of house ranging in size from stately Victorians to smaller bungalows dotted the blocks leading to the bay.

"My grandparents' home is now just a summer rental cottage. I'll show it to you later. They used to live there before they moved to New Jersey to help my grandfather's mother. Then they just stayed there with the rest of my grandfather's relatives."

They walked onto the small beach and spread out the towels Lucy was carrying. The water lapped lazily at the shore, and birds scanned the water for breakfast.

"That's Fire Island. You take a ferry to get there," Tavis advised, pointing. "Marlon Brando was discovered at Cherry Grove drinking at a bar."

"Wasn't Lana Turner discovered at a soda fountain? Drinking at a counter seems to be the key to success in Hollywood," Lucy noted.

"If drinking was the secret code, there would be a lot more celebrities, believe me," Tavis chuckled. "The booze flows freely, as well as plenty of other nefarious substances."

"You're not getting sucked in?"

"Me? Did you see that church on the corner? That's my parish, St. Lawrence the Martyr. I was an altar boy there, even though I didn't go to parochial school. Do you think I could face the parish priests if my face was plastered in some gossip column? No, thank you."

Lucy opened the basket and withdrew egg, pepper, and potato sandwiches. Sliced melons in a container and fresh-baked blueberry muffins completed the meal.

"It seems to me every Italian associates eggs, peppers, and potatoes with eating a sandwich on the beach," Lucy said.

"I know. It sure beats peanut butter and jelly, though, on a hot summer day. Sand, salt, and these," he said, raising his sandwich, "just seem to go together."

After eating, they stuck their feet into the water, which was warm. Lucy collected a few perfect seashells.

"My grandfather drilled holes in seashells that I gathered at the beach when I was little. Then he'd thread a ribbon through them, and I'd have a necklace, or if I had a lot of small ones like these, a charm bracelet. I thought he was a magician."

They talked for well over an hour. As they were cleaning up, a young mother arrived with her three children. They returned to the house to drop off the picnic items, and Tavis took her on a tour of Sayville.

"This is the Kensington Hotel, one of the great summer tourist spots. Rumor has it that it may be torn down next year."

"Whatever for?"

"A supermarket. There were tons of summer hotels here at one time. Sayville was a big resort town. A lot of boarding houses too."

"There's my high school," Tavis said. "Old Eighty-Eight."

"Will you go to your tenth high school reunion?" Lucy asked.

"I will if I can. I had a great time in high school."

"Mmm. Just like my brother, Dan, I'll bet."

"I can't wait to meet him."

"I can't wait until he's home so I can introduce you."

A powerful wireless station built by Kaiser Wilhelm of Germany had been erected in West Sayville in 1911.

"For many years, Sayville was the only spot for wireless communication between America and Europe," Tavis informed Lucy. "There was a station in Germany, and messages were sent in German code."

"No kidding."

Tavis nodded. "In fact, when a code was deciphered, they realized it said that the Luistania had passed by Sayville. That's when the president, I think it was Wilson, confiscated the towers. Now they belong to the FAA, which uses them for international flights."

"Wow. A piece of history right in your little town."

They reached Main Street, which was now open for business.

"Hey, Tom. How're you doing?" asked a man in overalls and cap exiting Heinlein Hardware Store.

"Hi, Mr. Siddon. Great, thanks."

"Congratulations on your success."

The smell of fresh bread drifted from the Fritsche's bakery, and the five and dime was setting out a table with items reduced to two cents.

"Really can't beat this," said Lucy, fingering a doll in a hula skirt.

At the corner soda fountain, Tavis headed over to the penny candy table. Taking a paper bag, he began tossing in Tootsie Roll Midgets, Mary Janes, wax bottles, licorice, and big red wax lips.

"How ya doin', Tom?" asked the woman behind the counter. "Wantin' a coffee hot fudge sundae? It's on the house for the big-shot movie star."

"The big-shot movie star can afford to pay for his own," said a voice from a booth.

Tavis turned. "Hey, Mr. Keenan. How are you?" He went over and shook the man's hand. "How's Deb and Alan?"

"Great. Deb has a baby daughter and Alan's at Cornell."

"That's good news."

"So, Tom, who's the pretty lady on your arm?" asked the counter woman.

"Oh, I'm sorry. Fran, this is Lucy Salvatori. Lucy, Fran, our sweet shoppe owner."

Fran walked over to the candy table.

"Here, little lady. This guy has a reputation." She handed Lucy a Sugar Daddy lollipop.

"That's not nice, Fran. I'm trying to win her affections, and my own townspeople are spreading rumors about me."

They moved down the block to the Beers Confectioners, where giant glass showcases displayed shelves of chocolate-dipped nuts, raisins, coconut, almond bark, creams, caramels, jellies, and more.

"Want something?" Tavis asked.

"I couldn't. I'm stuffed."

"They make homemade ice cream here. It's softer than regular ice cream and my favorite ice cream in the whole world. Hey, Joe!" he called out. "What's the freezer-fresh flavor today?"

"Peach. How ya doing, Tom? Ma'am?" he added, nodding. "Get you something?"

"I'd love to try it but some other time."

"I'll hold you to that," Tavis said, squeezing her to him.

"Your town is charming," Lucy said honestly. "What I like best is that you're just Tom DiGregorio here."

"No place like home to chop off the throne legs."

"It's picturesque and kept up beautifully."

"That's the Village Improvement Society. My mom is a member."

"Tom!" called a woman behind a fence. "Tom, dear. Good to see you. I loved the movie. Any talk of an Oscar nomination?"

"I doubt that, Mrs. Stahlberg."

"Well, it's an oversight if you don't get one. Here," she said, reaching over the fence. "A consolation prize." She handed over several figs that she had been picking from the tree.

As they continued walking, Tavis remarked, "More like a booby prize."

"What do you mean?"

"I loathe figs."

"No! Don't say it. I adore figs. My whole family adores figs!"

"What can I say? I'd sooner wear a fig leaf than eat a fig."

"Hmmn. Very interesting."

"Want to test me on that?"

"Oh no, you don't. Why are we stopping?" Lucy asked.

"This is the former John E. Roosevelt Estate, Meadowcroft. He was the nephew of President Teddy Roosevelt, who visited here several times."

"Very impressive. Quite a lot of history packed into such a small town."

They meandered along and eventually headed south again toward the Great South Bay. Tucked in a cove of trees with the water glinting streamers of brilliant sunlight at the windows, a small restaurant sat hidden from the unknowing passersby. A lazy fan circled above a small room with wooden floors and wooden tables. The room led to an open deck where a few more tables were located. Tavis led Lucy here, where a waitress was cleaning off the one open table.

"I'm glad we can sit outside where we can smell the water and hear the seagulls flying overhead."

"Are you sure they don't dive-bomb the tables?" Lucy asked as a particularly loud squawk caused her to check overhead.

"You're such a city girl."

"Maybe, but Hollywood news just reached the country. That waitress is tripping over herself telling the other one that you're here."

"Oh boy."

The girl returned bearing two menus, a shy smile, and a flustered manner.

"Hi, my name is Kristin. Can I get you something to drink?"

"I'll have a beer. Whatever's on tap. Lucy?"

"An iced tea, please."

"Here are your magazines. I mean, menus. I'll be back in a few minutes to order you…uh, take your order. Jeez! You're Tavis Gregg, aren't you?" she finally burst.

"Yes, Kristin."

She smiled vacantly and returned inside.

"Not Tom to the younger set, I see."

"She must be in high school, right? I'm too old for her to know me from around. I'm having the clams on a half shell. They're the best in the country."

"You don't say?"

"Really. Sayville used to be the premier oyster fishing town, but now it's clams. The best. Try them."

"I'm not overly fond of raw clams."

"Have the Cove's clam chowder. There's nothing else like it."

They placed their orders and chatted amiably through the soup and clams.

"Try one of mine," Tavis insisted.

"I'd rather not. I know what they taste like."

"These are special. They're like a kiss sliding down your gullet."

"Well, there's an appetizing review for you," Lucy said with a laugh.

Tavis held one up to her lips.

"That's not exactly what I'd want sliding down my gullet," Lucy persisted.

"Oh? OK, then. I'll remember that for later."

"Bad boy."

As they passed by the Edwards homestead on Edwards Street, Lucy leaned in to Tavis.

"We're being followed."

"Huh?"

"There's a posse of girls behind us. I just hope they're not armed."

Tavis stopped and turned. The girls jammed into each other in a fit of giggles and squeals.

"How are you all doing?" Tavis asked.

One bold blonde stepped forward. "Hi, Tom. Don't you remember me? I'm Jeremy Reiss's sister, Peggy."

"Oh yes. Haven't you grown up! Are you at Sayville High School?"

"I'll be a senior this year."

"Well, lots of luck."

"Can we have an autograph?" one small girl with glasses and a ponytail asked.

"Sure. Do you have something I can write on?"

After signing one handkerchief, five strips of paper ripped from the pages of a magazine, and an eyeglass case, Tavis obliged one saucy bobby-soxer by also signing her upper arm.

As they continued on their way, Lucy commented. "If girls are asking you to sign body parts in Sayville, I can't imagine what's going on in California."

"Actually, it's more laidback there. Movie people walking around are as commonplace as fireworks on the Fourth of July. Nobody gives you a second glance."

"Hard to believe."

They returned to Tavis's house, where his father had just finished mowing the lawn.

"Dad, I'd like you to meet Lucy Salvatori. Lucy, this is my Dad, John Di Gregorio."

"A pleasure," they said in unison.

"I would have mowed the grass for you," Tavis scolded.

"It's just about the only exercise I get anymore. I'm going to finish up a little trimming and take a shower. Your mother started preparing a raspberry shortcake when she came home on her break. She wants to sit with you two when she gets back."

"Great. We'll be out back."

Tavis led Lucy to the yard, where he pointed out the raspberry bushes that the berries came from. "Ugly-looking things, but they produce fantastic raspberries. When my mother doesn't feel like using them, she picks pints and sells them to the confectioner. They dip them in chocolate."

"Sounds delicious."

Tavis picked one and led her to a hammock suspended between two maple trees. Sitting on the hammock, he turned to Lucy and said, "Open your mouth."

"Why?"

"Just do it."

She obliged, and he put a raspberry between his lips and on a breath of air shot it into her mouth. Lucy stopped it with the back of her tongue before it tumbled down her throat.

"Are you trying to choke me?" she gasped.

"Just checking how agile that gullet of yours is," he teased. "Let's see if we can both squeeze into this thing," he said, nudging her to turn sideways.

Side by side he rocked them gently, with one leg dangling over the side. He gave her a gentle kiss, and Lucy sighed.

"What's next on your plate, Tavis?" she asked.

"I'm leaving for Rome to film a movie. It's named *IX Times IX.* At least it is right now."

"What's it about?"

"It's a romantic adventure. Intrigue, a great chase sequence on a Roman train, a missing masterpiece, and lots of kisses."

"Who's the lucky lady? Is Audrey Hepburn skipping around Rome again?"

"I wouldn't mind that, but I doubt it."

"She's adorable. I loved *Roman Holiday.*"

"She's adorable, but you're spectacular. I'd love a Roman holiday with you. Would you join me for part of the time?"

"You're not serious?"

"You bet I am."

"I couldn't possibly. First of all, there's my work. Second, my father would kill me."

"How old are you?"

"Almost twenty-three, thank you, which makes absolutely no difference in an Italian family, as you well know. I missed my senior prom because no date met my father's approval. I truly doubt he'll wish me *bon voyage* as I go traipsing through Rome with an actor."

"Not just any actor. Me. Who is falling in love with his daughter."

"Oh," Lucy said weakly.

Tavis turned, and their bodies collided in the concave center of the hammock. Holding her face, he kissed in the raspberry-sweetened depths of her mouth. He kissed the lobe of her ear and the tip of her nose. His hand traveled to her breast, and Lucy was helpless to resist in the afternoon sun.

"Come with me," he repeated.

"I can't, Tavis. I have pupils and classes at Julliard. I have…stop it!" she whispered as his hand traveled under her dress. "We're outside, and you have neighbors behind not very high hedges. And your father is home and…"

Tavis withdrew his hand and kissed her deeply once again. He kissed each eyelid till they burned. "I'm imprinting myself on your eyes, Lucy, so whenever you close them, it's me you see. I may be in Rome, and you may be in Brooklyn, but when you go to bed at night, it's me you'll see. I may be in Hollywood, and you may be in Manhattan, but when you rest for a moment, I'll be before you. I won't let you forget about me. Promise you won't try."

"It would be a little hard to forget about Tavis Gregg."

Chapter 31

"Ma?" Giuliana prodded her mother, who had stopped midsentence. Her eyes looked vacant. "Ma? You bought the dried figs at..."

Anna snapped back. "Fi..figs. I buy..." She closed her eyes and keeled over.

"Ma!" Giuliana screamed, catching her before she fully tumbled to the floor. Laying her on the kitchen floor, she grabbed the phone and called the operator for an ambulance. She then called Rinaldo, who was home on this November Sunday morning. He arrived in his car just as the ambulance pulled up, and they followed it to the hospital. Anna was whisked into the emergency room, and Rinaldo called the opera house, where he knew Lucy was working with the new conductor.

"Lucy." Valentino touched her arm gently. "Your father is on the phone. He needs to talk to you."

"Ask him if I can call him back. We're just…"

"Lucy," Val repeated. "It's your grandmother."

Lucy turned in a flash and with Val at her heels entered Phil's office. "Maestro?" she said into the receiver.

She cradled the receiver and faced Val who was hovering nearby.

"My grandmother is in the hospital. They think it's a stroke. I have to go. Give Ignacio my apologies. I have to go." She scrambled about for her purse. "Do you have a token for the subway? I don't have a token. I have to buy one. Where's my wallet?" She started fishing through the opened bag.

"Lucy. Take a deep breath. You're not taking the subway. I'm calling a cab. I'm going with you. Sit down." He physically grasped her shoulders and put her into the chair. "I'm calling the cab, and I'm telling everyone we're leaving. I'll make sure Ed has the key to lock up."

Lucy nodded. "I'll pray," she said aloud, reassuring herself with a purpose.

* * *

Anna's own grandmother, Calogera, had emigrated from Sicily to Florence when she was a young woman. She liked the city well enough, its architecture, culture, and shops, but she never really lost the ache in her heart for Santa Margherita, the little town where she was born. Grinding poverty had sent her parents fleeing from the rugged mountains that bore testimony to the people's strength and survival. The lush golden fields, grapes the size of your eyeballs, and olives dancing among the silver leaves of their trees were just a few of the sights no longer at hand to soothe her soul. Florence may have been sophisticated, but Sicily was intoxicating.

Calogera eventually fell in love and married, her kitchen an altar to her Sicilian upbringing. Among her recipes, the most cherished was *cucciddati,* traditionally prepared for the Christmas season. She gathered the dried figs, raisins, and nuts, both almonds and filberts. She mixed in the family ingredients of chocolate, honey, spices, and a homemade orange marmalade, complaining all the while that the oranges in Santa Margherita were as big as the rising sun and these Florentine marbles could not be expected to do the job. With a flick of her wrist, a dash of black pepper settled on the mixture. All that was left was the *vincotto,* the thick sweet syrup made from the homestyle pressing of grapes and aged in oak barrels. Her supply had traveled with the family from Sicily, and when it ran out, she'd have to search out a new source. She rolled out her dough, filled it with the fig mixture, etched cuttings on the top, and baked tray after tray. She passed along the recipe to her daughter, but it was her granddaughter Anna, who, with sticky hands and muscle power to grind the dried figs, stood on a bench next to the table and perfected the technique. *Giusta, giusta,* the Sicilian tradition became the centerpiece of the Florentine household through the ages. "After all," as Calogera used to tell little Anna, "Italy is shaped like a boot because it had to take its first steps on Sicily."

* * *

When they reached the emergency room, they were ushered immediately inside. The nurse looked grim but said nothing as she pointed to a small room. As they appeared in the doorway, Maestro rushed over. Lucy could hear her mother crying inside.

"She is gone, *cara.* Nonna Anna is gone. She had a massive stroke."

Lucy shook her head. "Noooo, noo…" She ran to her mother's side and enveloped her in a hug.

"Lucy, Lucy, my mother is gone."

"I know, Ma." She stepped around her mother, who was sitting on the bed, and kissed her grandmother's forehead.

"She was planning her fig cookies. She bought the figs…somewhere. We were planning the date to do it."

"OK, Ma."

"We'll have to make the cookies, Lucy. She'll be mad if we don't make the cookies for Christmas. She was going to freeze some for when Dan and Phil get home. That's why she bought so many extra figs this year. For Dan and Phil…" Her voice drifted off into another stream of sobs.

"We'll make the cookies, Ma. We'll do it."

Could they possibly taste the same without her grandmother's stories of the *cucciddati*?

* * *

Valentino stood by Lucy's side, arm around her shoulders as they entered the room in the funeral parlor to view her grandmother's body. Lucy had volunteered to be the first to inspect the handiwork of the funeral parlor's cosmetician, to determine if her grandmother looked "natural." She moved forward on wobbly legs, eyes focused on the raised lid of the casket, avoiding the body of her beloved grandmother settled within. She looked down at the softly powdered wrinkled face framed by a bonnet of white hair from which no stray wisps straggled, as had always been their wont. Anna's "good" navy-blue suit was tasteful, but…

"What is this tulle netting around her shoulders?" she asked the funeral director.

"It is traditional. It is how deceased women go onto their glory. There is no charge for it," he added as an afterthought.

"It's hideous. I don't like it."

"Ma'am, you're mistaken. It is ethereal. It's a symbol of the glories of heaven."

"I don't think my grandmother wants to enter the hereafter with something like a butterfly net wrapped around her neck."

"It's standard, ma'am."

"Remove it." Valentino's instruction was quiet yet firm.

He pulled Lucy aside and said, "Let's look at the flowers."

Lucy inspected the obligatory red rose "bleeding heart" arrangement from her parents. Tino had sent a magnificent arrangement of mixed blossoms, including Dan and Phil's name on the card. He would be arriving from Las Vegas tomorrow. Lucy looked at her own vase filled with calla lilies in respect for Nonna's devotion to her grandmother, Calogera. There were other baskets and arrangements standing on easels, but the most breathtaking was a giant wreath of lilies, roses, peonies, out-of-season tulips, berries, and autumn-colored leaves. It was from Thomas DiGregorio.

"That's that actor, isn't it?" Val whispered, not wanting to even acknowledge his name.

"Yes. Imagine him taking time out of his shooting schedule to order flowers."

"Imagine," Val said in a strained voice. "I'm guessing he had someone do it for him."

"Is this to your satisfaction, ma'am?" the director asked.

Lucy returned to the casket. "Yes, thank you." She smiled at her grandmother. "There you go, Nonna. Refined as always." She knelt on the kneeler to say a prayer with Valentino at her side.

* * *

Lucy sat beside her mother, accepting condolences while her father stood to the side deep in conversation with his brother-in-law, John Vetrano. Married for thirty-one years to Giuliana's sister, Natalia, the couple had moved to Chicago early in their marriage and had rarely visited New York in the years since. The Arditos had traveled to the Windy City several times in their younger years, especially to see their grandchildren, Clotilda and Johnny, but eventually the visits had tapered to a trickle and the connection was maintained via telephone and photographs.

It was the biggest heartbreak of her parents' life. Giuliana resented her sister's neglect and disinterest and was surprised they had managed to pay their final respects to Anna. She had already endured minute descriptions of Natalia's latest decorating projects in their home in one of the ritziest sections of Chicago. Gratefully, as Natalia continued to babble about a tennis match, Giuliana focused on Jimmy, who arrived at the casket and was praying at the kneeler. When he rose, he opened an eight-by-eleven briefcase, unfolding four legs within. This produced a small stepstool made of wood that stood about a foot off the ground. He could now look into the face of Nonna Anna, who had been so kind to him through the years.

* * *

Even though they were both twelve years old, Lucy having had a birthday the week before, Nonna Anna held both their hands as they crossed the busy Manhattan street after they emerged from the subway. A quiet family celebration was all the party Lucy had wanted on the actual day. Her father wouldn't have permitted her to invite Jimmy to a birthday party, so she chose to do without. Nonna Anna promised her a day in the city, with Jimmy in tow, and now they were headed to Radio City Music Hall to see a movie and the Rockettes.

It was Jimmy's first trip to the grand theater, and he skipped about in awe of the murals, sculptures, draperies, and chandeliers. It seemed to him the massiveness of the house would make anyone feel small. When the Mighty Wurlitzer pipe organ materialized in its showcase corner, he could feel the vibration of its music through his bones. The Rockettes were dazzling, and if there was a dwarf or two running around on the stage, he could only congratulate them for their magnificent venue.

Afterward Nonna took them, by the hand of course, to the Horn and Hardet Automat. There, loaded with a handful of nickels, they made their choices. Not to be deprived the fun of slipping his own coins in the slots and turning the handle, Jimmy dragged a chair from window to window making his choices. A manager came toward him, and Nonna gave him a stare that dared him to interrupt the little boy. Both children chose macaroni and cheese and milk chocolate. Nonna had chicken potpie, the famous baked beans, and creamed spinach. Waiting on a tray was lemon meringue pies all around.

"Try the beans," Nonna insisted. "They are delicious."

"I don't like beans," Jimmy said.

"You've never had any like this. Here, Lucy, taste."

Lucy opened her mouth. "They *are* good," she told Jimmy.

"OK. I'll get my own," he said, sticking his fork in Nonna's beans.

"Well?" Nonna inquired.

"Good."

"See. You have to give things a chance."

"Lucy's father won't give me a chance. He hates me. He always has. I don't know why." He said it matter-of-factly, but Nonna detected a note of pain in his voice.

"He doesn't hate you, Jimmy. He just doesn't know you. He doesn't really see you."

"How can he not see him?" Lucy asked defiantly. "He's not *that* little."

"Let me tell you a story. Where I grew up in Florence, there is a building called Orsanmichele. It was a giant grain market. Then it was converted into a church for the trade guilds." "What are guilds?" asked Jimmy, sipping from his straw.

"Like a union. You've heard of unions?"

"Uh-huh," he nodded.

"Now mind you, this is all hundreds of years before I was born."

"Some old building."

"You might say," said Nonna resignedly. "Anyway, on the outside of the building, there were these niches. The city told the guilds to commission artists to sculpt statues of their patron saints to display in the niches. The linen weavers commissioned Donatello…"

"Who's Donatello?"

"A very famous artist and sculptor. They asked Donatello to sculpt a statue of St. Mark, who was their patron."

"Didn't St. Mark write a gospel? What does he have to do with linen?" Jimmy asked, taking another forkful of beans.

"Yeah. Shouldn't it be like John the Baptist? He walked around in only that loincloth thing. He could have used some linen," Lucy observed with glee.

The two friends went into howls of laughter.

"All right. Forget the story. Forget about Maestro."

"I'm sorry, Nonna. I want to hear the story," Jimmy apologized.

"So. Donatello was very smart. He looked at the final setting where the statue would be placed. It was very high up. So he changed the proportions on the statue."

"What does that mean?" Lucy asked.

"Maybe he made the hands too small, or the nose too wide or the head too big. Why, you may ask?" Nonna continued, beating them to the punch. "Because when it was raised high above the street, the perspective would be different. Then all those features that were distorted would look perfect. But when the linen merchants came to view the sculpture in Donatello's studio, they thought it was grotesque. He had created a monster. They refused to put it in the niche and told him he had to fix it. Donatello knew they didn't understand about looking at things in perspective, so he covered up his statue for a few weeks and then under cover of darkness he had it placed in the niche himself. He then called the guild members to see it. From where they stood on street level, it looked perfect. He said they had to pay him extra for the additional work, and they happily did. They never realized it was the exact same statue. They had just been standing too close to it to really see it."

"OK, Nonna. That's a nice story, but what does it mean?" Lucy asked.

"Yeah. I don't get it," Jimmy agreed.

"You see. Maestro is standing too close to you."

"He never gets anywhere near me."

"No. He only sees you're different. You're small. Something about that bothers him. I don't know what it is, but he associates you with it. Because of that he can't stand back and look at you from the right perspective. If he did, he'd see you are a lovely, talented, good boy who is a faithful friend to his daughter. Someday, God willing, he'll see you in your proper setting, and he will recognize the error of his ways. Until that day, you just have to realize he doesn't understand perspective. Always remember, Jimmy, it's all about perspective."

* * *

Jimmy stepped off his stool and folded it. Lucy covered her smile with her hand. He gave his condolences to Giuliana, Natalia, and then Lucy.

"What's that contraption?" she asked.

"Nick just invented it for me. Isn't it great? It looks like a briefcase except that it's wood. I can use it in all sorts of places. Like at the box office at the movies, or at the tellers at the bank. I don't go anywhere without it anymore."

"Pretty clever. He should market it."

"Maybe if there really was an Oz, he could. What's he gonna do? Go from town to town looking for little people?"

"Jimmy! Hello." Valentino extended his hand. "I read that piece you did on arts in the schools. Excellent work."

"Thanks."

"Lucy is going to be in a fund-raiser at Carnegie Hall in a couple of months. It's to raise scholarship money for Julliard, isn't it?" Val asked.

"Yes. They're contacting agents right now to get some known artists to participate."

"I'll attend. Maybe I can do a follow-up piece with benefit concerts as a fund-raiser for the public school arts program."

"The seats are going to be pretty pricey," Lucy warned.

"The paper will pay. Haven't you noticed the high lifestyle I've been leading?"

"Yeah, right," Lucy said disparagingly.

* * *

Later in the evening, the Salvatoris and Vetranos sat around the dining table drinking coffee and choosing from the buffet of desserts that had been sent over by thoughtful neighbors.

"I'm sleeping in my old bedroom tonight," Natalia mentioned. "I can't bear the thought of sleeping in Mama's bed."

"Well, I'll sleep there. I'm not squeezing into that twin-sized bed with you," John informed her. "Can someone cut me a sliver of that pumpkin pie?"

"It doesn't look anything like my room anymore," Natalia said.

"That's because Mama fixed it up for the boys so they'd be more comfortable when they slept over. My old room is pretty much the same, though, because that's where Lucy would stay."

"Well, it's all going to have to go when we sell the house. When do you want to go through Mama's things, Guiliana? I don't want any of the furniture, I can tell you. But there's plenty of other stuff to sort through."

"I really don't feel up to it right now," Giuliana said, glancing at Rinaldo with tight lips.

"Well, I can't stay here forever. I can stay a couple of days past John, but that's it. Do you have a Realtor you work with, or do we have to search one out?"

"Natalia, I wasn't thinking about selling the house immediately. What's the hurry? It's not going anywhere. You see what you're interested in taking, and I'll take my time with the rest."

"No. I want to know that action is being taken on the house. I've learned the hard way that when you leave matters to others, it never gets done."

"I wouldn't think you'd consider me 'others.'"

"You know what I mean."

"No, frankly, I don't. You haven't set foot in that house for over a quarter of a century, and now you're looking to make your mark on it."

"It's not good to make these decisions in haste," added Rinaldo, trying to put a cover on the boiling pot.

"Haste?" questioned Natalia. "Now Brooklyn is the Garden of Eden? People are falling over themselves to buy the house so we don't have to worry about it sitting like a lump of coal for months on end?"

"Are you so desperate for the money you would get for the sale?" Guiliana asked, indulging herself in a bit of cattiness.

"That's not the point," John said. "We live far away, and this would be unfinished business eight hundred miles away. We just don't run our estate that way."

Giuliana opened her mouth to retort, but Val, who had been invited to join the family after leaving the funeral parlor, intervened.

"You should know that the market isn't quite as good as it could be at the moment. Believe it or not, the Korean Conflict has had an effect on real estate prices. If you give it a bit more time, perhaps not even a year, prices will rise for sure. You could rent in the meantime. People are always looking to rent in this neighborhood. You'll have a nice monthly income and then cash in when the market swings upward."

"Valentino is an accountant, and there isn't a number he doesn't know how to analyze and coerce into a more impressive sum," Rinaldo added fondly.

"Well. I suppose that's an option. Is the house ready to be rented, or do you have to do massive restoration on it? I haven't really been inside except to drop our bags and freshen up."

"It doesn't need much in the way of repairs. Mama always kept it looking nice. If there is any painting to be done, we will handle it," Giuliana said in a calmer voice.

"Then I'll take notes in the morning when it's light and discuss it with you tomorrow. We really should be going, John," she added, rising from her seat.

"Would you care to take some of this cake back to the house with you?" Giuliana asked.

"No, thank you."

"I might. I'd like that coffee cake for breakfast," John replied.

"I'll wrap it for you," Giuliana said, jumping up and heading to the kitchen.

She returned with the cake and sniffed the air. "John! You're smoking? There's no smoking in this house. Rinaldo, why didn't you say something?"

Rinaldo shrugged and looked sheepishly at Val.

"We're leaving so you don't have to worry about the smoke in your house," Natalia said with tense fury in her voice. "C'mon, John. We'll see you all tomorrow afternoon."

"Whew," said Lucy after they had gone. "I guess it's not such a bad thing that they've never been around. Are my cousins anything like them?"

"Who knows? They're probably fat from cake and smell like smoke," Giuliana said, continuing to clear the table. "Believe me, this isn't over. The devil makes the pots but not the lids."

"What's that?" asked Tino.

"An old expression," said Rinaldo. "The devil stirs up the pot until it spills over, but leaves it to others to clean up the mess."

Val smiled at Lucy. "I've never seen your mother so pent up with anger."

"Well, you can see the sisters are very different," Lucy replied as the others scattered.

"Your mother was left to care for aging parents alone."

"Thankfully, neither Nonna nor Papi were a burden. They remained in good health and sound mind until they died."

"And your father's parents?"

"Never knew them. They lived in Italy, some small island. No one ever talks about them. It's strange. I think about it now that I'm older. Something must have happened with them. There are no stories, no memories from my father."

"That *is* strange from a man who can turn a trip to the post office into an opera."

"Exactly. Now it seems it has become a family code not to ask about it. Maybe someday."

"I'd better get going. I'm not sure I'll make it to the afternoon viewing tomorrow. I'll be there at night."

"You've done too much already, Val. Thank you for all your help." Lucy put one hand on his face and kissed his other cheek. "Even tonight. You saved the day with your real estate analysis."

"I had visions of that apple pie flying across the room." He kissed Lucy back on the cheek, and his heart leaped in his chest. "If there's anything else I can do, please don't hesitate. I'll be at the theater all day tomorrow." He squeezed Lucy's hand and left.

Chapter 32

After Sunday Mass, Giuliana, dressed in a black dress and sweater, robotically churned the figs and raisins in her mother's meat grinder. Lucy chopped the nuts and kept up a steady stream of talk about her classes, Louisa, and a guy named Casper, of all things, whom she would not be seeing again. Not unless she ever intended to take up fly-fishing, that is. She talked about the opera house and how glad she would be when Phil returned. And Dan. But they weren't back yet, and this Christmas loomed just three weeks away without any of the boys at home, Anna gone, no Christmas tree or decorations other than a wreath on the front door, which had replaced the funeral wreath, at Lucy's insistence.

"I don't know how she did this at her age," Giuliana commented, grinding away. "This is so hard to do."

"Let me take over for a while," Lucy said, moving her mother aside. Giuliana picked up a jar of orange marmalade. "Nonna's grandmother used to make her own orange marmalade for the cookies."

"Like they didn't already have enough to do back then," Lucy commented.

Giuliana picked up the bottle of *vincotto*. "After next year we'll be out of this. Then what?" she asked as if the future of Christmas depended on the answer.

"Talk to Mr. Coltri next door. He makes home-made wine. Maybe he can do whatever it is to make that stuff," Lucy suggested.

"Maybe," Giuliana said listlessly.

They worked a while longer until Lucy tired of her job.

"Hello!" greeted Maestro. "Any cookies ready yet? I can taste them already." He looked at Lucy and raised his eyebrows questioningly.

She shook her head at him.

"This is hard work."

"Maybe it's a man's work. Eh?" He took off his tie, unbuttoned the top button of his shirt, and rolled up his sleeves. He took over at the grinder and began singing a Neopolitan folk song about feeding figs to pigs and pigs to cows.

Both women watched in amazement at Maestro's first-ever foray into the kitchen. He insisted on mixing the remainder of the ingredients in with the figs and raisins while Giuliana and Lucy prepared the dough.

"OK. We should take a break before we fill the dough and bake them, no?" Maestro suggested.

"I'll prepare lunch," Giuliana said, rising and moving toward the refrigerator.

"No! I will order pizza, eh? We haven't had pizza in a long time. Then tonight the three of us will go out to dinner. But we'll come home for dessert. Fig cookies!"

Lucy smiled at her father. "Wonderful idea, Maestro. Maybe afterward, Ma, you can play the piano, and Maestro and I will sing."

"We'll see," said Giuliana, inexplicably fascinated by the blob of fig filling on her husband's shirt.

* * *

After dinner on Christmas Day, Louisa, Joe, and Val all came by for a visit and a cup of coffee. The fig cookies, prominently displayed on a three-tiered dish, sat alongside Lucy's first attempt at cheesecake and Maestro's purchase of spumoni. Louisa brought a box of homemade chocolate-covered cherries from a confectioner a few doors down from the hospital. Joe was liberally splashing the bottle of "special" sambuco he had brought into the espresso, while Val's foot-long bar of *torrone,* a nougat candy, was cut into pieces.

"I love *torrone,*" Lucy said, popping another piece into her mouth.

"I know. You've mentioned it," said Val.

"How is your family, Val?" Giuliana asked.

"Great. There's a mob of relatives at the apartment. Too many for the size of the rooms. It's good to get away for a while."

"Never complain about being too crowded with family," Giuliana advised.

"I'm not complaining. I'm just catching my breath." *And feasting my eyes,* he thought, looking at Lucy, pretty in a black skirt and red and white striped blouse.

The doorbell rang, and Lucy rose to answer it.

"Hi, Jimmy. Merry Christmas."

"Merry Christmas to you, doll."

"Doll? What's with that?"

"I thought it sounded suave."

"It sounds like you're looking for a joint to roll dice in."

"Oh. Then forget I said it. Here," he said, handing her a small package.

"I have yours inside. Come on in."

Jimmy hesitated. "Just here in front," he said, stepping through the doorway.

"Come into the parlor. There's no tree this year, but that's where the gifts are." She retrieved his package. "There weren't too many presents this year. Mom didn't feel like shopping or receiving, so we kept it simple. Maestro bought her a fantastic royal-blue dress and said there are only thirty days to return it, so she has to try it on. If it fits, he gives her one week to wear it."

"He's forcing her out of the mourning clothes."

Lucy nodded. "I'm so glad. Here. Open."

Lucy's gift was a pink neckerchief with small black music notes scattered on it. "I love this, Jimmy. Thank you. I have a pink sweater it will go with perfectly."

"Wow!" said Jimmy, opening his box. There were four-dozen clear-barreled, smooth Bic ballpoint pens.

"They're guaranteed non-leaking. I read that the ballpoint pen has finally been mastered."

"This is great. I'll always be prepared, and I don't have to worry about a fountain pen leaking or my pencil points breaking. Thanks, Luce."

Lucy looked across the entryway into the dining room, where five mismatched people sat. She picked a pillow off the couch and said, "C'mon inside and try a fig cookie. Ma and I made them for the first time by ourselves."

"For real?" Jimmy asked, holding back.

"Like you said, Jimmy. We have to grow up sometime." They crossed over and entered the room. "Everyone knows Jimmy, right? Oh, maybe not Uncle Joe. Joe, this is my lifelong friend Jimmy Ferraro. Jimmy this is Joe Gallino, managing director at the opera house."

"Only until Phil gets home. Then I'm semi-retiring. How do you do?" he asked, extending his hand.

"Hi, Jimmy," and "Merry Christmas," circled the table, except for Maestro, who nodded his head at the visitor.

"Ma, Jimmy wants to taste our cookies," Lucy announced as she plopped the pillow on a chair Giuliana dragged in from the kitchen. Lucy waited, while all arms and backside, Jimmy lifted himself onto the chair. She then pushed the chair closer to the table.

"These are gorgeous, Mrs. Salvatori. Much prettier than the ones my mom buys at the bakery," Jimmy said, inspecting the cookie. He took a bite. "Wow. That's fantastic. Those bakery things don't even come close. I wonder why my mother never made them."

"They're a ton of work. In fact, even Maestro had to pitch in to help," Lucy said.

"Good job, Maestro," Jimmy said, toasting him with the bitten cookie.

"Thank you," Maestro said stiffly.

"I'd sure have liked to see that," chuckled Joe. "Tell me, did you order the ingredients to blend harmoniously, or did you merely threaten that they would not make an appearance at your table if they didn't get their act together?"

"I beat them to death with everything in me," Maestro replied with a smirk.

"Sometimes that's what it takes, Maestro. You have to beat something into some people's heads," Jimmy said reaching for another cookie.

"Or out of it," Giuliana added, looking Maestro in the eye.

Afterward as they said good night, Jimmy told Lucy, "Remember when I went to the Golden Gloves as a kid? Well, I felt like I was fighting for my life in there tonight."

"Oh, I'm sorry you felt that way, Jimmy. But you know what? I think you won round one."

* * *

On a clear February 1954 day, the royal-blue dress made its appearance when Dan arrived home from overseas. Over an especially requested meal of lasagna with meatballs, fried veal cutlets with broccoli rape, stuffed mushrooms, salad with plenty of olives, and crisp Italian bread, the family set their stage of renewal and thanksgiving. Dan didn't speak much about Korea; he was a bit more forthcoming about Tokyo. Louisa asked about geishas, whom he denied visiting, and she believed him from the way he kept grasping her hand and leg under the table.

The scene was repeated four weeks later, different menu, Tino added to the table, when Phil returned home. Giuliana gazed at animated faces around her dining-room table. Talking, teasing, taunting each other as though the last two years had never intervened.

"An Allelulia day," she whispered to herself as she carried yet another culinary offering to the table. Although buried under domestic chores, Giuliana ecstatically floated about the house. She even found time to go downtown Brooklyn to buy another new dress for Phil's first night back at the opera house. The family would be sitting in their box, except for Dan, who was in the orchestra section with Louisa, her parents, and two sisters. Just before the bows, Dan leaned over and whispered to Louisa.

"Phil is signaling me to come backstage. Something is up."

Immediately after the bows, Phil stepped from the wings.

"Good evening, everyone. It is so good to see all of you and be back home in this theater. I look forward to working with my father and everyone else at the opera house to bring you the wonderful music that you love. If you can spend a little time with us this evening, there will be refreshments set up in the lobby as a 'Damn, I'm glad to be back' celebration. But if you'll remain seated, you'll learn there's another reason the Salvatoris are celebrating tonight."

Phil walked off stage right and the curtains opened. The entire cast of the evening's *Don Giovanni* stepped forward in chorus line formation. Dressed in velvet and antique satin breeches, capes and waistcoats, leggings, jeweled bodices, and dresses with fringed hems, the cast belted out Maurice Chevalier's 1929 hit, "Louise." Halfway through, they broke into a comical kick line as the music soared, and Louisa realized that the "whispering breezes and twittering birds" of the song were actually singing for her. The audience roared and applauded enthusiastically before hushing as if on cue when a newly tuxedoed Dan walked center stage.

"While overseas, the only peace of mind I found was in thoughts of my family and the girl back home.

As Don Ottavio so beautifully expressed a short while ago on this stage, 'what pleases my love gives life to me and what grieves her wounds me to the heart.' Louisa," he said, now getting down on bended knee, "unless we share our days and join our lives, I cannot know happiness. Louisa, will you marry me?"

The audience erupted, and Louisa's hands flew to her red, tearstained cheeks. While her parents clung to each other, her sisters jumped up and down and hollered. Lucy stood in the family box waving one hand at Dan and one at Louisa, neither seeing her. Tino ran downstairs and escorted Louisa to the stage. Once in Dan's arms, she whispered her acceptance.

"She said yes!" Dan shouted. Phil came running onto the stage carrying a sack. From it he withdrew a ball and chain, which he attached to Dan's ankle. As the audience applauded, the cast withdrew, singing "Louise," giving the newly engaged couple a few moments of privacy when the curtain closed.

"Wasn't that incredibly romantic?" Lucy asked no one in particular.

"I knew it was coming," said Mike Livalli, Louisa's father, "but I didn't expect an entire production."

"That had Felice Salvatori written all over it," said Lucy.

"Oh, great," groaned Maestro. "He's home a couple of weeks, and my theater is already renowned for a Felice Salvatori production!"

"Never mind that," said Dan, joining the group with Louisa flashing her one-carat diamond ring. "I chose the song. Phil did change it from a serenade, though, since I refused to be the one to sing it after these people had just heard such grand voices. I'm so relieved Louisa is happy and not mortified," he added, squeezing her close.

"I told you she'd love it. We haven't been friends forever for nothing. And now we'll be sisters," Lucy rejoiced, dashing over to give Louisa a hug and kiss.

"You can have her," Lori, the next sister in line joked. "Maybe then I can find my own shoes and makeup when I want them."

"You're a lucky man, Dan," said Val, slapping him on the back.

"Isn't it time you started settling down, Val?" asked Dan.

"I'd like nothing better."

"You have to get out there more," Lucy told him. "You're not going to meet anyone with your nose in those books all day long."

"Maybe if your nose wasn't in those movie magazines all the time, you might notice someone for yourself too," Val said with a bit more bitterness in his voice than he intended.

"Touché," Lucy said with a bow. "We're both misfits. Here comes Phil with champagne. Great job, Phil," Lucy congratulated as she ran over to help him.

Val picked up two glasses and handed one to Lucy when she was through serving. "Here, Lucy. Let's toast each other. May this misfit be more bold and that misfit," indicating Lucy with his flute, "be less blind."

"C'mon then. Let's go mingle out front," Lucy suggested, linking her arm through Val's. "Maybe our intendeds are nibbling on a piece of cheese while we're standing backstage."

* * *

Two weekends later, the plans for the wedding reception were the main topic of conversation among the Livallis and Salvatoris. Millie Lavalli put out an elaborate spread of foods to pick on while they discussed the arrangements.

"This artichoke spread is delicious," Giuliana said sincerely. "If it's not a family secret, I would love the recipe."

"I'm so glad you like it. Louisa has told me what a wonderful cook you are."

"My wife is a wonderful cook too, as you can tell from my stomach," said a jovial Mike Lavalli, patting his round belly.

"A man lifting heavy garbage pails all day long needs his energy," Millie confided.

"The children have looked at several catering halls for the reception. I know they like the Regency, but I'm afraid that's a bit out of my pocket's depth. I have two more weddings to think about," Mike explained, nodding his head at Louisa's sisters, Lori and Lettie. "So we're looking at the Palm Garden and one hundred guests, not counting our immediate families. That's fifty guests apiece. How does that sound?"

"I would be happy to contribute toward the reception. They can have it at the Regency, and you can invite more guests," Maestro interjected.

"Thank you, but no. This is my daughter, and I will provide the party. I must insist."

Maestro started to object when Giuliana grasped his forearm. "There are certain things the groom's family pays for by tradition, though, no?"

"I suppose," replied Millie.

"Yes. The flowers, Maestro. You can buy the flowers. And the rehearsal dinner," Dan offered.

"Our pleasure," Giuliana said with a smile.

"Please let me provide the music also. I know so many people," Maestro solicited.

"Well...," Mike stalled.

"That is very kind of you. Of course, we bow to your superior knowledge of music," Millie acquiesced.

"Again, I know a lot of people, so if you'd like to invite more than fifty...," Maestro continued.

The proud sanitation man stood up. "I can't allow that, Maestro Salvatori. I will provide the best I can for my daughters. Each, God willing, will have their father give them away on that blessed day, and then celebrate at the party I can throw for them."

"That's a beautiful sentiment," Giuliana said, squeezing Maestro's arm for silence.

"Come. The coffee is ready. Louisa baked an apple pie, and Lettie made cookies. Two kinds."

"Oh my, Dan. You'd better watch out. Sounds like these Lavalli women want to fatten you up," Giuliana teased.

After coffee the parents went inside to watch Ed Sullivan while the young women and Dan headed to the kitchen to clean up.

Dan was putting a stack of dishes back in the cabinet when he almost dropped them.

"Oh! With all the reception talk, I forgot to tell you! I've been offered a job at WKAD. My own radio show! Get this...Dazzlin' Dan's Dynamite Chart Toppers."

"For real, Dan?" Louisa said, swinging from the sink and getting suds in Lettie's face. "That's wonderful. My husband, a disc jockey."

"Yeah. There are great sponsors on board already too. Jell-O Instant Pudding, Brylcreem, 'a little dab'll do ya,' and Anacin."

"For 'Fast Fast Fast Relief' from listening to your show?" Lucy kidded.

"For fast, fast money in the pocket for the station. I get to play all the latest hits, but I can play older chart toppers too. I love how the station is saying the program will run."

"What's with the call letters of the station… WKAD. Cad? Did they choose you specifically?" teased Louisa, drying her hands with a towel.

Dan grabbed her arm and drew her to him. "Don't even kid about that anymore, Lou. Not when we're in front of your sisters, in front of others, or even when we're alone. That was then. I've grown up. All I want and need is you. Are you clear on that?"

Louisa nodded breathlessly.

"Now the three of you can either go inside and watch television, or you can take a seat at the kitchen table and watch me kiss Louisa until she thoroughly gets what I'm saying," Dan said to the three young women standing agape.

Hastily they retreated from the kitchen.

"Oh my God," Lori whispered. "He is so dashing."

"And on the radio. I wonder if he can get me to meet Eddie Fisher," added Lettie.

* * *

In the car driving home, Maestro grumbled, "I do not understand why he will not let me help make the reception more elaborate."

"Everything isn't an opera, Maestro," Dan said from the backseat.

"But I know so many people. They will be insulted not to be invited to my firstborn's wedding."

"I'm sure if you explain that it's an intimate party, no feelings will be hurt," Giuliana soothed.

"A hundred people isn't that small," Lucy added.

"Poof," Maestro said, blowing air. "We get fifty. That doesn't cover friends and family. Forget about the theater and business acquaintances."

"Well, I can guarantee Natalia and the Chicago brigade won't bother showing up, so that's an extra six spots right there."

"Louisa asked me to be a bridesmaid, so even I won't count as family," Lucy announced.

"You didn't count anyway. He said in addition to family," Maestro reminded them. "I feel embarrassed. It is too lowkey. There is no glamour."

"Rinaldo. The glamour is in the sentiment of the day. In the vows being exchanged, and the promises being made. For once in your life, forget about production value. Mike is a proud man. He has worked hard to provide for his family. He lifts garbage cans all day. This will probably be the most glamorous thing he's ever done in his life. Don't even think about snatching it away from him."

Maestro sighed as he parked the car in front of the house. "You are right, of course." They climbed out of the car. "How many floral arrangements do you think the altar at St. Mary's can hold?"

Chapter 33

"Why do you have a Nativity set out in August?" Maestro asked as he watched Giuliana rearrange pieces on the window seat of the parlor window.

"I'm just deciding if it's shown to its best advantage here."

"Ever since Phil brought it back from Germany, you're like a little girl with a dollhouse. You're going to wear it out before Christmas."

"Isn't it just beautiful? I've always wanted a *presipio.* Even though he bought it in Germany, it was crafted in Naples."

"I know. Phil told us. You told me," Rinaldo said, sitting down with his newspaper.

Giuliana tapped her fingernail on a low-lying house. “When will we tell Dan and Louisa about the house, Rinaldo? I’m bursting with the secret.”

“You said they are coming for Sunday dinner. We’ll tell them then.”

“I hope Louisa is happy with the news.”

“What’s not to be happy? We’re giving them a house as a wedding present,” Rinaldo said with a snort as he folded the newspaper.

“Who’s getting a house?” asked Phil, entering the room.

Giuliana moved from the window. “All right. We’ll tell you, but don’t ruin the surprise. We bought Aunt Natalia’s half of Nonna Anna’s house, and we’re giving Dan and Louisa the house as a gift.”

“Wow. That’s cool. To keep the house in the family, I mean.” He thought for a moment. “Aren’t there tenants right now?”

“Yes. Their lease is up in February. So Dan and Louisa will have to stay somewhere else for three months.”

“They can stay here in Dan’s room if they want,” Giuliana said.

“I’m never getting that room, am I?” Phil kidded.

“You’re almost twenty-seven with a good job. You can get your own room if you want,” Maestro suggested.

"Shush, you," Giuliana said. "You stay here until you settle down and get married."

"We'll see, Ma. Speaking of the job…I wanted to go over my thoughts for next season, and I haven't had a chance at the theater."

"Fine. Let's go inside, and leave your mother to her dolls."

In the music room, Phil shuffled some papers. "While I was in Germany, I had the good luck to see Wagner's *The Ring of Nibelung*. It's a series of four epic operas. Unfortunately, I missed the third one, but…"

"I know what it is. I'm not interested."

"Maestro, it was terrific! I loved it. Something really different. You have to draw people in nowadays. Broadway musicals are taking over. This is a fantasy based on Norse myth—"

"No."

"What's the matter with you? There are heroes and gods, mythical creatures, and a magic ring that grants domination over the world. It's a saga of generations. The music is incredibly rich, and with each ring cycle it gets more complex. I'd think you'd be falling over yourself to produce something like this."

"Let's do *Aida* again. People loved it."

"You're going to have to do better than that. Every character, object, emotion, whatever, has its own theme music. I was swept away. One of my buddies came with me one night. The guy doesn't know opera from a hole in the wall, and he loved it."

"It is an opera I swore I'd never do."

"No. That's unacceptable. I'm not Uncle Joe. I want reasons."

* * *

Rinaldo was in his last year at the Conservatory of Milan. He had sung many leads and supporting roles during his studies, and was well loved by the audiences who attended these productions. The adulation was amusing; the girls and women who threw themselves at him were satisfying. The energy that possessed him when he inhabited a character would produce a volcanic transformation in his soul. Yet amidst the congratulations or jealousies of others for his having been chosen to sing Siegfried in the *Ring*, Rinaldo nursed serious reservations. Neither the director nor his professors would honor his disquietude. Hence, he set about his tenure as Siegfried, the adopted son of Mime, the evil dwarf, who had rescued the infant Siegfried. Rinaldo understood the opera's plot, yet in his own heart he faulted Siegfried for allowing all the beasts of the world to mean more to him than his father, Mime.

Rinaldo knew that Mime was depicted as a despicable character. Roberto, who portrayed Mime, did not truly resemble the twisted, shrunken figure when he was out of makeup and costume. While members of the company joked and played tricks on the small-statured Roberto, Rinaldo hurried away, feeling sick to his stomach. When the dwarf playing Alberich and other real-life dwarfs took to the stage during rehearsal, Rinaldo reclused himself to a backstage room or outdoors, not to hear the laughs and hooting that went on amongst the company audience. Rinaldo struggled through his scenes with Mime, and by opening night, he felt himself in a panic. He had begged his parents not to attend, and they had promised they wouldn't. Through the years they had seen only two of the operas Rinaldo had appeared in since the trip to Milan was long.

Rinaldo made his entrance and sang. He was in a cold sweat; the lights blinded him. The emotions were wrong. Mime had schemed to win Siegfried's affections. The plan failed so he taught him fear. But Rinaldo blamed Siegfried. He was the selfish one. He was the one who couldn't love. He was the one who grew in Mime's nurturing, and then thrust it from him like a shackle. The music that spilled from his throat felt drenched in hot, red blood. Dizziness overcame him. From far away he heard low mumblings in the audience. He staggered from the stage and collapsed in the wings. His understudy took over for the remainder of all performances.

Everyone was solicitous, but Rinaldo could not shake the panic, self loathing, and humiliation that enveloped him. He chose to emigrate to America, forge music as his sword, and wield it for others. Never again would he set foot on the stage as a performer.

* * *

"So are you telling me that your refusal to do *The Ring* has something to do with Siegfried not being Mime's natural child? Have you refused to do it because I'm adopted? Not even adopted, just not your natural son?" Phil asked with an unfamiliar tenseness to his voice.

Maestro looked drained and tired. "No, of course not. It has nothing to do with that. It just brings up terrible memories and feelings. I do not want to face them at this point in my life." He rose and stood by the window facing the garden. The fig tree was bursting, the peaches hung heavily, the roses vowed one final burst of greatness. His own robust season was nearing its end; Phil's future held bounteous promise.

"Go ahead. Do it. But I cannot be involved. Get your director, musical director, whatever you need elsewhere. Go to the Met, Kings. Your masterpiece will cost you a fortune."

"Forget it, Pop. I won't do it," Phil said softly.

"Pop? What's Pop? You think I'm an old man? Not the maestro anymore?"

"No, of course not. It just came out. I see my father in some kind of pain. I don't understand it, but I see it."

"Do the opera, Phil. I want you to have the joy of doing something you obviously have so much enthusiasm for. I have plenty of work to keep me busy. Just do not be disappointed when I do not come to see it. Because I cannot."

* * *

"I saw it in his face. For a moment, he was horrified," Rinaldo whispered to Giuliana as they lay side by side in bed.

"You imagined it. Horrified for what? I think he's confused. You're upset because your secret is starting to fall out of your pocket, and someday you may not be able to shove it back in." She sat up. "I think that will be a good day."

"Too late. Too long ago."

"No."

"You know your parents weren't evil like Mime."

"They brought out the evilness in others. Every time, every time. I hated the laughter. I hated the evil. I tried to escape. I fashioned my own magic helmet like in the opera. I became the famous impresario. Not Adela and Marcello's son, Rinaldo, hidden away on a small island or in the dusty corners of a theater. But a flamboyant persona of my own fashioning. I tried to become invisible by sticking out like a sore thumb. So they would only see the thumb, and ask nothing more."

"Nonsense. You are who you are. You became who you were meant to be. You have choices you regret? So does everybody." Giuliana bent over and kissed Rinaldo's forehead. "Go to sleep. You'll feel better in the morning."

"In the morning I will still be sixty-two years old and kicked out of my own theater while my son produces an opera that makes me sick to my stomach."

"Tomorrow we will be alone for dinner. You are taking me out. Then we'll see just how well a sixty-two-year-old man copes with a fifty-four-year-old wife who adores him."

* * *

Lucy loved her 1952 Chevrolet Belair, which she had bought secondhand from a violin professor at Julliard. It was an autumn harvest shade of wheat. It reminded her of rich coffee lightened with heavy cream. She parked in front of the house, ran inside and up the stairs, calling out, "Ma, I'm home. Have to hurry. I'm meeting some friends for dinner and a movie."

"I know," Giuliana called back. "We're going out to dinner tonight too."

The phone rang. Giuliana answered.

"Hello?"

"Hi. Mrs. Salvatori? It's Tavis Gregg."

Giuliana smothered a giggle by clearing her throat.

"Why, hello, Mr. Gregg. Lucy just came in. I'll get her."

"Thanks. And please, it's Tavis."

Lucy came charging down the steps.

"Don't forget you're in a hurry," Giuliana reminded her with a grin.

"Hi, Tavis."

"Hi, Mousey. How're you doing?"

"Great."

"Sorry I haven't called. I was on location in Canada for a while doing *Strangers in Quicksand.* Now I'm on the lot filming *Pledge of Victory*. I'm on a break. My hair is blond. It's awful."

"Send me a picture. Or should I just wait for the next *Photoplay*?"

"Well, pictures have been taken. My mother cried when I told her. She said it ruins the texture of your hair."

"I'm certain it will be fine. *IX Times IX* got rave reviews. I loved it."

"Yeah. I think that's my favorite to date." Tavis paused. "Thanks for the letters. I miss you terribly."

"I'd like to see you too."

"Isn't there any way you could come out here for a visit?"

"No, Tavis. The new school year is just about to begin. And I have my brother's wedding in October."

"I wish I could come. Although that would prove to be an unholy mess, I'm sure. I really hate not being able to step outside unaccosted."

"Or with a gorgeous actress on your arm?"

"Most of what you see is a setup or a publicity shot. Means nothing. Have you been seeing anyone? Wait! No, go ahead, tell me."

"I went out with the widowed father of one of my piano students, if you can believe it. Nice guy. Until I found out he loathes theater. Can you imagine? Luckily, they moved at the end of the school year, so I can't teach his daughter anymore. I don't know what I was thinking. I'm going out with a bunch of friends in a little while. We're seeing *Dial M for Murder.*"

"Good one. I met Grace Kelly."

"She's beautiful."

"Yeah. She is. Lovely person too. Uh-oh. They're calling me. Listen. I can't get back to New York until before Christmas. Keep every day open in December until I can set a day to see you."

"Oh, that should be no problem," Lucy responded sarcastically.

"I'm not being high and mighty, Mousey. I just want to see you. The minute I know my schedule, I'll let you know. I have very little say in these matters."

"OK, Mr. Gregg. I'm at your beck and call."

"Love you, Lucy. I really do. You're like…a plate of spaghetti in a room full of cotton candy."

"That's romantic. You really do need a scriptwriter."

Tavis laughed. "Well, the analogy stinks, but what I mean is you're real. The real thing. Everyone else out here is a whole lot of fluff. Gotta go. Love you."

"Bye, Tavis." Lucy set down the receiver and sighed. He still sounded like the Tavis she knew. Her heart was still doing a little shimmy at the sound of his voice. She hoped the Hollywood dragons didn't get him.

* * *

Lucy bent over the railing above the orchestra pit.

"Tino, we're here!" she called, waving at her brother as he set up his drums.

He waved, rose, silenced the cymbal he banged into, and walked over to greet her.

"Hi," he said straining upward as she bent over the rail to kiss him. "Hi, Val."

"Great gig, Tino. I can't wait to see the show. I hear it's great."

"I'm loving it. It's a lot of fun."

"Sorry I couldn't make it last week with Mom and Maestro for your debut performance."

"That's fine. I was nervous as a cat on a hot tin roof. Ha. That's an inside joke. That play is in rehearsal."

"I can't understand why you'd be nervous. You've played with the best for years now."

"I know. But it's Broadway, you know. And they specifically offered the job to me. I didn't want to mess up. Well, I'd better finish up. See you after the show?"

"Sure thing. We'll be stage-door johnnies," Val said as he put his hand on Lucy's waist to lead her to their fifth-row seats.

"I'm so glad he's happy. My mother is reeling. He's been staying with a friend until he got settled, but now he's coming home to live. Dan and Louisa moved in last week. A full house. She's in paradise."

"They had a nice honeymoon?"

"Sure. They could only get away for five days because of his new job. They both loved Niagara Falls. They just got their pictures back, and it looks wonderful. I'd like to go there sometime."

"I'd be happy to take you."

"Wouldn't that just dampen Maestro's affection for you."

"I guess I'll just have to marry you."

"The way the two of us are going, that may be our final option."

My first and only choice, thought Val as the conductor entered, and took a bow.

After the show Tino joined the couple for drinks.

"You don't mind if Jake joins us, do you? He plays Joe in the chorus," Tino asked.

"Of course not. Jake, you made a beautiful high leap during 'Once A Year Day.' Do you have springs under the soles of your shoes?" Lucy joked.

"I pulled a hamstring muscle a couple of months back. There were no leaps going on for awhile, let me tell you."

The foursome found a quiet booth in Benny's Bar and ordered.

"You haven't been staying at Jake's, have you?" Lucy inquired.

"No. That's Jack. And his sister Emmy. She's a dancer too. I knew Jack from before. He played saxophone with me for a while when I was with the Swing Time Sounders."

"So, are you two an item?" Jake asked.

Lucy laughed. "We've known each other forever, right, Val? He's a big shot at the opera house now. Apparently, the key to success is to begin with a little vandalism."

"Huh?" asked Jake.

They told him the story of Val's initiation into the theater business.

"It was truly fortuitous. My father is wheelchair bound. He was injured during the war. The First World War. I've really only known him that way. I was a baby when it happened. He sorted mail at a law office, and my mom cleaned those same offices at night. It's tough on a kid having a dad who can't play with you like the other fathers and a mother who isn't home to tuck you in and read bedtime stories. I tried to be a good kid and not ask for much. I knew we didn't have the money. Plus I loved them and didn't want to give them anything more to deal with. I don't know. That night, I just sort of caved in. I felt like being reckless and free. Not having to think. It was stupid, but in retrospect, it saved my life. I would have never known that I love opera and being involved with the theater. We didn't even have a radio."

"Maestro would say, 'Destiny has decided.' That's why it all happened."

"I'd say so too," Val added, planting a kiss right on Lucy's lips.

"Whoa! What's that? I think you've had too much to drink, Valentino."

"Well, then. I'll have another."

"No, you won't. Or you can…but I have to still drive home."

"I really don't like you driving home by yourself at this time. You can stay at our place. Mom and Dad are both snug in bed at this time."

"What's with all you native New Yorkers still living at home with the folks?" Jake asked.

"Well, I help my mom with my dad," Val explained.

"I'm sorry. I wasn't thinking," Jake apologized.

"Don't be silly. They are actually talking about moving down to Florida. My mother's sister went, and they love it. Of course, they'll have to get some kind of aide to help out."

"Well, if you want a ride home, you'll have to forego that drink because I'm off," Lucy announced.

"I'm coming. But I'm not happy with you," Val said.

"Too bad, sir. You have no say in the matter." Lucy reached across the table and took Tino's hand. "Great job tonight, kiddo. I'm so proud of you. We always knew all that racket you made would amount to something."

"Thanks heaps."

As Lucy and Val reached the door, she turned to wave at Tino one last time. With his arm draped around Jake's shoulder, deep in conversation, he didn't notice her good-bye. She turned to look at Val.

"Surprised?"

"Tino? I guessed."

"It's not easy."

"I guess not. It's harder on him than the rest of you."

"True. He's always careful. In fact, I'm surprised…"

"Did you look around that bar?"

"What do you mean?"

"It pretty much looks like a theater crowd to me. More of the same and lots of people who are used to it and couldn't care less."

"Oh." Lucy walked a few steps and slipped her arm through Val's. "I'm glad there are places where Tino can feel totally at ease."

* * *

"Don't get home too late. Remember, tomorrow is fig cookie day," Giuliana reminded Lucy as she headed for the door.

"I know, Ma. Who could miss the mountain of ingredients you have spread out all over the place?"

"Mr. Coltri gave me a nice jar of *vincotto.*"

"Christmas is saved. Is Louisa off tomorrow?"

"No, but Dan is."

"Good. He can help with the grinding. See you in the morning probably."

"Say hello to Mr. Movie Star. Tell him I enjoyed *Strangers in Quicksand.* He makes a good doctor."

"Will do." Lucy placed the poinsettia arrangement she had bought on the floor of the back of the car. She turned on the radio, and drove the sixty or so miles to Sayville, listening to her brother captivate his audience with banter filled with his charm and humor.

Lucy pulled up in front of the DiGregorio house, and Tavis trotted down to the curb in a blue cable-knit sweater that matched his eyes.

"Hello, beautiful! I can't believe you're finally here," he said joyfully, taking her in his arms. "C'mon in. Everyone is waiting."

"Everyone?"

"My brother, Bill, and his wife, Claire."

"Let me get the flowers from the back," said Lucy, opening the back door. "Good. They look like they made it in one piece."

They went through the front door festooned with garland and a pine wreath. The house smelled of roast pork and potatoes.

"Welcome, dear. It's so good to see you again," Mrs. DiGregorio said, kissing her cheek.

Greetings and introductions were made all around.

"After dinner we're all going down to the Village Square for the community Christmas tree lighting and carol singing," Tavis told her.

"That sounds like something out of Dickens. How lovely," Lucy responded.

"This poinsettia arrangement is beautiful, Lucy. So different," Tavis's mother commented.

"Well, my brother got married in October, and my father festooned the church, our house, the bride's house, and the reception hall with the florist's yearly income of flowers. The florist was only too happy to see me and show off his holiday displays."

"He certainly succeeded. Dinner is just about ready. Everyone take a seat."

Lucy enjoyed learning more about Tavis's childhood. The affectionate sibling rivalry reminded her of her own brothers, but the conservative chemistry teacher, Mr. DiGregorio, held no resemblance to her own colorful and theatrical father.

"After the carols, we'll go down to Mill Pond and ice-skate for a bit," Tavis suggested.

"I've only ice-skated a few times in my life," Lucy warned. "I'm not very good. Besides, I don't have skates."

"We have a basement full of ice skates in all sizes," Mrs. DiGregorio promised.

"I doubt you have anything that will fit my clodhoppers," Lucy said.

"I hope you're not the same size as I, because I've appropriated the biggest woman's pair down there," Claire admitted.

"If not, I'll just skate with you sitting on my shoulders," Tavis teased.

"I'd like to see that. Should I call the *Suffolk County News*?" Bill asked. "That will make a great front-page story."

* * *

The Village Square was already filled with people when they arrived. Members from the high school band were warming up their instruments, while small children squealed with anticipation and energy. Lucy noted that although people greeted and congratulated Tavis, no one pestered him or imposed on his good time. When one gaggle of teenage girls breathlessly surrounded him, he staved them off by promising them autographed pictures if they came by his family home the next day. Mollified and imagining greater possibilities than an eight-by-ten glossy, they staked themselves quietly on the outskirts of the growing crowd, where they could watch his every move. After the requisite oohs and aahs when the tall fir tree suddenly sparkled in a multicolored burst of Christmas lights, and after the band led them through a medley of carols and popular songs that ended with "White Christmas," Tavis took Lucy's gloved hand and led her to the spot where they had parked the car. They drove to the pond, which had been cleared by hand shovel a few days earlier after a snowfall. Tavis parked the car in line with other cars facing the frozen rink, with headlights left on to provide illumination for the skaters.

Lucy stepped gingerly onto the ice, clinging to Tavis's arm for dear life.

"I'm just not very good at this," she moaned.

"You'll get the hang of it. Just hold onto me."

They circled a couple of times, Lucy's ankles turning every so often. She fell once and narrowly avoided causing a major collision of several skaters.

"Let's move more to the center where people aren't circling as much," Tavis suggested.

"No! That's worse. Look, that girl is practicing figure eights and that boy is doing turns."

When she fell again, Tavis purposely went down with her and fell on top of her. As he kissed her on the mouth, she could feel the cold ice on the back of her head. A flashbulb went off, and Tavis recognized three skaters huddled on the outskirts of the pond as the culprits.

"Don't worry about it," he comforted Lucy. "They won't get anything. It's too dark."

Lucy got up and wiped down her coat. "That's it. I've had it. If they make a movie about Sonje Henie, they won't be auditioning me."

"All right. I've had enough exercise for tonight too."

As they pulled up in front of a small bungalow, Lucy asked, "Where are we?"

"This is my grandparent's bungalow I told you about. They rent it in the summer. It's closed up now, but I came earlier and turned on the burner. There's no water, though. You can use the bathroom in the house next door. I've already spoken to the neighbors."

"Oh geez. Thank you, but I don't need to. Not yet, anyway."

He opened the front door into a small vestibule.

"Wait here while I light some candles," he instructed, picking up a flashlight from a table to his right. After several minutes the parlor to the left was alight with a romantic glow. The room had a welcoming ambience of low-key comfort and well-loved familiarity. A deep, comfortable sofa faced a stone fireplace already set to be ignited. Two armchairs saluted each other from either side of an area rug that covered the battered plank floor in front of the hearth. Mugs had been set out on a low coffee table beside a thermos of hot cocoa and a box of Mallomars. After lighting the fire, Tavis led Lucy with a candle and flashlight in each of their hands through the kitchen, dining area, and two bedrooms. They then sat in front of the fire, each with a mug of cocoa and the box of cookies between them.

"I'm going to be a presenter at the Academy Awards this year," Tavis said.

"I'll be watching on television."

"Good. When I kiss my two fingers and point them out to the camera, like this," he said, demonstrating, "that means I'm thinking of you and wishing you were attending with me."

"That would be fun."

"I get a guest ticket."

Lucy shook her head. "I can't. But thank you. I'll be green with envy for whomever you bring."

"More likely whom the studio sets me up with." He set his mug on the table and rose. From the top of the mantle, he took a small box.

"Merry Christmas."

"Oh, Tavis! Thank you. I have something for you too, but it's in my car. Don't let me forget to give it to you."

"Ha! You weren't going to give it to me unless I had something for you," he snickered.

"That's not true. I didn't want to bring it into the house. I would have liked nothing better than have you feel like a heel for not reciprocating," she said with a grin.

"Well, you lost that bet. Open."

Lucy undid the ribbon and removed the wrapping paper. The black velvet box of a local jeweler was inside. She opened it gingerly.

"Tavis. How beautiful," she exclaimed as she looked at the two small clamshell earrings made of rose gold.

"To remind you of Sayville Beach and how you collected shells that day. I still keep the one you gave me on my nightstand back in LA."

"That was a special day. You'll see when you get my gift."

"Do your folks ever say anything about me? How they feel about you seeing me?"

"Not really. We're together so infrequently. But my mother did say to tell you that you made a very believable doctor in *Strangers in Quicksand.*"

"Really? Because I *did* learn quite a lot."

"How do you mean?"

"Well," he said, scooting closer. "The cheekbone's connected to the jawbone," he explained, drawing a line from one to the other. "The jawbone's connected to the neckbone." He kissed the hollow of Lucy's throat. "The shoulder bone's connected to the breastbone…" His hand traveled over her breast and lingered. "Actually, this doesn't feel too bony. Maybe I should check this out."

Sweeping her back over one arm, he slowly lifted Lucy's sweater. "Hmmn. I'm not sure I can visualize the problem." He lifted her bra, and Lucy's breath caught in her throat. "As far as I can tell, you look absolutely perfect. Nothing remotely wrong here."

His hand caressed one breast as his mouth found the other. The slight chill on her skin was replaced by a warm flush of pleasure. Tavis brought his lips to hers and kissed her deeply. He removed her dangling sweater and bra before kneeling to remove his own sweater and undershirt. He resumed kissing her throat, drifted lazy kisses down her arms to her fingertips and back up her stomach to her breasts, where he maddingly lingered. As his hand began exploring beneath her skirt, Lucy experienced a jolt of sober-mindedness. Her brain flashed a warning while her body ached with ardor.

"Tavis," she said, reaching for his hand. "No."

"No?"

"We can't. I'm sorry."

"Okaaay," he said, corralling his passion and ordering his thoughts. "It seemed right and natural to me. I'm the one who's sorry for jumping the gun."

"It's not that." Lucy sat up, crossing her arms over her nakedness. "I do love you. But I'm not ready for this with you. We have a long-distance relationship. Very long distance. And very occasional. I can't make love with you and not see you for a year. I can't live with that."

"I can respect that."

"I hope so. I hope you're not angry. I'm sorry."

"Don't say you're sorry. You're right. I wouldn't want you living with regrets about us." He reached for her arms and removed them from her breasts. "But God, you sure are beautiful. I can't look at you and not want to love you. Here," he said, handing her clothes to her. "No sense torturing myself."

"And me. Me too." She kneeled beside him and kissed him gently. Her breasts brushed his chest.

"Don't be a tease, Lucy. There's only so much rejection I can take."

Lucy's hands flew to her chest. "I didn't mean to…honest…"

"I'm joking. But let's get dressed."

"I have to get going anyway." She looked at her watch. "It's almost eleven. I have to get home."

"I hate you driving home in the dark. We can stay here in separate rooms, or you can sleep in my room at my parents'. I'll sleep on the sofa."

"No, thank you. Tomorrow is a big day with an early start. It's fig cookie day."

"What?"

"We have to make the fig cookies for Christmas."

"Great. Another reason to hate figs. They're taking you away from me."

Lucy laughed as they blew out the candles. While Tavis locked up, Lucy's mind congratulated itself on her wisdom while her body yearned for fulfillment. She stared at his handsome profile and almost wept. When they reached her parked car, she retrieved Tavis's gift from the trunk.

"Here you go, Mr. Gregg," she said, feigning light-heartedness. "I will use your bathroom before I hit the road."

When she emerged from the restroom, Tavis was sitting by the lit Christmas tree in the parlor.

"Can I open it now?"

"Of course."

He ripped off the paper. "This is beautiful. It's Sayville, isn't it?"

"Yes. My friend Jimmy had a photographer from the paper who lives in Ronkonkoma snap a photograph of Sayville Beach. The mother of one of my students is an artist, and I had her paint it for me. Then I had it framed."

"Are those two figures us?"

"Kind of. I told her the woman should have dark hair. And the man's hair should be the color of that famous actor."

Tavis examined the kneeling woman in the painting whose extended hand offered the seated man a small clamshell. His upturned palm seemed to beg for more than just the gift of the ocean ornament.

"I love it. The play of color from the setting sun on the water…the sand is so…sandy. And you and me. This will go on my bedroom wall back home."

Back home in Califiornia, Lucy thought. *Miles that can't be bridged by wishes or dreams.*

"I'd better get going. Thank you for a wonderful evening."

"I love you, Lucy," Tavis said, kissing her tenderly. He helped her slip back into her coat and walked her to the car. Once she was settled inside, she rolled down the window.

"Merry Christmas, Tavis. Thank you for the earrings."

"Thank you for the painting. Call me when you reach home."

"I'll wake your folks."

"I'm staying up until I hear from you." He kissed her again. "We could call your folks, and tell them you're too tired to drive back."

"Can't. Fig cookies first thing tomorrow."

Tavis groaned. "Merry Christmas then. Be careful."

A bit over an hour later, Tavis picked up the phone on the first ring.

"I'm here," Lucy whispered.

"Good. Wish your family a Merry Christmas from me."

"I think I saw my mother at her bedroom window when I got out of the car."

"I hope that doesn't mess up your baking tomorrow," Tavis joked.

Lucy laughed. "Good night, Tavis."

"Good night, Mousey." He hung up the phone. *Damn it! Outmaneuvered by a bunch of figs.*

Chapter 34

President Lincoln and Dante shared a birthday. In the year 1955, this meant a Saturday that Louisa didn't have to work on a day that Dan was home. Cause for celebration. They had moved into their new home the week before. The rooms were a bit spare on furniture, but they had a bed. They decided this was also the day they would begin trying in earnest to have a baby. They tried before breakfast and then again before they went out for a movie matinee. They strolled through the park before heading for dinner at Dante's favorite Chinese restaurant. They sat on a park bench, watching children swing, teeter-totter, and climb the monkey bars.

A group of small boys played cowboys and Indians with toy guns, bows and arrows, cowboy hats, and feathered headdresses. Somehow a Daniel Boone with a coonskin cap was allowed to be part of the posse as they hid behind benches, trees, and shrubs dodging each other's popgun blasts and rubber-tipped arrows.

Dan and Louisa laughed at their antics until a pigtailed little girl came sliding out of a metal tunnel that landed in the sandbox. Several cowboys turned on the unexpected intruder at once, firing guns and arrows at her. She started to cry, and Dan broke into a cold sweat. As the little girl's mother scolded the boys and comforted her child, Dan grabbed Louisa's hand and said, "Let's go. I don't feel well."

Instead of eating out, Dan took two Anacin and lay down on the bed with a cold compress over his eyes. He felt queasy and sweaty; he just wanted to be left alone. Louisa ate a lonely sandwich, her present for Dan unopened on the kitchen table. When she crawled into bed, she could tell Dan was awake.

"Feeling better?"

"Yes."

"Do you want something to eat?"

"No, thanks."

She spooned in next to him. "Want to try and make a baby again?"

"No. Too much effort might ruin the final product."

"Wha..." Louisa bit her tongue. "OK, then. Good night."

She felt Dan toss and turn until she finally fell asleep herself.

In the middle of the night, she was jerked awake by a feverish toss and Dan abruptly sitting up in bed while crying, "No, stop. Stop. No! Stop!"

"Dan! What is it? Wake up! Wake up!"

Slowly Dan shook himself awake and looked desperately at Louisa.

"You were dreaming." She felt his sweaty forehead. "Let me get a cool washcloth." She picked up the cloth he had used earlier and rinsed it in the bathroom. Returning, she replaced it on his brow.

"Do you remember what you were dreaming?"

"No. I'm all right now. Go back to sleep. Thanks."

The next day Dan seemed fine although uninterested in baby-making. That night again, however, he awoke in a frantic, crying sweat once again. The pattern repeated itself every night except one for a week. Dan began to look haggard and a bit disoriented. Lucy was listening to him on the radio one afternoon when the record ended. There was dead airtime for a good thirty seconds before Dan came on, stiffly animated.

"Sorry, guys and dolls. A wee bit of technical difficulty. Seems that *Sh-Boom* by the Crew Cuts nonny ding-donged and alang, alanged our system here. But we're all straightened out now, so how about a little "Hey There" from Rosemary Clooney?"

He sounded false and strained to Lucy, and that evening she called Louisa.

"He's in bed. He hasn't been sleeping all week."

"What happened?"

"He didn't say a word to me. I'll find out, though. Thanks for calling."

Dan finally admitted he had fallen asleep in front of his console. The station manager had run around and shaken him awake.

"Dan, you have to see a doctor. Something isn't right."

"I've just got a bit of insomnia. It will go away."

"You haven't come near me all week."

"I've got a bug, I think."

"Look at this place Dan. I come home from work, and your stuff is thrown all over the place. It's not like you. It looks like a pigsty."

"For Chrissakes, Louisa! This isn't a goddamn hospital! I don't have to be sterile in my own home. The house *my* parents gave us, if you'd care to remember."

Louisa burst into tears and ran into the parlor. She threw herself sobbing onto the sofa. What was the matter with Dan? Who was this stranger? She waited for him to come out and apologize. She fell asleep waiting.

The following week was punctuated by icy comments, abrupt outbursts, unrecollected nightmares, and sleepless nights. Thoughts of a baby were on hold, not that Louisa wanted anywhere near this stranger.

Coming to a decision, she approached one of her favorite doctors at the hospital.

"Dr. Murray, I'm concerned about my husband. I think something is very wrong. It's like a virus has infected his brain and is destroying the man I know. He refuses to come in to see a doctor."

"Has your husband sustained some trauma?"

"Not that I can think of. Unless getting married was more traumatic to him than I knew."

Dr. Murray allowed himself a chuckle. "No. I don't think that's it. Wasn't he in Korea?"

"Yes."

"I think Dan should come in and see Dr. Gerard."

"He's a psychiatrist, isn't he?"

"Yes. He spoke about research he is doing at a conference not all that long ago. It is in regards to being shell shocked. He thinks the impact from an experience such as war or a particular event during the war can cause psychiatric wounds as real as gunshots or shrapnel. It's not widely accepted yet by any means, but he'll explain all that to you and Dan. I'd highly recommend Dan make an appointment and come in to see him."

Louisa begged and pleaded and finally resorted to having the entire Salvatori clan intercede. They came marching in one Sunday morning and refused to leave until Dan agreed to get help. Any kind of help.

"Fine. Make the damn appointment with Dr. Nutso. I'll go since you're all so sure I'm crazy."

"You're not crazy. It may be some kind of a reaction. It happens to people all the time," Louisa said tearfully.

"Enough of this nonsense," Maestro said sternly. "You are a married man with responsibilities. You do what you have to do."

"I go to work. I bring home my paycheck."

Phil faced his brother head on. "Do you love Louisa?"

"Of course."

"You're going to lose her. She shouldn't have to live with this kind of tension and stress."

"And that mouth," Lucy interjected.

"Do you like your job?"

"Yes," Dan said less defiantly.

"You're going to lose it. How many times do you think you can go in bleary-eyed and conk out at the station? Or screw up the commercial and prerecorded messages on the tape player?"

"Have you been spying on me?"

Phil ignored him. "Don't come to the opera house when you're out of work. We have nothing for you," Phil added as a parting shot.

Later that week Dan sat before Dr. Gerard.

"I became fascinated by Dr. Kardiner's clinical study entitled, 'The Traumatic Neuroses of War,' which was published in 1941. He talks about physioneuroses, which indicate that the body can be involved in psychological traumas. There have been numerous accounts of combat reactions during Korea and World War Two. Oftentimes they were dismissed as the desperate attempts of a frightened soldier to get out of combat. But we're since learning that these situations can cause abnormal behavior in people who had previously been your average Joe. It isn't just wartime trauma. It can be natural diasasters such as earthquakes and floods, victims of crimes, fire…It's called 'gross stress reaction.'"

"Yeah, I hated Korea. Most of the guys I knew did. But if that were the case, we'd all be walking around like zombies because of nightmares. Which I can't recall the second I wake up, by the way."

"That's a defense mechanism. A kind of amnesia. I'd like to administer sodium amytal, better known as truth serum, and see if you can recall and describe the trauma."

"I can describe it. I haven't forgotten one moment of that bloody war."

"Maybe."

"I just don't get why it happened now. It's a year since I'm back."

"Not unusual. I think I can help."

"They say I've become a monster. Well, not exactly, but I do hear what they're saying. I can't stop myself, though. Worse, I don't want to when I'm doing it. Frankly, I'm restraining myself right now from walking out of here because they forced me to come in."

"All part of the symptoms. Something triggered this reaction, and now your mind is defending itself. Make an appointment with my receptionist, as soon as possible, and we'll get started."

At his next appointment with Dr. Gerard, Louisa joined Dan. Pictures began to flash in Dan's mind, and the horror spilled from his throat. He saw the naked family, the little children. The North Koreans, half dressed, reaching for their guns. He saw the little boy, dark straight hair overgrown into his eyes. If only it could have shielded him from seeing his dead family. He crawled out warily, eyes wide with trepidation. Gunshots. Gunshots. Gunshots. The small boy lay dead.

"He had a page ripped out of some American magazine in his hand. It was a black-and-white picture of a kid with a bicycle. All this little guy wanted in life was his family and a two-wheeler. And we killed him."

Dan clutched his stomach and groaned. Louisa stifled the cries that caught in her throat as tears streamed down her cheeks.

"All right, Dan. Now we can begin," Dr. Gerard said gently.

Within a month Louisa would have pronounced Dan cured. He still visited Dr. Gerard on a regular basis, but he slept through the night, and he was sweet, charming, teasing, and loving. Dr. Gerard warned there was no way of knowing if the disorder was gone or if the symptoms might return.

"If they do, you make an appointment immediately. We'll know even more in a few years time."

"I don't know how to thank you, Doc. You've given me my life back."

"You just thank that pretty wife of yours. Make babies."

"The thought of a baby was making me sick just two months ago."

"That's understandable. We've discussed all the reasons and resolutions. Go. Live. Love. Be happy."

* * *

Maestro was talking with two women in his office when Phil poked his head in.

"Oh, sorry. Didn't know you were busy. I'll come back."

"No, come in, Phil. You remember Dai Jiang? Maybe not, you were a small boy."

"Of course I remember. Revolutionized *Tosca.* Nice to see you again."

"This is her niece, Ami Huang."

Phil looked the woman full in the face and felt his stomach do a belly flop. A perfect oval face framed by gleaming black hair. Eyes dark as coal that sparkled with the spirit of diamonds, a small nose and perfect lips. A small lithe body graceful in movement as she extended her hand.

"Nice to meet you," the young woman said in a musical voice.

"I stopped by to show my niece the man and the place that gave me my start," Dai said.

"I'll be happy to show you around," Phil offered.

"I was just about to do that," Maestro explained. He noted the normal twinkle in Phil's eyes was replaced by the pitiful expression of a puppy being teased with a biscuit. "Perhaps it would be better if you do the honors. I have a few things that need attending."

Phil gave them the grand tour and returned them to Maestro's office at its finish.

"You've certainly grown since I was here," Dai said. "The theater is beautiful. Of course, it always was. I noticed a backdrop up in the flies that looks quite impressive. That has changed."

Maestro grinned. "The critics gave me the most grief over my sets. Once I could afford it, it was the first thing I spent more money on."

"Not the first, but he made improvements along the way," Phil corrected. "May I take you ladies out for a cup of coffee? Or tea? Isn't this considered teatime?"

Maestro raised an amused eyebrow.

"I'm sorry. I can't," Dai said, lovelier than ever at thirty-eight years of age. "I have a meeting with Rudolf Bing at the Met."

"Are you free?" Phil asked Ami.

"Why, yes. I was going to go to the library to do some research, but I can do that another time."

"Great. I'll be back in awhile," Phil called to his father as he ushered Ami toward the door.

"I must be going too." Dai smiled. "Young people. It wouldn't even occur to Ami to ask me if it was OK to go for tea."

"Not to worry. It's my Phil."

"I know that. That's why I didn't say anything."

When Dai left, Maestro stood by the window looking out at Ninth Avenue.

Phil, Phil. Be careful. She's lovely, I'm sure. But the world isn't ready for that. You'll get hurt. You'll both be hurt.

Maestro shook his head. Something in his heart told him it was too late already.

"Destiny has decided," he said aloud.

* * *

"I work as a production assistant at ABC Studios."

"Where did you go to school?" Phil asked.

"I graduated from NYU two years ago."

"You went straight to ABC?"

"Yes. I was really lucky. They had just merged with United Paramount Theaters, and last October was a whole new beginning for us."

"How so?"

"ABC invested half a million dollars in cash and guaranteed bank loans for Disney. Walt Disney is building a park near Los Angeles called Disneyland. Construction begins in a couple of months, I believe. ABC is getting thirty-five percent of the park and all the profits from the food concessions. That's because Paramount knows how profitable food is from the movie theaters."

"I've heard of Walt Disney. He couldn't get backing for this dream of his."

"Well, ABC stepped up. MGM, Twentieth Century Fox, Warner Brothers have all been producing programs for us now. In July we have a new variety show called the *Lawrence Welk Show.* The *Disneyland* show we already have is doing very well. In October it's going to become the *Mickey Mouse Club.* You should see the ears the kids on the show will be wearing."

"Ears?"

"Mouse ears. Really cute."

"Marketing TV to kids also is probably a good idea. I should think about it for the opera house. Do *Hansel and Gretel,*" Phil mused.

As they got up to leave, Ami said, "Thank you. This was lovely."

"May I see you again? Have you seen *Pajama Game*? My brother is in the orchestra. I can get tickets."

"I'd like that very much."

Ami gave Phil her phone number, and they parted. Phil whistled badly all the way back to the theater. He thought he sounded just like Fred Astaire.

* * *

"Set your TV dial next month to the Philco Television Playhouse," Tavis said to Lucy as she curled up on her bed with the new phone she had installed in her bedroom. "I'm going to be in a live production of *The Gift of the Magi.*"

"Isn't that a Christmas story?"

"Yes. But Philco is closing its doors, and a couple of other playhouses are taking over. They have the script and want to do it."

"Let me know as soon as you have the airdate. It gets pretty hectic around here."

"What have you been up to this summer?"

"Actually, I'm rehearsing. Julliard is having a fund-raiser in October for scholarships. At Carnegie Hall! I'm so excited."

"That's the big time."

"I know. Instructors are performing, some students and a few actual big names."

"Like who?"

"Uh, I'm pretty sure Robert Merrill, Jennie Tourel, Mel Torme, and I think Peggy Lee."

"Wow. I don't know the Jennie person."

"Famous opera singer. Can you come?"

"I'll be in Majorca in October. Filming *Satin Sky.* I wish I could, though. What are you performing?"

"I'm playing Mozart's Piano Concerto No. 26, K. 537."

"I'm such an ignoramus."

Lucy laughed. "Wait. And I'm singing 'Adele's Laughing Aria' from *Die Fledermaus.*"

"Singing and playing, and I have to miss it. I hate my job."

"Do you?"

"No, but there's a lot I do hate about it."

Why don't you quit and come back here? "You still have to meet my family. Next March there will be a new member. My brother and his wife are expecting a baby!"

"That's great news. I'd love to be a father. Hell, I'd love to be an uncle, but no word on that front yet either."

"Beat you to it. Will you be around for Christmas this year, Tavis?"

"I'm afraid not. I won't even bother asking you to come out here. I know the stupid fig cookies outrank me."

Lucy laughed. "They are sweet and satisfying."

"I asked my folks to spend it out here, but they won't. My mother's afraid to fly, and this is their year with Bill and Claire. Cousins. A whole catalog of reasons why they can't come."

"You won't be alone, will you?" Lucy asked worriedly.

"No. I'm not as pathetic as all that. I have friends out here. Good ones, actually. I think I'll pick one who's married with kids, though. That kind of makes the holiday, you know what I mean?"

"I do."

"Although, if it was just you, me and mistletoe, I wouldn't ask Santa for one other thing."

"We've got to stop kidding ourselves, Tavis. We won't ever be a couple," Lucy said with sadness. "I think we need to face that."

"I'd rather have hope."

"I think I'd rather have a hope of marriage and family. I'll see you as a friend the next time you're in New York."

"What's this about?"

"I'm just a bit disillusioned knowing it will be well over a year before I see you again. Maybe much longer. I have to get my head on straight, actor boy. Friends?"

"Friends, Mousey. Always. Love you. Forever."

* * *

Lucy was stunning in a gown fashioned from black silk satin. The bodice was decorated in a whimsical beading pattern of rhinestones, beads, and sequins. Seams ingeniously controlled the fullness of the skirt over the hips. The gown was attached to a complete underdress that featured a built-in boned undergarment that eliminated the need for any other "foundation." Crisscrossed fabric in the back gave a gentle "train" effect over the buttocks. She headed for the room where she could hear the performers on stage as she awaited her own vocal performance.

"Lucy, your Mozart was magnificent," said Josef Klaus, one of the professors at Julliard. "Absolutely delightful."

"Thank you, Professor."

"I look forward to your vocal presentation."

"I enjoy doing it. It's a fun aria."

A woman approached them carrying a gigantic bouquet of two dozen yellow roses. "Lucy, these are for you."

"Thanks, Edyth." She read the card. *"Who knew they had mice in Carnegie Hall? Congratulations. Love, Tavis."* Lucy laughed in delight. "There's an air mail envelope dangling from this side," Edyth remarked. Lucy handed her the bouquet and opened the envelope. Inside there was a check made out to Julliard in the amount of $2,500. "Oh my. Put this in the coffers, Edyth."

Edyth took the check and looked at it. "Tavis Gregg? As in the Tavis Gregg in *Pledge of Victory*?'

"Old friend," Lucy acknowledged, reclaiming the bouquet and heading for the waiting room.

After the concert the entire family with the exception of Dan and Louisa, who couldn't stay awake a moment longer, remained for a celebratory reception. Valentino designated himself Lucy's official escort and beamed with pride at the praises directed her way.

"That was quite a theatrical performance," the *NY Times* critic commented. "Any chance you'll sing Adele at the Salvatori Opera Company?"

"I'm afraid my schedule is too busy for full-time performing,"

"Lucilla, you sang such a sassy Adele. It is remarkable the ease with which you handled your coloratura."

"Thank you, Maestro. If you approve, I know I hit the mark."

"What was amazing to me was your diction," said Renata Lanzo, one of Lucy's former vocal instructors. "The higher the notes go, the more difficult is the diction. Yet your diction never wavered, and the laughing aria goes very high indeed."

"I appreciate that. It was a challenge to accomplish that during practice," Lucy said honestly.

Val lifted two glasses of champagne off a passing tray. "I don't know about all the technique they're talking about, but I certainly fell in love with that saucy chambermaid. Although, I must say, I've never seen a maid dressed in a gown like this."

"Hopefully, my acting aided the illusion."

"I'm sorry. It didn't. Why would I want my eyes to forego your spectacular presence on that stage? Lucy, I am so proud of you," Val said tenderly.

"Thank you, Val. And thanks for being here tonight."

"Did you think I would want to be anywhere else? Do you have an inkling of how much I care about you?"

Lucy gazed into his dark eyes, gentle and reserved. His lean face was handsome, still almost boyish. He would be one of those men who grew even more dashing with age and graying temples. In her high heels, they stood eye to eye. The well-built form beneath his black suit belied the hours he spent sitting at a desk. She suddenly wondered how he spent his weekends.

"You adore me, I know. Ever since the year I tossed you an extra fig," Lucy said with a grin. "And I've adored you ever since you offered to take that spindly legged girl to her prom."

"That never happened."

"Maestro thought you were too old."

"I'm not too old any longer."

"Alas, I'm too old for the prom."

"I don't recall you ever having spindly legs either."

"Oh sure. It was one of the reasons I never learned to ice-skate. They couldn't hold me up." A shadow crossed her face. “Well, that was then, and this is now. Listen. Someone is playing the piano on stage. Let’s go there and waltz. I want to say I danced in Carnegie Hall too.”

“I can’t waltz.”

“Twirl me around. I just want to get dizzy tonight.”

“I’ll learn to waltz if you’d like,” Val offered. *I’d like to be the one you get dizzy about from now on.*

Chapter 35

"Table for six," Dante said as they entered the Spumoni Gardens, pointing at Louisa's stomach.

After they were seated, Dan asked, "Feeling better, Buttercup?"

"Don't call me fat," Louisa said testily.

"Did I say fat? Did anyone hear me say fat?" Dan asked.

"Butter is fat. Like me."

"You're wearing yellow. I called you buttercup." Dan groaned.

"I swear I'm carrying twins. I feel like a house."

"No problem there. I just got a two-turntable system at the station so I can alternate between records for continuous playback. I'm a whiz at handling two at once."

"Great. You'll be spinning the baby around on the changing table to clean his *culi*."

"Whatever works," Phil said with a laugh.

"So why are we celebrating your birthday today instead of on the actual day?" Lucy asked.

"Because I'm working a sock hop for Valentine's Day at the Knights of Columbus on Sunday."

"You do a lot of those?" Val asked.

"Some. The station sets it up. Good publicity. Kids love to meet the face behind the voice. We give them all kinds of stuff. This one is going to be fun. Tino is coming."

"What's he doing?" asked Phil.

"What do you think? Playing the drums. It's pretty popular now. He maintains the beat between songs so the dance floor doesn't empty."

"Maybe I should come. Tino's drums might just vibrate this baby out of me."

"It will be over all too soon," Ami said. "It is a beautiful occasion to be carrying happiness in you for nine months."

The food arrived. Ami looked at Louisa's plate.

"You're really going to eat that?"

"Don't ask me why. I have a craving for *scungilli* salad. I don't normally eat it."

"What is it?" Ami asked.

"Damned if I know."

Dan looked startled. "Louisa! What's the matter with you?" He turned to Ami. "It's a kind of mollusk. I've never seen her eat it before."

"I ask because Chinese believe what a pregnant woman eats affects the child."

"Well, I hope eating a whole pint of pistachio spumoni ensures green eyes and curly hair, because that's what I'm ordering next," Louisa said, slipping her feet out of her shoes under the table.

* * *

Adriana Starr Salvatori arrived as a pretty pink package exactly on her due date.

"Look at those fingers! Long like a pianist," Maestro said proudly.

"Sings like an opera singer too," Dan informed them. "I heard her crying."

"She's beautiful, Dan," Lucy said, wiping away tears as she gazed through the hospital nursery window.

The attending nurse smiled at them, picked up the baby, and brought her closer to the window.

"Looks like she may have the curly hair," Dan mentioned. "But those eyes are already dark as can be. Aren't babies' eyes usually blue?"

"Where would she get blue eyes in this family?" Maestro scoffed. "She's long, right? Your mother said she's long."

"Twenty-two inches. Louisa said that's pretty big."

"She's our little star from heaven." Giuliana's voice glowed with happiness.

"Don't get too mushy. Louisa picked Starr because she loves the Brenda Starr comic strip."

"It's a beautiful name for our beautiful granddaughter."

* * *

As Giuliana reached for the two quarts of milk in her milk box, cries from the open window next door wrenched through the morning air. Setting the bottles in the refrigerator, she ran upstairs to Rinaldo, who was shaving in the bathroom.

"Something happened at the Coltris'. I hear crying. Loud crying, like screaming."

Rinaldo wiped the remaining shaving cream from his face and grabbed a shirt from his closet. He was still buttoning the shirt as he raced down the walkway and banged on his neighbor's door.

Paul Coltri opened the door in an open robe that did not conceal his boxer shorts and undershirt.

"Paul? Is something wrong? Can I be of assistance?" Rinaldo asked.

"Come in. Come in. No, you cannot help. We are supposed to pick up Tessie's nephew at the pier today, but we just heard on the news about a collision at sea."

"Collision?"

"The ship, the *Andrea Doria,* crashed with another boat from Stockholm, I think. Or that was its name. I don't know. Renzo is coming to stay with us. He thinks he wants to immigrate to America."

A wail from the parlor cut through his words. "No word yet on survivors. It happened before midnight near Nantucket. They were almost here and now this."

"I'll call up Dan. He can get news early from the radio station. I'll let you know if I find anything out."

"Thank you, Maestro." A small smile brightened his features. "By the way, your shirt is buttoned crooked. I never seen you with a thread outta place before."

"You should talk, Paul. Your fly is flapping in the breeze there."

Paul looked down and started laughing. "Honest to God. I forgot I wasn't dressed."

* * *

The following Sunday the Coltris invited the Salvatoris to dinner. Only Tino was home, and he joined his parents at the happy occasion of Renzo's safe deliverance from the disaster at sea.

At twenty-six, Renzo was a good-looking man with startling green eyes and enough dark curls to hide the fact that his hair was beginning to thin. He stood two inches taller than Tino and spoke in school-learned English. Over steaming bowls of spaghetti and meatballs followed by fried chicken and vegetables, Renzo detailed the life-threatening experience.

"We leave Genoa. The ship, *mama mia*, so *magnifico*! The people, all kinds, so rich, so poor. I peek the room one night with the musica and dance. Like a…princess story. *Bella*! I swim the pool. The ship, she hasa three pool! It'sa like a whole town, she moves on the water." He reached for another piece of chicken. "This chick is a good, Zia Tessie."

"*Mangia, mangia.*" She looked at Giuliana. "We called my sister long distance so she'd hear Renzo's voice."

"I was look a movie with a new friends when it happen. It'sa call *Foxfire* with Jane Russell. I learn more better the English with movie. The ship she go boom, and I fall the floor. The peop scream. I run get life jack. I look out the…how you say...like a the window…"

"Porthole," Tino suggested.

"*Si.* Porthole. *Grazie.* The water right there wherc sky she was. I think the world upside over."

"It must have been terrifying," Giuliana commented.

"Terror all the ship. After is my turn to go down lifeboat. The rope almost she broke up when I take. I'ma think I be Jonah in the whale soon. *Ma,* no. I hita the boat. We go forever, it feel like. The…" he waved his hands in the air. "Clouds, fat..."

"Fog," Tino submitted in his new interpreter role.

"Fog? Oke. Fog, she go up. We reach ship, the French one. They pick us up into ship. Never I so hap to see French. We come New York, and here I eat the fried chick! *Grazio Dio.*"

"Thank God, indeed. What an ordeal," Giuliana murmured. "There were lives lost, though. Not many in comparison to the number on board, but still. Their poor families."

"As soon as you feel up to it, you must come to my opera house and see an opera. We have a good season this year. You can choose. Or see them all if you like." Maestro looked at the Coltris. "You come with him, of course."

"If you'd like to see a Broadway show, I can usually get tickets," Tino offered.

"You can hear Tino play also. He plays in the orchestra on Broadway," Giuliana said.

"You play the music? What you play?"

"Percussion. Drums."

"Oh! I like! I come."

"Great! I'll introduce you to New York after theater life."

Giuliana glanced at Maestro without lifting her eyes. He was studying the Coltris. They were oblivious.

* * *

"Excuse me. I think I hear the baby." Louisa rose from the dining-room table.

"Bring her down if she's awake. I'd love Tavis to see her before we go," Lucy said. "She's a beauty. Although not a very good sleeper."

"She's curious. She doesn't want to miss anything," Giuliana said proudly.

"What's this new movie you're filming?" Dan asked.

"Called *Litterally Yours.* Cute romantic comedy. I'm a wealthy playboy type who becomes enamored of a Rockette. My buddies say I could never win her if I was just an ordinary Joe without money. So I get a job with the sanitation department to prove them wrong."

"Do you get the girl?" Lucy asked.

"Eventually. And learn a lot in the process. We're only filming outdoor scenes here. The rest is on the lot in LA."

"Your parents must be thrilled to have you closer. I don't know how I'd cope if my children lived across the country," Giuliana observed.

As Lucy and Tavis left, Louisa called out, "We'll be watching the TV. Sometimes Ed Sullivan announces who's in the audience."

"I hope not," Lucy said sincerely. She settled herself in Tavis's car. "I swear, Mrs. Rossi has Tavis Gregg radar. She's standing in front of her house again."

"Who?"

"The woman you charmed a couple of years ago."

Tavis grinned and slipped out the driver's side. "Hi, Mrs. Rossi. How is it possible you look more gorgeous than last time I saw you?" He got back in.

"You're dreadful," Lucy groaned. "She's going to have a stroke."

Tavis pulled out, and Lucy turned around to watch Mrs. Rossi, with arms flapping, run across to Giuliana, who was still at the door.

Tavis and Lucy were seated at the last possible moment along with Anne Baxter and Phil Rizzuto. The reaction to these entrances was less than might be expected due to the anticipatory hum of the audience. Elvis Presley was making his second appearance on *The Ed Sullivan Show,* and only the hysteria of the crowd outside the theater made the inside fans look almost refined. Ed Sullivan walked out before the camera, stiff, slightly stooped, and rubbing his hands together. After greeting his audience, he described the reeeeally big show he had prepared for them that evening. The camera then turned on the lovely Anne Baxter and baseball shortstop, Phil Rizzuto, when he introduced them.

"Not only do we have a larger-than-life singer on tonight's stage…"

Screams broke his statement. Ed waited for them to subside and continued awkwardly, "We have a larger-than-life actor in our audience too. Tavis Gregg."

The camera turned on Tavis and Lucy.

* * *

"There she is! There's Lucy!" yelled Tino, sitting at home in front of the television.

"Looka that! There's a you sister," Renzo said with glee, sitting on an ottoman in the Salvatori parlor.

* * *

Tavis grinned and waved while Lucy smiled sweetly, all the while kicking his leg beneath camera range.

"You're a brat," he kidded once the camera was off them.

"You loved it."

"I'd love it more if I was making the fifty thousand Elvis is reportedly making for this appearance."

"Holy cow!" Phil Rizzuto turned in the seat in front of them. "Is that for real?"

"Rumor has it." Tavis extended his hand. "Nice to meet you. Great win in the World Series this year, by the way."

"Thanks," Phil said and smiled at Lucy.

Lucy said, "Nice to meet you." She shrugged helplessly. "I'm from Brooklyn. I was kind of rooting for the Dodgers."

"Beautiful, but not too bright," Tavis explained.

Lucy socked him in the arm.

Elvis sang "Don't Be Cruel," "Love Me Tender," and "Hound Dog."

"Do you want to go backstage and meet him?" Tavis asked after the show.

"No. That's all right. Here comes security. Let's just follow them out to wherever it's safe."

"My agent has a small apartment he keeps in the city. He said we could use it after the show." Tavis raised his hand. "Just to have a drink or a cup of coffee. I know the rules. We really can't go any place in public. It's gotten that bad."

"I've noticed. OK. Let's go."

Tavis found a parking spot on the Upper West Side and let them into the one-bedroom apartment.

"Here's a note. 'I told the cleaning lady to leave out the coffeepot. I hope she did. Ron.'"

"Here's another note. 'I did!' Must be from the cleaning lady." Lucy chuckled. "I'll put up the pot."

"I'm surprised you didn't want to meet Elvis. Or did you just not want to be cruel to me, the one with the heart's that true?"

"Funny. Frankly, I'm keeping my eye on someone else. I saw him in *Rumble on the Docks.* Bit part. Have you ever met James Darren?"

"No. That's not fair. You can be interested in someone on the East Coast, but no looking at other guys on the West Coast."

"I didn't realize those were the rules."

"I'd rather we didn't have any rules."

"I know. Me too. But they're set in place."

Tavis took her in his arms and kissed her. They fell in a tumble to the sofa, and his hands began to explore. When his fingers began to tug at the zipper on the back of her dress, Lucy sat upright.

"The rules are engraved in stone, Tavis. You promised."

"Scout's honor, I only wanted to look."

"What kind of scout might that be? Wide-eyed owl scout?"

"You're one tough broad. OK. Let's sit here and do a little necking while the coffee perks."

Chapter 36
1957

Lucy stood on the front lawn, hands on hips, as little Adriana made stumbling efforts to catch a butterfly.

"Here, Adriana. Let's play ball," Lucy suggested.

"No!" Adriana turned around. "Where go? Where bird go?"

"Butterfly. Not bird. A butterfly."

"Budfly," she screeched, spying it again and giving chase.

"Hey, Jimmy!" Lucy called as she noticed her friend pass on the sidewalk.

Jimmy stopped and opened the gate. "Lucy, hon. How've you been?" He buzzed her cheek.

"Great. You?"

"Busy, busy. I'm going to Reno, Nevada. "

"For what?"

"A convention. Billy Barty is holding a convention for people like me."

"Smart-mouthed, no-holds-barred journalists?"

"Well, I will do a story. No, dwarfs. He's a dwarf. You've seen him in a lot of movies. An actor."

"I don't recognize the name. Was he in *The Wizard of Oz?"*

"I don't know. I'll ask him. He's pretty famous."

"Is there a point to this convention, or is it just a social gathering?"

"He's looking to form an organization to help make life easier for us. He calls us little people."

"Sounds like a great idea. Adriana!" Lucy ran over and extricated her niece from a shrub she had fallen into.

"She's a beauty," Jimmy observed, looking at the mop of dark curls, rosy cheeks, and serious dark eyes.

"She's a handful. Louisa works part time now, and my mother helps out. So does her mother. But Aunt Lucy had to fill in this afternoon. I'm exhausted."

"I'm going to spend some time in Vegas while I'm out there."

"Fun. See a show; win some money."

"That's the plan. How's everyone?"

"Good. Tino is playing for *My Fair Lady* now. He moved back to the city. He's living with Renzo, the Coltris' nephew. They're a little upset."

"Surprised?"

"I guess so. Mr. Coltri didn't give my father any homemade wine this year. Although he talks nice enough to him if they should meet. Between my father and Tino, they got Renzo a job at New York City Center."

"What does he do?"

"A tailor. Apparently quite adept at his craft too. He loves working on costumes. He's involved in whatever it takes to get permanent residence here."

"Does your family like him?"

"He's a sweet boy, man, I guess. Tino is happy, so I'm happy."

"Your father is OK with this?"

"Never said a word that I heard."

"He's a strange man, your father. No problem with fairies, but dwarfs freak him out."

"Jimmy! Don't say fairy. You of all people should be more sensitive than that."

"Sorry. You're right. Common parlance; it slipped out. Did he tell you we sat next to each other on the subway about a week ago?"

"No."

"Yeah. He was by the window, and I got on, and sat against the wall next to him. He nodded and said, "Good evening, Jimmy," before I even said hello to him. I couldn't believe it. Then he had to stare out the window at the dark tunnel the whole ride or sit there staring at my profile. As I thought about it, I had to concentrate not to laugh."

Adriana ran over and grabbed Jimmy's hand.

"Budfly. Budfly."

"Some other time, sweetheart," he said, rubbing his hand in her curls. "I'd better get going."

"Good night, Jimmy. Let's get together when you get back."

"Will do, Luce."

* * *

Phil stepped out of the specialty shop in Chinatown and hailed a cab.

"Plaza Hotel," he told the cabbie.

When they reached the hotel on Central Park West, he instructed, "Wait here." He ran through the lobby to the Palm Court.

"May I help you?" the gentleman at the restaurant desk inquired.

"Yes. Hi. I've spoken with the chef. He's expecting this. He's going to arrange them around a special floating island dessert for dinner tonight. Can you see that he gets it?"

"Your name, sir?"

"Phil Salvatori."

"I will see that your instructions are carried out."

"Thanks," Phil said as he ran back to the cab.

After picking up Ami at her apartment, he instructed the happy cab driver whose meter hadn't stopped clicking for an hour to take them to the Museum of Natural History.

"What's going on?" Ami asked. "You're so secretive today."

"I've planned a special July Fourth. That's all," Phil responded innocently.

In the museum, they headed for the Planetarium. A sign outside said Closed.

"How can it be closed? I checked. It's open daily," Phil moaned in a huff. "Hey," he called at a museum staffer, "how come the planetarium is closed?"

"Fourth of July. No shows today."

"Damn. I never thought to ask about that."

"Let's just visit a few other exhibits. Why the Planetarium?"

"The sky, the solar system. I was going for romance. Besides, I heard the current show is amazing."

"That's sweet. We passed the Hall of Man and Nature on the first floor. What could be more romantic than what comes naturally to man?"

"Fine. I like your way of thinking." His tone held a hint of disappointment.

When they left the museum, they strolled through Central Park.

"Let's take a carriage ride before dinner," Phil suggested.

As they ambled through the park to find a walk-way to the street, the sky got ominously dark. Fat, cold raindrops began to fall like paint splotches on their clothing.

"Ride," Phil said to a carriage driver as he helped Ami into the seat. As they got settled, lightning etched a brilliant zigzag through the dark sky and a crack of thunder quaked through the air. The horse whinnied and bobbed uncomfortably.

"Sorry, guys. I can't take Hercules out in this. He'll turn skittish and run."

"For crying out loud!" Phil groaned as he grabbed Ami's hand, and they bolted for an art supply shop nearby. "Some Hercules. He should rename him Wimpy."

"What are you so angry about?"

"Everything is getting messed up."

"Let's walk through this store. It looks like it has some nice merchandise."

Ami picked up an origami kit and a few greeting cards with original artwork designs.

"We can go to dinner now," Phil said, looking at his watch. "I made a six o'clock reservation."

When they entered the Palm Court with its marble columns and gold leaf, Ami commented, "I guess we're not having barbecue."

"If you tell me you've been craving a hotdog all day long, I will boycott Nathan's for the rest of my life."

They looked over the menu and decided to share an appetizer of Maine lobster and Alaskan crabmeat salad before their individual entrees. The waiter was approaching their table when a commotion erupted out of sight. The waiter did an about-face and ran in the direction of the noise. Soon waiters were scurrying about to their tables.

"I'm sorry, sir. You have to leave. There's a fire in the kitchen."

"Should we wait in the lobby?" Phil asked.

"Hurry. Hurry. Please evacuate."

A nose-pinching stench of burned oil began to filter into the dining room. Phil and Ami joined the exodus past palm trees into the lobby.

"Mr. Salvatori!"

Phil turned. The maitre d' approached him.

"I believe this belongs to you." He handed Phil the bag he had arrived with earlier. "The chef remembered in the midst of the catastrophe. He said to tell you he is sorry."

As they stepped onto Fifth Avenue, Ami asked, "What is that?"

"Just a little surprise I had planned."

"Can I see it?"

"In a bit, I guess, when we're not standing on a steamy sidewalk. At least it's stopped raining. Let's walk to the subway."

As they neared the station, they passed a hotdog vendor who was returning to his spot after the earlier downpour.

"I'm kind of hungry, Phil. I'll take that hotdog, if you don't mind."

"What the hell," Phil said, discouraged.

As they stood on the platform waiting for the train, Ami took the bag from Phil's hand.

"I'm dying of curiosity."

"There's a bench. Let's sit," he suggested.

She opened the bag. "Fortune cookies?"

"They were supposed to be surrounding a floating island dessert. Go ahead. Break them open."

Ami snapped the first one and read the small piece of paper tucked inside.

"'Example is not the main thing in influencing others. It is the only thing.'"

"What?" Phil shouted, grabbing the slip of paper from her hand. "I don't believe it. Open another one."

Ami took a second cookie. "'In great attempts it is glorious even to fail.'"

"If I didn't want to kill someone right about now, I might take that as my motto today. Go ahead, try again."

"What's going on?" Ami asked as she popped a broken piece of cookie into her mouth and opened another. "Even the longest of days will come to an end."

"At this point, I hope that's true," Phil said wildly. "I'm sorry. This is not what I had planned."

"What did you plan?" Ami asked gently.

"I had personal notes made up for the cookies. I went to a specialty shop in Chinatown. Needless to say, the word *fail* wasn't in any of them."

"What did they say?"

Phil thought back carefully. "One said, 'I saw only your face.' The next one said, 'A hundred million miracles began the day I met you.'"

"A hundred million miracles! That's poetry. How beautiful."

"All right. I cheated on that one. Remember how I told you I want to get into producing musicals in the theater too?"

"You said your father objected."

"Yeah, well, what else is new? I did some legwork on my own. I went to producer previews of new musicals. There's one called *Flower Drum Song*. Rodgers and Hammerstein. It's a Chinese love story set in Chinatown, San Francisco. There's a song called "A Hundred Million Miracles." I couldn't afford it, but I did invest a little something in it. I'm still working on finding something I can actually produce at the opera house."

"What did the third fortune say?" Ami asked, slipping her arm through Phil's.

"'Love conquered me.'"

"Truly?"

"Truly and absolutely."

Ami kissed him tenderly. "Me too."

Phil looked at his watch. "Where is that train?"

"And Impresario Phil is back."

"Huh? Oh, sorry. But I have a timeline here."

"Always the producer. It's a holiday. The trains are running slow."

"Uh."

"They didn't check with you first?" Ami teased.

* * *

When they reached Brooklyn, Phil directed Ami to his car parked near the station.

"I'm almost afraid to ask what's next," Ami said with glee.

"Sssh. If I were a superstitious man, I'd have thrown in the towel two hours ago. There's still plenty that can go wrong."

"The trouble with you is you think you can organize everything. You always have to be in control."

"Start outlining my failings. That will cap off the evening nicely."

"I love your failings."

They pulled up in front of an apartment building.

"What's this?" Ami asked.

"A friend's place."

They took the elevator up to the twelfth floor. Phil pulled a key out of his pocket. The door opened. "Ah. Finally something that works today," he said.

Ami looked around the apartment. It really wasn't anything special. Two bedrooms, a kitchen, and a large living room, all visible from the entryway. Phil led Ami through the living room to sliding doors that led onto a balcony.

"Have a seat," Phil instructed, "while I get something to drink."

Ami didn't dare disobey. She was grateful for the green canvas that was attached to the three sides of the balcony. It offered privacy, but more importantly, it suggested security. If she couldn't look down, maybe she could pretend she wasn't twelve stories high. Somehow she didn't think Phil could handle a request to sit indoors.

"Here you go, my lady," Phil said, returning. He handed Ami a flute of champagne. "To us."

Ami clinked glasses with him. "To us."

They lay together on a lounge chair as the sky darkened, kissing and touching. Suddenly the sky crackled and golden arrows shot through the night.

"Oh!" squealed Ami, sitting upright.

"Fireworks!" Phil announced. "Coney Island fireworks."

The sky exploded in red, green, white, and gold as starbursts and waterfalls of color descended on them, punctuated with staccato explosions of sound.

"They're so close you can almost catch the light," Ami exclaimed.

Phil grabbed his cue line and got down on one knee.

"Ami, I have found my light. You are the light of my life. I cannot imagine facing the years ahead without you by my side. I will cherish you and love you all the days of my life. I know we'll face problems and hurt because of the stupidity of some people. But we'll get through anything they can throw at us together. I love you. Will you marry me?"

A circle of golden light like a wedding ring danced in the sky. Ami's heart filled with joy at the promise of a lifelong love to share with Phil.

"Of course I'll marry you. There is no miracle in that. How could it happen any other way?"

She knelt down on the floor beside him. Tenderly he took her face in his hands and kissed her. "This is the happiest I've ever been."

Ami nodded in agreement. Slowly they sank to the floor.

As they made love passionately, the sky was an asterisk to all they were feeling. They lingered over each sensation, touch, taste, and desire.

"I'm done for," Phil eventually whispered. "I've finally lost any semblance of control."

* * *

Jimmy hoisted himself into the booth at the ice cream parlor. Lucy took off her sunglasses as she slid into the seat opposite him.

"How was the convention?" she asked as she glanced at the menu uselessly. Did she ever order anything besides a hot fudge sundae, vanilla ice cream, whipped cream, nuts, no cherry?

"Amazing. Billy Barty is a fascinating guy and such a nice man. And by the way, he wasn't in *The Wizard of Oz*. Too young at the time. Children were allowed fewer work hours, so the producers weren't interested in dealing with kids."

"Interesting. I'll have to see the movie again sometime. I thought they were all children when I was a kid."

"Billy is third-generation Italian American. His real name is William John Bertanzetti. He told funny stories about how he used to spin around on his head as a child to get the stuff out of his pockets."

"What?" Lucy asked, taking a sip from water glass the waitress had filled.

"His arms were too short to reach into his pockets, so he twirled upside down on his head. It's practically the reason he got started in show business."

"Imagine something we all take for granted being such an ordeal."

"That's exactly what this convention was about. Integrating little people into mainstream society."

"How?"

"Education. So people realize we're not just in the circus or extras in movies. But also in concrete ways."

"Like what?"

"Helping to get rid of architectural barriers that make it impossible to do certain things. Organizing support groups that can work as a force to get adaptive aids invented and tooled, special furniture, clothing. I'm heading up a chapter of Little People of America here in Brooklyn."

"That's terrific. I'll be your first donor."

"I know you will, Lucy. You've always been there for me."

"How was Vegas? Did you win?"

"I hit the jackpot," Jimmy said, smiling broadly.

"No kidding? How much? Playing what?"

"Aw. Just about seventy-five bucks at blackjack. I hit a different kind of jackpot."

"What do you mean?" Lucy asked, trying to assemble ice cream, hot fudge, cream, and nuts all on one teaspoon.

"I met someone."

"Honest? Tell me more."

"Her name is Jane, and she's from New Jersey. She works in a podiatrist's office. She's blonde and blue-eyed and gorgeous. She was at the convention and luckily she and her friends had planned to visit Vegas for a few days too."

"And?"

"And after the first day in Vegas, she kind of ditched her friends and spent most of her time with me. I mean, I spent time with her group too, since I was on my own, but evenings we took off."

"You fast worker, you."

"Lucy, I'm crazy about her."

"I'm so happy for you. Just don't jump into anything blindfolded."

"She calls me Tarzan," Jimmy said sheepishly.

"Tarzan? What, is she a comedienne?"

"Thanks. It's better than Dopey. No, like, 'Me, Tarzan, you, Jane.' Get it?"

"Okaaay. Can't wait to meet her."

"I was hoping we could get together on Sunday. Maybe you can bring Val."

"Since I don't have anyone special like you?" Lucy kidded. "Actually, I can't. We're having one of my father's musicales on Sunday. Want to come?"

"This time I sincerely mean no. I'd rather be alone with Jane if I can't be showing her off to you."

"We'll make it another time. You can practice your Tarzan yell in the meantime. When you've perfected it, just give a holler, and we'll come running to meet up with you."

* * *

"I went to a good deal of trouble, Mousey. Don't turn me down."

"You know I'm not crazy about this kind of thing."

"For me. It's a big deal. Starting off the holiday season with a premiere of my movie. It will be fun, I promise. I really have no other time to be with you. They're flying me in for the premiere of *Litterally Yours,* and then I have to go back again."

"Will we arrive on the back of a sanitation truck?" Lucy kidded.

"No. A limo. A white one if you want. They wanted me to escort Noreen Morrissey. Trying to stir up rumors about us. I really had to work this, Lucy."

"All right. I want to see you too.

"You could pretend to be a little jealous of me. It might heal my bruised ego where you're concerned," Tavis suggested half kiddingly.

"I *am* jealous of all your movie starlets. They're in the right place at the right time."

"Nothing to be jealous of, Mousey. Like you said, they're starlets. You're the whole damn galaxy in my eyes."

Chapter 37

1. Movie, *Desk Set.*

Work on my sly repartee. She seems to love it.

2. Hayride with Jimmy and Jane on Long Island.

Great for holding her close.

3. Dinner at Monaco's. Back to her house to watch *Gunsmoke.*

Luckily, she's not into Westerns too much.

4. Bowling with Phil and Ami.

Wish she was a better bowler. Jumped into my arms or lap for the three spares she managed to score.

5. Babysit Adriana. Yay! She finally fell asleep.

Wow!

6. Ride to Bear Mountain. Antique shopping.

Most romantic to date. Fell asleep on my shoulder on drive back.

7. Pumpkin Festival in Amagansett.

Almost too exhausted to neck later on, with all the pumpkins she made me carry. Almost.

8. Tonight.

Lucy was going to the theater after leaving Julliard. They'd grab a quick bite to eat and head for the Forty-Second Street Library. They were taking in a sight and sound presentation on "The Beauty of Florence." Lucy was excited to experience the city her mother had known as a child.

"That settles it," Lucy reported to Val as they stood alongside one of the famed New York Public Library marble lions after the event. "I have to visit Florence. What an incredibly beautiful city. So much to see!"

"I'll be happy to go with you," Val said. "We'll tour the Uffizi, where Venus has nothing on you. We'll eat in a little trattoria, and I'll buy you leather shoes, leather purses, leather hats, leather coats, leather belts…"

"Just what are you suggesting, sir? Does my father know you're trying to seduce me with cowhide?"

"You can really kill a moment, Lucy. I'm trying to be gallant, and you bring cattle into the picture."

Lucy took Val's hand and kissed it. "You don't have to act at being gallant. You are naturally charming, considerate, and a total dear."

Val drew her closer and moved to kiss her. People scurried on the street before them. Lucy put her hand to his chest.

"You're not going to start a romantic encounter here on Fifth Avenue."

Val sighed. "I'm also brother to these lions," he said morosely.

"What do you mean?"

"Don't you know their names?"

Lucy shook her head.

"Patience and Fortitude."

* * *

Anger swept over him like a tidal wave.

"I'm not happy, I don't approve, and frankly, I won't have it," Val said in a tight voice. The tension in his expression emphasized his well-shaped jaw line and taut brow.

"Be reasonable," Lucy said soothingly. "I promised Tavis I'd go to the premiere with him months ago. We weren't officially dating back then, if you're keeping score. I can't go back on my word. Besides, we're only friends. How can you be jealous of someone I haven't seen for over a year?"

"He's like an annoying rash that never fully heals, but flares up every so often to drive me crazy."

“He may be a rash to you, but he’s a dear friend to me.”

“I don’t like this whole red carpet, photographers, late-night party thing.”

“And I don’t like this whole ‘I don’t approve, I won’t have it, your friend is a rash’ thing. We haven’t made any commitments to each other, Val. We’re only beginning to know each other on a different level.”

“I’m not going backward with you, dammit.”

“Nor do I want to. But Tavis is my friend, and he will always be my friend. We talk, write occasionally, and once in a blue moon, we get to see each other. I can promise you this. In the future, when he visits New York we’ll spend time with him together. I’m sure he can dig up a girl to be with.”

“No doubt.”

Lucy smiled tenderly at Val’s huffy tone. She stepped comfortably into his arms, and kissed him with the intensity of his own emotions.

“Need any further reassurance?” she asked.

“So you’re going to give up these private rendezvous as easy as that?”

“Now would be a good time to keep your mouth shut.”

* * *

Lucy glided down the stairs and faced her parents seated in the parlor. Maestro put the pen he was using to make notes down on the coffee table and removed his glasses. His lips trembled slightly even as his heart jerked in surprise.

"You look heartwrenchingly beautiful," he whispered hoarsely.

Giuliana stared at her daughter, dressed in the body-skimming gold silk gown she had worn to the opening of the Salvatori Opera Company over twenty years before.

"Was I ever that beautiful?" she asked, in awe of this child of hers.

"*Si,*" Maestro replied, transported back in time. "You looked identical in that dress. You are even more beautiful now."

"Ever the charmer, your father," Giuliana observed, breaking the mood.

"The limousine just pulled up," Maestro noted.

A few moments later, there was a knock on the door, followed by the bell. Lucy opened the door. Tavis's eyes grew wide, and he took a step back.

"Lucy, you are without a doubt the most magnificent creature I have ever laid eyes on."

"Likewise. I'd say you might do for tuxedos what Marlon Brando did for undershirts. Come on in."

Both Giuliana and Maestro rose to greet him.

"Congratulations on the premiere. It seems they expect big things from this movie," Maestro said.

"It's just a romantic comedy. The Christmas show at Radio City gets play in it as well as New York all dressed up for the holidays. They are hoping it does really well over the season."

"You'll be eligible for the Academy Awards," Giuliana suggested.

"I doubt that. Like I said, it's light fare, but it's fun. It is a big deal to get a premiere at Radio City itself. We'd better be going, I'm afraid. It was good to see the two of you again."

Lucy picked up a small suitcase by the front door before exiting.

"What's the suitcase for?" Maestro questioned testily.

"She's staying at Tino's tonight. It will probably be a late night."

"You're certain?"

"That's what she said."

The chauffeur opened the car door for the couple. As Lucy slid in, Tavis asked, "Where's my fan club?"

"We didn't mention that I was going to the premiere to a soul."

"But Mrs. Rossi! How could you not tell Mrs. Rossi? You could have met me at the Music Hall had I known I wasn't going to get to see her."

"I can run across the street and see if she wants to slip into this dress and go with you," Lucy teased.

"Christmas will be over before she manages to stuff herself into that gown. No, I guess I'm stuck with you."

They caught up on each other's lives as they crossed the borough into Manhattan. Fifth Avenue was closed off for several blocks on either side of Radio City Music Hall to accommodate the throng of exhilarated fans.

"There really is a red carpet," Lucy commented as their limo waited in a line of cars waiting to sacrifice their cargo to the hysteria beyond. Lucy jumped as a hand pounded on the back window. She could see the faint impression of it on the tinted window. The driver rolled down his window a few inches.

"Please keep your hands off the car, ladies," he warned.

The car bounced as someone sat on the trunk. A police officer shooed the trespasser away.

"This is crazy," Lucy gasped.

"The premiere is by invitation only. Everyone will be normal inside. Well, at least as normal as show business people can be," Tavis amended.

When they pulled up to the spot to disembark, the chauffeur stepped out and opened the back door. Tavis emerged to a roar of squeals, cries, and exclamations. He waved to the crowd, whispered to the driver, who stepped aside. Turning back to the car, he extended his right hand to Lucy. She clasped it, and as she started to emerge, Tavis whispered, “Don’t tell me I never take you any place nice.” Lucy threw back her head and laughed. Both of them were momentarily blinded by a flashbulb popping off in their faces.

* * *

Lucy felt like her eyes were still glazed with flash-bulb stars as she scanned the crowd at the after-theater party. Famous faces came over to congratulate Tavis. Men ogled Lucy; women wondered whether she was a new actress with whom they’d soon be competing. Lucy stood to the side while Tavis took a series of photos with his lovely co-star. He came hurrying over when he was through.

“Sorry. It has to be done.”

“I don’t mind. While you’re dallying with all the gorgeous ladies, I’m searching the crowd for James Darren.”

“I made sure he wasn’t invited.”

“Spoilsport.”

Tavis kissed her swiftly on the lips. "A few more minutes of this, and then we can blow this crowd. Is that OK with you?"

"Very."

They hustled out a back door and into the waiting limo.

"Where are we headed?" Lucy asked.

"Waldorf. That's where they set me up. Pretty cool, huh?"

"To think I knew you when."

"When was that? Before you loved me?" Tavis asked, taking her hand.

"Before we became dear friends."

"Platonic."

"Just think of me as your girl in the New York port."

"That's not what a girl in every port means."

"Consider it drydock."

"Don't I know it."

* * *

Upstairs, Lucy ogled the city lights from the suite's living-room window.

"Takes my breath away every single time. I've known the heartbeat of New York City my entire life, and it still gets to me."

"It's magical," replied Tavis, coming up behind her and putting his hands on her shoulders.

Lucy put one of her hands on his. "Are you finding your way out there in LA? Are you making a real life for yourself?"

"I'm trying. It's not easy. Movies aren't real life, and I'm filming all the time. Girls screeching and crying isn't real unless you mean my mother yelling at me when I was a kid. Magazines asking inane questions about my life, and my picture being plastered on everything made of paper isn't real either. If I didn't love the actual work so much, I'd give it all up. Perhaps I should have tried to be a Broadway actor. I don't think their lives get this nuts. Plus, I'd be close to you."

Lucy laid her head back against his shoulder. "That would have been nice."

Tavis took a step back and moved to face her. He kissed her tenderly once. Taking her hand, he led her to the sofa. Lucy kicked off her shoes and tried to bend her knees under her, but couldn't manage it with the slim skirt.

"That won't work," she commented. "I guess I'm stuck here like a mermaid."

"You could take it off."

"Tavis."

"Lucy. I'm asking you to come back to California with me. We can be happy. I promise you that."

"You know I can't."

"I'm asking you to marry me, Lucy. Please consider it. Please say yes. I love you with everything in me. If you think my being an actor is hurting our relationship after five years, I'll give it up. I swear this to you."

"Oh my God, Tavis," she said in a voice barely above a whisper. "Don't do this to me. I love you. Of course I do. But we can't marry. I'd never ask you to give up your career. In time you might come to resent me for that."

"Never."

"You can't know that. We can only try and prevent that kind of heartache. Tavis, I'm trying to make a life for myself here. One that includes you as a friend for all of it. It can't be anything more. It just wasn't in the stars for us, Thomas DiGregorio."

"I don't want to hear you saying good-bye."

"I have to say good-bye because I can't go with you. Someday, when we're both more settled in our lives, we can meet together as devoted friends."

Tavis reached into his jacket pocket. As his hand withdrew a blue velvet pouch, Lucy cried, "Please, no, Tavis."

"It's not what you think, Mousey. If you had said yes, I would have taken you shopping in the Diamond District to pick out the ring of your dreams. This, instead, is because I knew in my heart what you would say."

Lucy loosened the rope tie. She shook the pouch and into her hand tumbled a crystal heart with a single tear suspended in its center.

"That's my heart, Lucy. It will always belong to you. It will always cry for you. If you cannot love me as my wife, then treasure me as your beloved friend who loves you from afar."

Tears glistened on her cheek and lashes. "You've sure learned how to say your lines, Mr. Gregg," she said, trying to inject humor into the depressed doleful air that surrounded them.

"When the words are from the heart, they don't need to be rehearsed."

"I think I'd better go."

"I'll let Stephan know we're coming down."

Lucy shook her head. "Stay here, Tavis. Let me say good-bye right here." She kissed and hugged him and turned blindly for the door.

"Lucy."

She turned.

"I played fair. Did you notice? I remembered the rules."

"I did notice, Tavis. More's the pity."

* * *

Lucy slipped her key into the lock.

"Oh! Hi, guys," she greeted Tino and Renzo seated at the small table in their living room. "I hope you didn't wait up for me."

"No, hon. We just got in about a half hour ago. Do you want a cup of tea?" Tino asked.

"You look absolutely gorgeous, Lucy," Renzo said with only the barest trace of an Italian accent.

"No to the tea. I have to get out of this dress."

"How was the premiere?" Tino asked.

"Fun. The movie's terrific; the party was incredible. I'm beat, though. There's more to tell, but I'll tell you in the morning if you don't mind, sweetie."

"Sure. The couch is made up, see? We'll just take these into the bedroom and leave you to do your thing. C'mon, Renzo."

* * *

Tino groaned and reached for the ringing phone. He burrowed further under the blankets as he answered.

"Hello?"

"Tino?"

"Maestro!" Tino hoisted himself upright, alert. "What's wrong?"

"Nothing is wrong. I was doing some work, and I need to ask Lucy something."

"At six o'clock in the morning? Are you kidding me?"

"Oh. Is it only six? I've been up working. I lost track. Is she there?"

"Yes, she's here. Wait. I'll get her," he said, swinging his legs out of the bed. "She's not going to be happy," he murmured under his breath. He put the receiver down on the night table.

"Tino, Tino."

He could hear his father's voice calling from the rested receiver. He picked it up again.

"What?"

"Never mind. Let her sleep. I'll talk to her when she gets home." Maestro put the phone back and in his pajamas padded contentedly from Lucy's room back to his own bed.

* * *

Lucy sat at the table over a cup of coffee telling Tino about the previous evening.

"The proverbial star-crossed lovers," Tino said sadly.

"That's what I said."

"What about Val? He's crazy about you."

"I know that. I'm extremely fond of him too. Which is why I had to tell Tavis good-bye. I want a real life with a real marriage and real kids. I can have that with Val." Lucy played with the crumbs from her toast. "Don't tell him that, though. I don't want him proposing next week."

At the sound of a key in the lock, they turned to look at Renzo.

"Newspaper and milk," he announced, kicking a pair of sneakers out of his path.

"We drank the coffee black. There's more in the pot," Tino said.

"Lucy, dear. You're in for a bit of a surprise," Renzo advised.

"Now what?"

"I had to wait to pay for the milk, so I started looking through the paper. Look, right here on page six."

Lucy looked down and saw herself, head thrown back in laughter, hand in Tavis's, emerging from the limousine. She read the caption:

"Tavis Gregg, who plays a sanitation man in his new movie, *Litterally Yours,* is also a chauffeur as he lends a hand to his date for the premiere, Lucilla Salvatori."

"Lucilla? Boy, they really did their research," Tino noted.

"Oh boy. Val is going to have a cow," Lucy acknowledged, closing the newspaper with concern.

Chapter 38
1958

The February-stiffened limbs of bare trees twisted over the remaining patches of snow alongside the highway.

"I'm glad we didn't get that storm they were predicting," Lucy said.

"I know. Do you think she'll be surprised to see us?"

"I'd think so. I haven't seen Sister Grace in ten years, although we do write."

"I've been bad about writing, but Nick sends her my regards."

"A fiftieth Jubilee as a nun! How old do you think she is?"

"She's eighty. I asked Nick."

"Ha. We thought she was eighty fifteen years ago."

"How's your dad doing?" Jimmy asked.

"He's seeing doctors. He appeared to have the flu, but he can't seem to shake it. He's got this strange feeling in his toes, like being weak. In fact, his legs are weak. He truly uses that walking stick for support now."

"I hope they figure it out."

"Thanks, Jimmy. It's good of you to even ask."

* * *

Jimmy pulled into the parking lot at St. Joseph's in Brentwood, where the celebration was being held. They entered the auditorium of the school, which had been festooned with crepe paper and balloons.

"No haystack," commented Lucy with a nudge at Jimmy.

As they worked their way to Sister Grace, who was standing with a punch glass in her hand and talking to several people, Lucy groaned.

"Maybe I'm crazy, but that looks like Sister Agnes from St. Aly's to me."

"*The* Sister Agnes?"

"Uh-huh."

"Oh boy. OK. You're a big girl now, and you can show her who's the better person."

"Do I have to?"

"Luce," Jimmy warned in a low tone.

"Oh goodness! Oh my!" Sister Grace got misty eyed. "I can't believe what I'm seeing! Lucy! Jimmy!" She wrapped her arms around each of them individually.

"Surprised, Sister? How're you doing?" Jimmy asked.

"I'm thrilled. Even though you're a terrible correspondent for a journalist. Why don't you ever write?"

"Because there's no chance the editor will hit me in the back of my head with an eraser if I don't."

The group laughed.

"Let me introduce you. These are my two favorite students of all time, and I was lucky enough to have them both the same year." She made the round of names.

"Sister Agnes and I already know each other," Lucy said. "From St. Aloyisius."

"Of course. That's right," Sister Grace agreed. "Sister Agnes is still teaching there. She's also Prefect of Discipline."

"Things must be shipshape then," Lucy said. "Hello, Sister. It's good to see you again."

"Miss Salvatori," Sister Agnes said, inclining her head. "Nice to meet you, Jimmy."

"Nice to meet you, Sister."

"So you've known each other since Sister Grace's class."

"Before. Since first grade. Jimmy's always been my best friend."

"Are you a couple?"

"No, Sister," Jimmy injected.

"Jimmy has a girlfriend he's pretty serious about, Sister," Lucy tattled to Sister Grace.

"Where is she? I would have loved to meet her," Sister Grace asked.

"She had a family wedding. We couldn't do both, and I had to be here."

"Well, I hope I have the opportunity another time."

Jimmy and Lucy moved off to get some food.

"I can't believe that girl allowed herself to be seen with someone so different when she was a teenager," Sister Agnes whispered to Sister Grace.

"Lucy? She's one of the most wise and warm people I know. As a youngster she may have trembled where her own efforts had to be demonstrated, but she has always shown a heroic indifference to anyone's opinion about her choice of friend. She was always Jimmy's staunchest defender, and he is her shoulder to lean on and biggest booster."

* * *

After everyone had eaten, there was entertainment. A former pupil read a poem from her recently published book of poetry. Another young woman played the harp. Three nuns sang "Boogie, Woogie, Bugle Boy," much to everyone's delight. Lucy sat at the piano to play and sing, "You Made Me Love You," with some especially revised lyrics. The crowd loved it. Afterward, Sister Grace sat down with her gifts. From her brother Nick and his wife, Suzanne, there was a rocking chair crafted by Nick with a seat cushion by Suzanne.

"That's magnificent, Nick. You should go into business now that you're retired from the paper," Jimmy suggested.

"We'd starve to death. Do you have any idea how long something like that takes him?" Sue said.

Sister Grace opened Lucy's gift. "An electric blanket! Wonderful. These old bones are always cold nowadays."

"Hoping to electrocute a nun, Lucy?" Sister Agnes asked. The touch of humor was genuine, unlike the sarcastic barbs of yesteryear.

Lucy recognized the difference and admitted to herself that she had been full of sass and teenage superiority in her high school days.

"No, Sister. Just trying to thaw any remnant of ice in her veins," she kidded back.

Jimmy's gift was a beautiful plush bulldog, which brought a roar from the crowd, who knew Sister Grace's nickname. Sister Grace immediately christened him Fidelis.

As they bid their farewells, Jimmy said, "I have one more thing to tell you, Sister. You too, Lucy."

"Good news, I hope," said Sister Grace. "Are you getting married?"

"I'm working on that. No, it's something that you had the opening hand in. I've been nominated for a Pulitzer Prize."

"What!" Lucy squealed.

"That's wonderful," said Sister Grace. "I'm so proud of you."

"Aw. I'll never win, but it's a huge honor in any case."

"For what are you nominated?"

"I did a five-part series called, 'The Hard Climb Over the Rainbow.'"

"I read it," Sister said.

"That was an incredible series, Jimmy. I'm sure you have a real shot at the prize," Lucy insisted. "It called attention to a national problem. Not just for little people, but for anyone with a handicap."

"Talking about the Pulitzer?" asked Nick as he joined them. "Did I bring the *Daily News* a star or what? A true humanitarian. The piece calls for public and private agencies to notice and take action for people who wind up being second-class citizens due to disabilites."

"More important than the prize would be to see some results. Maybe even laws that make public places more accessible for those with handicaps. By the way, Nick, there's someone at Little People of America I'd like you to talk with. He's seen the aids you've come up with for me, and he wants to see about putting a line together."

"Well, look who's giving whom a job now," said Sister Grace with a loving gaze at her two favorite men in the world.

* * *

In the blossoming days of spring, Dan and Louisa announced they were expecting another child. Amidst that joy, Phil and Ami married. They were living in Ami's apartment in the city until they could find a larger place. Three of the apartments they had viewed in Brooklyn had suddenly become unavailable. Sadly, Sophia Titziani passed on at the age of seventy-nine, having been predeceased by her sister Rosa a year earlier. Phil imagined he could assuage his sadness by living in the apartment that had become a second home to him.

The landlord, who had known Phil since childhood, stared stonily at a distant tree while explaining that his nephew had just announced his desire to have the apartment. With Ami at his side, Phil squelched the torrent of angry words that threatened to erupt from his mouth. He had other battles to fight at the moment. Phil would have preferred to stay closer to home because Maestro was exhibiting increased signs of weakness. He struggled through the wedding on crutches, refusing to use the wheelchair that Dan and Phil delivered one evening.

"I will not have the world staring at a crippled old man," he roared, the infirmity not affecting his stubbornness or voice.

"It's hardly the world," Giuliana argued.

"The guests will be looking at Ami, not you," Phil pleaded.

It was useless. He hobbled into the reception and held court at the family table. He sounded robust and enthusiastic. Yet beneath the handsome visage crouched a feeling of panic, lying somewhere close to the surface and heartbreakingly apparent to Giuliana.

Stubbornness could only carry his legs a short distance farther. As Maestro sat in the abhorred wheelchair, the doctor pronounced he had Guillain-Barre syndrome.

"We are perplexed by the slow progression of your illness. Usually it happens within days of the patient having the flu. However, it definitely appears to be Guillain-Barre. Sometimes the paralysis continues to move upward. If it affects your diaphragm, you will need to be hospitalized and put on a ventilator. For a while, at least."

Maestro sat stonily silent, willing his body not to absorb these words.

"Doctor, what about his, er, bodily functions? Will he need help?" Giuliana asked fearfully.

"I am perfectly able to control myself," Maestro spit out coldly.

"We know, Maestro. Mom's asking about the future," Dan said.

"Chances are you will maintain control over your bowel and bladder. You will probably even maintain sexual function," Dr. Szabo reassured him.

"We will not discuss that in front of my sons," Maestro warned.

"Excuse me, Mr. Salvatori. Your family needs to know what to expect as well as you do. Your symptoms have worsened a lot slower than is often the case, so perhaps you will maintain a measure of use with your arms. I know you are frightened with the sudden onslaught of this paralysis. Let me reassure you. Oftentimes the symptoms disappear. It may take months or even years, but you may very well recover for the most part."

For the first week after the official diagnosis, Maestro rarely left his bed. He resisted the sponge baths Giuliana tried to give him. Eventually his fastidiousness won out, and he allowed her to help him into the tub.

"I'm like a suckling babe. You used to kneel at the side of the tub with the babies."

"I recall you doing the same for me one time on a trip to the Catskills. My mother was watching Dan and Phil. We stayed at that inn with a fireplace in the bedroom and the tub that was on legs. Remember? You went out to that speck of a town and came back with the most awful-smelling bubble bath ever made. You poured the whole thing in the tub, and then you searched for every part of my body through the suds. Eventually, you climbed in with me and..."

"Well, don't climb in now. You'll stop the circulation in my useless legs, and they will turn gangrene and fall off. I'm done. Help me out of here."

He maneuvered from wheelchair to bed or chair under his own power, oftentimes with Dan, Phil, or Tino hovering nearby waiting to assist. Lucy wasn't allowed anywhere near him when he needed to move from one seat to another.

Louisa warned Giuliana, "Be alert. Sometimes patients with Guillan Barre lose tactile sensation. Make sure he doesn't burn himself or get a bad cut he's not aware of."

"So far, he's aware of everything and makes sure everyone else is aware of it too."

"I guess that's a good thing in a way."

"He's driving me crazy. He won't leave the house. Phil tries to get him to go to the theater. He offered to pick him up in the car and get him there before anyone else arrives. He won't budge. Dan offered to take him to the radio station to watch him work. He's not interested. He just sulks and shouts."

"Give him time to adjust, Mom. Dan says he's always been a showman on his own terms only."

"It's true. He has hidden wounds that have always made him emotionally vulnerable. Yet there's a fire in his bones that I don't believe can be snuffed out. I just need to find the kindling that will get it blazing again," Giuliana said with more hope than conviction.

* * *

The podium stared down at her, solid and menacing. Lucy took another sip of water.

"I'd much prefer performing up there than giving a speech," she whispered to Val.

"Just let the music in your heart lead you, and you'll be fine," he reassured her.

They sat at a circular table with ten others in the Commodore Hotel. A congratulatory banquet hosted by the *Daily News* was being held in Jimmy's honor. He had been awarded a rare Special Citation from the Pulitzer Committee for his series, "The Hard Climb Over the Rainbow." Jimmy sat with Jane, his parents, Sister Grace, Nick and his wife, Suzanne, his editor, Billy Barty, and his wife, Shirley. Lucy was a featured speaker at Jimmy's special request.

After several congratulatory speeches and a brief recap of the winning series, Lucy was introduced. Val squeezed her hand, and she approached the podium in a sweep of peach chiffon.

> "Good evening, ladies and gentlemen. I was barely six years old and cowering under the teacher's desk the day I met James Ferraro. Jimmy got down on his knees and dragged me into the world of first grade. That was the last time I ever saw Jimmy bend down to anyone. I was immediately enchanted by his fun-loving spirit and amazing disregard

for what others thought about him. Over the years, that boy grew into a man who greeted the world with warmth, generosity, humor, and unparalleled loyalty to his friends. He befriended me with a devotion that is indicative of how he lives his life. Always minimizing his own difficulties, miseries, and heartaches, he taught me to believe in myself, to stand up for myself. Never angry or abrasive, he chose to teach others who were less than kind to him through example and forbearance.

I do not need to embellish Jimmy's attributes. They are pure, clean, and life sustaining. He is a gifted listener. So he learns. He is quietly firm. So he accomplishes. He is intelligent. So he recognizes inequities and strives to correct them. "The Hard Climb Over the Rainbow" is not a strident editorial crying injustice and spewing demands for equality. It is an eloquent statement from one who has known disregard and disrespect and is therefore sensitive and sympathetic to the plight of those in similar situations. He fights to make the world more accessible to those who have been callously shoved to the fringes of society. Jimmy never points an accusing finger; as always he gives the benefit of the doubt.

He seeks to inform those who are unaware and win them over by the righteousness of his position.

Jimmy has started a chapter for Little People in America here in New York. He saw a road to make a difference and immediately set his path. This journey did not blind him to others on different yet similar paths to his. His words encourage all of us to notice, to care, and to get involved.

The book of Sirach, chapter 6, says, 'A faithful friend is a sturdy shelter; he who finds one finds a treasure.' I have been blessed to know James Ferraro for most of my life. I have already found the treasure at the end of the rainbow. I can only strive to stand as tall as he. Together we can only wait to see how high his dreams of justice and goodwill lift all of us.

I love you, Jimmy."

The guests broke into thunderous applause as they rose to their feet. Jimmy scooted to the steps by the stage to escort Lucy down. They hugged, and Lucy lowered herself to sit on the edge of the stage to kiss Jimmy full on the mouth.

"Nice job, kiddo. You said all your lines without any prompting from me. It only took you twenty years to get over your fear of speaking in public. Who says I'm not a great teacher?" Jimmy said as he led her back to the table.

* * *

Jimmy caught up with Giuliana as she returned from Sunday Mass.

"Hi, Mrs. Salvatori. How's it going?"

"I've known better, Jimmy. Lucy is inside with the old grouch. She still has to go to Mass."

"Can I come in for a second? I have something for Mr. Salvatori."

"Enter the lion's den at your own risk," Giuliana said grimly.

"He's always been a lion to me. Now I can actually look at him a bit more eye to eye."

"For your own well-being, I wouldn't point that out to him."

Giuliana opened the front door. "Excuse the mess. We are having an elevator chairlift installed on the staircase. The job should be completed tomorrow."

"That's going to be a kid magnet," Jimmy observed.

"Giuliana! Is that you? What took you so long? Lucy couldn't find my blue shirt."

"I'm here, *caro,*" Giuliana said, brushing his cheek with her lips and rolling her eyes at Jimmy. "The shirt is in the laundry. Wear something else."

"That one is cool. I want that one."

"You have other cool shirts. I'm not doing the wash until tomorrow. Do you want chicken with olives today or not? I have to get started on that." She brushed a lock of hair that had fallen across his brow to the side. "Look. Jimmy came to see you."

Maestro's face tightened. "I don't want visitors."

"That's good because I can't stay. How're you doing, Maestro? Getting a fancy new gadget to climb those stairs, huh? I could have used one of those in school. I would have been pretty cool."

"You would have been a spectacle."

"I already was. But then I would have been a motorized spectacle. Way cooler. Anyway, I was talking to my friend Nick about you."

"What would you do that for? You making announcements all through Brooklyn? Why don't you see if Dan can run a telethon for his pathetic father on his radio show?"

"I don't think he'd raise much money on your behalf, Maestro. You're not as pathetic as you'd like to think you are." Jimmy winked at Giuliana, who stood with her mouth agape. "I spoke with Nick because he had polio real bad way back when. He suggests, Mrs. Salvatori, that you massage all of Maestro's limbs to keep the circulation going."

"You sure you don't want that honor, since you're such a know-it-all?" Maestro asked.

"Rinaldo. It's bad enough I have to put up with this attitude, but I am really embarrassed that you would focus it on non-family members too. Forgive him, Jimmy. The doctors say it's mostly his legs, but I think his brain is a bit paralyzed too."

"Your sarcasm is wasted on me. I'm supposed to improve. I'm not improving. I'm getting a Steeplechase ride in my house."

"The chair is not an amusement ride. And the doctor said you *might* improve. He didn't promise."

Jimmy intervened. "Well, in the event you do regain mobility, you need to be prepared. So do the massages. Plus," he added, opening the shopping bag he carried, "I've brought you these weights in the meantime."

"Am I going to pose as Atlas?" Maestro sneered.

"Not without that blue shirt. Your robe does nothing for your physique. No. I know about upper-body strength. I use my arms and shoulders to lift myself constantly. You'll need to develop those muscles so you can depend on them. These are light, only three pounds. Here, try it."

He plopped both weights in Maestro's lap.

"I'm not interested in your theories."

"Cut off your nose to spite your face just because I'm the one presenting you with the weights. That's real smart. Here, let me show you a few exercises. Mrs. Salvatori, maybe you want to take notes in case he forgets."

"I can't forget because I'm not remembering."

"Your choice. Let everything just shrivel up and atrophy. I'll leave the weights here for you. If you decide to use them, and you advance past these three pounders, we'll get heavier ones. In the meantime, I'm going to Riis Park with Jane today because no bully trying to kick sand in my face, or anything else for that matter, ever stopped me from doing anything. Today it's going to reach ninety-five degrees!"

Giuliana saw Jimmy to the door and returned to the kitchen. "Why can't you be more like him?" she asked in an annoyed tone.

"Because I was never crazy about the beach. Atlas! Hummph!" he said scornfully as he lifted one weight and did a bicep curl.

Chapter 39

Whirling sheets of water beat against the windshield as Lucy drove home from an interview with the family of a prospective piano student. The eight-year-old girl was enthusiastic and proudly pounded out "Heart and Soul" on the piano as her mother had taught her. Lucy jumped at the clap of thunder that shook the car as she leaned forward to better see through the streams of water. It was eight o'clock; she was starving. She knew her mother would have kept her dinner warm. Eating alone, away from her father's stone face and icy comments, might actually be preferable on this wicked night. The summer evening sky was already black, the streets ran with rivers of detritus, and the rain drummed on the roof of the car with a more frantic beat than Tino had ever attempted.

Once inside, Lucy shook herself like a puppy.

"I'm home," she called out.

"Dinner's warm," Giuliana called from the parlor.

"I have to change. I'm soaked. My umbrella collapsed when I left the Catanzaros' house. Where's Maestro?"

Giuliana joined Lucy in the entryway. "He went up to bed already. I think he does exercises with the weights before he goes to bed. He doesn't want me to know. He does them in the morning when he gets up too."

"He'd better not overdo it."

Giuliana sighed. "You know him…all or nothing."

* * *

Lucy came downstairs in pedal pushers and a blouse whose sleeves had been partially rolled up her arm.

"It's actually chilly," she commented. "What's for dinner?"

"Meatloaf, potatoes, peas. Salad is in the fridge."

The phone rang on the table next to the staircase.

"Got it," Lucy said. "Hello?"

"Hey, Mousey."

"Tavis! What a surprise. How are you? Hold on. Let me pull this cord so I can sit on the steps. I just got in."

"How are you?"

"I'm good," Lucy replied. His voice sounded odd. "Everything all right?"

"Not really. I have some bad news I have to tell you."

"OK," Lucy responded slowly. "I'm listening."

Lucy heard him suck in his breath. "I've got cancer."

She sat in stunned silence for a moment. "Where?"

"Pancreas. It's bad."

"Are you having surgery?"

"It's too far gone, Lucy. It's the size of a grapefruit."

"How could it get so far along? What kind of doctors do you have out there?"

"I didn't know. Reward for living a relatively healthy lifestyle. My body kept its secret as long as it could." Tavis's voice was melancholy.

"So what changed?"

"Abdominal pain. I didn't feel like eating. I lost six pounds. Mostly in my face, I guess, because my agent told me to see a doctor. He prescribed antacids and advised me not to get so stressed about making movies. But I wasn't stressed."

"Great doctor," Lucy said bitterly.

"Yeah, well, when I doubled over on the set while filming, it got taken more seriously. By then the damn tumor was gigantic."

"So what are they doing? Radiation?"

"No radiation, Mousey. It's too far gone."

Lucy became clinical. "Wait. I read something in *Time* magazine. Something about advances in medicine, some kind of chemicals to cure cancer. What about that?"

"Yeah. There's nothing out there for me, Lucy. I've got a spot on my liver too. It's spreading."

"No."

"I'm coming back East. I'm tying up loose ends out here. I'm going home to my folks' house to…I want to see you. Can you make time to spend with me?"

"Of course. Do you want me to come to Sayville?"

"No. I want to be alone with you for a few days, a week even. Away someplace. Maybe upstate. Just you and me. Rules intact, but I'd really like to be with you before I'm not able to see anyone anymore."

Lucy bit her lower lip and squeezed her eyes tight. A hammer thudding pain pounded in her head. "I'll make the arrangements. When do you want to go?"

"As soon as possible."

"I'll call with the details. Be strong, Tavis. I'll be praying for you."

"Thanks, Lucy. I love you."

* * *

Maneuvering like an undercover agent, Lucy put together the planned getaway. Robert Norse was a fellow professor at Julliard. He and Lucy were amiable colleagues and frequent luncheon companions. Robert's niece, Tricia, was part of an extended group of friends with whom Lucy socialized. The Norses were planning a two-week vacation upstate. Lucy didn't know where; it didn't matter. She told everyone she was sharing a room with Tricia Norse, who was joining her uncle's family upstate. Even Val was enthusiastic.

"I'm glad you're getting away. You've been working too hard. Since your father's abandoned us, my workload has increased dramatically. Phil's going to start interviewing for a staff assistant. I guess your father deserves to retire, but we're all sad that this is the way it happened. I'm going to try and clear the last weekend in August and the first weekend in September. Maybe we can plan some fun things for then."

Lucy made the reservation for a two-bedroom cabin at Villa Positano. They assured her meals could be delivered to the cabin if they preferred not to eat in the dining room.

"My husband is recuperating from an illness. We want to be quiet and by ourselves for the most part."

"The Sunset cabin should be perfect. It's right on the lake and is named for the breathtaking sunsets visible from your front door. We look forward to your arrival. Thank you, Mrs. Salvatori."

Lucy could see the outline of her promise to Val begin to blur.

* * *

The car was already waiting in the diner parking lot west of Idlewild Airport. Lucy honked lightly, and Tavis emerged carrying two cardboard cups of coffee. The driver retrieved Tavis's luggage and placed the two bags in Lucy's trunk. Tavis slipped into the front seat.

"Hi, beautiful. I feel like I'm in an espionage film."

"Hi, yourself." Lucy leaned in and gave Tavis a kiss. His face did look a bit thinner, but other than that he appeared healthy enough to her.

"Did you tell your folks where you were going?" she asked.

"I gave them the name of the resort. They wouldn't have let me out of the house otherwise. It's like I'm a kid again. They won't call, though."

"Good. You can't answer the phone. I'm sharing a cabin with a girl named Tricia."

"Oh good. I've always wondered what went on at slumber parties. Here, I bought you a coffee. It's pretty good."

"Thanks. You'll have to hold it for me. Let me take a couple of sips."

"How'd you hear about this place?"

"The woman in charge of costumes at the theater. She has wonderful things to say about it. Says the food is fantastic." Lucy grimaced. "Although I know you're not up to eating much."

"I've been eating a little better. I've been trying to eat healthy, although it kind of seems like a waste of time now."

"Don't."

"Right. No talk of tomorrow. We'll savor today."

* * *

Tavis remained in the car while Lucy went into the three-story white villa to register. She returned with brochures and the cabin key.

"We have to take this gravel road to the left. Then I have to bring the car back here to park." She handed Tavis the pamphlets. "It's beautiful inside. She insisted on showing me the dining room, the game room, and the nightclub. The lobby has a fireplace. There were fresh-baked cookies in there."

"You should have grabbed a couple."

"I did." Lucy pulled a napkin out of her shorts pocket. "One chocolate chip, one oatmeal raisin."

They carried their bags into the rustic cabin constructed of logs and bark. While Lucy returned the car to the parking lot, Tavis unpacked his toiletries.

"I didn't know which bedroom you wanted. This one faces the lake, the other one faces the mountains."

"I don't care."

"Then I'll take the lake. It's closer to the bathroom."

Lucy unpacked the supplies she had brought for the tiny kitchen area. "Do you feel like lunch? I can make a salad, eggs, tuna, cheese, soup. I have fresh fruit."

"Some soup sounds good."

"Campbell's Chicken Noodle?"

"Great."

After lunch, they lay in lounge chairs facing the lake, with a cup of tea in hand.

"Begin with your earliest memories, Lucy, and tell me about yourself. Don't leave out anything. Teachers, friends, relatives. Fights, tears, feelings. When you get to the part where you meet me, I want to learn about what you were thinking in that analytical mind of yours."

The next day they borrowed fishing poles and stood knee high in the water.

"The fish are circling the bait and laughing at us," Lucy observed, pulling in her baitless hook yet again.

"They recognize your defeatist attitude."

"I don't see where you're doing any better."

"They're judging me by whom I associate with."

"Well, excuse me. I'll go sit by the cabin and watch you catch our dinner." Lucy marched back to the lounge chair, happy to sit down out of the bright sunlight. She watched Tavis standing sturdily in the glistening water and felt a needle-sharp pain in her heart.

Dear God, he's only thirty-one years old. I don't understand. Please don't let this happen. Let us find a way out of this.

My ways are not your ways, a voice whispered inside.

No! Knock and it shall be opened to you. You promised.

Tavis let out a whoop. "I've got one!"

Lucy jumped up and ran to the shoreline. "He's not giving much of a fight," she observed.

Tavis grabbed the fish and walked back to her. He stared at it and started laughing. "He's been shot."

"What are you talking about?"

"Look." Tavis pointed to a hole that went clear through the fish's body. "I think it might have been a BB gun."

"Poor thing has suffered enough. Throw him back," Lucy said.

Tavis walked back into the lake and lowered the fish into the water.

"We're pitiful fishermen. Let's give it up," Lucy suggested.

"I'll have you know I'm a great fisherman. I grew up on the water, if you recall."

"Well, your glory days are obviously over."

"I know." The pain was thick in his eyes and voice.

"Oh God, Tavis. I'm so sorry. That was the wrong thing to say."

Lucy's hands fluttered helplessly. Tavis took her in his arms.

"No, sweetheart. It's better we face the truth. Hey, I feel like going over to the main house and see what's going on over there."

"OK."

"Let me get my sunglasses and hat."

They walked down the gravel path hand in hand. Families were swimming back and forth to a raft at that end of the lake. Seniors played shuffleboard, a checkers tournament was under way, and voices shouted from a bocce court nearby. They dawdled by picnic tables where kids were making jewelry. The younger children played with pop beads; older kids were stringing beads of assorted shapes and sizes. Teenagers were painting on flat wooden square beads. One talented girl had strung together a bracelet of squares on which she had painted tiny images from the resort.

"You're very good," Lucy complimented her.

"Thanks."

Tavis picked up the finished product. He recognized daisies, a trellis of roses, a bird, stars, water, a mountain, a fork and spoon. "What's this?" he asked.

"Our cabin door," the girl explained.

"Yes, of course. See the tiny VP in the center?" Lucy agreed. "I love it. I bet you can sell these to the proprietors."

"I want to be a designer someday."

"I'll be your first customer," Tavis said. "How much for the bracelet?"

"Oh no. You can just have it. I'll make another. I enjoy doing this."

"Absolutely not." He pulled a five-dollar bill out of his pants. "Here you go. No ice cream for you, Lucy. I'm all out of cash."

"Five dollars! Wow! Thanks. This is way cool." She looked closely at Tavis.

"Did anyone ever tell you you look like that actor Tavis Gregg?"

Lucy stiffened.

"Yep. All the time. I think I'm better looking, though."

"My mom's crazy about him."

"Your mom, huh?" Lucy snickered.

"Yeah. There she is, over there. The redhead."

Tavis and Lucy turned to see a startling pretty redhead in shorts and halter top talking with a group of women.

"Well, now. Let's hear it for the mom fan club," Tavis whispered to Lucy as she slipped the bracelet on her wrist.

That evening they ordered roasted chicken and yams from the dining-room menu. They sat at a small table and finished off with coconut cream pie.

"This is even better than the pie from Chock Full o' Nuts," Lucy commented.

"You can finish mine. I'm stuffed."

"No, I musn't. I'll put it in the fridge."

She brought the dishes to the sink and began to wash them.

"I don't think you have to do that. The staff will just collect them in the morning."

"I don't mind. I'd rather not leave them sitting dirty overnight."

"You look so domestic. Like we're married."

Lucy didn't respond.

"You didn't tell Val the truth, did you?"

Lucy turned off the faucet and wiped her hands on a towel.

"What do you think?" She ran her hand through her hair. "It would upset him too much. What was I supposed to do? I had to come and spend this time with you."

"I'm sorry you have to lie. But I'm glad you came. Will you marry Val?"

"Maybe. I don't know. I think so. He's a great guy, conscientious, considerate, loving. It's just that he's been part of the family for so long…"

"You have to get over the familiarity breeds contempt thing?"

"Not contempt. Not at all. I overlooked him. Neglected to recognize who he really is. I'm rectifying that. It's easy work."

"I'm glad. Truly. I want you to be happy."

* * *

Lucy's eyes flew open. She listened intently. Barefoot, she went into the small parlor and felt the wall for the light switch. The musty wood smell of a country night filled her nostrils.

"Tavis?"

An answering wretch sounded from the bathroom. She ran to the open door. He was on his knees over the toilet bowl. She got on the floor next to him.

"Tavis. I'm here."

"Go away," he croaked.

"No. We're married this week, remember? In sickness and in health."

She grabbed a towel and wet it under the faucet. Tavis flushed the bowl and leaned back against the wall, his knees raised. He groaned softly.

Lucy took the towel and wiped his face. She pushed his hair off his forehead and kissed it tenderly.

"Your stomach?"

He answered with a groan.

"Was it the dinner?"

Tavis shook his head. "Doesn't matter what I eat. When the pain comes, it charges through whatever's in its path. I'm sorry. I was doing so well."

"Let's get you back in bed."

"I may get sick again."

"I'll find something in the kitchen and bring it to your room."

Tavis was sitting up in the bed, two pillows behind his back when Lucy returned with an empty coffee tin.

"I found this under the sink."

She sat down next to him on the bed. "Smoosh over a little. I'm falling off the side."

Tavis moved and gave her one of the pillows. He leaned forward in pain again. "I have to curl up on my side."

"Go ahead. Put your head in my lap if you'd like."

Tavis shimmied down and did as Lucy suggested. She played with his hair, rubbed his forehead, his shoulder.

"Lucy, I'm lying here thinking, but it's no use. I can't gather the words together that can express how much I love you."

"Sssh. What do we need with words? Words can't change anything. Words won't erase the memories or ease the years ahead. Words will only give credibility to the grief that lies before us. Sshh. Try to sleep. I'm right here with you."

The stars seemed to have descended so low, they looked like a stage setting hung over the lake. Lucy sang the lullabies she hummed to Adriana until Tavis's chest gently rose and fell in sleep.

By noon the next day, Tavis was feeling better. They took the car into the town, such as it was, and browsed through the country shops. They drove on a bit farther, parked on the side of a road, and took a scenic walk. The sun played peekaboo from behind a veil of clouds painting a sloping meadow in brilliant green, a brook in chilly silver, the mountains in darkest pine. When Tavis began to tire, they watched two young girls on horses practice jumping and dressage in a field set up for practice. As twilight stole upon them, they walked back to the car in the deepening shadows.

* * *

"Rummy," Tavis said, laying down his spread. "Three to two. I think I'll quit while I'm ahead."

"Hi."

Lucy and Tavis looked up at Mina, the owner of the Villa. Her tightly permed hair covered her head like a sheepskin coat.

"I have a flat of figs here. I don't want you guys to miss out. You're never up by the villa."

"Thanks," said Lucy, reaching for a blackish purple fig. She bit into it. "This is delicious. So sweet."

"Take more." She offered the flat to Tavis. "Have one. They're full of nutrients and minerals. Good for whatever you've got."

"That would be something," Tavis murmured. He picked out one and bounced it in his hand.

"I also came to tell you that the rowboat you asked about is available now. I don't know if it's too late for you, though."

Lucy stood. "No, that's great. We just want to take a short ride. We'll be right down."

"I also wanted to tell you that tomorrow night we do a barbecue. The music is outdoors, and there's dancing. We've got a special treat. The Four Lads will be performing live."

"That's fantastic. Thanks for telling us," Lucy said.

When Mina left, Tavis handed the fig to Lucy. "I picked out the biggest one for you."

"Try it."

"Ugh." He took a bite and shook his head. "Nope. I don't know why. It's sweet, but I think it's the outside texture. It's like fingernails on a blackboard to my tongue."

"Give it over then," Lucy said, taking it from him and munching happily as they walked down to where the rowboat was waiting.

Lucy insisted on rowing, much to Tavis's chagrin. They paused to watch children up on the lawn play with sparklers. They jumped impatiently, waiting for their sparkler to be lit. Their childish squeals crossed the water as the sparkler burst into crackling brilliance and the falling pinpoints of light danced around their feet. Lucy rested the oars and scooted across to sit beside Tavis. The boat rocked and water splashed on their feet.

"Oops. Sorry."

Tavis put his arm around her. "You have chicken skin."

"It is getting chilly out here. Look. What's that at the water's edge?"

"A raccoon, I think."

Tavis turned to face Lucy and kissed her tenderly. "This week has been amazing. I can't believe we only have two days left."

"Savor the moment, Tavis," Lucy whispered, laying her head on his chest.

The next evening, they sat outside the cabin with coffee and s'mores that Lucy had confiscated from the barbecue. The sound of the Four Lads wound through the trees and circled around them.

"This is really nice," Tavis commented.

"Moments to Remember" drifted up to them.

"Dance?" Tavis asked, extending his hand.

Lucy crept into his arms, and they moved slowly to the music. The poignant lyrics, filled with the ache of anticipated absence, infused Lucy with a despair she was unable to squelch. She broke down in sobs, digging her nails into Tavis's arms.

"Hey, Mousey. C'mon. We've been doing great. None of this." He pulled away and wiped her face with his fingertips. "I won't have my best girl crying on my account."

He led her to the chair. He sat and drew her onto his lap.

"Let's pretend I'm going back to Los Angeles. I have this fabulous co-star in my new movie. Her name is, uh, Cissie LaRue. You know the type…blonde, bazookas out to here, legs the length of a giraffe's neck. I completely fall in love with her and marry her. I'm a big jerk. I never call or write you again. We're separated by three thousand miles, and you hate my guts. You never want to see me again." He kissed her lips, which had lifted into an amused smile. "Let's pretend that's what happened. That's the reason we're apart."

"Can you have been hit by a truck and been slightly brain damaged before you marry Cissie?"

"Sure."

"OK. Let's pretend."

* * *

Lucy was just about to turn down the gas lantern she had carried into her room when she heard the crash. Grabbing the lantern by its handle, she ran inside.

"Tavis? Are you all right?"

"Sorry, Mousey. I knocked the ashtray off the table when I went to turn off the light." He stretched down the side of the bed to reach it.

Lucy put the lantern on the dresser. "Stay. I'll get it."

Tavis sat back in bed.

"I'll put it on the dresser. No one's using it anyway," she said, picking the ashtray off the floor. "Good night then."

The lantern light shown through her pale-pink nightgown, which ended mid-knee. Tavis stared at the rise of her breasts through the thin fabric. Her waist eluded the pink cotton nightgown, which then flowed softly over her hips. The outline of her thighs was clearly visible in the soft light. He sat there staring, mesmerized.

"Tavis?"

"Do you have any idea how much I desire you right now?"

Lucy began to bring her arms across her chest. She stared into his eyes and resolutely returned them to her sides. She approached the side of the bed.

"How much?"

Tavis shook his head. "The longing is unbearable. More unbearable than some of the pain." He closed his eyes. "Go back to your room, Lucy, before something happens we'll both regret."

"No regrets, Tavis."

She reached for the hem of her gown and pulled it over her head.

"Open your eyes, Tavis."

He did as he was told. Her body gleamed in the lamplight. The night was silent except for the chirping of crickets creating their own midnight harmonies. The sound of lapping water could be heard through the screened window. Furry visitors had chosen the cover of darkness to play in the inky blackness of the lake.

Lucy put one knee on the bed and leaned forward. Her hair rippled across her face. Tavis reached up and moved it back. Hesitantly, she climbed in beside him. The feel of her nakedness beside him unleased a rapturous storm of desire.

"What about the rules?" he asked hoarsely.

"Rules are meant to be broken."

He urged her to her back and kissed her hungrily. He reached for her breast. Its fullness filled his hand completely. Tavis moved to his side to gaze at this miracle again. He skimmed his hands lightly over her breasts. He felt the softness, the firmness, the silkiness. His palms registered her growing desire, and he bent to kiss each breast in turn. Lucy clung to his back; her mouth trembled. She had not known this craving for fulfillment could be so excruciatingly painful. One hand reached for Tavis while the other tugged at his boxers.

Tavis assisted in the disrobe and continued to kiss her hips, her belly, her inner thighs, her knees. Sliding back up, he pressed his face in her breasts and used his tongue on each one until she was trembling. Their bodies cleaved together. Any pain Lucy might have known was overshadowed by the monumental fulfillment of their suppressed passion. Like a sparkler, a fire inched through her body until it exploded with a hidden brilliance for which she was unprepared. Lucy felt tears on her face; she realized they belonged to Tavis.

"I'm not sorry, Lucy. My life is complete."

"I'm not sorry either."

"I hope not. I've never been this happy. I will relive this night for the rest of my days."

Lucy curled into his arms. She could hear his thundering heart. Taking his hand, she replaced it on her breast. He squeezed gently.

"I want you to be happy. I love you so. Promise me you'll be happy," Tavis whispered.

"I'll try. It's too hard to think about here, now."

"You must. Or I'll never rest. You see, my heaven will be in your joy. Promise me."

"I promise."

Lucy lay with Tavis through the night. She dozed off and on, riding the crest of his breaths. She knew she would hide this euphoric liaison away like a cherished quilt made of love and memories that was too fragile to be exposed to the light or the scrutiny of others.

Chapter 40

"I've brought you five-pound weights," Jimmy said, dropping the box on the floor.

"Just leave them there," Maestro instructed.

"You know what? I want to try this lift chair. Here." He put the box on Maestro's lap and climbed into the chair. "Give me the weights. I'll bring them upstairs."

"This isn't Coney Island."

"Don't be such a killjoy. This is cool," Jimmy announced halfway up the staircase. "I may get one someday when I own a house. How much are they?"

"It's expensive," Maestro warned, wheeling himself into the parlor.

Jimmy descended and picked up the shopping bag he had brought.

"Want to play a game of Scrabble? We're having a Scrabble tournament at LPA as a fundraiser, and I want to bone up on the game."

"No, thank you."

"I'll play a game with you," said Giuliana. "Let's use the dining-room table."

They set up the board. A few words were down when Maestro rolled through the dining room on his way to the kitchen. He glanced at the game without comment. He returned with a banana in hand and paused at the table. Giuliana had set down the word *gadget.* Jimmy moved his tiles around and filled in *dwarves.*

"You did that on purpose," Maestro accused.

"What?"

"Wrote *dwarves.*"

"It's a legitimate word. Or hadn't you heard?"

"I know it's a word. You put it there for my benefit."

"You're not even playing."

"You could have spelled out....graves."

"Then I couldn't use the *w*, which is worth four points and on a double-score square."

"You're an instigator."

"Good word. But too long. If you want to play, I'll come back another evening. I can use all the practice I can get."

"You're a writer. You've got the advantage."

"You're taller. Your brain gets more oxygen."

"Very funny."

* * *

Two evenings later, the challengers met at the dining-room table.

"I'll go first," Maestro said, having lined up his tiles.

"You don't just go first. You have to draw a letter and see whose is higher."

"What's a higher letter?"

"*A* is higher than *B*."

"That's stupid."

"It's the rules."

"So James is better than Rinaldo because *J* comes before *R*?"

"Go. Go first. I don't care."

Meastro spelled out *obl.*

"What's that?"

"It stands for *obbligato.*"

"No abbreviations. No proper names."

"It's a music term. It means the instrument is necessary in the piece."

"It's a musical abbreviation."

"I'm not changing it. It's a good word."

"Fine. Keep it."

Jimmy put down his tiles. "O–a–f. Oaf."

In the kitchen making coffee, Giuliana covered her grinning mouth with her hand. She hurried inside to call Dan and tell him what was going on.

* * *

At the head of the stairs, Giuliana heard choking sobs from behind Lucy's closed door. She knocked.

"Lucy?"

No answer.

"Lucy, Lucy, answer me."

She turned the doorknob and peeked in. Lucy was curled in a tight ball on her bed. Her eyes were red, lashes in little clumps; tears ran a path down her lightly rouged cheeks. Her breath came in gasping sobs as she tried to gain control.

"Sweetheart, what is it?"

"Oh, Ma, Ma," she cried. "Tavis is gone. He's… he's gone." A new round of sobbing let loose.

"Oh, my poor darling. I'm so sorry." Giuliana sat on the edge of the bed and wrapped her arms around her child.

Short bitter cries of anguish and pain escaped Lucy's throat. "I can't stand it. It hurts so much."

Giuliana pushed her daughter's hair from her face. She reached for a tissue to wipe her streaked face.

"Tell me."

"His assistant called. He died this morning. The family is having only a one-day wake. They're afraid of the crowds and newspapers."

"We'll go. We'll all go."

"You can't. It's by invitation only. I've been invited. I can bring one person with me. A guest…like it was a wedding." Lucy started crying all over again.

"Val will go with you."

Lucy swallowed a knot of guilt and choked. "He can't. I can't. I mean I can't have him go with me. I just can't."

"All right. Do you want me to go with you? When is it?"

"I'm not going to the wake. I can't. I'll go to the funeral parlor on the morning of the service. Then I'll attend the Mass at his church." She reached for a piece of paper by her phone. "It's Thursday."

"Oh. Maestro has a doctor's appointment. I'll cancel."

"No. Don't cancel."

"What about Jimmy?"

"He'd have to take off from work."

"If he can, I'm sure he will."

Lucy sniffed. "Jimmy would be good."

"I'll call him for you," Giuliana promised, kissing Lucy's brow. She stood up and studied this wretched woman. What secret was Lucy hiding in her soul?

* * *

The mid-November air was cold and harsh, but the sun shone brightly through the windshield as Lucy and Jimmy headed east to Sayville.

Tavis's face floated before Lucy, and she covered her face with her hands.

"This is going to be unbearable, Jimmy."

"I'll be right there with you."

"I loved him," she said with raw-edged emotion.

"Of course you did. He was a great guy. This whole thing really stinks."

"Thanks for coming. Ma said you talked to Val."

"I told him I had to come out here for the paper anyway, so no sense him taking off from work."

"You're too good," Lucy sniffed.

"Is there something you want to tell me?"

"About what?"

"Why Val couldn't come."

"Just because I'm falling apart, and he's always been jealous of Tavis anyway. I don't think I can maintain my composure, and I don't want it to turn into a scene with him."

"OK."

Jimmy had to inch his way into the funeral parlor's parking lot through the throngs of curious surrounding the area. At the door, Lucy's name was checked off a list. They stepped into the room, which was stifling with the scent of flowers. Lucy could see Mrs. DiGregorio bent over in her husband's arms. Tavis's brother Bill hurried over.

"Lucy, thank you for coming."

"Of course. This is my friend Jimmy Ferraro."

"I'm sorry for your loss."

"Thank you. Do you want to see Tom?"

Lucy glanced quickly at the open coffin. His quiet profile made her bite her lip.

"Yes. All right."

Jimmy held her hand; Bill grasped her elbow. Escorted, she approached the open coffin and knelt down, grateful to be off her unsteady legs. She said a prayer and slowly raised her eyes. He was so much thinner than in August, but still beautiful. Was that an impish smile on his face? Of course not, it was the undertaker's handiwork. *The last time you had to sit for makeup, Tavis.* A sob escaped. "I'm sorry," she whispered to no one in particular. She stood up and leaned over Tavis's face. "I will carry you in my heart forever," she whispered as she bent to kiss his cold brow.

St. Lawrence the Martyr was surrounded by throngs of people. Television and radio stations had cameras and microphones aimed at the front door. Suffolk County Police managed the crowd and kept a path open for the mourners to climb the steps into the church. Jimmy was surprised at the highly wrought interior of the simple-looking country church. A huge altar was surrounded by ornate white latticework. Two four-tiered candelabras held burning candles. Flowers from the funeral parlor were clustered near the altar and lined the altar rail.

Lucy sat rigidly as the coffin was rolled down the center aisle, followed by Tavis's family. She kept her pale strained face focused blindly at the altar, but try as she might, she could not pray. *Why? Why? Why?* A low, guttural moan escaped unexpectedly, and Jimmy took her hand and kissed it. She tried to concentrate on the homily filled with the pastor's reminiscences of the young Thomas. Stories she had heard so recently told in his own sensitive, melodious voice.

She declined the family's invitation to return to their house. She couldn't face those rooms where they had spent time laughing and teasing. No amount of time at all, really, but in view of the actual number of hours they had shared, a lifetime.

They were quiet on the ride home. Lucy couldn't speak about any of her time with Tavis. It all seemed so fragile now, like a dream in the moment after you wake. She was afraid the harder she tried to hold on, the quicker it would all fade away. She was afraid she had messed up. Her heart was longing for yesterday. She felt herself hurtling hopelessly toward a calamitous unstoppable tomorrow.

* * *

"You sneaking away without saying hello?" Lucy paused on the bottom step, her hand on the banister.

"I didn't know you were home." Jimmy lifted a paper bag. "I came to steal some fig cookies to bring to Jane's house for Christmas Eve."

"How is Jane? I haven't seen her in ages. Say hi for me."

"She's fine. You haven't seen anyone in ages."

"I'm sorry. I'm exhausted at the end of the workday."

Lucy sat down on the stairs. Jimmy joined her.

"I know, kiddo. But people are worried."

"I'm OK. I need to refocus on what's happening now." She knit her brow. "Every time I try, something pulls me back."

"Like what?"

"I got a package in the mail today from Tavis's assistant. Two things he had set aside for me. Pulled the rug out from under me all over again. Plus, I feel like such a phony. Val mentioned that he read in the paper that there's going to be a memorial for Tavis in LA. He asked if I was thinking of going. I said, ever so casually, 'LA.? I wouldn't go there while he was alive. Why would I travel there now that's he's gone?' I was a perfect specimen of nonchalance."

"Did it make him feel better?"

"I'm not sure he was entirely convinced. He says I'm distracted and distant. He's probably right, poor guy."

"Can I tell you a secret?"

"Sure. Is it good?"

"The best." Jimmy hoisted himself up one step and whispered down over Lucy's shoulder, "I'm proposing to Jane on Christmas Eve."

"Jimmy!" Lucy turned to him. "I'm so happy for you. Lucky, lucky Jane."

"I bought the ring already."

"What's it like?"

"It's a cushion-cut diamond. Kind of a square shape because Jane never wears anything round. She says she's all round edges and doesn't need to add to the curvature. I hope she likes it."

"If she doesn't, I'll marry you, Jimmy."

"Too late for do-overs, Lucy. You missed your chance," Jimmy kidded, tugging at her hair.

* * *

From her doorway, Lucy stared at the brown paper wrapping strewn on her bed. Slowly she approached it and tossed the paper on the floor. She picked up the painting of the Sayville beach she had given Tavis for Christmas. Her finger traced her outstretched hand that almost, but didn't quite, reach Tavis's palm. She laid it down beside her and picked up a framed photograph. There she was, emerging from the limo, laughing with the naivete of those who believe life is fair. There was Tavis extending the hand she never held tightly enough. He had written on the photo: *To My Lovely Lucy…Love, your prom date, Tom.* How she wished she could climb back into that photo. Pull the car door shut and sit alone with Tavis.

Tell him she would be braver this time. She would be smarter. He always listened, he heard her, he understood her. She always questioned, she analyzed, she doubted him.

"Too late for do-overs," she whispered.

Chapter 41

1959

Knots in the stomach seemed to have replaced the comfortable familiarity of being together. Accusatory tones overrode sweet nothings. Lucy concentrated on putting one step in front of the other, step, by step, by step. She reminded her heart to beat; at times it felt like it had stopped and turned to point a denunciatory finger at her. Val swallowed each overlooked loving gesture, each unreciprocated word of devotion until they refluxed inside him and spilled acidly from his mouth.

"I'm tired of you trying to sabotage our relationship," he fumed in his office behind closed doors.

"I don't know what you're talking about. I'm just confused. We need more time."

"Until Tavis Gregg died, we were doing fine." There. It was out in the open.

"I'm in mourning. I admit it." Lucy looked at Val's stricken face. "Not just for Tavis," she equivocated. "For the waste of such a promising life. It makes me wonder if we really do have a purpose in life, or if it's just a crapshoot."

"Bullshit."

"When Dan was a kid, he almost died. I had never seen my fearless father enfeebled until then. This giant of a man was brought to his knees at just the possibility of losing his son. On his knees, but he couldn't pray. For him, God no longer existed. I understand now. I can't reconcile the God I know with what happened to Tavis. I feel like I have to start from scratch to make sense of the world again."

Val walked around his desk. He put his hands on Lucy's shoulders.

"I planned to ask you to marry me this spring. If anything, you're more skittish now than a year ago."

"It's not you, Val. You have to believe me. I'm truly making an effort. I want to have a family too."

She sat in one of the armchairs facing the desk. Val took the other and turned it to face her.

"I haven't told this to anyone yet. Alfredo Bevacqua at Julliard approached me several months ago with an application. I've been accepted to a master class in piano at the Chigiana Musical Academy in Siena."

"Is that Siena in Italy?"

"Yes. Alfredo promises it's an invaluable opportunity for me professionally. I'd only have this summer or next to be eligible. Piano students are limited to age thirty or under."

"It's just for the summer?"

"The master classes are held in July and August." She cleared her throat. "I also heard of a teaching position through the grapevine."

"Where?" Val asked suspiciously.

"In Siena. For the academic year. I'd be teaching music and English in what is equivalent to a high school here."

"You're running away."

"No. I just need a fresh start."

"You can be away from me for a year? Oh, wait. I forgot. That's easy for you."

"Now who's trying to provoke a fight? Your righteous indignation notwithstanding, it's an honor to be accepted to the master class."

"I'm sure it is. It's the Lucy withdrawal from life I'm more concerned with." Val stood up and strode behind his desk. "Out of curiosity, how are you going to communicate with your students?"

"I'm hoping my high school Italian will stand me in good stead. I've been reviewing. Besides, they're supposed to be learning English, and music has its own language."

Their eyes locked, each lost in a solo dance of denial. Val, nurturing the hope that her relationship with Tavis was never more than a friendship cut short. Lucy, reassuring herself that the residue from a broken promise could not leave a permanent stain on her conscience.

"I'd never wish you ill, Lucy, so good luck in your quest." He sat and swiveled the chair to face her. "I can't promise I'll be waiting for you when you return."

His boyish good looks had aged handsomely. The straight nose now appeared narrower as his nostrils flared. The strong chin tilted upward in defiance. His close-shaven cheeks were sunken, not from laugh creases but from the anger sucking them inward. Under the well-shaped brows, his dark eyes betrayed his sadness and fear.

"I understand," Lucy said simply.

* * *

Maestro raged. "It is inappropriate for a single girl to be on her own in Europe."

Phil wheedled. "You'll miss the birth of our baby in October."

Dan bribed. "I can arrange an introduction to James Darren. He has a movie about surfing coming out that he's promoting."

Tino cajoled. "Renzo was just hired by Balenciaga, and he's swamped with work. I was depending on your help in decorating our new apartment."

Giuliana implored. "You cannot run toward happiness if you leave everything you are at the departure gate."

"I'm not leaving everything. All the good is coming with me. I can't change the beginning of my story, but I can learn enough to change the end. I feel like it's written across the sky, 'Surrender, Lucy.' I want to stop directing and orchestrating every moment of my life. Let me just ride the tide and see what happens."

"Don't be meeting anyone over there and getting married."

Lucy laughed lightly. "That's not likely. This is just a bridge to figuring out my future. The return trip over the bridge ends back in Brooklyn."

Chapter 42

Eleven o'clock on a June morning. Lucy set her two pieces of luggage down in front of the massive wooden door and used the knocker to announce her presence. A woman in her seventies dressed in black, a huge white bun sitting on the back of her head like a spare tire on a '53 Buick Skylark convertible, opened the door.

"Signora Nappi?"

"Ah! Signorina Salvatori? *Entrata, per favore.* Come in, please." She called behind her. "Evelina! *Venga!*"

As Lucy moved her luggage into the stone entryway, a beautiful young woman with long, straight, blonde hair and striking hazel eyes came tripping down the staircase.

"Hello," she said, extending her hand. "I am Evelina. I am Signora Nappi's niece. Uh, how you say, great-niece. She ask I come to speak the English to you. I study in school."

"It's nice to meet you. You speak very well. Where do you go to school?"

"Oh! No more school. I finish long ago. I work at my cousin's shoe store." Evelina translated for her aunt, *Zia* Nina, who made a comment.

"She said I should work to look for a husband." Evelina winked at Lucy. "I do that too. Three boxes arrive last week. We put in your apartment. Come, I take you now."

The two women stepped back into the street almost into the path of a motor scooter.

"You must watch the scooter. You get used."

Evelina opened a huge wooden gate, which led into a courtyard. They walked around the building. A beautiful garden filled with flowers, orange and lemon trees, and a grape arbor spread before them.

"This is gorgeous," Lucy said.

"*Si.* You take the orange or lemon you want. Come. You are the stairs."

A travertine stairway led to a less-elaborate wooden door. Evelina opened it and handed Lucy the key. Lucy stepped into a good-sized living room, comfortably furnished with antique tables and armchairs. A modern pull-out sofa was the only nod to contemporary décor. Lucy stared in amazement at the ceiling painted with clouds, cherubs, vines, and flowers.

"Oh! My own Sistine ceiling."

"Sure. Many houses have painted ceiling and murals. Look at the kitchen. Modern icebox. Here's matches to light the stove. Dishes, pots in the cupboards." She led the way to the bedroom. It was a large room with a full-sized bed. Old photos stared back at Lucy from under glass on the dresser top. Lucy opened a door.

"I thought this was a closet!" she exclaimed, surprised to see a showerhead attached to the wall and a drain on the floor of the closet-sized room.

"No. Here is your wardrobe," Evelina explained, pointing to a magnificent armoire.

Lucy stepped to the huge French doors along one wall. Opening them, she stepped out onto a loggia offering a breathtaking view of Siena's hills in the distance. The streets and landscape were dotted with red-toned houses. She recognized where Crayola had gotten the name for one of the new colors in their box of sixty-four crayons, raw sienna. A rich earthy red.

"I think I'll be spending a good deal of time sitting out here doing my work," Lucy remarked.

"Don't do only the work. Siena is place full of life. You go out. Learn to live Sienese."

"I will. I didn't notice the restroom."

"Ah. This way."

Evelina led her back to the small hallway and opened a door. Facing them sat the toilet bowl situated like a throne. Jutting from the wall beside it was the smallest sink Lucy had ever seen.

"I may have to back into this room to use the toilet," Lucy commented, gauging the dimensions.

Evelina shrugged. "As long as the bedroom has enough room to play, who cares the *toilette*?"

* * *

Farmers' market stalls overflowed with brightly colored vegetables. Never before had Lucy seen artichokes more purple than green, wild asparagus as thin as pipe cleaners, figs the size of an egg. There were bins stocked with bright yellow zucchini flowers begging to be brought home, stuffed, and fried. No dinnertime fights among siblings here over who would get the last one from the garden. Gigantic sunflower heads reigned over a court of flowers at the florist's stall. Lucy meandered in and out among the stalls, filling her shopping basket from the day's bounty. She bought a fish for dinner, paying extra to have it cleaned. The mustached fishmonger teased and flirted with her until his wife barked orders at him, a wide knife flashing in her hand.

Lucy roamed the countryside. She wandered down winding alleys and up and down steep steps. She scrambled over the remains of an ancient wall and cooled her toes in a discovered pond while absorbing the incredible vistas. She visited St. Dominic's and viewed St. Catherine's head, still remarkably intact.

Not a bad arrangement all around, she thought. *Keeping head and heart separated could save you a lot of heartache.*

She visited the Accademia Musicale Chigiana to complete her registration. The magnificence of the palace took her breath away. Who was she to be studying in these incredible surroundings? Her heels click-clacked through a mezzanine reminiscent of the Renaissance. The concert hall, where she, Lucy Salvatori, would perform this summer was designed in the delicate colors of the eighteenth-century Venetian style. She was escorted through rooms with coats of arms, busts of famous Italians, works of art, masks, and pottery. Three rooms were set aside to house the instruments collected by Count Guido Chigi, who founded the Accademia. How could one not be inspired to create music grand enough to lift the spirit and sensitive enough to soothe the soul?

As she explored the medieval city, Lucy grew used to being constantly accosted with the attentions of men. A touch to the elbow, a pinch to the rear end, a low whistle, a smacking of lips. Flustered at first, she came to recognize it as part of the exuberance of Italian life. The same attention followed any woman not dragging a doll or bent over a cane. It was appreciation for the female form, no harm intended. She slipped out of her coat of New York indignation, tossed her hair, and smiled coyly as she shook free of her parochial upbringing.

The Duomo of Santa Maria dell'Assunta was a Gothic wedding cake of a cathedral. Guidebook in hand, Lucy examined its ornate Carrara marble pulpit, frescoes, paintings, and statues sculpted by Bernini, Donatello, and a young Michaelangelo.

"*Non si dimentichi di osservare giù*," a handsome young man at Lucy's elbow said.

Lucy translated in her head. "Look down?" she asked.

"*Si.* Do not forget to look down at the floor," he said in accented English. "The floors are the wonder of this church." He extended his hand. "Hello. My name is Orlando Bechi."

Lucy nodded, taking his hand. "Lucy Salvatori."

"You are a tourist?"

"Today, yes. But I will be studying and working in Siena this coming year."

"That is wonderful! Let me show you what I mean about the floors."

He led Lucy around the church, pointing out intarsia floor pieces ranging from simple drawings to inlaid marble scenes.

"There is as much to admire beneath your feet as above your head," Orlando concluded.

"Thank you for describing all this to me. I'm sure your explanation was more in-depth than this guidebook I'm using. Are you an artist?"

"So-so," he said, waving his hand back and forth. "I am an architect. I studied in your Harvard."

"Really? You traveled to America when the ancient architecture is still standing all around you here?"

"This architecture inspires me. It infiltrates my soul. For you, it is ancient; for us, it is but a moment in time. Life goes on; the past is with us today; tomorrow is already somewhere in the making. I went to your country to learn in the way we are taught by children, through fresh, exuberant eyes. My work suggests the complex composition of old and new to reflect the continuum of time." Orlando paused. "Besides, I wanted to see a real baseball game." Dark curls fell onto his forehead; thick lashes shaded his eyes. He was slender, an inch or two taller than Lucy, and charmingly forward. "You will have a cup of espresso with me, yes? I am falling in love with you, and I must discover if you are worth the trouble."

Lucy blenched until she noted the twinkle in his eye.

"I would enjoy a cup of coffee. But you're going to have to spring for a cappucino. Your espresso is much too strong for me."

"Spring for? I don't recall…but anything to do with spring and a beautiful woman can't be bad."

They found an empty table at a café on the shell-shaped Piazza del Campo. Orlando pulled out a cigarette and offered one to Lucy. She declined.

"I thought all Americans smoked."

"No one in my family does." Lucy went on to describe her familial background.

"To have grown up around opera must have been grand," Orlando mused. "There is a Puccini opera festival in Lucca next month. I will take you."

"Are you sure I am worth the trouble?" Lucy teased.

"Just looking at you is worth the trouble," Orlando replied.

"There is no cat and mouse game played around here, I see."

"Of course there is. It is not my way. I see something I want; I go for it. I learned more than architecture in America. You will come with me to the festival? I will research the schedule."

"If I can. I have classes and concerts to attend and perform in."

"I will come and cheer you on."

"A concert is not a baseball game. Which is your favorite American team?"

"The Boston Red Sox, of course. I went to Harvard."

Lucy groaned.

"Do not hold it against me. My baseball allegiance can be bought quite easily. Unlike my allegiance to my contrada for Il Palio."

"Yes, I'm learning all about this famous horserace. The excitement is mounting. There are seventeen contradas, but only ten take part in the race."

"They are chosen by lottery."

"And contradas are neighborhoods."

"In the smallest sense of the word. A contrada is your life, your family, if you will. Everything you are is within your contrada. We celebrate marriages, baptisms, holidays, parties only with our own contrada. It is not an easy thing to marry outside one's contrada. The Palio is the most life or death situation faced by a contrada."

"I have noticed that you Sienese will initiate a challenge at the drop of a hat."

"But the Palio is most important. There are two, July second and August sixteenth. Preparations are underway for the first one. What contrada are you living in.? Do you know?"

"Aquila."

"The Eagle. I live in Oca. The Goose. It is St. Catherine's contrada. Have you visited our St. Catherine yet? She was a brave and outspoken woman."

"Considering only her head is on display in the church, I'm hoping that's not how you deal with outspoken women."

Orlando laughed. "No, she died in Rome. It was a gift back to her hometown."

* * *

The streets of Siena became more frenzied and exuberant as each day grew nearer to the Palio. Lucy stumbled into rehearsals for the two-hour medieval pageant that preceded the actual race. She helped out at a sewing circle beneath the grape arbor as her landlady and her friends renounced their afternoon siesta to restore costumes. Evelina smuggled her into the studio of the artist who that year was painting the *palio,* or banner, to give to the winning contrada. Lucy learned that the Eagle contrada was one of the four noble contradas. She also learned to keep mum about her ancestral Florentine roots. The bitter enmity between Siena and Florence survived to this day. She could only imagine the fervor with which Phil would attack orchestrating this event. She bought extra film to document everything she saw for his perusal. The evening before the race, Lucy joined others from her adopted contrada at a huge outdoor feast held in the open air of the contrada's largest square. The evening light shimmered amber from the glow cast by torches and lanterns. Huge bowls of pasta, sides of boar, avalanches of vegetables, and vats of Chianti fed a crowd on the verge of hysteria. From every direction, voices shouted. Lucy could never tell if they were laughing or arguing. It didn't matter; they were alive, full of vigor and enthusiasm for what is and what would be. Signora Nappi gifted Lucy with a handkerchief in the Eagle colors of yellow with black and blue bands.

By the following morning, Lucy herself was bursting with excitement. She walked down to the Piazza del Campo to watch sand being spread for the track. When she returned to her apartment, she was accosted by Evelina and her brother, Paolo.

"My brother has arranged for you to come into the church before the race. You will be our good luck charm," Evelina gushed.

"Good luck charm?"

"*Si.* A foreigner living in our contrada should bring the luck."

"Why is that?" Lucy asked curiously.

"It doesn't matter why. Maybe it is true; we take the chance," Evelina insisted.

At two thirty, Lucy entered the smallest church she had ever seen. There were no pews. Alongside Paolo and Evelina, she stood near the altar next to the narrow center aisle. Lucy heard a snort and a clippity clop. To her amazement a horse pranced down the aisle while the altar boys swung enough incense to cause the eyes of the statues to water. A priest approached the restless animal, said a few prayers, and recited, "*Vai e torna vincitore.*" Go and return a winner. There was then a mad dash to get to a good viewing spot in the square. Lucy was not among the lucky spectators who had seats in reserved bleachers.

When the medieval pageant began, Lucy held her camera aloft and hoped for the best. Most participants were in costume: pages, drummers, flag wavers. Carabinieri, trade corporation members, academicians either marched or stood on floats and decorated carts. An ancient chariot led by two oxen rolled past, and Lucy jumped up and down trying to get a snapshot. Bells tolled, trumpets blared, tambourines clanged, drums thumped. People broke into victory songs while rival neighbors hissed and tried to overpower with their own anthem. At long last there was an explosive roar—a signal for the race's commencement. The noise got even more deafening. There was a collective groan. A false start. The horses needed to be lined up again, a woman nearby explained to Lucy. As she started jumping up and down once again, Lucy suddenly felt herself swooped into the air on a giant of a man's shoulders. She grabbed his hair for balance and kicked her heels into his massive chest.

"Rimanga ancora e goda la cors," he shouted up at her. Stay still and enjoy the race.

Lucy decided to follow his advice. She tucked her skirt around her legs. She thought she saw the Eagle jockey look in her direction. She waved frantically with her handkerchief, contributing to the writhing sea of color that surrounded her. The horses took off and in less than two minutes, the race was over. Eagle had won! Lucy whooped it up with the other contrada winners all the while surrounded by the jeers, shouts, and fury of the losers. Her human scaffold carried her to the judges' stand to see the *palio* being given to the captain of the contrada. The winning jockey was also aboard the shoulders of his jubilant friends. He shouted down to them, and they brought him face to face with

Lucy. He reached out for her shoulders and pulling her toward him, he kissed her long and hard. Hoots and hollers pierced the air. Lucy's handler lowered her to the ground. She was embarrassed and laughing all at the same time.

"Be glad this isn't ancient times. The winning jockey used to be entitled to the girl of his choice," the giant declared as he pinched her cheek and took off.

"Come, pretty lady. Come, celebrate with me," a young man beckoned in Italian. He grabbed Lucy's hand. "Follow me. We are both Eagles. We are young and victorious."

Lucy pulled her hand away. "No, *grazie*," she said firmly, shaking her head.

A toothless crone stood nearby. "Foolish girl," she cackled at Lucy in gleeful Italian. "A stallion from the winning contrada is the best ride you will have in your entire life!"

Lucy, exhausted from a full day of zealous excesses, retreated to her apartment. She couldn't face another feast even larger than the one the previous evening. She was physically and emotionally limp. Lying on her bed, the sounds of celebration blitzing her room on the roller-coaster wheels of drums, firecrackers, and whistles, she pictured the moments back home when excitement had reached exalted heights. Opening night at the opera house, the eighth grade graduation dance, Dan's homecoming from the hospital, Phil's parade down Times Square, Dan's proposal to Louisa, her Carnegie Hall concert, Jimmy and Jane's wedding day. The premiere of *Litterally Yours.* All events that filled her to the brim, trickled away, and left her with a residue of warmth and security.

But had she ever celebrated the first crocus in the garden, the predictable spray in the roomy shower, the smell of vanilla as her mother baked, or the touch of Adriana's chubby fingers? Here, she was swept along in her neighbor's enthusiasm for the moment. As the evening grew late, she fell asleep to the sweet sounds of mandolin strings. She dreamed she was astride a horse. She held the bay's mane while arms holding her close from behind directed the reins. She was happy; she was alive. She turned to look at the rider, but his face was covered by the winning *palio.*

* * *

Lucy tried to keep pace, but the banquet was too vast, the possibilities infinite, the destinations without horizon. The nobility of music staggered her mind; the tutelage of these master instructors humbled her. She was soaring through the air; she was pushing life through rich soil. She stood atop a mountain; she lay stripped of all pretense in a valley. Music rested upon her like the breath of God.

At times she felt fraudulent. Her plans did not include the grandiose dreams of concert performances and world renown as did those of her peers. She filled her evenings with lesson plans, tools, and techniques to showcase the majesty of music to her students. She had not begun to teach in Siena, but her head was filled with ambition for the talented young men and women at Julliard and her precious privately instructed youngsters. In the middle of the night, she climbed from her bed to record sleep-laced ideas to challenge and mentor them. She performed in outdoor concerts and in the grand concert hall of the Accademia with her fellow master class students. Bit by bit, Lucy began to remember who she was.

The school year was a busy one. Both her English and music pupils loved the *Americano.* The male students fought to carry her bags and books; the girls shyly approached her as a confidant. Lucy had mastered Italian by October. A good ear enabled her not only to comprehend, but also to sound like a native when she spoke. Loneliness had not knocked at her door quite yet, but it was tapping at the window. She had been unable to attend a Puccini opera with Orlando. They did, however, spend a day touring Lucca. It had been a fun, companionable outing; they seemed destined to be good friends.

On what would have been Thanksgiving if she were back home, Lucy sat with a cup of tea in the teacher's lounge and looked fondly once again at the picture of her newest nephew. Little Ronald Joseph was newborn in the photograph; it was difficult to tell whom the red crinkled bundle resembled. She sighed deeply.

"Ah, Lucilla. The weight of the world is on your shoulders today?" Giovanni Gaeta asked in Italian, sitting in a chair beside her.

Giovanni was a history teacher whose schedule was almost identical to Lucy's. They lunched and had breaks together. He enjoyed plowing her knowledge of American culture and traditions for his own enlightenment.

"Just missing my family a bit more than usual," Lucy responded.

"It is because this is your day of Thanksgiving, no?"

"I would be hard-pressed to find turkey, sweet potatoes, and cranberry sauce at the local trattoria."

"Why don't you come to my house this evening? My wife made a wonderful farro soup and boar stew."

"I've eaten boar, and it is delicious. But what is farro soup?"

"Farro is an ancient grain. Similar to barley. Say you will come. I will try to ease the pain of no berry soup. I have quite a few prestigious bottles of wine in my cellar."

Lucy chuckled. "Cranberry sauce. All right. Thank you, Giovanni."

* * *

A golden cast hung over the city as Lucy walked to the Gaeta house. It was a balmy fifty-eight degrees; shutters were open. Voices of mothers scolding children, families sitting down to dinner, and shopkeepers' calls of *"Buona sera"* to each other trailed her footsteps. Lucy entered the Gaeta house and relinquished her jacket. Giovanni led her into the living room. Through a doorway, she could see a table set for two.

"I brought these flowers for your wife. Where is Signora Gaeta?" Lucy asked, ignoring Giovanni's suggestion to be seated.

"You must have misunderstood me. My wife is not home. She is visiting her sister in Cortona."

"The farro soup?"

"Si. She made me meals for each day she will be away. Today is the farro soup and boar stew. It is heating on the stove. I made a salad on my own," he added proudly. He went into the kitchen and returned with two glasses of wine. "Tell me what you think of this. Please, Lucilla. Sit down. I am not going to bite you."

Lucy accepted the glass while scolding her suspicious attitude. "This is delicious. Is it local?"

"Of course. As is the olive oil on the table."

"Oooh. I've had freshly pressed olive oil. The flavor is intense. It is as green as liquid emeralds with quite a bite to it. I am preparing a package of foods to ship home to my family for Christmas. I bought a bottle of Baggiolino extra virgin olive oil to include."

The meal was delicious. Afterward Giovanni led Lucy to a small outside patio to finish with sliced pears, cheese, and espresso. Olive trees were silhouettes in the evening sky. Voices from neighbors engaging in their evening *passagiata* reached them in the darkness.

"Is it too chilly for you out here?" asked Giovanni.

"No. It's lovely. But I will take my jacket if you don't mind."

While waiting, Lucy eavesdropped as voices from the street discussed a movie entitled *Anna in Brooklyn* starring Gina Lollobrigida.

Giovanni returned and helped Lucy with her jacket.

"I think I'm going to the cinema one evening. I just overheard a discussion about a movie where Gina Lollobrigida lives in Brooklyn but returns to a small village in Italy to find a husband. I'll enjoy seeing Brooklyn if it was actually filmed there."

"Do you miss home?"

"Yes. Of course. My family and friends. I love Italy, the pace of life, the intense savoring of every moment. I'm learning to do that. But I'm also realizing I miss having loved ones to share those moments with. All summer long I could have raced home from class and talked all evening with my parents about what I had learned. Now, after school, I would be reminiscing with my brothers and friends about our own antics in the classroom. I play with the neighbor's children and know I am missing the never-to-be-recaptured moments in my niece and nephews's lives. I have a new nephew whom I won't even see until he's eight months old. All the sights and sounds of your beautiful country and no one to share them with."

"There is no *amore* waiting for you at home?" Giovanni asked, leaning forward. His narrow eyes seemed to glint in the moonlight.

"There is someone I care deeply about. I'm not sure he is waiting. We had words before I left."

"Perhaps a man cannot wait, but he will be there when you get back."

Lucy lifted an eyebrow. "Spoken like a native Italian male. We'll see what happens once I return, I suppose."

"He disapproved of your sabbatical." Giovanni shook his head. "He is a man afraid of a headstrong woman. I, myself, find women of temper and conviction both provocative and passionate."

"Aha. Is that how you would describe your wife?"

"Maria? At one time, yes. She is now less of everything…except body."

"That's rude, Giovanni. I'm surprised at you. Especially after we've eaten this wonderful meal that she prepared."

"I would like nothing better than for our marriage to be as it once was. But she is only interested in gossip and food. If I want to visit Florence or Rome, I tour alone while she shops. She was a beauty, I tell you. She bewitched me, and I failed to take notice that we had little in common. Fortunately, our daughters are a bit more levelheaded, and our son is studying law."

Giovanni poured them both wine from the bottle he had brought outside earlier.

"You, my dear Lucilla, will always be beautiful because you will always have something interesting to say."

"I have a big mouth."

Giovanni laughed. "I loved the way you argued with the principal over a second Christmas concert. Wagers were being made in the lounge over who would win."

"Did you make any money?" Lucy asked, grinning.

"But of course. I bet on you."

"It was only fair. When I agreed to take over the concert in September when Basilio's mother got ill, I began working those kids really hard. They've put their whole heart into what they are doing. I didn't want to eliminate the solos because the concert would run too long. With two evenings parents can attend the evening their child is featured."

"You were on fire. It was quite enticing. As you are now just speaking about it."

Lucy wrapped her arms around herself. "I think we'd better retreat indoors. It's getting quite cold now."

They gathered the cups and dishes and deposited them in the kitchen.

"I'll be right back, and then I would like to show you around the house. I have a painting by a young man named Vellagio. I think he may be someone to watch."

Lucy began washing the dishes. She set them on their sides in the wooden grates above the sink, where they would slowly drip themselves dry. She hummed quietly, picturing her family around the dining room table elbow deep in turkey and chatter.

"Lucilla! What are you doing? Come inside."

"I was waiting for you. Let me finish these last couple of dishes." She placed them on the rack above, dried her hands, and followed the sound of Domenico Modugno's voice singing "Volare."

Giovanni was standing by the record player in a dark red silk robe. His legs and feet were bare except for sandals. He was reading the back of the album cover.

"Have you heard Modugno sing 'Piove'? It is beautiful. I am looking to see which song number it is."

"Giovanni, what are you doing?" Lucy asked, her arms folded in front of her.

"Searching for 'Piove.'"

"Why are you in a dressing gown?"

"I always get comfortable at this time of night. I sit with a little brandy, a cigarette, and music. You, *cara,* I know, do not approve of cigarettes. So I shall refrain. We will find something else to do."

"It's time for me to leave."

"You haven't seen my Vellagio. Please, my Lucilla, do not revert to being a high-strung American."

Lucy straightened her shoulders and tapped her foot. "Where is your Vellagio?"

"In my library. Come."

"Oh." She followed him into a room lined with books on two walls, a desk, two armchairs, and a sofa. Above the latter hung a confusion of strokes, angles, and color.

"What do you think?" Giovanni asked, breathing over her shoulder.

"I think it's not my taste. I don't get this abstract art."

"So. The first thing we disagree on. I find it utterly fascinating and mysterious."

"I'm happy for you. I'm impressed that you can find something in it to relate to. It's beyond me." She moved to leave, but Giovanni put his hands on her upper arms.

"Lucilla," he whispered. "Let me ease your loneliness."

Lucy shook free and backed toward the door. "Don't do this, Giovanni. Don't ruin our friendship."

"I am hoping to enhance it. Make the rest of your stay in Siena more fulfilling and exciting."

"You're a married man."

"I don't deny it. Do not let that stand in our way. My wife would not care. As long as she can spend her days doing as she chooses, she prefers I stay out of her hair."

"Be that as it may, I don't just hop into bed with any man who comes along."

"I am not any man. We are bosom friends. You are sad; you came to me to cheer you up. Let me show you how it feels to be adored. In Italy it takes on a whole other meaning."

Giovanni stepped quickly in front of her and took Lucy tightly in his arms. Her breasts pressed into his chest, and his desire announced itself from beneath the robe. He leaned forward to kiss Lucy, but she turned her head while pushing him away. His mouth landed on her cheek.

"How dare you set me up this way? You think because I'm a woman on my own, I'm some kind of cheap trollop? You think I need a man to feel complete? What makes you think I'm sad? Lonely doesn't mean desperate! I may miss those I've left behind, but I'm not looking for sordid substitutes. I'm learning about life and how to live my moment. I'm strong. I need no entanglements."

She was in such a fury, she didn't realize she was shouting in English.

"Lucilla, Lucilla, please. I don't understand you. What are you saying? I am sorry. I thought it would be pleasurable for us both. When you said it was time to come inside, you looked dreamy. Inviting. I did not mean to offend you."

Lucy paused to catch her breath. "I'm sorry too. I'm sorry this happened. I should have known better than to come here without a direct invitation from your wife. My father has always been concerned with appropriate behavior. This was inappropriate, and I am partly to blame."

"I hope we can put this evening behind us. I will not deny that I am disappointed. Still, I value your friendship. Please continue to treat me as a friend and not as a spurned lover."

"Let's take it day by day. Hopefully, I can overcome my vision of you in that dressing gown."

"What are you saying? I look bad?"

"You look like a lascivious wolf in a third-rate Italian film."

* * *

Lucy refused Giovanni's offer of an escort home. She walked through the streets feeling completely safe. She could already chuckle at the incident. Giovanni's upraised hands in urgent supplication of friendship. The slightly loosened robe revealing wispy black and white hairs on his chest. The slight wetness of his lips and tongue on her cheek. The musky, woodsy smell of his cologne. She felt a tightness in her chest and groin.

She paused in front of a darkened *pasticceria.* Momentarily, she had been aroused. She recognized his desire, and in his longing, her own dormant passions awakened. She missed being held. She missed being touched. She missed being kissed. In less than a year, she would turn thirty. Loving Tavis had been glorious. That moment in time had been brief but filled with the splendor of the heavens. God's plan for Tavis was filled with reasoning beyond her powers to comprehend.

In the *pasticceria's* window, a raspberry tart stared back at her through the darkness. She recalled the raspberries in Tavis's Sayville garden. Memories of Tavis would endure. He was not dead in the intangible universe of time. Everything he brought to her, everything they shared would inform and color her future. She would not cling to a guilt that only served to deny a profound love. Nearby was a small church; its bell struck the hour with deep sonorous clangs. To be angry at God, to cry out to Him in fury was, in fact, a blessing. Only a heart that had known an overwhelming love could be anguished enough to despair at being left alone in this finite world.

Chapter 43

Suspicion of the late hour forced Lucy to open her eyes. The two Christmas concerts had been a huge success. She was exhausted from the effort and the late night of celebrating with a few colleagues. It was a Sunday morning; she had every right to sleep late. There was one week until Christmas. Presents had been mailed home. She had purchased the few gifts she needed for friends in Siena. She looked at her clock. Almost eleven o'clock. She could huddle under the blankets a while longer and then indulge in a leisurely shower. Perhaps she would go to Il Campo and lunch at one of the small trattorias.

Was that knocking at the door? Lucy groaned and turned on her side. Yes. There it was, more persistent. Her feet searched for her slippers while she ran her hand through her hair. Slipping into her robe, she glanced in the mirror. Touseled and bleary eyed. Too bad.

"I'm coming," she hollered in Italian as she finished tying her sash. She opened the door.

"*Buon giorno.*"

"Oh my God! Oh my God! What are you doing here?" Lucy flung her arms in a bear hug. "It's so good to see you, Val."

"That's a relief."

"Come in." She stepped aside.

Val picked up his two suitcases and set them inside the doorway.

"I'm sorry. I'm a mess. I just got up."

"Late night?"

"Yes. Celebrating our successful Christmas concerts. What are you doing here? Why didn't you let me know you were coming?" She led him into the living room. "Sit. Let me put on some coffee. No, first tell me what's going on." Panic suddenly shadowed her face. "Is everyone all right at home?"

"I came because your father asked me to. His blood pressure is through the roof not knowing how you are. I couldn't warn you because he wanted you surprised and unable to conceal any problems. None of your brothers could come, obviously, so he gave me a month off from work to check things out."

"A month? That's some exam I'm going to undergo."

"I'm sorry. I know this is awkward. I can tell right off you're none the worse for wear. Perhaps more *vino* and *tarantellas* than we would have guessed, but doing fine."

"I'm mortified, Val. Let me shower and dress. I was going to the Piazza for lunch. How does that sound?"

"Terrific. I can't wait to do a bit of sightseeing. I know you're working during the day, so I'll have to find my own way."

"I have partial weekends and some time off after Christmas. I was planning to go to Florence. I can't believe I've been here six months and haven't made it there yet." She smiled tenderly. "Geez, it's good to see you Val. Make yourself comfortable. There's lemon soda in the fridge." She hesitated. "You'll be staying here?"

"That's up to you. If you're uncomfortable, I can go to a *pensione*."

"Uncomfortable? I'm ecstatic to have company. I'll have to clear it with my landlady, though. She watches over me like a hawk."

"I like her already," Val said, scanning the family photographs on a side table and noting there were none of him.

After lunch and a tour of the Duomo, Lucy knocked on Signora Nappi's door.

"Lucilla, come inside," she said in Italian.

Lucy and Val both stepped indoors.

"*Signora*, I will be having a houseguest for a month. My father sent him to check up on me. This is er, my cousin, Valentino LoMuscio."

Signora Nappi looked Val over skeptically.

"*Un cugino che la latta handsome conduce soltanto a difficolta,*" the elderly woman said through tight lips.

"What did she say?" Val asked.

"A cousin that good looking can only lead to trouble," Lucy translated.

"Look, *Signora*, you can call Lucy's father if you want. He'll confirm he sent me here," Val suggested.

"*Che cosa?*"

Lucy translated again.

"Hummph. *Venuto con me.* Come with me," she said, leading them into the kitchen. She handed Val a jar of capers and indicated he should open it for her.

With a twist of the wrist, Val removed the lid.

"*Forse puo essere utile me anche.* Perhaps he can be useful to me too," she said, giving Lucy a hard glare.

"Now what?" Val asked again.

"Oh, she just said you're very strong," Lucy replied, taking his hand and leading him outside.

Lucy emptied the one small closet that had been built into the apartment and jammed those clothes into the armoire in her bedroom. She emptied a dresser drawer for Val and piled her things in the corner of the room.

"Sorry. I don't have much in the way of storage."

"I'm sorry to inconvenience you. I can pile my stuff in the corner of the parlor."

"No, the bedroom isn't visible if anyone visits. Your stuff spread all over the parlor will look like a dorm room. Come and see the view from my loggia."

They stepped through the French doors.

"Val, I haven't greeted you properly yet." She put her hands behind his head and lowered it toward her. She caressed his lips with her own.

Val's hands rested briefly on her hips until he withdrew them to his sides.

"I've missed that," she whispered.

"Have you?"

She nodded.

"I couldn't help but notice that you don't have a picture of me inside."

"I know. I didn't want to fixate on it. I didn't know if you'd be there when I got home, so I rehearsed the separation on my own."

A slight breeze ruffled Val's hair, which fell becomingly onto his forehead. The dark-green turtleneck sweater he wore emphasized the firm line of his jaw. Lucy could still feel the sweet pressure of his well-shaped mouth on her lips.

"Will you be there, Val, when I return in June?" Lucy asked.

"That's six months away. A lot can happen in six months." There was a steeliness to his voice. A wall that blocked all breaches.

"Fair enough. Let's talk like friends. Have you been seeing anyone?" she asked.

"I've gone on dates. There's no one special."

"Me either."

They stood in silence, staring across at the panoramic view before them.

"Speaking of pictures, I have recent ones from your family."

"Oh! Do you have one of Ronald?"

"They call him Ronnie. Except your father, who calls him Rinaldo. He's a cute baby. He has Ami's eyes and nose and this blond spikey hair that looks like he's been electrocuted. I swear to God, the kid smiles like he's already been up to mischief. Phil and Ami found an apartment on West Eleventh Street. The father of a friend of Phil's from high school lost his tenants. He's renting to them."

"Ma must be thrilled. They're so close."

"She keeps busy with the three grandkids. And your father."

"No sign of him regaining mobility?"

"Not yet. But his temperament is much better. He exercises with weights, but we're not supposed to know. Jimmy goes over and plays Scrabble, Monopoly, and *briscola* with him. They're always harping at each other, but your father looks forward to their time together."

"Who would have ever imagined?"

"Life is a gigantic puzzle, Lucy. You only get to see the big picture after struggling to fit all the pieces in one by one."

* * *

On Christmas Eve Lucy and Val joined Signora Nappi, her sister, her sister's daughter and husband, with their children Evelina and Paolo. Fasting from meat, the meal included seven fishes: fried eel, scungilli, clams, baccala, calamari, flounder, and the famed anchovies from Vernazza in Cinque Terre cooked with potatoes, tomatoes, oil, white wine, and herbs. Evelina sat next to Val, forcing Lucy to sit opposite him. Evelina peppered him with questions and flicked her blonde hair so it brushed his shoulder. She misused words Lucy was sure she had never stumbled over before, absorbing Val's corrections with wide-eyed gratitude. With the excuse that she had some sights she wanted to show him before midnight Mass, Lucy escaped with Val before the rest of the group organized to leave the house.

The church looked beautiful decorated with wreaths, garland, poinsettias, and a magnificent *presepio.* Afterward Lucy and Val stood arm in arm and watched children portraying the Holy Family in a live Nativity scene. Real shepherds came down from the mountains dressed in traditional leggings, sheepskin vests, and leather trousers. They sang songs of old accompanied by lutes. A choral concert was presented in Il Campo, which was decorated with little white lights. Lucy leaned back against Val's chest, his arms around her, keeping her warm and peace filled. The holiday was truly a holy day here in Siena. Although she missed her family, the lack of bustle and exhausting rituals was just what her spirit needed to rejuvenate this year. They walked back to her apartment, hand in hand.

"*Buon Natale,* Val," Lucy whispered, kissing him lightly on the lips.

"*Buon Natale,* Lucy," Val replied, watching her close the door to her room.

He removed the cushions from the sofa bed and set them on the armchair. His eye caught something familiar on the end table. There, in a gold-etched frame, sat a photograph of himself, laughing in the Salvatori backyard. He recalled that he had just stolen the last fig from Lucy's lap, and she was pelting him with the unsatisfactory grapes he had replaced in its stead.

* * *

Orlando was already waiting beneath the Torre de Mangia when they arrived. Following introductions, Orlando escorted them to where his Fiat 500 was parked. Lucy insisted that Val sit in the passenger seat. She tried to get comfortable in the small space allotted back passengers and settled for sitting with her legs curled beneath her.

They reached the medieval town of San Gimignano in no time. Fourteen medieval towers greeted them, and Orlando was an architectural font of knowledge. They visited a Romanesque church filled with Renaissance frescoes and scaled a castle for a grand view of the surrounding area. They then headed for Volterra with a lunch break at a truck stop. A wall-length spit and grill just inside the door filled the air with mouth-watering aromas. Burly drivers, skinny drivers, young and gray-haired drivers alike all paused in conversation when the threesome entered.

"*Mamma mia…*" and something unintelligible to Val's ear stopped him dead in his tracks.

"I don't think this is the best place to bring Lucy," he said in an undertone.

"Don't be concerned," Lucy said calmly. "See that woman in the corner?"

Val looked over to see a solid-looking middle-aged woman with salt and pepper hair, wielding a rib bone in the air.

"Yeah."

"Guaranteed she generated the same attention. If nothing else, a woman always feels beautiful in Italy."

They enjoyed a feast of sausage with onions and peppers, cinghiale or wild boar ribs, peas with sage and garlic, roasted potatoes, and local red wine. Afterward they headed to Volterra, where they viewed crumbling cliffs, a ruined monastery, and remnants of Etruscan and Roman life. Such was the success of the day, Val hired a tour guide to take Lucy and him to Montagnola the next day. Their journey was briefly impeded by a flock of sheep that ambled across the road. Lucy got out and stood among the milling sheep while Val took a picture. The guide honked his horn, but the sheep took twenty minutes to scatter enough for them to pass. They visited a twelfth-century cloister, a Roman bath with a spring, and a local crystal and glass artist. Val bought Lucy a crystal fig, which brought a faint smile to her eyes. Val handing her the fig was tantamount to someone else giving her a heart. The slight clutching she felt in her chest was no longer insupportable. More importantly, Val had kissed her cheek and brought his lips close to her ear.

"My parting with the only fig available this time of year is proof of my undying devotion to you."

Lucy hoped so. Since his arrival Val had treated her like the cousin he was pretending to be.

* * *

Back into the routine of school, Lucy missed the idyllic holiday Val's presence had initiated. He left for a two-day sojourn in Rome and then again for a two-day visit to Orvieto and Assisi. His descriptions and photographs only exacerbated her incipient resentment of the rigorous teaching curriculum. The unforgiving schedule had been vital to her resuscitation, but now with lighthearted excursions by Val's side as the alternative, she found herself restless and distracted.

She waved an absentminded good-bye to bewildered colleagues who asked her if she wanted to join them for drinks one evening. She hurried to the coffee bar where she was meeting Val, who should have returned from a visit to Montalcino. They were planning a day trip to Florence, which he had resisted visiting thus far in order for Lucy to accompany him. Stepping inside, letting her eyes adjust to the change of light, she scanned the crowded room for him. He was standing at the end of the bar, head bent low, deep in conversation. When a whip of swinging blonde hair flipped into view, Lucy's teeth clenched. Standing in a perky pose, breasts poised and ready to fire, lids skillfully fluttering over hazel eyes, Evelina stood talking with Val. As Lucy approached, Evelina's hand reached for Val's arm, and she pulled him toward her conspiratorially. Then straightening and wrinkling her nose, she asked guilefully, "How was your day, schoolmarm?"

"Intense. Saving the next generation from meaningless employment, I hope," Lucy parried. "*Buon giorno,* Val. How was your day?"

"Wonderful. As all days here in Italy are. Evelina was giving me a must-see list of things in Florence."

"Oh, I already know where I want to go. Unfortunately, we can't do it all in one day."

"I will be happy to accompany you, Valentino, to see what you miss with Lucy. We can spend a few days there. I get time off. My cousin, she is generous with giving me the time off from work. It is good to have a generous cousin, *si*, Lucy?" She turned to Val. "So what you say? We go Firenze together? You save seeing the David for me. It is my favorite thing."

"I'll bet," Lucy sneered. "I'm afraid the David is a must-see with me. Right, Val?"

"Whatever you say."

"Lucy, you act you want your cousin all yourself. That's not nice. I think you not be, how you say, *primo cugino,* first cousins. Maybe *secondo or terzo*, eh? Second or third."

"We're very close in my family."

"I prefer to be very close outside of family." Evelina stroked Val's face with her slender fingers.

"It was nice seeing you, Evelina, but Val and I have plans for this evening," Lucy, clearly upset, stated.

Val raised a quizzical eyebrow but didn't comment.

"I think we'd better go pick up the *bistecca* for dinner and make our plans at home where we can sit at a table."

Val swallowed the rest of his coffee while Evelina leaned back against the bar and pouted prettily.

"I think you already have your meat for dinner at hand, Lucy." She smiled at Val. "A near neighbor is better than a distant cousin, Valentino. If you need walking shoes, you know where to find me."

* * *

"This was unexpected," Val said, popping a bite of steak into his mouth. "I thought we were eating out tonight."

"I'm tired from work. It's much more comfortable here in my sweatshirt and slippers."

"Hmm." Val sipped his wine. "If I didn't know better, I'd say you were a little jealous of Evelina today."

Lucy started to argue but instead speared a tomato. She looked at it thoughtfully and said to Val, "What if I was? A little."

"Nothing. It's just an interesting turn of events."

"So are you going to take her up on her touring expertise?"

"What do you think?"

"From that crummy conceited expression on your face, I'd say you're getting too big a kick out of all of this."

"When you're compared to a hunk of meat, it does kind of go to your head," Val said with a wide grin.

"You smug creep," Lucy said, trying not to laugh. "If you haven't noticed, this piece of meat stinks. It seems you can't get good beef in Italy."

"That must be why I'm so popular."

"You're beyond conceited."

"You're right, though. This is the only bad food I've had since I'm here."

"Good. You don't deserve any better tonight." She emptied her glass of wine in one gulp.

* * *

Buy a train ticket. Stamp it in the machine. Sit with it expectantly for the whole trip.

"I don't get it," Lucy complained. "Never once since I've been here has anyone come around and collected or even looked at these tickets."

"I'm only here a few weeks, and I've already figured it out. It's all part of the cutthroat competitive spirit. You buy the ticket, or you don't. They catch you, or they don't. The ticket evader lives for the free ride, and the conductor waits for the 'Ha! I've got you' moment. Just adds to the gusto."

The thirty miles to Florence were accomplished swiftly, and soon both Lucy and Val stood in awe before the pink, white, and green marble of the Duomo. Its massive bulk hovered over the narrow streets of the city like a sentinel swathed in a soft-hued dawn. They viewed the Baptistry and bell tower. Speechless from viewing Michelangelo's

David, they hurried to Orsanmichele, where Lucy told Val her grandmother Anna's story about perspective. With only a gelato to keep them going, they crossed the Ponte Vecchio, shopping in the many stores and asking a stranger to take a picture of them with the water and view of the city in the background. As they hurried to catch a bus to visit Piazzale Michelangelo, they passed an artist drawing Raphael's cherubs in chalk on the street, only to be washed away by the street-cleaner's hoses in the early-morning hours. From the Piazzale, high atop Florence, they looked over the slopes dotted with villas and dark green cypresses as firmly rooted in history as the Renaissance city. Brunelleschi's dome atop the Duomo dominated the landscape like a huge sparkling diamond in a jewelry box of precious gems. An artist dressed in a thick wool sweater dabbed at an easel set before him; a vendor in open-fingered gloves hawked torrone and candied almonds. School children on roller skates, metal wheels clacking across the pavement, darted past youngsters on scooters. Young lovers walked past, arms entwined, kissing, gazing only at the landscapes visible in each other's eyes. Lucy swallowed the lump in her throat and suggested they find someplace to eat before catching the train back to Siena.

Red-checkered tablecloths, a simple menu, a liter of red wine deposited automatically on the table.

"I'll have the homemade spinach tagliatelle with wild mushroom sauce," Lucy ordered.

Val pointed out the ravioli in pesto sauce to the waitress/ owner/mother of the family-owned trattoria. When the food arrived, Italy once again surpassed culinary expectations.

"I can't believe after such a full day, there's still so much left undone," Lucy said, trying to fold the long tagliatelle gracefully into her mouth. "I can picture my mother as a young girl in this city."

"Yes. It's like her. Elegant and classy. You can always come back," Val comforted. "With all your brother's ideas, I don't know if I'll ever get away again."

"Don't let them take advantage of you. What's Phil up to now?"

"I told you he wants to get into producing musicals. Right now he was negotiating with some producers to have the opera house used as an off-Broadway site for limited runs. It's not always attractive to directors, though, because the stage is so huge. Anyway, when I left, a deal was in the works for a musical called *Burying Belinda Butter*. Let me tell you, we could have used your father to orchestrate the meeting with the producers, director, and the rest. What a bunch of prima donnas! I don't know if Phil is making a mistake with taking away from the opera season. He has a good public following. It does give everyone a breather, though. Without your father there contributing, the workload has been stifling for the artistic director and the others."

"It's hard to believe he can keep himself away from the theater for so long."

"Your absence didn't help."

Lucy didn't respond. Turning playful, she teased, "Do you wish you had come here with Evelina?"

"That joke is old," Val said, using his fork to halve a tender ravioli. "She's a little twit."

"She was wrong, though."

"About what?"

"You *do* treat me like a cousin. Maybe even a sister."

Val's eyes narrowed. "I wasn't the one who needed to find myself. You needed breathing space, remember?"

Lucy fell back in her seat. She dropped her fork, and her hand fluttered until it landed in her lap. "I know that. And I'm not sorry. This time has been good for me."

"I'm glad. This trip has been good for me too. I see you thriving, more beautiful than ever. You've mastered a language, a culture, and a new way of life. You are an independent woman in the year

1960 AD. I'm proud of you." He lifted his wine glass in a salute.

"You're drunk."

"Just a bit tipsy. The liter is almost gone, and I've drunk most of it. I only have two days left in Italy. Then it's back to numbers, purchase orders, investments, and Phil. I'm sorry if I offended you, Lucilla darling. I think you're *magnifico.*"

* * *

Val stepped out of the shower and slipped into his pajama bottoms. Still rubbing his wet hair with a towel, he found Lucy in the kitchen preparing a care package for his plane trip the next day.

"I never thought I was claustrophobic, but that shower might just do the trick," Val announced.

"I know. With all the incredible…" Lucy looked up. Val's bare chest glistened, with a few drops of water falling from his hair.

"…Roman baths and aqueducts, you'd think someone could have figured out a better system," she finished, averting her eyes.

"You sure you won't get into trouble for taking a day off to go with me to the airport?"

"What are they going to do? Fire me?"

"Thanks for the snack kit."

"You're welcome. I put in half that *panforte* we bought the other day." Lucy turned and faced Val. "I'm really sad it's time for you to go."

"I'll miss you too."

Lucy could feel her heart thundering in her chest. "You said you didn't want to go backward. So let's start moving forward."

"I said that back home. It's different now."

Lucy slipped off her robe and threw it on the counter. She stood in a white cotton nightgown delicately laced at the curved neckline and puffed sleeves. Her hair cascaded about her face and shoulders in a chestnut shower. Val's heart buckled under the weight of her gorgeousness.

"You know I've never been reckless in love. I'm ready to take the next step."

"Go to bed, Lucy," Val said, turning to leave.

"Don't treat me like your cousin. Don't worship me. Don't be proud of me. Just make me feel alive again," she begged.

Val turned angrily. He grabbed her hand and put it to his chest.

"Can you feel my heart pounding with desire?"

He pressed his fingers tightly on her temples. "Can you feel that?"

He ran his hands down her back till they rested in the curve. "Can you feel that?"

His palms ran up and down her sides. "And that?"

His hands moved further up, and he cupped her breasts. "Are you alive now?"

His hands slowly slipped over her ribs to squeeze her waist and rest on her hips. He took her buttocks in his hands and pushed her into him. "Can you feel that?"

Lucy legs weakened with excruciating desire. Val steadied her and walked into the parlor. "I'm not doing this," he shouted.

Lucy followed him inside.

"I'm not doing this," he said in a softer tone. "I'm not acting on mistaken cues all over again. It would be real easy to take you to bed, Lucy. And if it could be fun and uncomplicated, I would do it. But I'm not going to be a horse's ass a second time. You have another five months over here, and God knows what can happen in that amount of time. You wanted this year. Now take the full goddamn year. I'm not asking you *not* to fall in love with somebody over here. But I'll be damned if I make love to you and carry that home in my heart only to find out that you've met someone else. I won't be blindsided again."

Lucy bit the knuckles of her hand as her eyes filled with wretched tears.

Val turned away from her. "I'm immune to the tears. I'm immune to your scent. I've already forgotten the feel of your body in my hands." He stared out the window. "Besides, I wouldn't betray your father this way. He trusts me."

Lucy silently backed out of the room. She crept under the covers and smothered small gasping sobs in her pillow. It had taken over a year to cast off the shadows and live in the given sun. Now, instead of warmth and light, clouds hung low and threatening.

"Lucy?" Val opened the door. "Let's pretend tonight never happened. Tomorrow we part as friends. Five months isn't so long to wait to find out the future."

* * *

Glimpses of ocean could be caught beneath the patchy clouds as Val stared out his seat's window. An image of Lucy standing in heartstopping loveliness on a cracked linoleum floor was indelibly etched in his brain. His arms and hands ached to know her once again. He shifted in his seat and closed his eyes. *There's no point in embracing futility.* After all the years of yearning, all the soaring hopes, and all the mind-numbing despair, there remained only the prayer that Lucy's unexpected desire would not be diverted during their separation.

Lucy waited until Val's plane was in the air before allowing herself to tremble at his departure. Her shoulders sagged, and she rested on a bench before leaving the airport. His farewell kiss, more friendly than passionate, burned on her lips. *Hope is my roommate for the next five months.* After all the years of friendship, all the moments of discovery, and all the life lessons, there remained only the prayer that Val's love and devotion could conquer his embittered heart.

Chapter 44

Wild purple, blue, and white violets dotted the hillsides. Lavender and gold crocuses greeted Lucy at the foot of the stairs to her apartment. April had arrived in Siena; the air was perfumed with pastel, sharp-green, and bright-yellow fragrances. A basket hung from her doorknob, indicating Lucy had received mail. Charging up the steps, Lucy plucked the single white envelope from the basket while turning the key in the lock. Dropping her large satchel and purse on the floor, she kicked off her shoes and settled in the armchair. Her mother's cream-colored stationery emerged from the nonmatching envelope. Strange.

My darling daughter, Lucy.

Lucy turned the letter over. Her father. In all her years, she could not recall ever receiving anything in her father's hand. Her mother signed birthday cards, report cards, and wrote absence notes. Her mother had written all the letters this past year, sharing any information her father wished to impart. He wrote with black ink in a florid, Old World script. Wildly anxious with concern, she began to read.

I am hoping this missive finds you in good health and happy in your surroundings. We are counting the days until you return home to us. Your mother is thrilled with the bags of chestnut flour from Firenze that you sent her. She is making us wait for your homecoming to make castagnaccio with it. She is also pleased that her beloved city met all your expectations.

I write with a request. If you can find the time, I ask you visit Ventotene, the island of my birth. Once there, look up Francesca Mantovino. She is the niece of my one-time mentor, Gaetano Ripolli. She has something to give you. I make this request with a full yet heavy heart. I hope when you return, you can forgive your father for his secrets.

Everyone sends their love. Danny has his first tooth. Adriana can recite the alphabet. Little Rinaldo likes to sit in my lap and go up and down the stairs. I am now, truly, a carnival attraction, but it is worth it when I hear him laugh and clap his hands.

Your loving father,
Rinaldo Salvatori

Openmouthed, curious, and confused, Lucy tried to make sense of the letter. What secrets? Why now? Ventotene was never mentioned at home. It would have never occurred to her to visit there. Overflowing with inquisitiveness, she inquired into the arrangements immediately.

* * *

From the ferry, the island looked lushly green with dots of pink, yellow, and white. She was astonished to note that the small pink houses resembled the dusty pink of the Salvatori home. Rejecting offers of motor scooter rides, she hailed a cab and gave the driver the address of Francesca Mantovino. The car pulled to a stop in front of a two-story buttery-yellow house resting in refined simplicity in the shadow of budding fruit trees. As Lucy emerged from the cab, a woman in her early seventies dressed in a skirt and white blouse outstretched her arms in welcome. Ribbons of black streaked her white hair, which was pulled back low on her neck. Her skin was wrinkled from years in the sun; the gray eyes were lively and full of welcome.

"Lucilla? I am so happy to meet you. I remember your father well. Such a voice! And so handsome! I am anxious to hear his story in America."

She ushered Lucy into her home, and showed her the comfortable room she had insisted she stay in that night.

"I was surprised to hear from you," Francesca said, offering Lucy an espresso and homemade biscotti. "So many years, so little news."

"I must confess, my father never speaks of his childhood or his boyhood home. His request that I visit came as a complete surprise."

Francesca tugged at the side of her eye with one finger and nodded her head slowly.

"Your father was a good boy and a loving son. But then…what he did…it was not right."

"Please, *Signora*, can you start at the beginning and tell me what this is all about?"

"Better I should take you around our little island while we talk."

Fishing boats of every description were tied in the harbor, bobbing up and down in sync with the rhythm of the water. Off to the right, Lucy could see a beach area jutting forward of high gray cliffs. One hearty couple lay on towels in the sand.

"You can take the stairs down to the beach, if you'd like. It's too much for these old legs to handle anymore," Francesca told Lucy. "There are caves to explore. Over there," she said, pointing in the direction of an island in the distance, "is Santo Stefano. It is a prison commune."

They left the starkness of the jagged cliffs jutting over the coastline for the pastoral countryside covered with fruit trees of every description. Birds migrated from one tree to the next, perched on tree limbs, singing to each other, or chased butterflies against the blue sky. After a short distance farther, Francesca stopped and pointed.

"That is the house where your father grew up."

Lucy faced a one-level dwelling with walls so thick, she imagined the Etruscans might have built them. As they walked up the stone path, she noted the faded green shutters and tile roof. The mistress of the house, seeing the visitors from a front window, opened the door and greeted them. Francesca, who knew Bianca, introduced Lucy. The woman clapped her hands and invited them inside. The thick whitewashed walls made the house cool. They were standing in a large room that had been designated as both a dining area and parlor, the distinction suggested only by the placement of furniture. To their left was a kitchen so tiny, the three of them couldn't fit inside at one time. There was a concrete sink, an old-fashioned icebox, but a fairly modern stove. Left of the parlor was a rectangular room with one window overlooking the water.

"This was your father's room," Francesca said.

Lucy tried to imagine her imposing father engaged in youthful activities in the narrow confines of this room. On the opposite side of the parlor was a large square bedroom.

"Indoor plumbing and a third bedroom were added by the previous inhabitants," Bianca informed them.

Lucy noted that whoever did the work had copied the arched doorways of the original bedrooms. A large stone fireplace was set against the back wall. Standing before it, Lucy noted something odd. The parlor had three separate large windows with windowsills that were hosting several plants in clay pots. Beneath each window were small windows about a foot square, with wavy glass and what appeared to be a navel in their center. They were about a foot below the larger windows.

"I've never seen anything like those windows," Lucy said, nodding in the direction of the unusual duets.

"We were told…" Bianca began.

Francesca cut her short. "I know about the windows. I will tell Lucy in a while. Let us go outdoors. There is a beautiful view from the back of the house."

In the front yard was a cistern. Bianca explained it was about ten feet deep with a concrete floor and dirt walls that had been plastered over.

"Years ago people used it for all their water needs. They drew up the water with a bucket. Now, you see, there is a pump. We use it only for irrigation."

In the backyard was a small vegetable garden and fruit trees. There was a stone grill, a large toolshed, and a rope swing hanging from a tree. Under an awning, a table for eating alfresco was set up beside a much smaller table for the children.

"How many children do you have?" Lucy asked.

"Two. A boy and a girl."

"This table looks like an antique," Lucy noted.

"It is. We keep it in the shed during the winter. It came with the house."

Francesca spoke quickly with Bianca, who excused herself to begin dinner.

"Sit," Francesca suggested, taking a seat herself. "What do you think of your father's home?"

"It's charming. Although I can't quite picture him in this remote setting."

"I do not think he could picture himself here either. He was a sensitive boy. Took things to heart. Some people were simple and cruel back then. Not all people. Your grandparents' neighbors were kind. And they loved them."

"Why would it be otherwise?"

"You see what you called the children's table?"

Lucy nodded.

"That table belonged to your grandparents, Lucy. Your father's parents were little. They were dwarfs."

Slack-jawed, Lucy's eyes popped, and her throat's airway constricted. She gagged, choked, and lowered her head to feel the blood rush back to her brain.

"I'm sorry this is such a shock to you. I knew Adela and Marcello. They were good people."

"You don't understand. My best friend in the world is a little person. For my entire life, my father has given me a hard time about him."

"None of your siblings are dwarfs?"

Lucy shook her head.

"Your father probably feared for his grandchildren. Are there any grandchildren?"

"Yes. They are all…none of them are…Why would he keep this such a dark secret?"

* * *

Sixteen-year-old Rinaldo sat backstage on a stool, idly playing with items on the prop table. Ordinarily he would have preferred to stand beside the conductor during a rehearsal or watch the director block a scene. This afternoon, however, was the day before opening night, and a crisis had been uncovered. The lead soprano singing Gilda did not fit into her costume. The Salvatoris had been beckoned, and now Adela's nimble fingers ripped and pinned, chalked and basted. Marcello stood to the side, adjusting the fall of Rigoletto's jacket over his prosthetic hump.

"Keep your mousy fingers off my skin," Vera Chiara barked at Adela.

Adela continued to work without comment.

"Again, you sideshow refugee! Do not touch me!" Vera whirled angrily in a circle. "Alfredo," she yelled to the manager, "Why can't we have normal costumers? I cannot abide this mouse's touch."

"If you had not eaten your way through Venice on your last tour, perhaps we would not be in this predicament," Alfredo replied.

Vera swung back to Adela. "Don't touch my skin. Your hands give me shivers. I cannot abide it."

"I'm sorry, signorina. I will do my best," Adela said, adroitly finishing her task.

Marcello worked nearby without raising his head. Rinaldo fumed and lowered his long legs to the floor.

"Apologize to Signora Salvatori," he snarled at the soprano.

"Or you will do what, young man?" Vera said coyly, always confident of her seductive charms. "Give me an example. I may be interested."

"Or she will leave you half naked to appear on the stage tomorrow night."

"You would like to see that, wouldn't you, young man? Why should you care what I think of the elf?"

"She is my mother."

Startled, Vera took a step backward and pointed to Marcello.

"Is he your father?"

"He is."

Vera started laughing hysterically. "How is that possible? How could that twig of a woman produce a giant oak like you? I have a feeling the twig fell under a cypress tree, and this is the result."

Rinaldo's hands clenched until his knuckles turned white. A muscle in his jaw worked as he held himself back from punching her. Alfredo, seeing this, ran to his side and walked him away.

"She is an ignorant *puta* who cares for no one but herself and her own pleasures. The venom she spits is not worth one speck of your dignity."

"Dignity?" Rinaldo yelled. He drew back his arm and punched a stage set. The force behind the impact bruised his knuckles, which began to bleed. Worse, the flat now had a giant hole in the wall of a room in the ducal palace.

Vera screamed and ran off in the opposite direction.

"Stupid bitch should stay in her tight costumes. Maybe then she could hit the high notes she sang flat this morning," Rinaldo fumed. "I'll be back later," he yelled to his parents as he raced out the stage-door entrance.

It was seven o'clock when Adela and Marcello emerged from the theater. Rinaldo was leaning against the back wall.

"You go inside and apologize to Alfredo for destroying his set," Marcello instructed him.

"I will not," Rinaldo balked.

"Vera's behavior is not Alfredo's fault. You go back and apologize. You say you are sorry to the stage crew also. They have to repair the damage you caused," Adela insisted.

"I caused? Why didn't you say something? Why do you let her get away with that?" Rinaldo cried.

"It is this work that gives us the money we need to make plans for the future. We cannot risk our dismissal," Marcello answered.

"What plans? Scurrying back and forth on the ferry from our hole on Ventotene to the dark corners of the theater. She is right. We are all like mice."

"Go inside now and apologize," Marcello ordered, raising his voice slightly. "We will wait for you here."

Sullenly Rinaldo obeyed and reentered the theater. Adela and Marcello stood with their sewing kits that Marcello had especially fashioned. They had optimum storage with minimum depth so the cases would not drag along the ground when they carried them. They were a bit unwieldy because of their length. Rinaldo usually carried his mother's when he was with them. Hearing voices from an upstairs window, Adela stepped into the street to look up. Just then, three young men were passing, and as she turned, she swatted one of them in the knees with her case.

"Forgive me. I'm so sorry," she apologized rapidly.

"Well, what have we here? *Un rana verde piccolo*? A little green frog."

The drunken man picked up Adela, who was dressed in a green dress and shawl.

"Jump, frog, jump!"

"Leave her alone," Marcello said, running over.

"We have two frogs, fellows. Jump, frog, jump!"

Amidst hilarious guffaws, two of the men contined to bob the couple up and down. Marcello's fist reached back and connected with his tormentor's nose, which began to bleed.

"You rotten midget!" he yelled. "Paolo, grab his legs!"

Taking Marcello between them, they swung him back and forth and flung him down the street. Marcello rolled over and looked back. They were grabbing Adela. He charged forward and butted Paolo to the ground.

"Protecting your fair lady, are you, gnome? Who are you? Rigoletto in the opera?" he asked, pointing to the poster plastered on the back wall. "Is she your Gilda? Do we have a sack to put Gilda in, fellows? Remember what happened to Rigoletto's Gilda because he interfered?"

"No sack, Paolo. How about this?" the first drunk cried, pointing to a barrel used for refuse and waste. He picked Adela up and tossed her headfirst into the barrel. Her feet stuck out the top, and she kicked frantically while pushing with her arms to move her head back from the vile and decayed garbage. The barrel fell over and began to roll down the street. Just then, Rinaldo emerged. He took in the scene immediately and shouted into the theater for help. He lunged at the nearest attacker and threw him to the ground, pummeling his face mercilessly. Alfredo and two stagehands came running out. The other two drunks took off, and the men pulled Rinaldo off his victim. Nose and mouth bleeding, one eye closed, he took stock of the four men and ran after his comrades.

Adela crawled backward out of the barrel. She was covered in decayed scraps, moldy food, and horse and dog droppings.

"Come inside, Adela. Let us clean you up. We'll find something that you can wear," Alfredo offered.

"No. Just get me to our pensione for the night. I just want to get to our pensione. In the morning, we take the first ferry home."

"Please, let us help," Alfredo begged.

Marcello went over to his wife and began peeling the layers of filth off her. Her face was streaked, and her hair was wet and slimy. Marcello took off his jacket and cleaned her face with it. When he was through, Rinaldo took off his jacket and put it over his mother's ruined clothes. He rolled up the sleeves and buttoned it as far as her knees so she could walk. Alfredo crawled on the ground collecting the contents of Adela's sewing kit, which were strewn in the street. The three shaken Salvatoris walked the half mile to their pensione.

All through the night, Rinaldo lay on his cot and listened to Marcello comforting Adela with soft murmurings. He covered his head with the pillow and raged at his father's docility and impotence. His stomach churned, not at the attackers but at his parents for their humble acceptance of the world's scorn. When in the early-morning hours, he heard his parents discussing their scheduled trip back to the Teatro di San Carlo the following week, he tasted bitter tears of humiliation and revenge. With unflinching determination and precision, he began to plan for a future where he would never lack for respect. A future where no one would ever point at him and snicker. A future where his parents' groveling could never rub off on him.

Within a few weeks of attendance at the Conservatory at Milan, Rinaldo knew he did not enjoy performing on the stage. All those eyes staring from the darkened theater. What were they thinking? The instructors scribbling notes during rehearsals. What snide comments might they be jotting down in the margins? Were the clusters of girls laughing at the tall boy with his distinctive long hair? Were the male students guffawing at the country boy's lack of social skills? Even as he became aware that he outdistanced the others in musical talent and abilities, he worried his audience was scrutinizing every note, every gesture, every expression for a fault.

By the time he emigrated to America, Rinaldo had abundant confidence in his abilities. He warned his parents he would not return to Ventotene. As his reputation grew, so did his insecurity. He feared communication with his parents might encourage them to visit. He was afraid they would beg him to visit home in their letters to him. He didn't know if he was strong enough to resist persistent pleas. He stopped writing. He did keep in touch with Professor Ripolli, who in turn kept Adela and Marcello abreast of the events in Rinaldo's life.

He did not plan to marry. Women were enamored of him, and Rinaldo believed he could live his life slipping in and out of the bedrooms of the women he courted or who coveted him. Children were not in his future. He could not take the chance of revealing his past. Thus, when he saw Giuliana behind the counter at B. Altman, it was like a javelin to his chest. Immediately, he knew he must have this woman.

After speaking a few minutes, he knew the only way he would ever have her was to marry her. He spent a sleepless night reconfiguring his future. By morning's light he admitted to himself that he was tired of the faceless lovemaking and lonely apartment. When he told Giuliana about his parents, she did not care. She loved him. She would love their children. She was not pleased with his rejection of his parents but thought with time his stance would soften. It did not.

With the blessing of each normal-sized child, Rinaldo became more enmeshed in the fable of an American root for the Salvatori genesis. Then, like a cruel joke of fate, his daughter developed an impenetrable friendship with a dwarf. If something ever came of their relationship, the genetic pool might tip back to the past. Even worse, Jimmy was a guilty reminder of the parents he had abandoned for self ennoblement.

Rinaldo's guilt grew with each passing year. Having children of his own, he now realized how devastating his betrayal must have been to his parents. He may have broken most of the Commandments at one time or another, but his sin against the fourth Commandment, "Honor thy father and thy mother," was the most unforgivable. That sacrilege was compounded with sins of pride, betrayal, anger, and indifference to their suffering. His egregious neglect was beyond mercy. His children's happiness depended on not knowing that the wrath of God could strike at any moment.

* * *

"Your grandparents sent your father money they had saved back in 1936. He believed the money came from my uncle. It was your grandparents' wish.

However, when your mother wrote in about 1939, I told her where the money really came from. I also told her that both of Rinaldo's parents were dead."

"How did they die?"

"Your grandfather died from something with his stomach. It was very painful. He had been living with pain in his legs and joints for years. He was not well. Neither was your grandmother. She ached all over every day. People here were kind to them. I myself remember bringing over meals so she would not have to cook. Neighbors would come with a cart and wheel her to the market or someone else's home to visit. But she couldn't get over her loss. She missed Marcello too much. One day she wrote a note and climbed to a cliff where Rinaldo used to practice singing. No one knows how she managed to get up there. She threw herself off the cliff."

Lucy gasped in horror. "My father knows this?"

"I do not know. Your mother knows. What she chose to do with this news, I have no idea."

"She couldn't have told him. Yet it was my father who asked me to come here. To visit you specifically."

"Yes. I hold a letter from your grandmother. I am to give it only to your father or a member of his family. If someone cared enough to visit the past, she had a message for him. For you."

Lucy shook her head. "I can't open it. I'll give it to my father when I reach home."

"Would you like to visit your grandparents' gravesite?"

"Yes. Very much. They found my grandmother's body?"

"She washed up on the beach a week later."

They rose and walked around the side of the house.

"Oh yes. The windows. Your grandparents had them put in so they could view the outside world. That's the original glass in them. It suggests that their tailoring actually provided quite nicely for them. It's not likely there was another family on this island in the latter nineteenth century that had glass windows. They put in windows at regular height for visitors. Adela always said how pleased they were with their foresight since their son would have never known you could look out a window without squatting."

The yellow house had turned to bronze in the setting sun. Just down the road, a headstone marked the final resting place of Lucy's fraternal grandparents.

MARCELLO SALVATORI
b. 1878 died 1938
ADELA SALVATORI
His beloved wife

b. 1878 died 1938
A Great Heart Can Beat in a
Thimble-Sized Space

Walking through the setting sun's shadows, Lucy dwelt on how she had left this side of her family history unexplored. The snippets of history her father shared were always codicils to a larger America-based story.

"When my friends went fishing, I would sing on the cliffs."

"We swam five abreast in the sea. We were racing. I never won."

"My friend and I soaked apricots in wine and hurled them at some boys who had stolen his pig."

"My first girlfriend's name was Gianna. When her mother began discussing dowries, I hid in my house for a week. I was fourteen."

How had all their lives been diminished because Maestro believed his past was beyond forgiveness?

* * *

"Your grandmother had considerable savings," Francesca said. "She left instructions with my parents to sell the house. When my uncle passed away,

Adela could no longer send the money incognito to your father. She must have followed the music world quite closely, for she decided to send the proceeds from their estate as a scholarship to a music school. She wouldn't send it to Milan or Rome or Naples, which had instigated such bad memories in your father. She heard of a new center for advanced musical studies in Siena. We followed her instructions and sent her endowment to the Accademia Musicale Chigiana in Siena."

Chapter 45

The dull thud of the wheels on the runway initiated a subtle thrill of expectation through Lucy's body. Her heart and head took on a life of their own and raced ahead to the arrivals terminal. In the minutes before exiting the airplane, she freshened her lipstick and rouge, ran a comb through her hair, and studied her reflection in a small pocket mirror.

"Meeting someone special?" her seatmate asked.

"Yes. At least, I hope so," Lucy responded.

Immediately upon entering the terminal, Lucy spotted Val standing to the edge of the crowd. He wore khaki pants, white shirt, and a navy-blue blazer. His face lit up at the sight of Lucy, and he stepped forward, waving and calling her name. Throwing reserve out the window, Lucy ran into his arms.

"Val, Val, it's so good to see you!"

"You too, Lucy. Here," he said, presenting her a dozen red roses. "They're —"

"Thank you! They're beautiful."

"They're not from me. They're from Dante and Tino. Neither one can come tonight. They're working."

"Oh."

"But your mother is planning a big family dinner on Sunday for everyone, Jimmy and Jane included."

Lucy refocused. "That will be great. I'm kind of pooped right now anyway."

"You're not getting away so easily. She's been cooking up a storm all day."

"I'm sure the minute I see everyone, I'll perk right up. It's so good to be home. Listen to all that English being spoken around me. I feel like I have to retune my ears."

As they started to walk to the baggage claim area, she said formally, "Thanks for picking me up."

"Of course. Your mom is busy, your father doesn't leave the house much, the others are working. I'm playing hooky."

"Uh-huh."

Once settled in the car, Lucy asked, "What's Dan doing tonight?"

"Emceeing some preliminary contest for the Miss Teenage America pageant. I think Bobby Rydell is appearing."

"How's work been?"

"Busy. That musical I told you about is running in the theater for the summer. Your father isn't happy." Val paused. "Remember my friend Jake Morrissey? He started his own investment firm on Wall Street a few years back. He's doing quite well. He's asked me to join him."

Lucy faced Val in astonishment. "Are you going to?"

"I haven't decided yet. Time will tell."

"I can't imagine the Salvatori Opera Company without you. Have you told Phil?"

"No. Like I said, I'm thinking things over."

As they pulled up in front of the dusty-pink house, Lucy's face softened. Here it was, the repository of so much love and so many memories. Her family's tears, triumphs, blood, and harmony had seeped into the very foundation. A luminous crown of welcome home appeared to hover above the stucco facade. She might travel the world, but the connection to this corner in Brooklyn could never be severed.

The front door swung open. Louisa stood there with Adriana and Danny clinging to her skirts. She shouted into the house, "She's here!" and ran down the steps to greet her friend. Inside the doorway

Giuliana appeared, smiling broadly, an apron covering a mint-green dress and her good pearls.

"My darling girl. Welcome home!" Unable to stop herself, she burst into tears.

"Ma, Ma, don't cry. You'll make me start. You look beautiful. Where's Maestro?"

"We have a surprise. Look," she said, inclining her head toward the parlor. There stood Maestro before his armchair, leaning on the walking stick, so natural and comfortable in his hand.

"Come to me, my Lucilla. I cannot walk, but I can greet you standing like a man," he said, stretching out his left arm.

Lucy was in tears as she raced into her father's embrace.

"Why didn't anyone tell me?"

"Then there would be no surprise," Maestro said matter-of-factly. He looked into Lucy's eyes and smiled thankfully. The haunted expression was gone from her gaze.

"All right. I have only a few appetizers. I don't want you ruining your appetites. Dinner will be ready in a little while."

"What smells so good?" Lucy asked.

"Spaghetti carbonara with pancetta and osso buca."

"Jeez, Ma. I thought the big celebration is Sunday."

"The big celebration began the moment you set your foot through the door. The food cooks itself when my heart is happy."

"I don't know. Seems to me we've been chopping and sautéing all afternoon," Louisa chimed in.

After setting down her appetizer plate and chatting for a while, Lucy turned to Val.

"Take a walk with me in the backyard before dinner? I want to see how Phil's garden is doing, now that he's not around as much."

"A bit more weedy and scraggly, but still productive," Maestro said.

"Sure," said Val, rising.

They walked among the flowers; the roses were in glorious bloom. An herb garden was planted, and vegetable seedlings were marked off in neat rows.

Lucy turned to Val and took his hands in hers.

"I've missed you terribly since you left Siena. I'm hoping you missed me too."

"I have. Are you saying you've come back with no attachments?" Val asked warily.

"I'm attached all right. To you. Val, I realized something after you were gone. We belong together."

She stepped into his arms, and Val held the back of her head in his hand. He felt the planet plunge beneath him.

"*Now* I've arrived home," Lucy whispered. She looked up into his face, and he lowered his lips to hers. "Val, will you marry me?"

With great effort, Val maintained his composure. "*You* are asking me?" he asked incredulously.

Lucy nodded.

"The only reason I considered changing jobs was because I couldn't bear the thought of running into you if your life had taken a different direction."

"You would have lived a life without music and all these people who love you because of me?"

"Lucy, you know I can't sing or play an instrument. You are the aria in my life. You are the thought, the dream, the reason behind every move I make, every breath I take. Without you, there could have been no music."

"Is that a yes?" she said, teasingly running her finger along his jaw.

"Let me answer you this way," he said, taking her into his arms and kissing her passionately. "I will be devoted to you. I've loved you since I first saw you as a fifteen-year-old girl standing by that tree hoarding figs for your breakfast. I knew from that moment what you only now have discovered. We belong together."

* * *

At dinner the family erupted with cries of joy at the news of the engagement.

"Finally got the guts to pop the question, huh?" teased Phil. With his new crew cut, he looked amazingly like his own baby pictures. He bounced Ronnie on his knee and fed him small pieces of bread dipped in tomato sauce.

"You might say that," Val replied as he squeezed Lucy's thigh under the table.

When everyone had left except Val, Lucy joined her parents in the parlor. In her hand she held the letter from Francesca Mantovino.

"Maestro, you know I visited Ventotene. Here is something for you."

Maestro took it from her gingerly and placed it on his lap.

"What did you think of the island?"

"It is beautiful. I saw your home. They've added a bedroom and a bathroom. I saw the small windows."

"Yes," he nodded. "The windows. And what do you think?"

"I wish I had thought to ask you more questions about your parents and where you came from. I would have been happy to know all your stories from when I was a child. We have a lot of catching up to do. Are you going to open the letter?"

"Perhaps I should leave," Val said.

"No. No. Stay. You are family now," Maestro insisted. "I will read the letter."

He opened the envelope and reached for his reading glasses. He cleared his throat. His face looked ashen and fearful. A criminal awaiting his sentence.

Our beloved son, Rinaldo, his sposa, Giuliana, and our grandchildren,

Over twenty-five years have passed since we looked into your face. That time has not diminished our love for you or our sorrow at our separation. From your letters to the Professore, we know of your life circumstances and the gift of your family. We like to imagine you intended him to share your life with us, although we do not know this to be true. It does not matter. You had great promise, and you have fulfilled it. We are proud of you.

With age comes mellowing. If we are lucky, wisdom follows. We do not know if you are reading this letter as a young husband and father or as a bent-over old man. Perhaps if you are old as we, you will appreciate what we have to say all the more. Or your children can rest easy knowing that there have been no curses cast on your family line.

Forgiveness need not come from our direction. The truth is, we beg for your forgiveness. You fled to another world because of what we taught you about this one. We taught you shame. We reclused ourselves where we could maintain the least contact with the outside world. We did our business in the dark corners of a theater or in the seclusion of our home. We traveled at odd hours and under cover of darkness. From shame followed fear. We are to blame. You feared what people were thinking, what new trial would need to be faced on the morrow, what escape might elude us if we veered from our routine. Your anger with us was justified. It should have spurred us on to behave more courageously, to face our detractors and present a small but dignified presence. We did not do this. Instead, we partnered together against you, our son, who was part of that huge world. Instead of following your lead, we tried to submerge you in our narrow existence. You were right to rebel. It was only natural that you left.

Remember the good things. The days on the beach, the whittling of whistles, the meals by the fireside, songs on the cliff, and fresh peaches in homemade wine. Know that your good looks come from you mother's parents and your music comes from your *father's mother. Your bravery comes from your Uncle Giorgio and your good heart comes from your father's sister, Sister Maria di Cristo. They were all good people, and they all suffered because of our selfishness.*

So, dearest, one request only. That you forgive us. If, however, your own heart bleeds with sadness and remorse, if you need to hear the words from us that are not necessary, we say them so you can live the rest of your years with an easy heart. We forgive you.

Your loving mother and father,
Marcello and Adela Salvatori

The rustle of the pages falling to Maestro's lap filled the hushed room. Lucy squeezed Val's hand. She had much to tell him. Tears streamed down Maestro's face. Giuliana ran to his side and wrapped her arms around him. She kissed the tears on his face one by one.

"It's an Allelulia day, my love. An Allelulia day."

Chapter 46

The breeze that whispered through the screened window carried the clean, brisk scent of the recent rain. Giuliana and Rinaldo lay in bed on their backs, hand over hand, Giuliana's ankle entwined with his.

Rinaldo spoke softly in the darkness. "Remember last year when Lucy left for Siena? I said that the day she married, I would not walk her down the aisle; I did not want to ruin her entrance in a wheelchair."

"I remember."

"I have been thinking. Maybe it would not be such a bad thing. Maybe by the time they plan the wedding, I will walk."

Giuliana squeezed his hand.

"I know it will probably not happen. But I have decided. If I can't walk, I will roll down the aisle with my daughter. Do you think she will be embarrassed when I tell her this?"

"I don't think she expected to walk down the aisle any other way."

"Tomorrow, before everyone gets here for the welcome-home dinner, I will tell her."

Giuliana turned on her side and covered his mouth with two fingers. "Hush, Rinaldo. Don't let her know you ever thought otherwise. It is the way it should be."

"Yes. My heart feels right."

Giuliana kissed him. "My heart is full of happiness. Wisdom is very seductive."

"Seductive?"

"Yes, my love, seductive. You have been neglecting me for a long while."

Rinaldo closed his eyes. "I know. I am sorry. It is not you. It is me; it is age; it was sorrow."

"Well, then. It's time to remedy that." Giuliana climbed atop him.

Rinaldo's arms automatically wrapped around her. "I don't know, Giuliana, it's been—"

She cut him off with a kiss and removed her nightgown. In the darkness, lit only by the faintest light from a streetlamp, her face was that of the girl behind the counter, the girl on the hilltop, the woman in the attic.

"I think you underestimate yourself, Maestro," Giuliana said knowingly.

"Sssh. Lucy is in her room."

"Do you want me to get up and lock the door like we used to?" Giuliana teased.

"I want you to act like a grandmother so our daughter doesn't think we're crazy."

"But I am crazy. Still crazy in love with you. And if Lucy finds out that passion can outlive pain, heart-aches, and thirty-six years, how much happier will her wedding day be?"

* * *

Maestro thumped his walking stick on the floor before plopping back into his armchair. The impresario was reemerging, and he was getting as much mileage out of his theatrics as his legs and Giuliana would allow.

"Your mother and I have something we need to discuss with you before the others arrive," he explained to Lucy and Val.

"OK. Go ahead."

"For some time now, we've been contemplating building a bedroom here on the first floor. Next to the music room. We'd also add a full bath. It would be so much easier for your father," Giuliana began.

"Even though, any day now I may take a stroll down to Kings Highway." Maestro looked at the three solemn faces and burst out laughing. "I am joking. It will take longer than any day soon."

"Rinaldo, either we're going to tell them what this is about, or you're going to interrupt with your silly games," Giuliana said with aggravation.

"*Scusa,*" Maestro said, pursing his lips and making bug eyes.

Giuliana covered her mouth to hide her smile. "It would be just as easy for us to include a small, serviceable kitchen in the renovation."

"The bedroom makes sense, but why would you add a kitchen? You love your kitchen."

"Two women in one kitchen is a recipe for trouble." Giuliana cleared her throat importantly. "Maestro and I want to give you this house as a wedding present."

Lucy's hands flew to her face. She turned to Val, who sat in astounded silence.

"You realize the fly in the ointment is that your parents would be under the same roof. We would try not to get in your way."

"Perhaps we even build a sitting room where we can put our own TV!" Maestro announced as if the idea had just occurred to him.

"I don't know what to say. I'm overwhelmed. Val?" Lucy said, turning to him.

"I know what this house means to you. It's a magnificent offer, Maestro, Mrs. Salvatori."

"Mom," Giuliana corrected.

"I'd love to bring up my children surrounded by these walls that know us so well. To hear footsteps in the attic and yell at some little guy sliding down the banister. But…is it right? I mean, you gave Dan Grandma Anna's house and me, this one. What about Phil and Tino?"

"Don't you worry about your brothers," Maestro said firmly.

Giuliana looked at him. "Your father is giving the opera house to Phil. As for Tino, my parents had nice savings that they left me besides the house. We've set a portion of that aside just for Tino. If you take possession of this house, we will give Tino that money. You did not think we would favor one of our children over the other?"

"Of course not. That's why I didn't understand." Lucy was perched at the end of her chair. She looked at Val. "Can you picture yourself living in this house?"

"If this is where you'll be happy, this is where I picture myself. As long as you, Mrs. Salva…Mom, agree to come into the kitchen and cook sometimes. I've heard all about those newlywed dinner disasters."

Lucy punched his arm, kissed him, and jumped up to give her parents an enormous hug.

* * *

Jimmy loped into the house bearing a blueberry pie baked by Jane and a smile that nipped at his ears. "Where's my Luce?" he hollered.

"Jimmy!" Lucy came running out of the kitchen and dropped to her knees to hug him desperately.

"Hey, lady. Hands off my man," Jane ordered with a smile.

"Jane. You look wonderful," Lucy said, kissing her. "Thanks for the pie."

"We asked first. Louisa said to bring it. She said something about some special dessert that might be more trial than treat?"

Lucy chuckled. "She's only on stage three, I think."

"Huh?"

"We'll explain later."

The dinner was rowdy and rambunctious. The grandchildren were still too young to be set apart at another table, so whining, a spilled glass of water, and a meatball rolling across the floor were part of the mix.

Renzo tapped his glass with his knife. "Lucy, dear. I want to make an offer. I'd like to design your wedding gown for you. I've already begun several sketches for you to examine."

"What do you say, Lucy?" Tino asked, brimming with pride.

"I don't know how much more excitement I can handle in one day! Renzo, I'm honored. And flattered. I know you're a brilliant designer. Thank you so very much."

"You will look like a princess, I promise," Renzo said, toasting her with his wineglass.

When it was time for coffee and dessert, Giuliana carried a huge platter piled with brownie-sized squares into the dining room. She handed the dish to Lucy.

A culinary proclamation of where my grandmother grew up, of what my mother has learned, and of where I am going.

"I've never used chestnut flour this dark in color. They smell wonderful," Guiliana announced excitedly.

"What is it? Brownies, I hope?" asked Jimmy.

"No, it's *castagnaccio.* It's made with chestnut flour, has raisins and pignoli nuts, just a bit of sugar. It's not too sweet."

"I'll say," Louisa interjected.

"It's a Florentine tradition," Giuliana said. "My family grew up with it."

"We all love it," Dan said.

"Can you pass it around and stop talking?" asked Maestro.

"The thing is," Lucy began, looking specifically at Val and Jimmy. "Most people don't care for it the first time they try it. They don't get the fuss we make over it. The second time they try it, they say, 'Well, that isn't as bad as I remember,' and the third time they eat the whole thing and say, 'That was pretty good.' By the fourth time, they're grabbing at the dish for more."

"That's a ringing endorsement," moaned Jimmy.

"I'm on step three," Louisa informed them.

"I'm only on two," Ami said with a slight moan.

"Well, go on. Give it a try, honey," Phil said.

Ami took a bite, chewed, and swallowed. "I guess it's because I'm not as surprised as the first time. It's not too bad."

Louisa sighed and said, "Here goes," as she took a bite. "I think you used more raisins or something this time. It doesn't taste half bad."

"And the pattern continues," Lucy proclaimed.

"OK. I'm up for this," Val said. "No one's kicking me out of this family over a piece of cake or whatever the heck it is." He took a huge bite. "Mmnn. Uh, very, uh, Florentine?"

"What's that mean?" Lucy asked with a grin.

"Kind of fits into the *bistecca* category, if you recall."

"Which means?" Giuliana asked.

"He's holding true to form, Ma," Lucy said. "Go on, Jimmy and Jane. Your turn."

"I've never taken part in a food-tasting exhibition before. You people are nuts," Jimmy declared as he stuck the *castagnaccio* in his mouth. "OK, maybe it wasn't such a bad thing when I wasn't invited to eat over here. I'm sorry, but where's that blueberry pie? Jane's a great baker," he said, looking at her cow-eyed.

"Jimmy! I'm ashamed of you. You can do better than that. Be a man," Maestro chuckled. He took another square of the *castagnaccio* and popped half of it into his mouth. "Have another."

Jimmy glanced around the table and rolled his eyes. "That's a tall order, Maestro. A really tall order."

Epilogue
August 2016

Sienese *ribolitta* soup made with summer fresh Swiss chard simmered on the stove.

"I'll give you a container to take home for dinner with Jeff," Annie promised Julie.

"I don't think you should have to feed her anymore now that's she's married," Tony griped as he rummaged through the refrigerator. "Where's the leftover chicken?"

"I had it for lunch," Julie said smugly.

"See what I mean? Why isn't she working or something?"

"Because I'm a teacher, and I have the summer off. You, brain surgeon, will never have the summer off. Even if you do eventually graduate college."

"I'll graduate just fine," Tony said glumly, settling for an apple. "I bet Uncle Marc can help me get into med school if my MCAT scores aren't dazzling, which no doubt they will be."

"Don't count on that. I've never known my brother to bend the rules," Annie warned.

"I don't know. Didn't he and Uncle Jimmy's son Nick go to George Washington Medical together? They both just happened to get in there? Danny didn't pull any strings?"

"Leave my cousin Danny out of this. Everyone got where he was going on his own merits. As you will too, if you crack a book this coming year instead of dating every girl on campus. Even Grandma said you remind her of her brother, Dante."

"Speaking of Uncle Jimmy, it's kind of funny how his three sons are all these huge, big guys," Tony remarked.

"Yeah. Only his daughter is a little person," Julie said.

"Yes, she is. Grace is also a US Senator," Annie said, rummaging around in her cabinet for a take-home container for Julie.

* * *

Lucy ate her *ribolitta* soup on a bed tray that evening. She was quite tired, and she preferred to sit up in bed and look out at the fig tree laden with the thin-skinned purplish brown fruit. There would be a bountiful harvest this year.

A movement beside the muscular tree caught Lucy's eye. She shifted to a higher position and looked closely. Yes! It was Tavis! He was standing by the tree and grinning slyly. He picked three figs, juggled them, and then tossed them one by one at the window.

"Oooh, you," Lucy said. "Don't you waste good figs like that! You'll be sorry."

She raised her fist to him, but her eyes were laughing.

He beckoned her to join him.

"I see him."

Lucy turned. Val was standing beside the bed. "I'm sorry," she said.

"It's OK. We're friends now," Val said.

"Good. I'm glad."

"I miss you."

"I miss you too."

"Everyone's waiting for you. How's Tino and Renzo?"

"I saw them last week. They went to a benefit concert at Carnegie Hall. Tino brought me the program.

They look really well, but," Lucy said, resigned, "we're all old."

"Not you. You're beautiful."

"No," she whispered, shaking her head and pushing her still-thick white hair away from her face. "You look the same as you did in Siena."

"It's good here," Val said softly.

"I know. It won't be long now," Lucy said, stretching her hand to him.

Annie entered the room. "Who are you talking to, Ma?"

"Your father. Guess what? He and Tavis are friends now."

"Oh." She sat on the side of the bed. "How are you feeling tonight?"

"Tired. But happy. It is good to see your father and Tavis. I'll be joining them soon."

"Sssh. Don't say that," Annie choked. Her eyes scanned the room and out the window for any trace of a spectral visitor.

"Don't cry, darling. Don't cry. It's been an Allelulia day."

Acknowledgements

First and foremost, I thank my beautiful daughter, Brandi Danielle Russano, for invaluable information about vocal training and singing arias. I also appreciate the proofreading she managed to fit into her busy schedule.

My beloved mother, Dorothy Giarratano, was an invaluable source of information regarding daily life in the 1930s and '40s. Her recollections were sharp, succinct, and often quite funny. Several of them found their way onto the pages of this book.

I am grateful for generosity of time and knowledge to Glenn Boyar, MD for his help with cardiac contusion of the heart muscle, and Albert Szabo, MD for his assistance with Guillan Barre syndrome.

My aunt, Audrey Giarratano, and my cousins, Pamela Smith and Patricia Postle, were a valuable source of information regarding nursing and St. Vincent's Hospital.

As always, without my husband Jack's computer virtuosity, I would be at a complete loss. In addition, his proofreading skills are only surpassed by his love and support.

My editor, Elizabeth Smith who found the baffling typos that somehow elude multiple proof-reads and taught me a few points of contemporary grammar usage.

Finally, my family, friends, and fans, who have besieged me with requests for "the next book." Thank you for making me feel like my writing skills are the next best thing to an Italian feast.

Made in the USA
Columbia, SC
30 May 2018